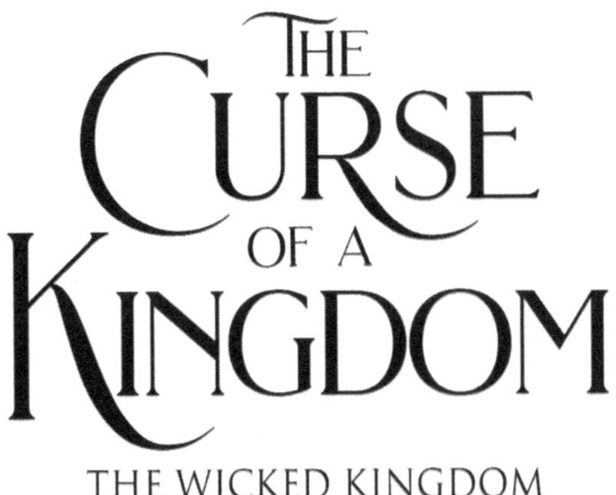

THE WICKED KINGDOM

ABBEY FOX

"Zar,
Thank you for being my critique partner."

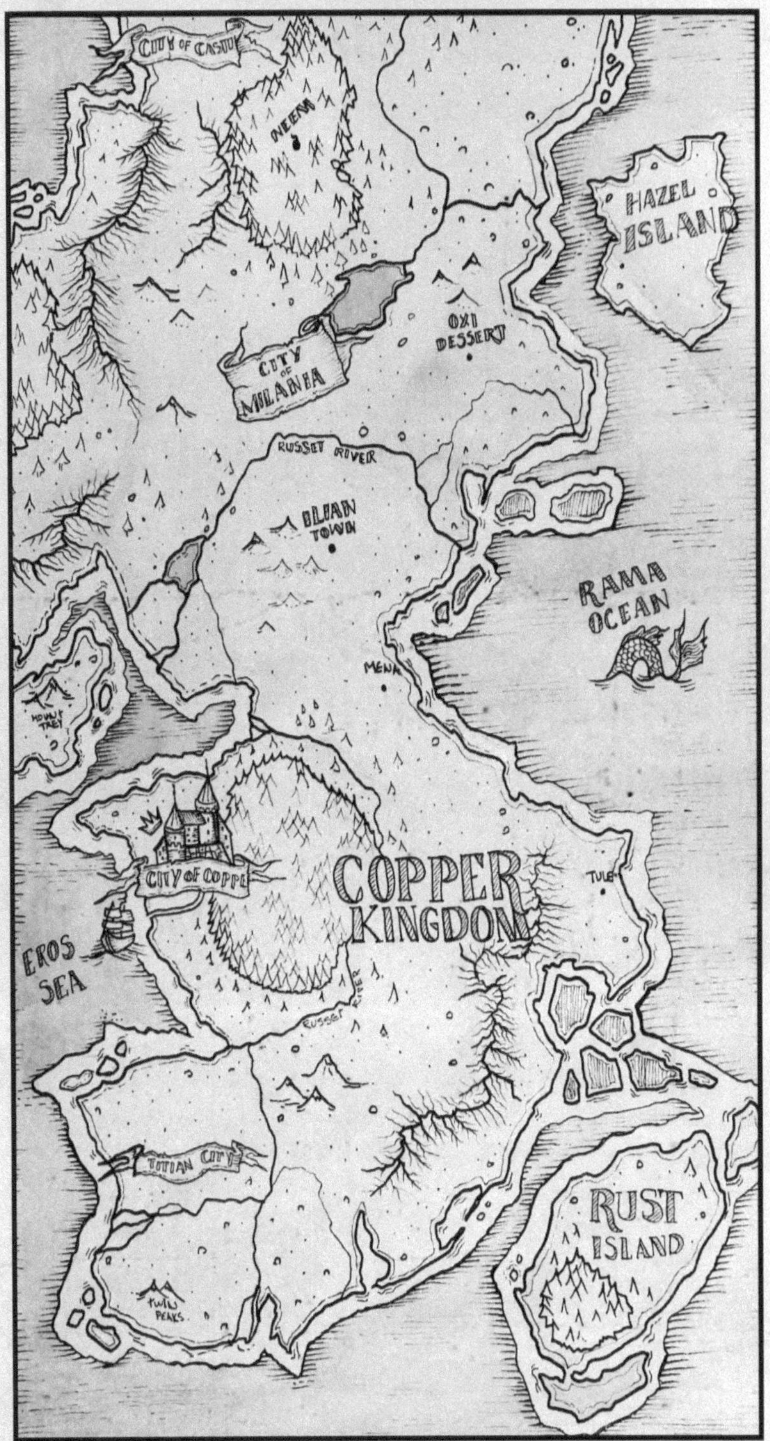

CITY OF CASUL
ONEEM
CITY OF MILANIA
OXI DESSERT
HAZEL ISLAND
RUSSET RIVER
OLIAN TOWN
RAMA OCEAN
MENA
MOVNT TREY
COPPER KINGDOM
CITY OF COPPE
TULE
EROS SEA
RUSSET RIVER
OUTIAN CITY
RUST ISLAND
TWIN PEAKS

The guard nearest to her fumbled over his feet. He reached her in a matter of seconds, and the smooth texture of his gloved fingers touched her wrists. After Arkimedes's earlier demonstration of magic with Herous, this poor soul was terrified.

"The woman is a witch, sir. Should we fetch the jewels first?" the second guard asked.

Arkimedes's aura exploded around him. Dark tendrils of magic emanated from his body, showing his temper. Both the guards shrank back. "Get the jewels, bring Callisto, and do not question my orders again, Rilu."

It was a part of him she had never seen before, Arkimedes Valeron the Crow. Someone she'd assumed he had left behind after a decade away from the kingdom.

"Yes, sir." Rilu's voice shook before he rushed past them and down the corridor.

Arkimedes, however, still refused to look at her. Could he feel her emotions right now? Or had the bond somehow been affected by the loss of his memories? Why didn't he remember her?

He and his captors had left that island so quickly, they had to have taken a portal, like what Devon created. Had Arkimedes been the one to pay the price? Had he been thinking of her at that specific moment and lost her?

Her chest squeezed and the knot in her throat became giant, making it hard to swallow, let alone breathe. Her eyes prickled as tears blurred her vision, and she forced her gaze away. Unsure if her emotions were only acting this way because of the possibility of him never remembering what had happened, but also because of the possibility of her never regaining whatever she'd lost.

"Stop frowning, kitten. You're going to wrinkle," Devon said.

She narrowed her eyes at him; however, she didn't trust her voice not to crack if she spoke a word.

The metal around her wrist loosened, and the discomfort in her skin eased slowly. The guard stepped away but stayed behind. She suspected he was buying himself time before his friend returned with whatever the jewels were.

"It has been a while since I have seen you, brother. Ever since you've been away from . . ." Devon let his words die down.

"The Iron City?" Arkimedes's voice deepened, and she could barely see his expression from his sharp profile. "We can speak about it at another time—when we are alone." His eyes flashed to Nava, and her stomach sank.

Devon nodded but said nothing. She could feel her soulmate's shoulders grow tense. Perhaps he was sensing some of her despair. If he really didn't remember her, then that alone would be disconcerting.

"Is she always this quiet?" Arkimedes asked flatly, finally fixing his gaze upon her.

Devon laughed as the second guard approached him with careful steps, reaching for the cuffs on his back. "Not at all, but I'm enjoying it while it lasts."

"Well, you can start by asking me the question instead of asking Devon, Your Highness." Those last words tasted bitter. This was all too much.

Arkimedes's frown deepened. She heard the distinct noise of someone gasping in shock; she guessed the poor guard behind Devon was expecting Arkimedes to flail her for her response.

He opened his mouth, but the upcoming steps of Rilu and a fae woman had them all turning their way. She held a polished metal box in her hands and approached Arkimedes with wide, shiny eyes.

She was slim and tall. Her deep burnt-orange dress

THE CURSE OF A KINGDOM

CHAPTER ONE

NAVA

Nava had been waiting for a while for Arkimedes to join her in the bath. She stared at her pruney fingers, moving her arms over the milky water. What was taking him so long? Surely getting wine from their kitchen wouldn't have meant leaving her alone for the evening. Not when he'd been kissing her senseless recently.

"Ark?" she called, frowning at the water around her that now cooled her heated skin.

Her heart skipped a beat at the silence. She lifted out of the water, and there was a heaviness in her stomach that hadn't been there before, something that made her pause.

She got out of the tub, reached for her nightgown, and draped it over her body, not caring that it would get wet.

Thunder rolled, and the pitter-patter of the rain fell harder against the glass window. She walked to the door, unsure why she tried to keep her steps weightless, but the uneasiness grew more assertive.

The prick of panic settled in the back of her mind like a whisper. Nava's steps slowed down as she tried to understand what was happening. She stilled her hand, then extended it to the doorknob. The only sound other than the rain was her loud heartbeat.

Out of nowhere, a stab of pain rattled through her. Her soulmate mark was aching like someone had branded her with burning iron. A loud bang roared from downstairs, followed by the cracking of wood.

She couldn't move and her vision blurred with tears as the scent of cayenne wafted around the room. Magic always carried a spicy note.

Devon, the member of the Society of Crows who attacked the village a year ago, had frozen her under a spell similar to this one in the middle of a battlefield.

Her body glowed as her magic awakened. Bees made of light formed over her skin, giving her the power to snap out of whatever had her frozen. She and Arkimedes were under attack. Her fingers twitched, and Nava focused her attention on them and closed her hand into a fist, grasping at the door and stabilizing her body weight on the frame.

Arkimedes had taught her earlier in the year how to battle a paralyzing spell by focusing on each part of her body and funneling her magic to it. Her muscles spasmed before she regained control.

She rushed down the stairs, her power around her like a shield. Candlelight illuminated the first floor. The sound of soft crackling came from the fireplace. The door that led to their garden swung with the loud wind from the storm outside.

Nava studied the space. The green glass of the bottle of wine on top of the wooden table mocked her. Her stomach churned.

Arkimedes. She tugged on their mating bond like a string, but panic tasted bitter in the back of her throat at the lack of response.

She ran past the threshold of the door and out into the rain. Her bare feet pounded the ground as she followed the pull toward him. Arkimedes held his head in his hands, kneeling and hunched over. A gasp of pain escaped his full lips. Her heart wrenched as she felt his pain vibrate through her body.

Their bond was aching, unable to contain this anguish any longer.

The darkness of the night veiled them, but she knew this area well and could roam it almost blindly. The scent of wet grass and summer rain enveloped her in a humid embrace, the tall trees of the Grey Forest their constant companions.

Nava was closer to him. His white knuckles tightened around his brown hair, pulling harder. "Ark—" She reached to him.

Arkimedes's head snapped up, and his wild green gaze came upon her. "Stay back, bee." He forced the words through tight lips. His handsome face was usually bright and healthy, but it had lost all its color.

Shadows of mist and smoke billowed around Arkimedes. It had to be the aura of his power. But these were wrong, like an evil presence of torture—ghosts made of dark magic and ancient, raw power.

Her heart lurched as an icy caress went down her spine, and she stopped panting for breath. Her body broke out in a thin layer of sweat. The aura around him resembled Arkimedes's power when he was in a fight.

The smell of magic and a mix of smoke enveloped her. The weight of the shadows' stony gazes made the hairs on her arms stand. Nava watched with horror as Arkimedes's face contorted, his lips opening in a silent cry. She took a step closer, but he shook his head in a plea.

"*No!*" he shouted in her mind. "*Stay. Back. Nava.*"

The bodies became sharper, almost taking the appearance of a human. Tall, with slim waists and broad shoulders, something wicked blooming behind their bodies. Wings. She couldn't tell their shapes in the darkness of their yard, but the clear silhouette of feathers became apparent, so similar to Arkimedes's.

She counted seven, maybe eight winged creatures who flickered in and out of focus. Her chest burned, and she tried to swallow the thickness that had formed in her throat and made it hard to breathe.

The tendrils of a dark spell approached her. They grew like a weed over the ground, fingers extending at a rapid pace. Nava took a few steps back as a distance buzzing tickled the edge of her mind.

She was quick on her feet, backing away, focusing upon her soulmate. The ache emanating through their bond distracted her.

The bees surrounded her, but for the first time since Nava had learned she was a Beekeeper, they did not offer relief.

Nava was losing sight of Arkimedes behind the shapes of her insects.

No, *no.* She pushed her hand through the shield that enveloped her. Bees covered every inch of her body, constricting her movements. Her power blinded her, even as it tried to protect her from harm. But she didn't want this—she wanted to see Arkimedes, to help him.

Nava waved her arms around, the scorching sensation in her soulmate mark intensifying. The bees lifted her body in the air. The buzzing grew louder as a desperate cry left her lips. Was Ari controlling the bees? Was the second Beekeeper nearby? "Arkimedes!"

The bees uncovered her face, and the humid air of the

summer night hit her skin. From the ground below, his face lifted, staring at her with pained eyes.

And then he was gone, disappearing in a billow of mist.

"No!" she gasped, and heat spread through her veins and her skin. The bees flew away from her body, and she dropped a few feet down. She landed poorly, but even as she stumbled, a deep hollow pain in her chest grew like a festering wound, making it hard to breathe.

Nava made it to where Arkimedes had been but a few moments ago. The weight of his body depressed the grass. She dropped to her knees and ran her fingers over the blades of grass. They were warmer than the cool ground. He had been here, and they had taken him away from her.

She heard something land behind her, but she didn't need to turn around to see it was the creature who was bound to her and Arkimedes. Aristaeus's presence had become second nature. Her friend, companion, and the first Beekeeper.

"*He is gone,*" he said.

She lifted her head, and the raindrops were warm in contrast to her icy skin. Her chest seized as tears ran down her face. "Where?"

"*The Dark Ones' kingdom, I presume.*" But she couldn't form a cohesive idea as she gasped for air like she was drowning. Aristaeus tilted his head, wood groaning at the movement. "*Sleep, dearest one.*"

The hard sticks that were his fingers wrapped around her shoulder, the touch numbing. Her vision became spotted and the stale taste in her mouth was replaced by the sweetness of honey, and then there was darkness.

Nava squinted in the warm morning light. The storm had passed, giving way to a sunny morning.

The shapes of trees and twisty branches hung above her. Her body ached from sleeping on a bed of leaves. Nava sat up and took in her appearance. Her white cotton nightgown was stained with greens and browns. Mud crusted her bare legs and feet.

It wasn't her appearance or the fact that she'd slept outside that gave her pause, but the sinking inside her chest. The slow ache reminded her of all that had happened the night before.

Nava brought her shaky hand over her soulmate mark. Her chest caved in, and the wrecked sound that escaped her lips was empty. Not a dream. The shadows had taken Arkimedes.

She stared at a lost point between the trees as her body shook with the intensity of her sobs. The sparse grass made the puddles more visible.

Her body was numb and heavy like lead. She had not an ounce of energy to move, and her thoughts were muddled. From her vantage point, the movement between the trees called to her.

Ari's wooden frame appeared in front of her, thick trunks and branches covered in lichen and moss. He took her in with a gentle, ebony gaze. It was hard to read his expressions since he was a creature made of wood. But the underlying pain through their strange bond was present.

He'd used his magic to put her to sleep the night before. Had settled her on this pile of garden brush that Cameron had refused to throw away before he left for his travels with Gavin and Violet.

Her younger brother had taken an immediate liking to both sorcerers as soon as they'd moved to the village earlier in the spring. It had surprised Nava that Violet liked children. For someone who'd been so standoffish the entire time they'd traveled together, she had warmed up to her younger sibling rather fast.

"You put me to sleep." Her voice sounded broken to her ears, wobbling at the end.

"You were about to faint, and my magic has numbing qualities that would allow you to rest."

Nava rushed to sit down, and the hard edges of wooden sticks buried into her back and sides. "We should've followed the Dark Ones. Find Arkimedes and help him. I didn't need to sleep, Ari."

The Beekeeper tilted his head, slowly blinking. *"And how were we supposed to? Did you master your transporting skills overnight?"*

Her Beekeeper had been spending too much time with her little brother. His sarcasm levels had shot to the sky during the past few months.

Nava took a deep, calming breath. "I don't need the attitude right now," she huffed. "You know I haven't mastered it yet." It was imperative she learn to harness her Beekeeper's magic and transport, the way Ari could move around the forests. Magic connected them to nature, and thus they could become part of it. She rubbed her chest, going over the memories of the night before. Something came up. "Yesterday, you said you presumed he was in the Dark Ones' kingdom?"

The Dark Ones—the name people liked to call Arkimedes, the reason the entire town had was so afraid of him months ago when she and Ark had been in the village for the first time, battling Devon's army.

Arkimedes had once told her that everyone else but her always saw him surrounded by his power. Something wicked and dark. She hadn't understood what that would look like. Why would people be so afraid? Today, she knew better.

Ari nodded, and the tremor of dread in her stomach grew. The shapes from the night before were part of whatever he was from. When he shared about his past, he'd mentioned where he'd tracked his origins before he had stopped searching further.

She got up from the ground and dusted off her nightgown. "He found his kin in the Copper Kingdom. I have to go there. What does that mean for us?"

The Beekeeper nodded. *"Magic bound the three of us long ago. I shall go with you and stay in the forests near the city. We should be able to maintain the balance in nature from there."*

Balance in nature, words Ari liked to throw at her, even though she had a hard time grasping whatever he meant. It had been almost a year since she'd discovered she had a larger fate than being a potion maker in Willowbrook.

Not long ago, she'd thought she would always stay in that non-magical town. But once they'd returned after the Crown's attack, she couldn't take it for longer than a couple of months. They'd stayed there long enough to pack a few things and make their way back to this village. She wanted to raise Cameron in a life that embraced their newly accepted nature, and she also needed to be closer to Ari.

Nava wished she hadn't been coddled her whole life, so maybe leaving this island toward the unknown wouldn't add to the dread already piled over her. There was no other way, however. She had to get to Arkimedes as fast as possible; their soulmate bond demanded them to be close.

How long would it take her body to deteriorate now that he was continents away? How long did they truly have?

Weeks, months? She didn't even want to consider being away from him for longer than a few days. Nava wished she could ask someone about how her bond might affect her by being away from her soulmate, even though they were both still alive—at least she hoped that was still that case. Her heart constricted at the way her thoughts twisted, and after a forced intake of breath, she took her mind away from that line of thinking.

There was one person who knew more about soulmates than she did—Violet. However, the sorceress was away for a month to do research in the enormous libraries of the Pearl Islands.

Cameron had begged Nava to let him go with Violet and Gavin, fascinated to learn more, and the largest magical library in the world had made her little brother tremble with excitement. She could use his hug to bring back her strength.

"*We don't have long,*" Ari said, and Nava met his eyes, her stomach dropping. "*Your bond is fully formed now. We will deteriorate fast.*"

"You are full of good news, Aristaeus."

The bark that made his brows dipped. "*The Zorren will come for us in our weakened state and make sure they finish what they started months ago when we first met.*"

Great. The pit of dread in her stomach grew. She'd found Ari nearly dead almost a year ago. The Zorren, creatures of a shadow dimension that sought destruction in the world, had attacked him. The only information Aristaeus had given her was that they fed on life.

They were the mortal enemies of the Beekeepers. *Her* mortal enemies, even though she'd never seen one before. "So what then? We transfer there? How long would it take me to master this?"

"*We have been working for a couple of months. You tell me.*"

She tightened her lips. "Cut the sass."

As if to prove his point or to annoy her further, Ari disintegrated in front of her. His looming body faded to shapes of bees, dust, and pollen. He flew away from her and headed to the forest, leaving her standing on her land.

Whatever peace of mind Ari had given her was gone, throwing her back into despair. She walked to her home, ready to get on with her tasks at hand. First, get dressed. Second, get her weapons. And third, find Roman.

The Commander knew about the Copper Kingdom. She remembered that detail being mentioned before and was hopeful he would aid her. Nava couldn't march there and bring Ari along with no actual knowledge of what to expect.

Had she honed her power and transfer, maybe they would already be there. She took a breath to lighten her heavy heart, to not be annoyed at herself and her failings. She'd been doing magic for less than a year. Arkimedes always told her she was her own worst critic.

Nava lifted her hand, chasing the cool brass handle of the back door. The aroma of leather, lavender, and cedar hit her in a wall that reminded her of home, but also of the clear hole staring at her with a sense of growing doom. She'd be of no use to Arkimedes if she crumpled now.

Like the dining chair that lay on the floor, turned on its side, the leg twisted and broken. The sound of it falling had been the only alert she'd gotten that something had been wrong the night before.

Nava walked to it, grasping the cotton fabric of her nightgown as she went over the splintered wood. She kneeled down and studied it longer than time itself. A few drops of dried blood stained the floor, and a breath caught in her throat as anger exploded inside her stomach, spreading like wildfire through her veins.

Nava wasn't the scared woman who'd run from her town a year ago. She was powerful and determined, all in one.

She would find him, whatever it took. And they would pay.

CHAPTER TWO

NAVA

Midmorning sun passed through the tall foliage of the forest, hitting the cobbled roads of the center of town. The buildings that jutted out of the trees were spaced closer; their shapes loomed over her and increased the sensation of claustrophobia that squeezed her lungs.

She ran down past her favorite restaurant, and curious looks from passersby trailed her steps. The streets hummed with life, the warm humid air of summer embracing them all.

With every step she took, her heartbeats became louder, the pounding of her headache increasing. The distance between Arkimedes and her was already affecting her.

The Commander held meetings during the day. She spotted him from afar, his long salt-and-pepper hair pulled up into a bun, his skin golden from being under the sun. He wore a forest-green linen shirt and sat at a table in front of the largest building in town, the Commissary. As he listened to the first person in line, he crossed his leg over, nodding every so often.

Roman wasn't alone. Next to him was one of the law enforcement recruits who protected the village. Nava jogged to him, and her quick steps alerted them to her approach. Everyone was still on edge, even though it had been a year since Devon's attack.

Roman's rum-colored eyes met hers; his brow deepened as he took her in. "Nava, is there something wrong?" he asked, rising to his feet. He studied her face and then his eyes traveled down her body.

"The Dark Ones took Arkimedes last night."

His face lost its color as he rounded the table to meet her. "What do you mean?"

The heaviness in her throat settled and her limbs grew numb. "They came to our home, and they kidnapped him. I need to find him. Arkimedes once told me he traced his kin to the Copper Kingdom. I know you are from there. I—"

"Nava, I can't just go back there." Roman's brows pinched in the middle.

Her body broke into a sweat. "Why? I— We have to find him."

"To do what?" He pressed his lips together tightly, his hand going over his face. "It was always going to happen. I told her they'd come for him."

"You told who what?" A spike of nausea hit her in a wave that built up and weakened her stance. Light-headed with the information she could not follow, Nava swallowed thickly and took a step closer to the man. "It doesn't matter. We need to go."

Roman's lips tightened. "I can't leave the town, and even if I could, we wouldn't make it there in time. It will take us months to travel there by boat. My small force here won't stand a chance against the Copper Kingdom's army. The king hates me, Nava. If I step foot in that kingdom, not only will Arkimedes die, but so will anyone who comes with me."

Drops of sweat scoured her skin, and her world closed in. She steeled her back. Bees were coming to her in her panicked state, swarming with a loud buzz.

Roman looked to the darkening sky and swallowed. "Nava, please calm down. I can't go with you," he repeated. "We need the defense against any potential residual attacks. You know that."

They did. The village had been getting attacked in the subsequent months since Devon's arrival. The soldiers who'd escaped had traveled to the West Village—finding allies among the wicked. No one was impervious to the kingdom's gold.

She swallowed but pressed on. "There is much more than our lives at stake."

Not that she didn't understand his point. To him, it was just two people in an entire town. She didn't want to divulge that their destiny was greater than politics and wars. It was even more significant than her love for her soulmate.

"If it was on this island, we would lift every rock to find him. But this is across oceans. To a force stronger than what I offer."

She drew a step back. "I will find another way."

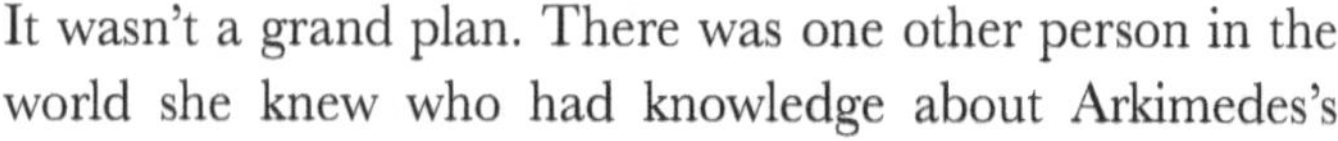

It wasn't a grand plan. There was one other person in the world she knew who had knowledge about Arkimedes's past and power beyond what was expected from a sorcerer, however scary he was. Devon Black had been a brother to Arkimedes once upon a time, and he was her only other choice.

She walked toward the building that held the prisoners. It was an asymmetrical construction built inside an ancient tree. The trunk was hollow but reinforced with many layers of magic.

Nava peeked from behind a home as the guards chatted in front of the rusted iron gate. Lunch hour crept in, and it always took them a few minutes for their replacements to come back. Arkimedes complained about this lacking system often, mentioning there would be a time someone would break in. Roman's answer was always to say no prisoner could escape on their own.

She swallowed, trying to keep herself from fading as her legs and arms turned heavy with the passing time. The soul bond affected every inch of her body with each breath she took, demanding to be near her mate. The Copper Kingdom had to be much farther than she'd originally thought.

Nava had to make it inside the building somehow and then find Devon's cell. Arkimedes had visited him often, ever since they moved to town. Her soulmate seldom spoke on the matter with her; she supposed it was normal since she wasn't Devon's biggest fan.

The bees hadn't stopped circling her body ever since she'd left Roman's company. Nava could sense Ari nearby, waiting for her to do the most stupid thing she'd ever done in her life. Judging by her failing health, there was little time to come up with a third idea.

The guards, one man and one woman, walked away, their long gray tunics billowing with each step they took.

The male's laughter trailed behind, masking the sounds of their heels over the stone ground of their path. Nava took a steadying breath and followed their retreat. After what she was about to do, she would forever be the enemy.

Her home for the last few months, the only place she'd ever fit in. She pressed her lips together tightly and allowed herself to wallow and then ran toward the building.

The heavy gates were unlocked, and they screeched as she lifted the lever and pulled it wide enough to squeeze through the hole. This would be a perfect opportunity to use her transferring Beekeeper spell if she wasn't feeling so weak.

Nava had transferred once before, only a few feet.

Her shoulders eased as she settled in the entryway. No one was here; she rushed to the front desk and rummaged through a rustic wooden box that was stained with age and held brass skeleton keys. The bees crawled everywhere, and the sensation of doom grew in the pit of her stomach, warning her.

Nava cursed under her breath and headed to the steps. She would have to release a man, who was hated by every-one, out of the prison she put him in, without the keys.

She ran up steps carved from live wood into the massive tree. The energy of it vibrated through every inch of her skin and blood, healing her body as she pushed forward. She was getting used to this part of being a Beekeeper, being the same with nature.

She and Ari protected it, whatever that meant. Nature, in return, responded to their calls, lending them energy when needed.

The sorcerer's magic bound the tree to repel people trying to release prisoners or prevent them from escaping. Nature, however, was aiding her, even though her intentions were clear.

Once, Ari had mentioned that they were one with the forest and its creatures, that it would help them and then would come around when it was their turn to replenish it. Nava had seen Aristaeus bring spring flowers out of thawing grounds before.

She climbed hundreds of uneven steps. The farther up she went, the stronger the surrounding magic became, almost suffocating her.

Nava took two steps at a time. Devon's ship still awaited his return to the ports in Willowbrook. They could take it to the Copper Kingdom, and maybe she wouldn't die before they got there.

Torches on the walls illuminated the top floor, casting long shadows that moved over the ground. The energy emanating from the tree's core enveloped her like a shield. Bees flew around her, crawling over the ground and the walls. The stairs stopped in the middle of the room; now that she was here, she counted nine cells.

Only one of them had the lights on.

Nava cleared her throat and made her way with tentative steps. She hesitated when she came upon a man sitting on a white cot. He wore simple black pants and a black striped shirt. His hair was longer than when she'd seen him in Willowbrook a year prior. It was similar to the way it'd been the day they'd met in the front garden of her manor eleven years ago.

Dread pooled in her stomach, and she stopped. Nava couldn't do this; she couldn't release this monster after all he'd done. Even if it meant she would die.

She took a step back. He was her chance of survival for both Arkimedes and her, and she had made it all the way here. Devon knew where the Copper Kingdom was and had the ship to take her there.

The world demanded two Beekeepers—Ari had

revealed as much. Even if she died, another would be born, right? It didn't have to be her. Arkimedes didn't need to be their protector.

She took another step back and froze, her soulmate mark throbbing as if in response to her thoughts. Tears dropped from her eyes, and a booming voice came into her head. It spoke in tongues, a language she didn't recognize. However, she understood.

"You will find your soulmate and defeat the demons."

It wasn't a voice she had heard before, and the sound of it made her hair stand on edge. Warmth rushed through her as she remained in her spot. Her insects crawled up her glowing skin. She understood with clarity; the Zorren's threat was much more significant than her, and a higher power refused to let her give up.

Nava steeled her fading resolve and walked a step closer to Devon. His head snapped up, and his lips parted as he took her in. She must be something to behold, with golden bees crawling over her body, her face visible and covered in sweat.

"Devon," she said in a commanding tone, or at least she hoped it was.

He came to his feet lazily, his head arching to the side, exposing his long, pale neck. "Now, this is something I didn't expect to see today." He walked closer to the cell bars.

"I need your help."

He barked a laugh that lacked warmth to it, shaking his head. "That might be the most ridiculous thing I've ever heard."

She took a couple of steps forward, closing the gap between them. "The Dark Ones took Arkimedes last night."

Her body almost touched the iron bars of the cell. It was so small in there, just a bed with thin blankets. The walls were plain dark wood, covered in a thick layer of moss that extended to the floor. A basin to the side of the room, nowhere left for privacy.

"Help me find the Copper Kingdom." Her voice wavered. She knew so little of the other kingdoms of this world. Geography and politics were not her favorite subjects. "We could take . . . your ship?"

Devon's eyes raked down her body, and one corner of his lips tilted. "Have you looked at yourself in a mirror? You don't have that long."

Nava didn't understand why her health deteriorated so quickly. It had taken her father much longer than a few hours to die after her mother had expired—a dreadful year of him suffering and sleeping.

The reality of his words hit her like stones dropping into her stomach. "Do you know any other way? To get there, to save him?"

He studied her quietly. "Perhaps I do."

"How?"

"You are thinking of sauntering to the Dark Ones' kingdom, and what? Politely ask them to return their prisoner back to you? You're naïve, and it will get you killed." He shook his head and added, "Not that I care if you do."

The Crow said it was the Dark Ones' kingdom. That information alone had her mind reeling. She'd always assumed it was just a village inside a kingdom, a continent, but if Devon's words were correct, elves ruled that land. Did they share it with humans?

The Iron Kingdom didn't welcome fae species openly. The name alone was a deterrent to most, if not all, as fae were allergic to iron.

"I will not ask them to return him to me. I will just—free him." Once she was in the same area as him, she'd have more time to come up with a better plan.

He scoffed. "Are you going there alone? Or have you somehow convinced that crew of greys who hung around you two last year?"

The greys Devon referred to, Gavin and Violet, weren't here. She wished they were the ones she had to rely on. This would be a lot easier with her friends around. Clearing her throat and taking a step closer, she realized that even in his cell, Devon stood with an air of grandness Nava almost admired. Further scrutiny showed he had ropes around his wrists that were tight enough to leave bruises on his skin.

She clutched the metal bars. Her energy dwindled immediately. They had spelled it to cancel magic, something she assumed would prevent a prisoner from escaping. She dropped her hand as if it had burned her. "You were so close, like brothers. Don't you care even a little?"

"It was always going to happen." His sharp jaw clenched as he avoided her gaze.

"It bothers you."

He bristled. "He locked me in this cell."

Nava ignored his words. "You probably were with him when he was doing his research on his past—before he found them. You know how to get to the Copper Kingdom and where he's being held."

Devon's inky gaze cut to her. "What if I was there? It's not like I can help you, even if I wanted to . . . And let's make something clear, *I don't.*"

"I can let you out if you help me," she whispered. The bees lifted from her body all at once, circling around her with an intense buzz.

Devon's back straightened. He took in the surrounding spectacle, his gaze tinting with a bit of panic. He remembered the bees that had almost killed him a year ago. "You would release me?" He took a step back, his long legs almost bringing him to the edge of his bed.

"I would, but only to go to the Copper Kingdom and save Arkimedes."

A bitter laugh escaped his lips. "Even if you could, why would you be so naïve as to think I would help you and not kill you myself as soon as I'm free?"

"You won't." Her voice came out strong, and she lifted her chin in the air.

His lips pulled back, revealing straight white teeth. "Please release me. I would love to prove you different."

"He saved your life, didn't he? He didn't do it for his own gain. He did it because he didn't want you to suffer." Devon's eyes came to meet her and his lips tightened as she continued. "You owe him a life debt."

His pale complexion turned green. "No."

"Yes, and I'm calling on it."

"You can't call upon this. You aren't him."

"But I'm his soulmate." Nava had been piecing this together, but as her confidence grew within, she knew this was the right path to follow. "Which makes him and me one soul. If I don't get to him soon, he will die, and you will fail to repay the debt I'm here to collect."

Devon shook his head. His skin glowed yellow, matching the color of her aura. The binding of the life debt settled between them like a strong rope tying them together in an unbreakable spell. "You conniving bitch." His wide ebony eyes looked at his glowing skin. Magic lit the cell. "How are you doing magic inside this building?"

He would never know that the tree was allowing her to

do so. "It doesn't matter how. What matters is to get you out of there so we can—"

"Die in that kingdom," he interrupted her, dropping his arms to his sides. "You seem like a fit mate for him, stubborn like no one else."

That, she couldn't refute.

CHAPTER THREE

NAVA

*H*er brain always worked in funny ways when put between a rock and a hard place. Nava was always good at making up plans to survive.

It wasn't like she was proud she'd ended up in this prison, making a deal with someone she hated. She wasn't sure if her shaking knees had anything to do with the tightness in her chest due to her betrayal of this town or the growing weakness in her body. It was likely both. She hoped Arkimedes would forgive her for calling a life debt in his name.

"So, how are you breaking me out of here?" Devon's voice was gruff and dangerously deep, his face disjointed with rage.

Nava took a step back, keeping a healthy distance from him. "I'm not, not until you say how you're bringing us to save Arkimedes."

He surged forward, taking a few steps to the cell bars but not reaching for them. It was then that Nava realized the palms of his hands were blistered, likely from holding onto the spelled iron bars. She almost pitied him. "It's of no use to me to reveal anything to you if I don't believe your skills will get me out of this fortified prison."

Her mouth became sandpaper, and the word "imposter" flashed through her mind. Even after learning she had a bigger destiny than just being a potion maker, she was unsure of her strength, in whether she was indeed worthy of all this.

Ari often told her this crutch stopped her from achieving her full potential, but what if the universe had been wrong all along? What if she couldn't do it?

She swallowed down the knot that had formed in her throat and took a step back before turning around to leave. Two could play this game. It wasn't like he had anyone else lining up to release him.

"Wait!" His eyes nearly bulged out of his head. "Where are you going?"

She shrugged, keeping her expression neutral as she fixed her gaze back on him. "I don't have time for your games. I will leave you here to rot and find another way."

He straightened to his full height, towering in the small room as he took her in a different light. Like he'd never truly seen her before. "I can create a portal that will get us both there."

Dark magic. A warning bell rang inside her head, and she blinked in silence. "You can make one that strong? What do you have to sacrifice in order to gain such power? Kill a baby?"

"Perhaps a kitten." His lips tilted up, but the gesture didn't reach his eyes. "You asked what I could do, no? I find it rich for you to judge me when you're so desperately trying to break a prisoner out of jail."

She hadn't been able to shake the damn nickname he'd

given her a year ago after his bounty hunters took her as a prisoner. Violet had thought the nickname fit, and it had stuck. "What's the price?"

"One I won't be paying, that's for sure." He turned, walked to the bed with lazy steps, and let his body drop on the mattress, crossing his legs and putting both hands behind his head.

She scowled. "What's that supposed to mean?"

"You know there's a price to open a portal, and I'm telling you I won't be paying it. It means you will be the one sacrificing something dear to you." He lifted his head and his eyes danced with mirth. "A hand? Perhaps your teeth? Your sight? The possibilities are endless."

Her stomach dropped; her skin prickled like a thousand ants were crawling over her.

"Does Arkimedes mean that much to you?" he asked.

"Yes, he does."

Devon sat up, his eyes wide like circles before he caught himself. "Fine. Now get me out of here. Because you, kitten, are on borrowed time."

Nava studied the cell in front of her. They'd secured the iron frame that held the bars to the wood with thick metal hinges and bolts.

"How are we going to make it out of this building? Have you even thought about that?" Devon's voice broke her concentration.

She was making her plan on the spot because no one had prepared her for the fae coming to her home and stealing the love of her life away in the middle of the night. She was also growing sicker by the minute and had gotten no help from the Commander or this town.

Gavin, Violet, Cameron, and Laurie were elsewhere, unable to support her. Her only companion, Ari, couldn't leave her behind and save Arkimedes on his own. She was alone.

"I have thought about it," she snapped back. "You will open the portal here."

He barked a laugh. "Here?"

"Shh, yes, here. You speak English, no?"

Devon crossed his arms and stared at her with an indifferent expression. "This shall be interesting."

Nava ignored his words and studied the tree. Her bees crawled on the roof and the energy of her surroundings became thicker as she called for more. She needed the wood to expand and contract, to weaken the iron gate, to crush it enough for them to kick it aside.

A tremor ran beneath her feet, and Devon stood from his bed. "I'll be damn—"

"It won't take much time for the guards to be up here when I break the gate. How long do you need to make the portal?"

His lips parted as his dark eyes studied the ceiling. "A minute or two."

"Good." She drew her dagger out of the sheath. Bees lifted in flight and surrounded her protectively. "You so much as move to attack me, and I'll finish what I started last year. Don't let my magic fool you. I intend on saving Arkimedes, whatever it takes."

"The life debt won't let me harm you, you know that," he said in a low tone.

"Get ready." She let her eyes drift to the tree and the moss. To the energy that came out of them and fed the power of her magic. The tremor became a full-on earthquake. Screams erupted from underneath, the prisoners' and guards' fear echoing around them.

Devon steadied himself against the wall, and the iron gate shrieked. The sound grew louder, and the wood above them contracted, the metal bending at weird angles. Heavy bolts loosened and fell to the ground; her knuckles whitened around the hilt of her blade as her stomach churned with fear, anger, and anticipation.

She felt a trace of an emotion that wasn't hers—pride. From Ari, not far away.

The screams came louder from the floors beneath, and she took a few steps back as the gate in front of her shook and then fell with a loud bang over the wooden floor.

Devon gasped. "No shit."

Nava's legs shook as the tremors of the tree died down. "The portal, Devon."

He lifted his arms, showing her the straps that prevented him from doing anything.

She swallowed and fixed her gaze on his. "Do not think about leaving without me."

He smiled. "Don't give me ideas, cat."

She ran the sharp edge of her dagger through the binds, and they fell to the ground with a heavy thump. Without the rumble of the tree, she could hear the clear voices of people beneath. She studied Devon as he rolled his wrists. For a breath, they stood in absolute silence, and she waited for him to pounce on her.

He stood a whole head taller. Nava squared her shoulders and brought her dagger closer to her body, assuming a defensive stance. Her magic soared around her as bees and a yellow glow.

"Open. The. Portal," she said.

Devon's own aura shifted, a color of indigo so dark it almost appeared black. Then his fingers shone with power. A crackling noise and the heavy scent of spice enveloped her. Peppercorn and cayenne.

A surge of wind whipped her wild hair over her face. Devon's brows dipped in concentration as he looked at his fingers, where inky trails came together and twisted into a circle that rose between both of them. The sizzle of static raised her hair, and she struggled to see behind the traces of debris and flailing insects.

A bead of sweat trailed down his temple. "When we cross, the portal demands a payment. The first thing that comes to your mind will be what it claims," he said. The black hole of dark magic was now the size of her whole torso.

She thought of Cameron and urged her mind to put that away, to not think of Ari or Arkimedes. "You mean the portal will claim my memory?"

"Yes, it will become his."

"His?" Nava repeated, blinking rapidly, trying to understand the information. "Who is he? Would he hurt me?"

Devon's black eyes flashed to her, and his lips twitched. "He is the guard and ruler of the shadow world. The portal will hurt you, but it won't kill you."

Nava swallowed, and her skin became clammy and cold. She hoped her mind wouldn't give something she couldn't live without or this would all be worthless in the end. "Why are you telling me this?" she asked, trying to distract herself.

"It will be of no use to my life debt if you wind up not remembering why we're there in the first place, would it?"

She guessed he had a point. The portal zapped, and behind the whirlwind of inky magic, she saw the mirage of tall buildings with patina-green rooftops and warm stones. A city made of copper. Behind the carriages, stone roads, and people, a giant castle loomed in the back.

"Now?" she asked. His hand shook as he dropped it to his side. She vaguely heard steps dashing up the staircase and met his gaze as he pointed to the raging circle in front.

"Ladies first."

"Oh, gee, thanks." Nava's voice dripped with sarcasm, but she stepped forward, lowering her dagger, and hesitated for a second. Then something—no, someone—shoved her in.

She staggered toward the portal. Her arms flailed for a moment, and then she couldn't see the prison she'd been standing in before as she fell down into the nothingness. Floating in a place without gravity or scent. Not cold or warm.

She wasn't even sure if she was breathing. Then her thoughts became sharper as she focused on her surroundings; the aching hole in her heart was present, and she still was sore and tired, but not dead.

Nava had to be careful what to think of next, as the portal—or the gods—demanded payment for magic such as this. They always wanted something. Then she smelled it, the soft scent of burning, like smoke over a fire.

Something moved through the darkness. It had to be a play of her imagination. Everything was as black as night. Her pulse quickened, and somehow she knew she was being watched. Her eyes strained as she followed the shape, sure it was a trick of her brain.

"Look, Father, a Beekeeper has come to us in our land," a whisper echoed in the cave, a sinister hiss that somehow hurt her ears and was familiar at the same time. Gooseflesh raised over her skin. The movement in her peripheral was choppy, like a nightmare coming to claim her.

Her throat clenched and her skin became cold with sweat. "Who is there?"

A laugh reflected in the empty shadows. Her skin glowed as her magic came to her calling, warm, bright yellow light. A pale-skinned man stepped back into the void with a hiss, black feathers moving to shield him from the light. His red eyes were forever burned in her mind.

A demon? Had she gotten stuck in the shadow world?

"This is not a normal Beekeeper. A human crossing *has* to pay," another voice said, this one deeper and detached, ignoring the pale man with red eyes who'd disappeared. "Give me a memory."

Nava held back a scream that threatened to spill as the same demon moved closer. He had wings, she realized, and was shielded by the shadows, however she sensed him coming near.

"A memory, girl," the deeper voice that came from everywhere reminded her, spiked with annoyance.

This didn't sound good. She tried to focus on anything but the winged man who approached her, wishing she could go back to the simpler days of training in the forest, camping on higher grounds, and the constellations above her. Like she'd done with her father.

No, no, no.

"Yes," the deeper voice gloated.

Memories flashed through her mind: starry nights, her father struggling to put the tent up when camping. The familiar burn of the rope fibers against her grip as she laughed at something he said. But his words faded.

Gasping, she screamed, "Not him, *please!*"

She tried to force her mind to focus on something else. The gods could take her hand, instead. But the rolling laughter of her dad disappeared, and so did the mornings eating brunch or him explaining how to make the perfect healing potion, which midnight flower would give her the strongest brew for migraine medicine.

Tears wetted her cheeks as the knowledge escaped her. One by one, they all flew away, even the bright blue color of his eyes. She brought her hands to her face as she tried to hold on to something, anything, a name.

Oliver Forrest—the potion maker of the Iron Kingdom. Her mother's soulmate.

But soon, that too disappeared.

CHAPTER FOUR

NAVA

*N*ava fell onto something soft but prickly and was blinded momentarily by the bright light around her. The scent of lavender and other florals enveloped her. She opened her eyes, blinking rapidly, and took in her new surroundings. The sweet, warm air of summer caressed her skin.

Sitting on top of manicured grass, she wiped her cheeks as her body racked with sobs that weren't as silent as she hoped. Tall hedges stood a few feet from her, crafted into the shape of a spire.

Devon landed next to her, his hands barely catching him before he fully ate the dirt. She might have laughed at his wild expression had she not felt so wrecked. She'd surrendered something so important. Her mind was struggling to provide her with what, but the hole left behind was too large to be anything but catastrophic.

Devon was up from the ground just as fast as he'd fallen, his face snapping to each side as he took in their surroundings. She followed suit, albeit slower, feeling her legs and arms shake under her weight. Her soulmate mark ache had lessened, and some of her energy was coming back.

Arkimedes was close.

She let go of a heavy sigh, relieved as the realization hit her that he wasn't the one who'd been taken from her. She scoured through her mind. Cameron's freckles came quickly, her mother's warm voice, Laurie— The soft trickle of a fountain nearby distracted her.

It mixed alongside her heaving breaths, a song of birds with melodies she hadn't heard before. A castle stood out in the background, hazed over by its size and distance, behind the layers of shaped bushes and vegetation that separated them. Yellow marble blocks layered neatly, and massive windows with lancet arches decorated the tall edifice. The towers' pinnacles were topped with aged copper-green roofs. Nava had seen nothing like this before.

"Snap out of it. They will be on us soon." Devon's sharp voice took her out of her reverie. With wide strides, he made his way past the hedge.

"Do you know where we are?" she asked, rushing behind him, glancing at beautiful white flowers that bloomed with geometric patterns. So similar to camellias, however . . . not. This enchanted vegetation followed their movements closely, angling their petals with their passing.

A chill ran down her spine as she hugged her arms closer to her body, eyeing the walls of flowers. The pit in her stomach grew.

"Do you even know where we are going?" she asked between clenched teeth.

He tilted his face, leveling her with a glare. "I have never been here in person. Since you talk to nature, apparently, why don't you tell us where to go before the guards are upon us?"

She reeled back, aghast. "What do you mean, you

don't know where we are?" She pointed to the wall of creepy flowers in front of them. "This is not normal. This is magic— Someone's tracking us."

Being in tune with nature had its perks.

His lips tightened. "We need to get out of this garden."

"You said you've been here before."

"No, *you* did. I just didn't correct you." Listening to his unaffected tone, she would've thought nothing was worrying him. What gave him away were his tense shoulders and traveling gaze. He continued down the path they were walking. The sun of the afternoon highlighted his profile. A straight nose, with proud, pale lips and large black eyes.

"Wait, wait. You didn't come to this kingdom with Arkimedes?"

"We have no time to get into semantics."

"Oh, no. We do." She quickened her steps, trailing him. "That changes things."

"Does it? You told me once here, you'll figure out a way to save him. I brought you here. So far, I'm holding my end of the bargain." He paused, and his gaze tracked down her face. "Now, you aren't dying. You're welcome."

She huffed her annoyance but chose not to dwell on his words. "Where are we, either way?"

He eyed the castle looming in the background with apprehension. "Looks like the castle's garden."

Her mouth dropped. "T—The castle, what?" She groaned as she looked at the marble statues between the bushes. It was carved into the likeness of someone beautiful. Were their eyes chasing them as well or was she going crazy?

This kept getting creepier by the minute.

"Why did you bring us to a castle? We just needed to

land near Arkimedes, in a safe place to come up with the next move."

"It's not like I had a lot of time to set up coordinates," he snapped, not pausing in his strides. "You were the one showing up to my cell, making demands and forging life debts."

"Believe me, you were the last person I wanted to ask for any help at all."

Devon stopped, turning to face her, and she almost ran into him. Reeling back, Nava tried to keep her distance. "Let's call it what it is, shall we? You forced me here, and now that your pathetic plan is backfiring, you need to put the blame on someone else."

Nava's mouth hung open. And she wanted to tell him to go to hell, except maybe his words had hit some deep guilt brewing inside her.

"Probably have never had to work with a team before, have you, kitten?" He continued walking after her lack of a response.

She cursed that this man's sharp tongue could get under her skin so fast. "I thought all of you Crows are supposed to be all-powerful," she breathed as she caught up with him. "To a truly remarkable, trained sorcerer, a portal would've been a nuance. Especially since I was the one paying the price."

"I hope they took something that pains you." His tone dripped with venom, and her heart contracted at the emptiness within herself.

"At least I had something to lose. You probably only have yourself—since you even lost your brother."

Devon reeled back, his expression shifting rapidly with fast blinking and paling skin. He pressed his lips together before his hand brushed away strands of greasy hair that had fallen over his face.

She could've felt the ugly grasp of guilt clutching at her, but she wouldn't allow it. Not when Devon had done all he had the year before. Nava cleared her throat. "You said the guards are coming?"

"You know what I said, you just like to hear yourself talk."

They took a sharp corner to what felt like a maze. It was hard to see where to go when the hedges were so dense, and the sweet scent of the blooms nauseated her. She might be in the only garden in the world she didn't like.

Something was very wrong with these flowers.

"In the name of His Majesty, stop at once or face the consequences!"

The sky darkened above them. Nava stood paralyzed at the sight of angels coming down from the sky, their large wings flapping in the air, contrasting against the copper shades of their shiny armor.

She turned at the sound of retreating steps. Devon had clearly decided he was not sticking around and was already eight feet away from her. A spike of panic ran through her as her instincts took over, and soon her legs were moving, chasing after the Crow.

Both Devon and she ran down the aisle of the maze, the hedges closing in. The sound of flapping wings wasn't far away. Bees came down around her body, circling her as her steps became lighter over grass; even though this bush wasn't helping her, her bees were.

"This way," she panted, and Devon turned and followed her blindly. His face morphed into a determined scowl.

She wasn't sure if he was annoyed at the soldiers chasing after them or at her. It was probably both. Air burned her lungs as the ground beneath transitioned from short grass to loose gravel, and the hedges were no longer covered in white flowers but were spires of cedar.

The sky darkened, and the air crackled with spices and magic, becoming humid out of nowhere. Thunder rolled, and mist appeared around them. It became difficult to see. Devon's magic was making an appearance, hiding them in plain sight.

They wouldn't make it; there were too many following them, even with both their powers combined.

"Shit!" Devon's voice echoed in the empty garden when a fae landed in front of him. The angel-like man assumed an attack pose, holding a two-bladed sword in one hand. His face was covered by a helmet of orange-and-pink copper, aged in greens and whites.

Wisps of ink bloomed around the fae's body, similar to what Arkimedes's magic did when he was amid battle—except not as impressive of a sight. Floating leaves and the shape of a dead tree embossed the center of his chest plate.

"Stop at once! This is your last warning." The fae's voice boomed in the clearing, and her steps faltered as she lost her footing over the loose ground.

"Fuck!" the Crow cursed louder, but he lifted his hands in a sign of surrender. His onyx gaze flashed to her.

Nava wasn't so ready to give up. She turned and faced the approaching shapes of the Copper Kingdom's army, their wings large and mostly black. The reminder of her soulmate made this moment that much more painful to bear.

She had gotten so close.

"We aren't looking for trouble," Devon said, though his eyes shone with murderous intent.

She dropped her arms to her sides, and the swarming of bees became larger, almost fully covering her body as the steps of the soldiers slowed around her.

"Stop that, witch," one barked, and indignation flared inside her stomach. Her skin glow intensified.

"Nava," Devon started.

"I'm not a witch," she said in a clipped voice, unsure why she was choosing to pick this battle. It certainly didn't help that winged shadows had kidnapped Arkimedes the night before. The portal bringing them to a place where winged fae lived was not a coincidence.

These were her enemies, and she would make them pay.

The soldier who'd spoken took a step closer to her, his shoulders wide and tense with anger. "I will kill you right now. You are trespassing, and the use of portal magic inside the palace is a grave offense."

Well, splendid news all around.

"Boys, boys—a simple miscalculation. We didn't intend to transport to the castle, clearly. Just show us the way out, and we'll be on our merry way," Devon said.

They all fixed their eyes on her, their weapons tilted toward her body. She felt the ground tremble beneath her feet as fear settled in with her anger. She wouldn't get captured, not without a fight.

"You will get to claim your innocence to the king. However, His Majesty does not easily dismiss the use of dark magic in his kingdom," said the one with the tarnished helmet. His wings were brighter than the rest, a light gray speckled with black spots.

The one by her took another step closer, and the bees started flying faster. The soldier swatted and hissed as some landed on his armor and quickly crawled to any open skin. "Stop that or we will kill you!"

"Don't come near me or I will—"

"Nava!" Devon snapped from his spot, his eyes wide. She stared at him as he shook his head almost imperceptibly.

"Kill them both now," one gravelly voice said from the background.

"I wouldn't if I were you." Devon's polite mask melted, his features twisting into the scary, confident face she'd seen the year before. "Unless you want this place to be swarming with the Society by midnight."

"A Crow." The fae swatting at her bees spat near their feet. "We don't fear you."

"I'm sure the king wants to prevent bloodshed, according to the accords he signed last year."

The one with the gravelly voice grunted a curse, and the one with the spotted wings took a step closer. "Then call off your magic if you care about the accords."

Devon's pointed look was not lost on her. She dropped her hands to her sides, calling her bees off. The bees flew away up into the clearing sky, leaving Nava naked among the enemy.

A hand clasped her arm, and she winced when he drew her closer to him, her body crashing against the metal of his armor. He brought both her arms behind her back and soon she had shackles around her wrists, the coolness of the metal a contrast to her skin.

They spoke in a language she didn't understand, but it sounded like a mix of elegant romantic-sounding words and beautiful unique tones. She walked with her head held high, her eyes prickling as her anger burned hotter. They were all men, taller than average and about the same height as Devon.

Muscular and built for battle, with wings as large and majestic as any painting of fae ever depicted. The rumors of faeries being fallen angels could be true—or demons that had escaped from the shadow lands.

They didn't hide their wings, unlike Arkimedes. Their armor was made to accommodate their shapes. A wispy dark mist radiated from their bodies in different shades of black, present at all times. The fae and the mist that constantly surrounded them gave her the creeps.

The castle wasn't far, and soon they were walking down well-kept stone pathways that led them to its back door. The entrance stood hundreds of steps away from them. Doors made of heavy metal and vaulted frames rose alongside majestic walls.

Now that she was this close, the variation between each brick of marble told a different story. Age had softened the sharp angles of the building as a whole. It was beautiful.

The fae who held her pushed her forward, and her foot caught on one of the uneven steps. Nava stumbled to the ground; every jagged edge of stone dug into her legs and stomach. A pained sound came out of her lips, and then she was hoisted up by her arms, sharp fingers digging into her skin.

She turned her face to the soldier and leveled him with a glare, trying to move out of his grasp. "Let go of me. I'm walking where you're taking me."

The Dark One pushed her forward with more strength than needed, and she almost tripped to the ground again. "Let's gag the witch," he said instead.

The one with the greenish armor and lighter spotted wings turned his head and studied her. "Calm down,

Herous. She is restrained, and the cuffs have taken the magic away. The king will tell us what to do."

A year ago, she'd had her first encounter with magic-canceling ropes and the horrible sensation that came from them draining her magic. These shackles had a similar burning feeling against her skin; however, this time it was different.

While her body wanted them off, her magic was alive and still running through her veins, even though she wore the cuffs. She wasn't sure why the shackles weren't working properly, not that she was complaining. Maybe it had to do with the fact that her magic as a Beekeeper didn't work the same as a warlock or sorceress.

She wasn't powerless here, not like they wanted her to be. Perhaps the fae had a reason to be dubious of her, after all.

The inside of the castle was bright. Tall, ribbed vaulted ceilings loomed over them, all a mixture of warm marble and copper. The tapestries hanging from the walls depicted moments in history she had no time to study, but what called her attention were the large stained glass windows that framed the aisles. Showing battles of beautiful winged figures, the bright colors kissed the floors in mosaic patterns that made her heart skip a beat.

Herous pushed her shoulder forward. She had fallen behind while staring at the surrounding beauty.

They walked for ages, down corridors and through rooms she supposed no one of importance frequented, if the subdued furnishings were anything to go by. She didn't encounter any other Dark Ones, beyond the ones escorting them. Was the king of the Copper Kingdom fae or human?

She had never heard of the kingdoms' royals being fae, but it was possible, considering all the Dark Ones around.

Arkimedes had told her very little of his time here in searching for his kin. He'd said he found them in a village here, so she'd assumed the faes weren't everywhere.

She hoped their luck would improve after seeing the king and that maybe they would make it out of the castle alive.

CHAPTER FIVE

NAVA

The doors in front of Nava were majestic, made of wood stained in ebony shades. Settings and images were carved into four panels. One was of a winged man standing over hills with both arms raised in the air; under his feet, roots grew deep into the ground. The second one was a beautiful blooming tree. The third was a queen who wore an intricately carved dress, and in her arms, she carried a child. The fourth was flowers, much like the creepy geometric ones that had spied on them in the garden.

Nava's eyes lingered on that fourth panel. Out of the four, this last one was odd, newer than the rest, lacking the details of aged gold leaf, and shinier in finish.

Nava forced her gaze away from the image, taking a deep, calming breath. She had never met a royal before. How was she supposed to address a king? She didn't even know his name. The king who apparently hated Roman. Maybe she needed to bow? Curtsy? If that was the case, how low?

Was she meant to go onto her knees and beg forgiveness so she and Devon could make their way into a forest village and find her soulmate?

Out of all she'd learned from Laurie, who had been Cameron and her caregiver since she could remember, how to address a king had never been a part of her studies. Much less if this king was a fae. One would think a book would have said as much.

The fae with the green armor, whom she assumed was the leader, took a step forward to the large doors, holding his double-sided sword all too casually in his hand. It was as if he expected someone to jump out of a dark crevice in the never-ending halls.

Perhaps he was expecting Devon to attack.

She swallowed and followed each one of his movements. They kept Devon and her in the middle, caged between the six of them.

"You will address the king as His Royal Highness. Do not look him in the eye unless he addresses you. Hold your tongue or you will lose it." He turned and faced her, and she could almost see his bright magical eyes behind the shadow of his mask. Her lips parted when she realized he was speaking to her.

The day kept getting better by the minute. She didn't need to be treated like she had no self-restraint when Devon Black was standing next to her, being a perfect little captive.

Nava's gaze traveled to the aforementioned man. He stood with his back straight, a calm but bored expression on his face. What the hell? What made him so relaxed when they were captives to these maniacs?

The doors groaned with their weight as they opened. Her stomach tightened as she tried to peek between the large wings of her captors, but the men were too large for her to get a clear view of what surrounded her.

The room was circular, with vaulted ceilings so tall she couldn't see the end in the haze. Light streamed in from the large stained glass around the room. Colorful shades of blue tinted the polished floors beneath.

Candelabras hung from the pillars that surrounded the room, and wax dripped down them, permanently suspended in mid-drip. The light of the flames burned hot, illuminating the space with orange light.

A shiver ran down her spine and dread grew inside her stomach as they walked in, their steps echoing in the mostly empty room.

She looked at the three thrones in the center of the room. The one to the right was empty. Large men occupied the other two. No, not men. Fae, judging by the large wings behind each of their backs.

The king of the Copper Kingdom was definitely a faerie.

Between the two, Nava wasn't sure who was the king. If she took a wild guess, she would think it was the one who was swallowed by black swirling power; she could barely tell what he looked like with the shadows that wrapped around his body.

This wasn't like the small ink emanating from the guards. This was genuine raw magic, the scary kind.

They were closer now, and she squinted, trying to see their faces, but still the shapes were blurry with the distance.

"Bow to the king, witch." Herous's voice took her out of her reverie, and her stomach churned when the warm air of his breath hit the side of her neck. He pushed her forward, and she stumbled to the ground unceremoniously.

Nava hated the man and struggled to get up as the other guards stood watching. She cursed, trying and failing to get to her feet, unable to use her arms and hands, which impeded her. She met Devon's gaze as it dropped to the ground, following her with a tensed jaw.

His chin twitched, and she understood. He was hurrying her to get on with it. The shackles that held her arms shrieked with her movements, and her joints protested from all the times she'd fallen today.

"Your Majesty, King Oberon Yearwood, and His Royal Highness, Prince Orion Yearwood. We found these trespassers in the west garden this afternoon."

Finally, taking pity on her, one guard came down and lifted her from her shoulders, settling her near Devon before he took a stance back.

"Keep your eyes low to the ground," Devon whispered between tight lips.

A voice deep and cold broke the silence. "How could these humans make it past our walls and gates?"

"They used a portal, sir. The man claims it was an accident—"

"An accident, you say. How would a sorcerer manage to portal into our heavily warded palace?" The king's voice was less than impressed if she had to guess. "That's a better question, Fael of Heira. Aren't my people's magic more powerful than that of a human?"

Nava frowned and chanced a look at Devon; his lips tilted up almost imperceptibly. He didn't need the ego boost, that was for sure. The silence that descended was charged. They weren't the only ones in trouble with the king.

"Of course, sir." Fael, head of the soldiers, dipped into a deep bow that showed her just how low she needed to go.

"Bring them forward. I'm curious to see the two humans who've challenged me." Oh, no. That didn't sound like a good start.

Alarm bells rang inside her head. She needed to get

out of here, quickly. A hand wrapped around her arm, so tight that pain extended through her limb and all the way to her shoulder.

Herous brought her forward, and even though she wanted to squirm and fight, she kept her eyes low to the ground. Her heart was beating so fast, it stumbled with double beats. Nava might have a panic attack if her sudden surge of fear was anything to go by. "I will enjoy seeing your head on a spike, witch." He whispered the words against her ear, and she winced.

Did the kingdoms around the world still do such macabre, ancient practices like put heads on spikes?

He halted, but his hand jerked her around, as if trying to get her to look up.

Fael's words echoed in her mind, not to look the king in his eyes unless he addressed her. Keeping her gaze low was imperative. If the king was the man covered in shadows, it would be hard to tell where his eyes were to avoid them.

"Why would magical humans be so bold as to come to my home without an invitation?" His crisp voice commanded answers, and she felt a spike of magic trailing down her skin, an icy caress that made her want to speak truths.

"The king asked a question." Fael's voice shook her out of her trance, and she lifted her head to the fae, and then her gaze trailed up, as if called by something larger. A prickle of recognition lit behind her panic state, a familiar warmth that extended through her body.

Her eyes came to the throne chairs. The polished wood was stained black. Then she studied a set of booted feet, pants black like a starless night. Her gaze went up and up; her heart stumbled in her chest when she met the eyes of forest and moss.

Arkimedes sat on the throne like it was made for him,

wearing a black silk tunic that hugged his broad shoulders and skimmed down his chest and narrow waist. They'd adorned the fabric with gold embroidery of a design she couldn't place from this far.

A copper crown, made of thorns and twisted branches, lay on top of his thick brown hair. He looked different from the night before, but it was the same man who'd been kissing her lips.

He stared back at her and his forehead twisted into a frown. Anger, she realized, burned in the pit of her stomach, but it wasn't hers anymore.

Had it been his anger driving her short mood this whole time? No, if she looked deep within herself, she could feel her own braiding itself with his. The fire driving her was his and hers.

His intense green gaze stayed with her for a while longer as the silence stretched. Her skin went cold and clammy all at once, confusion and horror settling in the pit of her stomach.

Why was Arkimedes sitting on the throne, wearing a goddamn crown that looked made for him? Why were his eyes so distant? What was going on?

"Arkimedes." The words left her lips with a gasp.

"No shit." Devon's voice was a whisper or maybe it was drowned by the loud drumming inside her ears.

Arkimedes looked down at her without any recognition in sight. She knew he was a master at masking his emotions, but he had never done so with her, not even when they hadn't known each other well. Much less now that they'd bonded and she could feel his powerful emotions, as if he were shouting them down their connection.

"Release them at once," Arkimedes growled. His features remained impassive. The only sign that he was as affected as she was the whitening in his knuckles against the arm of his chair.

The king's shadow twitched, and his voice bloomed with curiosity. "Do as he says." He waved a hand in dismissal, but she could feel the hot coals of his eyes burning her skin.

Herous's fingers dug deeper into her arm, and she gasped from the pain. The sudden movement was a shock to her system. "But, sir, this witch—" the man next to her started, but no other words came out, just a gurgling sound low in his throat.

She turned to him, and even though she couldn't see his face behind his helmet, the skin of his neck turned purple and blue.

The hand that held her twitched and dropped, and she skittered away. Her soulmate was now standing from his throne. His hand reached out toward them. Shadows enveloped him like a storm; wispy arms flared from him as his aura deepened to the color of slate.

Plumes of smoke emanated like waves, and the air around the throne room became musty with the scent of magic. Another gurgling sound and the guard fell to his knees. Other than his choking noises, silence descended upon the room.

No one moved a muscle to help or said anything.

"I said, release them." Arkimedes's voice was icy, unlike she'd ever heard it before. A shiver ran down her spine as the man next to her fell to the ground into an unmoving pile.

The king's hand grasped Arkimedes. The love of her life stepped back and sat on the throne once again, as if nothing had happened. His eyes avoided hers entirely. "Pick him up and take him to the infirmary," the king said to his soldiers.

Two men from the back rushed to pick Herous from the ground and dragged him out of the way.

The king stood from his throne, the shadows that enveloped him dissipating momentarily. His lips were full and youthful, as though he couldn't be older than thirty. Straight nose, thick black brows that framed cerulean eyes. His hair fell past his shoulders, silver, the color of starlight. He looked too much like Arkimedes.

She swallowed and looked away, hoping her curiosity didn't mean he would kill her now.

His frown deepened. "I must admit I'm curious as to why my heir has spared you two."

Heir, as in . . . Arkimedes was a goddamn prince?

CHAPTER SIX

NAVA

*N*ava understood why at first glance she hadn't seen that the prince had shadows around him. She had never seen what others did with Arkimedes's aura. He'd always looked normal to her.

Not like the scary fae hungering for blood—or like a prince.

What had they done to him? Her eyes raked down his face as he avoided her, his own fixed on Devon.

He'd almost killed a man. However, his face wasn't twisted with remorse like she'd expect him to feel. It was in his nature as her mate to want to protect her at all costs, but she knew Arkimedes often refrained from using his shadow powers, as she liked to call them since it absorbed parts of other people's souls.

"You called my son by his human name," the king said, and she squirmed under the weight of his gaze, quickly facing the ground. "Have you met this woman before, Orion?"

Nava brought her eyes up, meeting Arkimedes's heavy gaze. He narrowed his eyes at her, and her breath caught in her throat. Her skin was tight with pressure. Nava reached for the bond to find what was in store, but it told her nothing. There was recognition, yes, but none of the burning love he'd had the night before.

Her stomach tightened as her mind ran rampant with thoughts that were too wild and scary. Something was off.

"I have not met her before," Arkimedes spoke, standing from his throne, and took the steps down the polished marble stairs with a trot, his tunic billowing in the air.

What did he mean, he didn't know her? Her lips parted, and her body temperature dropped when she felt his confusion and wariness—toward her.

He didn't remember her? Then why was there a spike of something churning between them? She guessed it could be the bond making him feel something. Was this all a charade? Was he buying her time or was there something she was missing from his blank expression?

"I see." The king's intense blue eyes shone behind the dark smoke of his aura. Nava averted her gaze when she realized she'd been staring at him once again.

"Devon is my brother from the Society," Arkimedes continued, calling the king's attention back to him, and her entire world went still.

He is—as in, present tense?

"So, Devon . . ." The king's gaze reluctantly traveled to the man next to her, his hand moving in graceful circles as if trying to fill in the void of his name.

"Black, Your Majesty," Devon chimed in with a polite dip of his head.

"A Crow in my kingdom. That would explain how you could open such a portal." A frown morphed his gentle features into a wicked expression. His youthful expression fell apart as wrinkles tainted his face. "The Society isn't welcome in my castle. They stole my heir away."

No. Freaking. Way.

Nava had gone to sleep and had woken up inside a nightmare. Was Arkimedes the stolen heir? It was obvious by the crown resting on his pretty head.

She took a deep breath to calm her racing heart. The king's words didn't match the tale Arkimedes had fed her a year ago about him being dropped at the doorsteps of an orphanage.

"It took us too long to bring him back, where he belongs."

Her mouth opened in indignation. Arkimedes didn't belong here. He was supposed to be back home with her. Making hot chocolate and practicing magic in their back-yard. Building their life together.

Preparing for an attack from the Zorren.

"The Society also took Devon to serve them, Father," Arkimedes chimed in, and he stood next to Devon.

There was a silent conversation happening between the royals. Arkimedes's emotions were all but shouting down their bond. Confused but determined, her mate didn't waver or look at her.

How could she get him out of here if he didn't even remember her? Nava's whole plan, albeit not a great one, had been to get to him so they could work together in the escape. She'd expected to have time to come up with the next steps, but now, how was she supposed to do that from a cell with an unwilling partner?

Her powers were still there; she could transfer—even if it was a few feet at a time. There was also the possibility of doing the same thing she'd done at the prison on the island, to get to Arkimedes and somehow get him out of here.

"Well, if Orion considers you family, then you're welcome in our kingdom, of course." The king's tone was definitely not the friendly, welcoming kind. His gaze came upon her again, and she steeled her spine, ready to be accused of something. "What about the . . . sorceress?"

Would Devon let her burn now that he was safe and Arkimedes didn't remember her?

"She is my fiancée," Devon said without missing a beat.

Her mouth fell open as she took a step back, looking at Devon. *What?*

"Your fiancée?" Arkimedes echoed, and warmth pooled in her stomach with an unwelcome churn that didn't belong to her.

"Recently matched, I'm afraid. She is a spirited little thing. I can't leave her out of my sight." Devon nodded, and his onyx eyes came to her, a brow lifting at what was surely her dumbstruck expression. An unpleasant shudder ran through her.

"You shouldn't take your eyes off her. Humans with magic so earthy are hard to find." The king took a step toward his throne. His hand moved dismissively at them. "The Society must be rejoicing at the possibility of an offspring of you two."

She was going to throw up all over this polished ground, whether it was from anger or disgust, she didn't know. They spoke about her like she was a decorative piece and not a person. Was it common in the cities? Her scowl deepened, and she gave Devon her best murderous look.

"They're most eager." Devon's lips twitched with contained amusement. Arkimedes's complexion became sickly pale, and his scowl deepened.

The soft buzzing of a bee landing on top of her finger was a wake-up call. She swallowed down the rage burning through her. It wouldn't be helpful if she called on a swarm of insects and revealed that her magic was very much awake.

"You will join us for a banquet tonight. Orion can show you to the guest quarters. Take a couple of guards with you, son." It was an order, and a clear sign he didn't trust them.

Which made it mutual. Nava now knew who the kidnappers were. The reasoning was obvious, though murky. Arkimedes nodded and stepped away from the king, beckoning them to follow.

"Oh, and, Orion, make sure your guests get their jewels."

Arkimedes turned to face the king and his expression sobered. His eyes came to Devon, avoiding her entirely.

Guilt.

Whatever the jewels were, they weren't good.

This whole thing was bizarre, as if she had stepped into a different dimension. She blinked and wished to soothe her aching soulmate mark. It burned under the linen fabric of her shirt, like the first time it appeared a decade ago.

Nava dragged her feet past the heavy doors of the grand throne room, trailed by a couple of guards. She had found Arkimedes in less than a day, and that alone should be a cry of triumph. Had she stayed in the Northern Village, she would likely not have made it past tonight.

Arkimedes talked with Devon in a hushed tone that left their conversation in the shadows. The sounds around her were magnified, the clicking of their boots over stone, the guards' armor screeching with each step, the buzzing inside her ears.

Nava rolled her shoulders, trying to ease the pressure forming in her neck. Maybe if she focused on that woe, she might not obsess over the glaring issue walking in front of her.

She studied her soulmate's clothes; they were finer than anything she'd ever owned, the crown polished. Her brows furrowed as she focused on his hair. It was longer than she remembered.

How could that be?

The wind howled between the cracks of aged stone. They walked to an area of the castle with warmer, more inviting furnishings. Different from what she'd seen earlier that day. Clearly, these were areas of the palace meant for visitors, not prisoners.

The halls consisted of long, unbroken walls. Hanging tapestries of midnight shades decorated the place, and fancy arrangements of violets, white camellias, and other greenery stood on each side of the corridor.

Fae walked around, wearing silk clothes in similar shades of burnt orange, with delicate embroidery details of gold tones. Based on the tasks they were handling, these were palace staff. Some were carrying buckets and sweeping the floors. She even saw one lady cleaning cobwebs that had accumulated in a corner.

Didn't they use magic for these things? Nava had always assumed in these cities they would use magic for everything. She guessed that was the main issue the crowns were facing. Magic was disappearing. Nava had never considered it would affect the fae, as well.

She rolled her shoulders again. The dull ache in her joints wouldn't go away.

"Release them from their binds," Arkimedes commanded and turned to the guards, crossing his arms over his chest.

skimmed her narrow hips and hugged her chest. Her hair was pale and long, cascading behind her back with each step she took toward them. No wings showed behind her back, unlike the guards. Had she put them away with magic?

Nava didn't need a soothsayer to figure the fae was swooning over her soulmate. Not that she blamed her. He was handsome, dark, and powerful. The wide coquettish smile, and the wave of the woman's hips, made her blood boil.

"Your Highness called?" Her voice was tones of melody, and she extended the box to Arkimedes with a flutter of her eyelashes.

What a stupid question, because . . . duh. If Nava could vomit somewhere, she hoped it would be on the woman's dress—or maybe Arkimedes's shoes.

"Thank you, Callisto." Arkimedes opened the box, and inside were two gold bracelets encrusted with sapphires and emeralds. Rune letters in a language she didn't understand marked the sides.

"Is it necessary for me to wear this? I came here looking for you. Surely you know I won't leave," Devon asked. For the first time since they'd left the throne room, his calm mask shifted.

He would totally leave if it weren't for the life debt, right? Devon's expression showed a rare vulnerability she hadn't seen before. The way his Adam's apple bobbed when he swallowed, his crestfallen face.

It hit her then that Devon Black had never left Arkimedes. He had been searching for his brother for a decade. He wasn't going to leave him behind on the island. Nor was he going to leave him here. Life debt or not.

"I'm afraid so." At least that had not changed. Arkimedes was still a man of brief words. He handed the cuff to Devon, and the Crow hesitated for a moment, his eyes fixed on her.

This was it. Maybe now that the Crow had his magic, he could open a portal again and they could leave this horrid place behind. She still had her magic; they could stun Arkimedes for a moment and take him away. He would not expect it. This could be their only shot.

Devon's black eyes fixed on her as if he were reading her thoughts. Shockingly, he closed the bracelet over his wrist, and just like that, their chance of escape was gone.

Arkimedes took a step toward her but hesitated to approach. Maybe it was the way she looked at him, the churning in her gut, or a spark of memory? He lifted the delicate bracelet to her, and her jaw grew tenser. No, not a memory.

"I don't want your family jewels on me."

Devon snorted before his head tilted back with a deep, rolling laugh.

Arkimedes's lips twitched. "What's your name?"

"Nava."

"Nava," he repeated, and gooseflesh awakened over her skin. The way her name sounded out of his lips was like a prayer. "Is that your given name or your family name?"

"Given name."

His eyes danced with curiosity; however, his expression was null of further emotion. "The king demands you wear this bracelet while you're in his kingdom." He held her gaze, and Nava knew she had no choice.

As he fiddled with the jewelry, she could tell he wasn't happy to give her this; it had not been his decision. "Fine," she said in between her teeth, lifting her arm toward Arkimedes to allow him to put the bracelet on.

He appeared to debate whether or not he wanted to do

so. However, she felt the burning of something else through their bond, maybe desire. It was hard to tell when their connection was somehow fractured. It took but a second for the cool metal to touch her. The skin beneath the bracelet sizzled, but the soft caress of his fingertips warmed the ache left behind by the sting of magic.

Arkimedes didn't blink, look away, or move a muscle. His only reaction was the tightening of his jaw and the longing pushing through the bond.

"Sir, would you be requesting adjacent rooms for your guests?"

Adjacent—a room that shared a door between Devon's and her accommodations. Because they were supposed to be engaged. Something crawled in her spine at her horror, like fire-bending ants.

But then, upon further inspection, it might be the only way they could plan how to get out of here because she was running out of ideas. Even bad ones weren't coming to her.

Arkimedes's jaw was set at a sharp angle when he turned to Callisto. His aura darkened around him, and the air sizzled with energy and the scent of cayenne. "No. She will stay on the west side of the wing."

Devon eyed Arkimedes with an entertained expression, clearly enjoying their torment too much for his own good. "Oh, worry not, my brother. You don't have to protect her virtue. That ship has long sailed."

"Hey!" Her voice echoed in the hallway. "It's not like he's making it sound at all," she huffed but let her words die down, knowing Callisto still was around and eyeing Nava like she was below dirt level. Judgy wench.

Devon's eyes danced. "Sorry, that was uncouth of me. I merely wanted my brother to allow us privacy, my dear."

Arkimedes cleared his throat loudly, the vein on his

forehead becoming more apparent. "We don't have rooms next to one another."

Callisto opened her mouth, her delicate eyebrows wrinkling in confusion, but closed her lips as soon as Arkimedes's eyes landed on her. Nava didn't even need to feel his emotions to know he was lying.

"Please set the rooms, Callie. I will take Devon to the gold room and Nava to the green."

"Your Highness." She dipped down before she walked ahead of them, shaking her head.

Devon's eyes chased down the retreating shape of the woman whom Nava assumed was a maid. Her narrow frame was almost swallowed by the large hallways. "It's a shame I can't be closer to you, cat, really." He turned to her, and his straight teeth showed in a wicked smile. "No way to protect you if an assassin were to try to kill you."

Nava would have retorted that she didn't need his protection. But in this castle surrounded by enemies, she wasn't sure that was true.

CHAPTER SEVEN

NAVA

Callisto stood poised in front of what Nava assumed was the gold room, studying their approach with wide blue eyes. The imposing door reminded her of the one she'd seen before in the throne room, except this one was all bright yellow metal.

Devon whistled as he peeked inside, and his eyes cut to Nava with a smile. "This is an improvement to my previous arrangements from earlier in the day."

"Your apartment?" Arkimedes paused his movements, studying Devon as if looking at him for the first time. From the top of his greasy matted hair, the dark circles under his eyes, and the black-and-white prisoner outfit he wore.

If he found it odd, and the confusion pushing through the bond told her he did, Arkimedes didn't mention one single thing about it.

Devon blinked a few times before regaining his usual stance. "I haven't been in the city for quite some time."

Arkimedes didn't remember the island; he thought Devon had come straight from the Iron City. Eleven years of memories were gone.

"Where have you been?"

"Searching for you." Devon paused and sauntered into the room, peering in with tense shoulders. "You left and said little."

The Crow turned and met her gaze, and they both stared at each other in silence, understanding passing between them. This was not a lie. He had been searching for Arkimedes a year ago when he entered her shop that fateful afternoon.

Nava pondered if things would have been different had he not scared her off that day. Had he not sent the bounty hunters to chase her down, would their relationship be more akin to family now?

No. He would have still chased down deserters, destroyed families, and killed innocents he deemed useless. Devon Black was not a good man. She needed to keep remembering that, even if they were allies of sorts.

The bigger issue was Arkimedes's lack of most, if not all, of his memory from the last decade. It was odd that he knew everyone in this castle and also had a fair amount of comfort talking to the king, which would indicate he'd been here for a while.

It made no sense—he'd been taken from their home the night before. Maybe time in this kingdom worked differently or somehow magic was involved.

"True." Arkimedes's fingers went through his hair, making the thick strands stand on end. "I had not intended to stay for long. Callie, take Nava to her room. Make sure she has what she needs, as they will join us for dinner." Nava fought her urge to squirm under his gaze. "Rilu will come with you."

Oh, so he thought Callisto—or Callie—needed protection from her? Nava focused on the other woman, who was practically glowing, her face flushed and eyes glossy with desire. Maybe he had a point. After the day she'd had, her crankiness had gotten the best of her.

Though the one getting stung might be Arkimedes and not this girl.

"Your Highness." Callisto beamed with a bow and headed down the corridor. "This way, miss."

"Do you need me to call on a maid to help you wash?" Callisto opened the curtains that led to a sizable terrace. A pleasant view of the garden opened ahead and, beyond that, a vast forest. "Miss?"

"What? Oh. No, I don't need help bathing." Nava focused on the trees, wondering if Ari was waiting for her.

"The rooms in this castle are alive with magic," Callisto said. "When you want a bath, it will run on its own. The fire will turn on the moment you enter the room if the air is chilly. Clothes for you to wear are already in the armoire." She eyed Nava's clothes, and her brows met in the middle. "It's a great privilege to stay in this wing. Especially in this room."

Nava huffed and walked toward the terrace. She didn't need fancy accommodations. Something simple would be perfectly fine. Arkimedes was all she needed. "What do you mean?"

Callisto walked to the door, her pale hair shimmering with the sun. "This is the prince's wing. Where he hosts his guests." Her sneer swelled. "The guard will escort you to dinner tonight—don't be late. The king likes to eat before the sun sets." She opened the door and left before Nava could ask anything else.

Nava basked in the splendor around her, the warm tones of the stone wall, the imposing vaulted ceilings. The room alone was larger than the whole second floor in her house. Now that she was alone, she studied every detail. The linens on the bed were rich forest green. Multiple wool rugs were layered under the bed, in complementary shades of lighter greens that reminded her of Arkimedes's eyes.

The mantlepiece was green marble; carvings showed swirling rosettes and leaves, an imposing oil painting of a forest hanging on top of it. Her heart ached from what she'd left behind and what the men in the shadows had stolen from her.

The same flower arrangements she'd seen in the halls decorated each side of the fireplace in the room's corner. Nava paused as her gaze stopped on the weird geometrical flowers she had foolishly thought were camellias when walking down the corridors.

Spies.

Nava walked to the arrangements, plucked every single one out of the vase, and threw them out of the balcony. She breathed in, relieved that even if it was paranoid to throw away the beautiful arrangement, she would not let them spy on her.

The hole in her heart grew like a festering wound, unlike anything she'd felt before. Something was off with the encounter she'd had when crossing the portal. That shadowy shape was all too eager to have seen her.

She was unable to come up with what she had lost but knew it was something irreplaceable. Her cheeks dampened with tears, and she held the weight of her body against the cool banisters, feeling as if everything was closing in on her. This elegant room was a prison in disguise, oceans away from home, where she didn't know how to save her soulmate.

Nava had only her magic against an entire kingdom,

against powerful ones everyone feared. How was she supposed to start when she'd just learned about her magic a year ago?

She had never been this far away from Cameron and Ari—but there was one familiarity with her current situation: being forced to face everything she didn't know.

Her clothes constricted her breathing, and she stripped off the layers, taking a deep breath to calm the pressure forming in her heart. The shadows of the room traveled across the floor, and the warm, humid air of summer kissed her skin.

Her legs groaned with pain from standing for too long. She made her way to the washroom, ready to get the grime off and face whatever was coming for her next.

Just as impressive as the bedroom, green slate extended through the floor and up the walls. There was a tub—or a pool—in the center of the room. The water inside was steaming and a milky shade of blue, and the scent of honeysuckle drifted in the air.

Nava lowered herself into the hot water, hissing as it burned her skin but calmed her aching muscles. She picked a sea sponge from the side and dampened it in the water; she used to use these to make potions, her mind supplied, though she couldn't pinpoint what potion that had been.

By the time she got out of the tub, her fingers resembled prunes, and the sun grazed the treetops with orange hues. Nava wrapped her body with the most luxurious and fluffiest towel she had ever encountered and made her way to the bedroom.

The closet smelled like a mixture of sandalwood, mildew, and a side of peppercorn. She wrinkled her nose as she took in the wall of gowns in front of her, all in different shades of blue. Some shimmered under the afternoon sunlight.

She brought her hands to a specific gown. The color of sky blue reminded her of something she had a hard time placing. Her fingertips skimmed over it, and the knot in her throat grew thicker.

Why was she getting so emotional because of a dress, or the color of it? Nava picked it out of the closet and slipped it on, as if doing so would bring her closer to whatever was amiss. It fit like they'd made it for her, a modest high neck that covered the skin of her chest, hiding her soulmate mark under layers of sheer fabric and carefully stitched beads that formed a beautiful motif.

A knock on the door had her jumping in her spot, and she realized to her chagrin that she'd gotten little time to do anything with her hair, which still hung slightly damp against her bare back.

"One moment, please." Taking in her reflection in the nearest mirror, she ran her fingers down her locks. It was silly for her stomach to dance with the spike of adrenaline. Arkimedes had seen her at her absolute worst, covered in grime, mud, and blood, and had still fallen in love with her.

He'd always liked her hair—even if he teased her about it.

She reached the door quickly and took a steadying breath to give herself some gumption as she opened it, but it all escaped her when she met Arkimedes's gaze. "Oh, I didn't expect you to come and get me," she blurted.

His eyes quickly darted down her body. "I wanted to make sure you didn't get into trouble on your way there."

"What trouble was I supposed to get into?" She made her way out of the room, discreetly taking him in. He looked so handsome, wearing a black tunic and pants. His crown still rested over his head. He had brushed his hair back, making his cheekbones more prominent.

"Hard to know, but the guards were keen on monitoring you—and so was Devon."

"I'm not complaining. I enjoy spending time with you," she said boldly.

He turned to her sharply, his eyes narrowing as he took in her expression. "What does that mean?"

If destiny was going to hand her this crappy situation, she was going to make the most of it. There were some benefits in knowing you were irresistible to the person you loved. "That I'd like to get to know you better."

He grabbed her wrist, stopping her mid-walk. "Do you make it a habit of bewitching people you don't know?"

"I'm not sure I'm following."

He stepped closer, towering over her. "You need to stop this nonsense. I'm not interested."

Her skin heated at his words. "Still not following."

"I've been dreaming of you for months." The familiar scent of cedar and leather washed over her.

Months?

The soulmate dreams wouldn't spare him if he'd been here for a while without her. Without all their memories from a year together, he was likely remembering part of their past while he slept. That gave her hope.

It also fed into the idea that the way time passed in this kingdom was different. This was the only explanation of why he'd been dreaming of her for months.

For her it had been a day, but their souls had been apart for much longer. No wonder she had deteriorated so quickly yesterday.

She grinned. "You lied to your king."

"What?" He shook his head, taken aback.

"You told him you had never met me before, but you just said you met me in your dreams."

He scowled. "Dreams don't count. I have never met you in my life."

"What dreams have you so worked up?" She refused to back away from whatever intimidation tactic he was trying to enforce.

He swallowed, and she rejoiced in the way his cheeks turned a bright shade of red. "Nothing important."

"Well, then I guess I don't see the problem." She shrugged and stepped away.

He pulled her back, his body colliding with hers. "It is a problem. You are engaged to my brother—"

"I haven't put a spell on you. I just arrived in your kingdom, and the entire time I've been here, I've been wearing this." She lifted her hand and waved the bracelet in front of his face.

He dropped her hand. "I don't believe you, and I won't let you out of my sight."

"Good, I already said I like that." She continued down the aisle with a smile. Even though she didn't know where to go, she assumed he'd follow.

He reached her in a few strides. "How old are you? Usually the crown doesn't match members of the Society so quickly."

"Twenty-five."

He turned to her, raising a brow. "Devon is too young to be matched, especially with someone older than him."

"Well, aren't you pleasant?" she said between her teeth. "He hasn't complained to anyone. He actually seemed quite pleased by the match."

She would own up to the fact that her words were a cheap attempt to hurt him like he'd hurt her. In reality, she doubted Devon would have been pleased to be matched with her at all; their disdain for one another was quite mutual.

Arkimedes's brows dipped as he studied her features. It was hard not to get caught up by the intensity of his emotions. Mistrust and jealousy.

Nava wondered if this would've been how their interaction would've gone if her mother hadn't taken her away when they met eleven years ago. She found herself rubbing at the spot where their mark lay. "When you look at yourself in the mirror, do you see anything new? Maybe a scar that wasn't there before?" She remembered the old stab wound he had received last year. "Maybe something more . . . ?" Like their soulmate mark.

She could just reveal right now what they were to one another. Show him her mark and explain it all. But then, what if he didn't want her? He had told her a year ago that at first, he hadn't wanted the soulmate bond, either. And this version of Arkimedes was from a decade prior to that.

He wouldn't want her. Her breath burst out in a whoosh, and she struggled to keep her steps steady.

She couldn't tell him they were soulmates—yet.

A loud crash broke the surrounding silence, followed by the sound of splashes over stone. Arkimedes's arms wrapped around her and brought her behind him before she could blink. Her nose itched with the scent of pepper as his aura expanded around him.

"I'm *so* sorry, sir. I didn't mean to startle you. It slipped my hand." A youthful voice came from the open room to their side. A young maid exited, holding both her hands in front of her. She wore a dress the color of tangerines, the fabric darker in areas where it had gotten wet. Her shaky hands pushed back strands of bright red hair behind her pointy ears.

"Leela." Arkimedes nodded and stepped away from

Nava. His face grew darker. "Listening to other people's conversations won't be tolerated. You won't speak a word of what you just heard to anyone."

Her face lost all color and her wide eyes came to Nava as she nodded. "Yes, Your Highness."

Arkimedes strode off, and Nava followed, shaking with pent-up adrenaline. He didn't trust her yet, but she got the idea that he trusted this kingdom much less.

CHAPTER EIGHT

NAVA

They walked in silence past Devon's gold room and down long corridors that led them to the dining area. The castle was breathtaking, with decorated arches that faced the expanse of royal gardens, where her eyes lingered.

Her steps were heavy over stone, and the closer she got to where he was taking her, the larger the pit in her stomach grew.

"Is there any way I can skip this dinner?" She turned to Arkimedes the moment she realized the words had actually left her lips.

"Aren't you hungry?"

She shrugged. "I've been hungrier before."

Arkimedes's lips tightened. "The king requested for you to join us tonight, as my guests."

"He wants to monitor us because he doesn't trust us." She wrung her hands together, the bangle on her wrist pulsing against her skin. Even though the damn thing didn't cancel her magic, it zapped her like a current that didn't fully die off.

Arkimedes's eyes flashed to her and then toward the room in front of them. "Yes, and neither do I," he said after a moment, the words slowing her steps down to a stop.

"Fine. Though not sure I have done anything to deserve your mistrust."

"If you can put a spell on me from a continent away, who's to say Devon is not under one as well? He looks . . . different." He was saying he didn't trust her, but Nava got the impression he was battling with himself on this.

She could feel his interest grow as his gaze met hers; this was so different from the first time they'd gotten to know each other. A year ago, he had held back his emotions because he'd known she meant more.

Now this "younger" version of him threw her off. He was a bit more direct and guarded. He had no clue who or what she was to him but was clearly feeling something. Much like what she had dealt with a year prior, except they hadn't fully formed the connection then.

"That is the most absurd thing I have ever heard," she said. "If that was the case, why don't you lock me away somewhere else, far away from you?"

He clenched his jaw. "Maybe I will."

She took a step closer and challenged him. "Do it—but just so it's out in the open, I believe you are under a spell. But I sure as hell didn't put it on you."

"What do you mean?"

Nava turned around and started off toward the dining area, following the scent of food and baked goods. "I have no reason to say anything since you won't believe me either way."

She was ready to put distance between the two of them after letting part of the truth out. Nava clutched her stomach, trying to bring warmth back into her body.

The dining room was grand and meant to hold large gatherings. The scent of roasted pork, potatoes, and something buttery draped over her, making her stomach rumble as she took in the variety of dishes in front of her. Maybe she was hungrier than she'd thought.

Dark stained wood wainscoting encased the bottom half of the room's walls, and vibrant painted murals decorated the top, depicting scenes of hunting, woodland animals, and fae surrounded by shadows. A long wooden table occupied the center of the room, carved with intricate patterns and motifs. The room was mostly empty except for a group of Dark Ones who were sitting together while they talked in hushed tones.

All of them stood at once as soon as they noticed Arkimedes had entered the room. Their wings were of various shapes and colors. Soft gray mist emanated from their bodies, almost like they were starting to catch on fire.

"Your Highness." They bowed as one, keeping their shifting expressions low.

Nava studied the mood in the room, unsure if it was reverence or marked with a tinge of fear. The prickle in her skin intensified as soon as their gazes landed on her. She swallowed and slowed to a stop as she tried to avoid fidgeting.

"Please take a seat," Arkimedes said to the fae, and even though all of them sat at once, the room stayed quiet. The tension was palpable, and she startled when Arkimedes's breath hit the side of her neck, awakening goose bumps down her body. "You may sit next to me." His voice was like honey and sex all in one.

Her lips parted at the same time her body grew warm, longing pooling in her stomach. Still, she had to keep her head on her shoulders if she was going to survive the night. "Would that be near the king?"

"Are you afraid of sitting close to the king? He won't hurt you, you are my guest."

"Right . . . I'd rather not."

"Are you afraid of me?"

She met his gaze, trying to decipher his turbulent expression. "No. I'm not. Does that disappoint you?"

"Yes, and no." His lips twitched into a shadow of a smile. Nava got the impression he was more surprised she didn't fear him when everyone else around him always did.

Even if Arkimedes believed that his father wouldn't get rid of her, she wasn't so naïve as to count on it. How was she supposed to get him away from this kingdom before the king got rid of her?

A portal could be their only way out of here. She had to get the bracelet off Devon, so he could open another one. They might be able to leave and explain to her soulmate the truth at a later date.

Would that make her any different from the king? Kidnapping Arkimedes when he didn't remember her? Her shoulders sagged as she lost some of her gumption.

Nava couldn't do it. Neither could she tell him they were soulmates. He would just send her away, and that wasn't an option.

She might have to camp in the forest nearby, biding her time, like he'd done for a decade when her mother took her away. She didn't have Arkimedes's patience.

Maybe the only option would be to convince him to leave with them, to help him remember.

His hand hovered near her lower back. However, he held himself back from that intimate touch. A day ago, that touch would've been as easy as breathing for either of them. The sudden loss of it had her heartache growing.

It was then that she caught sight of Devon, standing by one of the large windows, staring at them from afar. He wore a dark blue tunic with silver embroidery down the lapels of it.

"Finally, you two. I started getting worried," he said with an indifference that didn't match his words. "I see who gets the preferential treatment here."

"It's not you he mistrusts," Nava whispered.

Devon's face brightened with delight. "Smart man."

Arkimedes ignored their words. "You two can sit next to me."

"Next to your father? I'd rather stab my hand with a fork, repeatedly."

For the first time, Nava agreed fully with the Crow.

The king entered the room then, followed by a group of women and a couple of guards. His aura billowed out of his body like smoke in a campfire, and his gaze landed on the three of them. However, his steps took him all the way to the head of the table.

All the fae at the table stood and bowed. "Your Majesty."

"Sit," he commanded, but his attention never left them. "Orion, would you join me?"

"Father." Arkimedes dipped his head, and at that same time, his hand actually touched the skin on Nava's back, jolting her as a wave of warmth traveled through her body. She swallowed and met his gaze, finding she had lost all the air from her lungs. "Stay out of trouble."

She very much intended to do so, but Devon spoke instead. "And where is the fun in that?"

Arkimedes's lips tilted up into a shadow of a smile before he walked away

They sat away from the royals, in wooden chairs with thin but tall backrests that were meant to accommodate wings. The king's attention never came to her directly, but she knew he had been the one who'd sent his guards to kidnap Arkimedes and was likely plotting a way to get rid of them.

She picked at the flaky butter bun that had appeared on her plate soon after. Nava peeked behind her hair to where they sat and wished that she sat next to Arkimedes, even though he didn't remember her. She missed the warmth his presence gave her.

Roasted pork, salted fish, and a casserole of peas and golden roasted potatoes appeared next. Her mouth watered as she took it all in before she followed the rest of the party and served herself a heap of food.

The idle chatter stopped when the king stood. The black fabric of his tunic billowed with an unnatural movement that mixed with his shadows. "We gather today among my court to celebrate the fortune of our kingdom. This year we welcomed my heir back home." His eyes shone across the table, and he raised his glass in the air. "To our prosperity. Our forces will take out those who try to break us apart, again."

Nava swallowed as the king's aura grew and the candlelight flickered under the constriction of his power. Even though his words were light, the ambiance of the room was anything but. As everything grew darker by the moment, the wood of the table shrieked and trembled under the pressure building around it.

"Father."

The king's hard gaze fell upon Arkimedes. "Orion's good friend from his past life, and his *fiancée*, join us today," the king continued, and Arkimedes stilled in his seat. His magic billowed around him, so similar to the king's. No one would be able to deny they were related.

Nava's back crawled with an icy touch, and her

stomach contracted as it grew more suffocating. Her knuckles whitened around her silverware, but just as it had started, it stopped. The room's darkness retracted to the man sitting at the head of the table, and the candlelight stopped flickering as it settled into a gentle dance.

"Please enjoy your meal. We will do a full celebration in a week's time during the summer solstice."

The room's ambiance shifted as the king took his seat. Nava let out a breath and focused on the plate in front of her. She had been so hungry a moment ago, but now her stomach churned with nausea.

The message was loud and clear: stay away from the heir or die a horrible, suffocating death. She guessed she knew where her life was taking her.

They ate in silence, and slowly everyone forgot what had transpired a moment ago. The idle chatter resumed once again.

Nava took a sip of her wine, her gaze fixed on a nonspecific point by the wall. Her hand came over her heart, massaging an ache that didn't go away. It had been easy to forget, if just for a breath, what had happened in her travels here. Tossed inside a palace to find out her soulmate was a prince and had completely forgotten her.

But now that she had filled her stomach and the looming pressure of what she needed to do weighed on her, it was obvious she had not only lost Arkimedes, but something else as well. Someone important she couldn't place.

She faced Devon, lowering her voice below a whisper. "Is there any way to regain what was taken from me when we crossed the portal?"

He shrugged, his cool, calculating gaze crossing the room, following the shapes of a couple of court people who were excusing themselves from dinner. "Not that I'm aware of. It wouldn't be much of a price to pay if you could take it back."

The weight inside her chest grew heavier, her breaths coming shorter as the world suddenly became too small. She had lost it forever—him, her? What? "Well, who took it . . .?" She hesitated. The shadowy shapes in the portal felt different from the voice that had spoken with her when she'd released Devon from his cell. "There was someone there with me—multiple people. Did they speak to you as well?" There was one in particular who'd been more interested in her.

Devon's attention snapped back to her as he dipped his head closer. "You saw someone when we crossed?"

She nodded, moving her mashed peas across her plate with her brass fork. "It was a shadow." But was it? No, it was a male, pale and familiar. "It— He *knew* me."

More importantly, he knew she was a Beekeeper.

The silence extended for longer than she'd expected; Devon was a bit too close for comfort, and his scent of mint and blackberries hit her straight in the face. She pulled her head back, eyeing him warily.

His skin had lost whatever little color he had to begin with. "What did he take?"

"It's not like I could know, would I?" she said between clenched teeth. "I can't remember what I lost, only that it feels important."

Devon tsked before bringing the brass goblet to his lips and taking a healthy swig of fruity wine. "I warned you it will take your first thought. Not a smart move to think of something important."

"It wasn't like I consciously picked." Nava tried to keep her voice down. "It felt like he took my first simple thought, and it pushed me to spiral. He took more and more, until it left me with emptiness."

"It might've been the Lord of the Shadows. The ruler of the place in-between. We don't know if these legends are true or not, but he is supposed to be a demigod. It's said he likes to lurk between worlds." Devon put his glass down and warily looked at the king at the end of the table.

"Have you met him before?"

He let out what sounded like a forced laugh, shaking his head. "No, he doesn't just show up to people. Even if he is claiming his portal fee." Devon's eyes narrowed on her. "Which makes me think, what is it you have to capture his interest?"

Well, so much for getting unfiltered information. She had gotten too close to the lion, and it had scented fresh blood. "You know well who I am," she blurted. "I was living my very peaceful life, in my boring-ass town, until you showed up."

"Kitten, I showed up way before that."

"Right, but you weren't alone then." She looked across the table toward Arkimedes and found his green eyes staring right back at her. He stiffened as his attention moved from her to Devon.

When had this all gotten so messed up? How would she be able to get him out of here when he was so keen to play the prince?

"I enjoyed finding a flustered miniature version of your mother eleven years ago in the manor," Devon said with a side smile, his focus lost somewhere in the room. "I didn't expect what followed, but that afternoon was entertaining."

"How are we going to get hi—"

"Shh." He dipped his head and gave her a hard look. "Long, pointy ears are bound to hear you."

She growled. "You thought to remind me of this now

that we've been talking for a while?" Her tone was so low, she was surprised he even heard her at all.

"Talking about a payment for crossing is something our host knows."

"Right," she said, and silence descended over them, while they just listened to the muted conversations around. No one else paid them any attention, but Nava knew better.

"You have my interest now. When we can talk at ease, I can't wait to hear more about you speaking to a shadow figure while crossing a portal," he whispered.

Dropping her fork, Nava gave him a hard look. The sound of metal against porcelain echoed across the room. "I'm not one hundred percent confident I want to confide in you with anything."

"You must." Devon's poised stance grated further on her nerves. His grin extended through his features. "After all, we are in this together, fiancée."

The lie hung heavy over her; she allowed herself to look upon her mate one more time. He had been away from both Devon and her the whole evening, chatting with the king and all the women who'd come with him.

Devon was her ally in this. She had been the one to release him after the king kidnapped her mate. What she hadn't expected was eleven years of his memories gone, taking away not only her and their bond but all the emotional growth he had done while away from politics and power.

CHAPTER NINE

NAVA

The air was heavy, like the storm raging above. Wet ash and smoke burned her eyes. She stood perched on the tree. Embers of red-and-yellow fire lit beneath blackened wood. A soft cry escaped her lips, encouraging the critters around the forest to scurry and survive.

The scent of death hung thickly in the air. Sulfur and burnt flesh.

The roar of the flames competed with the thunder in the sky. A dark shape of a demon surfaced from the smoke. Two horns shaped like antennas grew from each side of its head. Charcoal skin wrapped tightly against a plated thorax, a narrow waist, and long, segmented legs that bent in weird directions.

It looked like a wasp, except its face was demonic, with a flat, wide nose and a mouth that opened with jagged teeth.

It wore no clothes, nothing to shield it from the elements, much less from the fire it was causing. Hell had arrived in this land, burning it to ashes with fire from below, leaving no life behind.

She moved on her perch, feeling the rough texture of bark beneath her wooden claws. Anger flared in her chest as she took in the destruction. Embers blew in the wind with fallen trees, and the cry of animals surged within the chaos beneath.

Her body faded, becoming pollen, dirt, and leaves as it traveled to the ground. Pain scorched through her skin at the heat. She bared her teeth at the demon; its black, beaded eyes came to her and the rumble of a growl started in its chest as it lunged for her.

Nava moved out of the way, and her sharp wooden claws slipped over the demon's chest. Her hands burned from the contact, but its chest split open, showing embers of magma behind the wound.

It screamed, and the fire behind her claw marks subsided as nature reclaimed the demon's body. Branches grew from its heart, and its pained scream filled the air.

At some point, Nava would've been sorry to see a life sucked away like this, but not with a Zorren, their mortal enemy. Not when she was so angry.

It was the nature flowing through her that called on the dying trees, and its branches swung low, catching the demon and sending it flying up in the air. It became a pile of ash and fire when it landed.

The demon materialized back in front of her, and she attacked it again, slicing over its head and neck. It cried out, its eyes staring right at her before they grew slack, and slowly it dissipated in the air, following the ash of the burning forest.

Nava gasped for air as she woke, drenched in sweat beneath layers of silky blankets. She studied the room but found no ash and no forest, and definitely no demon.

In the green room, she was still a prisoner in the Copper Kingdom.

However, she knew deep within this had not been a dream but a reality for Ari. It wasn't the first time she'd dreamed of him this way. He usually was awake in the forest while she slept. It had been the first time she'd seen a Zorren, however, and she hadn't been there to help him.

A ray of lightning illuminated the dark sky, and a few moments later, thunder rolled in the distance, and wind swept into the room like a storm. Nava rushed to her feet and ran across the room to close the terrace's doors as the rain fell sideways, drenching everything in its path.

The gods were angry, and the Zorren had arrived in this kingdom. A coincidence? Unlikely. The three of them in this land just meant the demons would gravitate here, right?

Unlike the rain in Grey Island, this was unnaturally warm, as if the sky was telling her hell was coming. Releasing Arkimedes from this new curse of amnesia was her first job.

After quickly closing the wood doors, Nava wrapped her arms around her body and stared out past the terrace to the forest that surrounded the palace. It had been raining a storm where Ari was, much like this one, which meant he was there, waiting for her.

Nava needed to get to that forest, away from these four walls that constricted her. It was true the bracelet didn't work on canceling her magic. However, it numbed her skin with whatever power it had, like mild poison.

The likelihood of her leaving the palace was low, and making a plan with Devon had become another hurdle. In hindsight, she wished she had gotten an adjacent room to the Crow. Maybe both of them would have better luck finding a way out of this mess.

Where was her soulmate? He had to still be in the palace and close by since she hadn't been dreaming of him. She'd half expected to see him at some point.

They had locked the doors of this bedroom, and even though she had been speaking to the door every day, no one answered. It was almost embarrassing that the first couple of days in the room, she hadn't wanted to get out of bed, the heaviness in her heart too strong. She had cried until she'd had no tears left and her head hurt.

Nava wasn't sure what she was mourning. Her stolen memory or the fact that Arkimedes also didn't remember her and their love story had been sabotaged in such a horrible way. She missed Cameron, Aristaeus, and Laurie.

Then after sadness had come anger. He had been the one locking her in this room, even though he didn't intend to visit. Devon had likely gotten more attention since he was remembered fondly, maybe had even been outside of his gold room.

Leela, the redheaded maid, had brought her food every day but hadn't stayed or said much. The message was loud and clear. Arkimedes didn't give a flying rat's ass about her. After getting a sneak peek of the nightmare Ari was going through, Nava understood she had been wallowing in her self-pity long enough.

The sun had come up to the highest point in the sky, casting sharp shadows. Nava couldn't stay inside this room for a moment longer. She grasped the brass door handle, shaking it with pent-up frustration. The thing didn't budge.

She pounded on the heavy wood so hard the skin at the heel of her hand discolored purple and blue. "You can't keep me a prisoner here forever!"

No answer.

A sensation crawled over the back of her skull, and the oppression in her chest grew stronger. The energy in her body had dwindled since this morning, and she didn't know if it was because Ari needed her. Not being able to touch the rough texture of wood or the leaves and dirt and bask in the scent of the forests had to be affecting her.

There was no guard by the door. She hadn't heard or seen anyone during the time she'd been locked inside the hellhole. Hitting the door again, she put more strength into it this time. "If you are there, let me out at once."

Silence.

The weight of her skull touched the cool surface. She took in air deeply, trying to calm her ragged breathing. Not knowing how long she stood there, she opened her eyes with new resolve.

It was time to stop avoiding using her Beekeeper magic. Nava had transferred before—granted, with the direct guidance of Aristaeus, but she knew how to do it. She was not as helpless as the king intended her to be, and the thought comforted her.

Resolve settled in her with each step she took toward the balcony in the room, the only connection she had with nature. Soon her eyes drank in the wonderful visuals of the trees beyond the garden. The sky was hazy. With smoke, perhaps? Knowing her dreams weren't dreams, and the Zorren were causing havoc, only made her more eager to get out there.

She had no plan on how to get Arkimedes out of here yet, but at least she wasn't standing still.

The light summer breeze hit her skin as she focused on a place behind the palace's palisades. Closing her eyes, she allowed her magic to come alive, feeling weightless as the air carried her away.

She could taste freedom, so close as she floated over the banisters; however, her body just hung there, suspended in the air. She was stuck in between wanting to leave and being too afraid of not being able to get back.

Her energy dwindled at a fast rate, unable to borrow from nature. Her body materialized and then evaporated again.

In her panic, instead of going over the balcony, she

backtracked inside her cell. She was unable to feel her limbs, and panic took over her senses.

Her body transformed into wind, pollen, dirt, and other organic things. It allowed her under the crevices of her door, and she rushed down the hall before her magic gave up on her.

She materialized with a pop and crashed onto the floor, pulling the runner with her. The skin of her knees burned from the friction.

A vase shattered as it hit the ground, and her blurry vision sharpened with the noises down the hall. Quick steps and deep voices approached. Nava was on her feet, looking around for a place to hide, but she found only long sections of unbroken walls and closed windows.

Other than the columns on each side of the hall, which provided little cover, there was nowhere to hide. Her heart pounded near her throat as she ran back toward the forest-green door of her room.

Nava closed her eyes and tried to transfer again, but her body remained solid and her anxiety wrecked her mind. *Please, please, please transfer.*

She reached for the forsaken handle but met resistance. The steps grew nearer as she pulled and pushed. Trying to get inside was proving impossible, but her body was too weak and her mind too panicked.

Her grasp became heated, but the handle didn't budge. "Please, please."

She could force her way in, but if she ruined this door, how could she explain such a thing? They would know the bracelet wasn't working, and then surely she would get killed.

A couple of guards turned the corner and froze when their eyes met her. Nava's stomach sank, and the ants that had been crawling over her scalp descended over her body.

They took off running toward her, and her adrenaline spiked. Not tired anymore. Before she could think twice, she bolted in the other direction.

"Stop there, witch!" one shouted, and she had a looming sensation of déjà vu.

Nava couldn't hear their steps over the sound of her heavy breathing. She ran and ran until freezing air sent her flying forward.

The scent of magic surrounded her as she collided with the ground. This time, her arms buckled under her weight and her jaw hit the cool marble floor. Her teeth went through her lip, and all at once, pain erupted everywhere.

The hiss of burning crawled over her back, and she turned around, screaming, trying to put out the fire—or calm the freezing crawling over her skin. The metallic taste of blood mixed in her mouth.

Their steps brought them to her too fast. She opened her watery eyes and gasped when a gloved hand grasped her by the neck. The same icy touch of magic from her back extended down her neck.

Why did they always go for the neck? She wished she could scream at them that they weren't that original.

Nava grasped his wrist and tried to pull him off as he lifted her from the ground, still choking her.

"You can't kill her," the other man said from the back, keeping his distance.

"For Herous, I should." The man slammed her against the wall, and her head hit the rock with such strength, sharp pain rattled through her brain and black dots danced over her vision.

"The prince will kill you."

"He can't. We found her outside her room. The king will protect me."

Their voices became muted, and the hand around her

throat tightened. It wasn't large enough to hold her entire neck, but magic aided him.

Nava's hold on his wrists tightened as she clawed his leather glove, struggling against his hold like a fish out of water. There wasn't any more air left and her vision closed in.

The man behind her assailant tsked loudly, taking a step back or forward, she didn't know. "I don't want to be a part of this."

Panicked, Nava kicked and pulled, and the man slammed her into the wall again. She picked up her leg and kicked his metal-clad crotch.

Even though protected, the metal screeched under her strength. The man hissed and briefly let go. She gasped for air, but before a scream could leave her lips, he was back on her, his magic overtaking her senses.

She flailed under his grasp. Her strength was so low, she didn't have it in her to fight. It was as if her life was being sucked away. A fresh sense of panic took over before the weight of the man flew off her.

Nava fell to the ground like a boneless pile of meat. The surrounding commotion was unmistakable. Footsteps running toward her, wind blowing over her face with the scent of cayenne.

Nava was too cold to feel much. However, she opened her eyes and focused on the looming shape of a man with ebony wings. Warmth spread through her body as relief took over, but it wasn't her relief.

"You shouldn't have done that." Arkimedes's voice was colder than the magic that had been used to attack her. For a moment, Nava thought he was speaking to her as the gentle caress of his glove touched the side of her jaw. His features sharpened when their eyes met. Arkimedes frowned before rising to his feet and turning away from her. "What made you think you could touch her?"

"Your Highness." The man's voice shook with fear. Nava guessed he wasn't so cocky now that he was face to face with her soulmate. Arkimedes grabbed the fae's neck, so fast Nava had a hard time following from her spot on the ground.

He slammed the guard against the wall, much like the man had done with her a moment ago, and his armor bent under such force. "Answer me. I'm not a patient man."

"We found her outside her room!" the fae said, trying to inhale behind Arkimedes's hold. "It's the law. We . . . execute . . . if we find a prisoner outside their cells!"

"She is not one for you to punish!" Arkimedes slammed the fae again, and the helmet caved before it fell to the ground with a loud crash.

That's when Nava took in the man's features. He was gorgeous, with a pointy nose and wide, round eyes partly covered by red wavy hair. His lips twisted in a grimace as his skin turned from golden to gray at an alarming rate.

The mane on his head reminded her of Cameron so much. She tried to speak but gasped at the sharp pain that awoke at her attempt to prevent Arkimedes from killing this man. Bringing a shaky hand toward her throat, she tried again, but the sound was croaky at best.

"I thought . . . she . . . was . . ."

"You thought wrong!"

She wasn't sure why she cared if this man died or not. He had been trying to kill her, no questions asked. But his bright blue eyes were so close to the ones of her brother— she couldn't allow it. "Ark—"

The second guard approached her with reluctant steps and reached out a gloved hand. She recoiled against the wall, trying to avoid his touch. Her heart drummed as adrenaline bounced in her body.

Arkimedes's gaze snapped back to her, and the swarm of anger that took over her body wasn't hers. "Stand away from her," he growled, and the other guard put both hands up and took a few steps back.

Her soulmate dropped the redheaded guard and was kneeling by her in a matter of seconds. His warm touch was gentle on her shoulder, and his eyes studied her closely. "Get Fael and Leela," he said to the standing guard, who bolted out of there so fast, all she could hear were his retreating steps.

Her gaze met one of green moss, and he reached over, picking her up like she weighed nothing at all. It didn't take him long to get her to her room. Nava had been so eager to leave, never imagining being relieved to be back.

He laid her on the bed, and a gasp of pain escaped her lips when the fabric of her covers touched her raw back. "I will get a healer."

"No," she said, not wanting any fae to touch or tend to her. However, her voice was a whisper; it hurt too much to speak. Nava rolled over, and the burning ache in her back subsided. Arkimedes gasped a moment before she felt tentative fingers over the uninjured expanse of her back. She had come so close to dying, and now, as she lay in bed, her adrenaline was fading, leaving behind her shaking body.

"You are cold."

"I'm fine," she whispered, closing her eyes, letting her body drift away into a more peaceful time.

"What were you doing outside? How?"

"Magic," she answered. Her limbs were too heavy, and she was too tired to care whether or not this got her into trouble.

He was quiet for a while, probably assimilating the fact that she all but admitted to doing magic. "Why leave when you must have known there were guards outside?"

"I got lonely." She didn't hear this reply as sleep pulled her under.

CHAPTER TEN

NAVA

The night before had been a blur of people coming in and out of her room. Besides a couple of the royal healers and a few female maids, Arkimedes had been hovering around most of the morning.

Her back and neck were healed for the most part, not just with salves and potions. Healers in this city possessed magic unlike what she'd seen in the village. Ancient healing powers. They weren't too happy to use them on her, but it was hard to say no to the prince when that answer could get you killed.

By the time the red-haired fae who'd brought her breakfast last week came over, Nava was already dressed. When she opened the door to greet the maid, her eyes met the golden gaze of a guard by her door.

The man nodded in acknowledgment before the red-haired fae closed the door behind her. "I'm Leela. We haven't met properly yet, though I have been bringing you your food."

"I remember you from my first night in this castle."

She smiled prettily, placing the tray of food at the end

of her bed. "I would love to fix your hair for you this morning."

Nava combed her fingers over her tresses in response to Leela's offering. She liked her hair the way it was, wild and free. However, she winced as her fingers tangled in fresh knots. "Has the prince put you up to this?"

Leela's face fell before she shook her head. "Oh, no. But I would love to spend some time with you. I know it gets lonely here."

In other words, yes. Arkimedes had commanded this poor girl to keep her company, and that alone had her stomach fluttering with a pleasant wave of gratefulness and hope.

"Thanks, and who's the guard?" Nava rearranged one gold jewelry box neatly placed on the dressing table, allowing the girl to play with her hair.

"Fael," Leela said, and she remembered that name. Arkimedes had mentioned it yesterday.

"So is he going to be guarding me from now on?"

Leela met her gaze from behind, her thin fingers pausing as she held a lock of Nava's hair. "After what happened, yes."

"Is the other guard all right?" Alive, she meant.

Leela dropped her eyes to what she was doing. "He will survive."

"Good."

"Good?"

"I don't want to be responsible for that man's life." Nava shrugged, unsure why she cared. But for some reason, she did.

"He is lucky our prince spared his life after he attacked one of his guests." Leela clicked her tongue, shaking her head. "Nimb should have known better."

Nimb, the faerie who looked like an adult version of

her little brother, had almost killed her for no reason other than being outside her room.

"You are precious to our prince. That alone should have sent a warning to the guards to keep their hands off you."

"What?"

Leela swallowed and stepped back, bringing a cup of steaming tea in her shaky hands. Nava grabbed it from her before it spilled all over. "He put you in the green room when he could have assigned you a room closer to Mr. Black." Her words startled Nava. "What happened could have been avoided, had Nimb used his thick head."

Both of them had red hair, and Nava couldn't help but wonder if they were somehow related, or maybe this kingdom housed a bunch of redheaded people.

"He is all muscle and no brain," Leela continued, and Nava got the impression that even if they were related somehow, the girl wasn't a fan of the guard.

"I don't know if that says I'm precious to him. Devon and I are . . . engaged. He didn't want his brother to lose his soon-to-be bride, that's all." That lie tasted more bitter than any other she had ever told.

The fae hummed, dragging the boar brush over Nava's hair. A spike of panic moved through her as she imagined how puffy her hair would be after such attention. This fae had clearly never dealt with curly locks. "Well, he placed you in the room next to his—he must want to ensure your safety. He's put no one in here since he returned."

"Oh, I don't think that's the case," Nava said in what she hoped was a casual tone. However, her lips twitched as she fought to keep a smile under wraps, and warmth settled in waves inside her stomach. "Has he—um, has he brought anyone to his room before?"

The mere thought of it had her in knots. Arkimedes

had no memory of her, and even if their bond prevented him from feeling true attraction to anyone other than her, he might have been trying to prove a point to himself. Much like she had done once upon a time in Willowbrook with Hale, the only man other than Arkimedes she had been with.

That whole experience had been a fiasco to both Hale and her since she couldn't have been less interested if she'd tried.

"Oh, he hasn't shown interest in anyone these last months." The girl clearly didn't notice how Nava's whole body relaxed at her words.

"Either way, him putting me here is more to ensure I don't do something reckless," Nava supplied with a smile. It wasn't that she had any reasons not to trust this girl, other than the fact that the king had kidnapped Arkimedes and she was under his allegiance.

"For that, he could have assigned you to any room with multiple guards. Instead, he put you right next to him." Leela worked on her hair with nimble fingers. Her wide blue eyes met Nava's through the reflection, and it was easy to see that this faerie was a hopeless romantic. Leela wasn't that far off, since in this case Arkimedes and she were soulmates, in love, and fully bonded.

"If it makes you happy to think this, then go for it."

"It does, my lady. It has been awfully dull in this castle for many years, ever since the queen—" Leela let her words fade and lowered her gaze back down to Nava's hair.

"Ever since the queen what?"

As she shook her head, her long locks of fiery red hair whipped across her face. "I can't say any more, my lady."

"Please call me Nava. I'm not anyone's lady." Except she was a prince's soulmate, however weird that was to grasp. Cameron would have a major freakout when he learned this. He had always been so curious about the royals and their kingdoms.

"Of course, miss. However, I think you're someone's lady. Aren't you going to be married to Mr. Black?"

Right. "That's what I keep hearing." Lies to appease Arkimedes and buy them time to form a plan she was struggling to come up with.

"How exhilarating! To have these two men fight for you! I mean, we both know who will win. Our prince is one of considerable power, and I haven't sensed the Crow's power yet since he is wearing the jewel, but he is very handsome."

Was Devon Black handsome? She guessed he could be considered a more typical handsome man if you took away the evil veil that covered him. With his height, muscular build, and sharp cheekbones. It was hard to see him as anything other than a bully who'd tortured her and her friends. Someone who'd tried to kidnap a whole village to take them back to the crown and enslave them.

However, the perk . . . or downfall of having a soul-mate was the lack of attraction to anyone other than the person the gods bound you to.

"I guess I never thought about it." Nava shrugged, inspecting the intricate braids around her scalp that met into a low bun behind her neck.

"But the prince, now he has the beauty of our royals. The women of this kingdom have been swooning over him ever since he came back." Leela finished pinning the bun back. "Wouldn't you say he is the most handsome?" This girl could give Nava a run for her money for fitting so many words in one conversation. Leela was an utter gossip and a breath of fresh air in this prison.

Nava felt her cheeks warm as her mind supplied

images too heated for someone who appeared as young as the fae behind her. "I agree. He is handsome—and seems tense."

She had known Arkimedes from a soul-sharing level for a year. He was different now, like his soul was weighed down by things he didn't have a week ago when they were back home together.

"He is also wicked," Leela added with a delighted expression.

"How so? Has he done something bad since he's been here?"

"Not quite." The fae placed a pin in Nava's hair, a large white pearl with a hanging charm. "But it is known that in the Society of Crows, they called him the Reaper."

"The Reaper?" Nava repeated, a wave of annoyance running through her. Why was it that everyone knew more about Arkimedes's past than she did?

"I have no idea why, but it sounds dark and wicked, doesn't it?" By the large smile on the fae's face, they had a different understanding of those words.

First thing she would inquire about next time she crossed paths with either of the Crows. "Where has he been going during the day? I half expected Devon and I would see more of him as his guests." Nava's casual tone could have fooled anyone. She tucked a strand of wavy hair behind her ear.

"I guess it won't hurt if I say anything. No one has told me to keep quiet." Leela exhaled, lowering her attention to the ground as her delicate eyebrows twisted. "There have been rumors of attacks in the forest. We dispatched guards during the week."

"He has to go?" Maybe seeing Ari would jolt some memories back.

"His Royal Highness likes to go on the hunt with the

guards. It's said around the halls that hunting helps him gain power—when he takes others, it happens with His Majesty the king as well. They are so alike. It's like the king was reborn in his son, and of course, none of the mixed blood is hindering his powers. The queen couldn't take our heir away, after all."

Mental note, say nothing to this girl that could paint the queen in a positive light. "So it's only the royals who have that power? I notice only them and the guards have wings as well. Are most of the fae asked to put their wings away?"

"Put the wings away, how could someone do such a thing? Fae that have been gifted by the gods with wings should proudly walk amongst us with them on display." Leela's brows almost hit the edge of her hair.

Why indeed? Arkimedes had always chosen to do so. Maybe it was an insult? Nava had a lot of learning to do.

"I—I don't know. I haven't met many of your kind. I grew up in the Iron City, and there aren't many fae there."

Leela relaxed a fraction and nodded. "Iron is toxic to us." She took a deep breath and continued in a lighter tone. "Not all fae have wings, Dark Ones do. So the royals and the guards possess them, but not me, for example."

"Oh." That would explain why so many of the people working in the castle were wingless. "I thought this was the kingdom of the Dark Ones."

"Eons ago, only Dark Ones walked these lands. But the Copper Kingdom is a habitat for many races, including humans. Fae have been intermixing for generations, and so I guess we all have a bit of Dark Ones' blood in us, just not any of their magic."

"So that's why only the royals have their aura?"

She nodded, distracted by Nava's hair. "Some of our most powerful guards have a fraction—but not quite the same." At those words, Nava swallowed and watched as Leela's face lost all of its color. "I think your hair looks beautiful, milady. I appreciate you letting me braid it today. His Royal Highness will be pleased." Leela could compete with Cameron over who was the best matchmaker.

"Thank you, Leela. I appreciate your time. I wouldn't have been able to get my hair to do this."

Even though the words being exchanged were happy ones, Leela drew herself away. It was as if speaking about the queen was forbidden, even if no one else was present to chastise her. The air in the room practically crackled with tension, and the fae was already walking away, her skin shining with perspiration. Why was the mention of the queen so bad? Was the king able to listen to them somehow?

Nava had gotten rid of the creepy flowers, but the castle was run by magic. "I'm sorry, I'm a bit confused. Did I say anything wrong? Is speaking about the queen bad somehow?"

"We loved our queen. I will never speak ill of her again," Leela rushed to say, though Nava wasn't sure she believed her. However, the weird tension in the room did ease. The feeling alone had her skin crawling with self-awareness. Was she being watched? Or was it the particular subject that made the castle react?

Looking around the room, Nava ventured to say something more. "I'm curious what happened to her."

Leela's gaze turned pleading before she said, "It's forbidden by the king. Even the prince knows little. If His Majesty learned of someone divulging false information or any rumors, he would . . . It would be bad." Had Arkimedes been asking this poor girl about it as well? How else would she know that he knew little about the queen?

"Don't worry, Leela. The king and I are far from pals.

I'm practically a prisoner here, so please don't feel the need to panic. I will keep your secrets, and I hope you keep mine." But Nava would never, ever divulge a secret to this girl, however sweet she was.

After a few beats, Leela grinned, relaxing her posture. "You have gained a confidant, milady. I will be on my way then. I will bring your dinner at the same time." She bowed and, without another word, rushed to the door.

Nava stood from her seat by the dressing table, feeling the walls of herself collide as she was left alone inside this room once again. Her chest constricted, and suddenly it was hard to breathe. She rushed to the door as it closed in front of her, reaching for the brass handle, half expecting it not to move as she turned it.

Click.

It opened. *It opened!*

She let out a whoosh of breath as she peeked out into the hall, meeting the expectant gaze of Fael. He held his rusted copper helmet in the crook of his arm, and his golden eyes studied her as if reassuring himself that she was fine before he lifted a brow.

"May I help you?"

"Uh, no. I mean, yes!" She cleared her throat, bouncing on the tips of her toes as she looked down the hall to the retreating shape of Leela. "I'd expected to be locked in here like I was before."

Fael turned to her, letting out a contained breath. She had a hard time deciphering what it meant. "The prince has been busy with his duties and has been unable to tend to his *unexpected* guests. He understands it's unpleasant to stay inside the room all the time, so I've been placed as your guard so you can leave your accommodations at times."

A little more friendliness or hostility would help Nava

place this man onto her friend-or-foe list easier. She straightened and crossed her arms over her chest. "So . . . will I be able to visit the castle grounds?"

"With limitations, and always escorted."

"What about seeing Devon?" So they could plan *something*.

"When the prince is around, you may see your fiancé."

In other words, Arkimedes didn't trust them together. Whether because of jealousy or whatever reason, she was on her own.

CHAPTER ELEVEN

ORION

His long mist of shadows followed him as Orion entered the forsaken area of the library. The sound of his steps was muffled as his boots met the bumpy terrain of fallen books over rotten carpet.

The walls of bookcases were as tall as a common house in the Iron City. Even though this had once been as majestic as the rest of this library, it was now black and ashen after a fire long ago. Crusted with age and destruction, like the remnants of an old campfire.

The king had forbidden anyone to rebuild, rummage, or dissect the area after its demise. To the few who could step inside, it was a constant reminder of what had been lost long ago. Their queen, who they believed had betrayed them; their heir, who they thought dead; and all the history that once had been rich inside these shelves.

Four months ago, he'd boarded a flying ship from the Iron Kingdom that had brought him here to search for answers about his lost family, never expecting to find who he'd turned out to be. However, in the beginning, accepting a role in this madness had been more about finding why he'd been abandoned, rather than anything to do with the kingdom or the king's expectations.

That was, until the ghost of the queen had haunted him for the first time. It had begun when he entered this very same library three months ago. She'd been standing by the window. A woman wearing a black dress, with a full skirt and a tight corset. Her hair had billowed in the air, as if submerged in water. The crown had been barely visible between the strands, and he hadn't realized who she really was, until she'd shown up in his nightmares days later.

After that, he'd learned quickly that no one spoke of the queen. The kingdom believed she had died in a fire, in this very same library. Orion had believed the same, but the nightmares had shown him otherwise.

It hadn't been ideal to alternate dreams of Nava—a woman he knew nothing of—with nightmares of his mother dying in a fire. Confusing didn't begin to cover it; he didn't know what was real or a figment of his imagination.

Now that Nava had turned out to be real, he couldn't ignore the nightmares any longer. There was something larger hidden here, and he was being asked in a not-subtle way to find it.

Orion wasn't afraid of spirits; as a matter of fact, they constantly haunted him. It came with being a Dark One. This ghost of bones and ashes, however, had had him freezing in true fear the first time he'd seen her.

That day, many months ago, he had questioned the keeper of the library if he knew a ghost haunted the space. The old man had actually laughed in his face, clearly unable to see the figure of said queen standing a few feet away by the window.

Orion's mixed feelings of whether he should be resentful toward the woman who had birthed and abandoned him pulled him in a different direction. He hadn't wanted to learn anything more about her at first. Still, seeing her suffering, nightmare after nightmare, and the ghostly remnants of silent sorrow that followed him around the castle, had taken down brick by brick the wall he'd put up throughout his life.

The guardian of this place claimed all records of the queen had been burned when she died. The man had expected Orion to blindly believe the tale everyone else did. That she had taken him away, then returned to burn all records and killed herself in the same fire.

No one needed to know that he didn't trust much of what anyone around here told him, not when everything sounded like a lie.

Much less now that Nava and Devon had landed in the castle, claiming something was off—or at least she claimed. He had to find time to talk to his brother about it.

Tucking his wings closer to his body, Orion scanned the shelves for anything that would call to him. Searching for a name, feeling for a pull of magic.

Why had the queen been killed? She'd stolen the heir away. However, according to the king, he would never order such a thing. She had been treasured by him. Orion brought his hand to his temples, trying to massage away the pounding headache that kept building up as the hours passed.

It was a fool's errand to return to this place every night when, for the past three months, he had found nothing other than growing frustration. It didn't help that all he wanted to do in this particular moment was go and see if Nava was, in fact, safe.

She was a magic wielder who had bewitched him from across an ocean and was engaged to his brother. A bitter laugh escaped his lips as he shook his head and walked deeper into the ruins that once had been a guarded part of his family's library.

The worst damage of the fire lay ahead, leading him to areas he hadn't fully explored yet. He wondered if the ghost of his mother would await him in the shadows of this place.

He closed his eyes and let his magic pull him forward, following the instinctive pressure forming in his stomach as the scent of mold and ashes wrapped around him. Destruction often spoke the same language.

The moans and whispers of those he'd taken long ago stirred to life in dark, misty shapes. His power consumed kernels of other people's souls if he ever took their lives. It didn't matter if it was for self-defense or if he had been forced to do so.

An echo of a soul, forever bound to him.

The king had been teaching him to block them out, and he *had* learned. He was able to block them for the most part these days, but every time he stepped foot inside this place, they came back with a vengeance.

"*There is nothing here, other than filth,*" one cackling voice whispered, angry and disgusted.

"*A waste of time, really,*" said another.

The debris crunched under his weight, and the heavy scent of burnt matter had his eyes watering in response. It was even more unsettling that all the voices sounded alike these days; he had forgotten who they came from. His mother, however, never spoke to him. But it wasn't like he was an expert on how spirits worked. Unlike the ones who followed him around, this was the first time he'd been chased by an actual ghost.

He traced a gloved finger over the decaying ledge in front of him and wondered if he would be escorted out of this place once again. If he would leave empty-handed.

The deeper he went into the darkness, the more his chest tightened with the wrongness of it all. He knew she was around when the icy whisper of a touch of bone crawled down the back of his neck.

Goose bumps awakened, and he turned his gaze, searching. It was dark like a moonless night, but his fae eyes never disappointed, and even this remote, lonely space still looked bright to him.

The drumming inside his skull intensified as he walked deeper into the shadows, his own power blending into his surroundings as he followed a sinking feeling in his gut.

The scent of pepper lingered in the air, faint enough that most wouldn't notice it. A spell likely to disorient and push people away. Orion was close to finding *something*.

The ghost appeared then, snapping movements of charred skin over bones and empty holes where eyes had once been. He had to fight his innate reaction to flee. She raised her hand, bone pointing toward the case to his right.

Sweat beaded on his brow as he reached for one of the books, his fingertip tracing over the spine of it, and just like that, it disintegrated under his touch. Orion's wary gaze flashed to the spirit, who preserved her pose, floating in the air with teeth showing behind worn lips.

He continued, touching books here and there; his shallow breaths had him on the edge of hyperventilating when one book didn't fall into a pile of mush and ashes, and an embossed gold letter peeked out from behind charcoal.

"*There.*" The three voices of his mist perked up, but the ghost of the queen disappeared in an instant.

Swallowing, he reached for the book with gentle hands. Chunks fell off, but for the most part, it stayed solid between his fingers. His wings twitched as his fear morphed into contained excitement that ran through him like a wave.

His fingers trembled as he brought the delicate tome under his tunic in the crook of his armpit. It wasn't like the keeper of this place could stop him from reading it, but taking this without anyone being the wiser would give him a chance to get a leg up in this situation.

Orion took a deep breath and exited the burnt wing of the library, looking around for the curved old man who guarded this place, listening for the shuffling of his feet or the feeling of being watched. But nothing came to him, and he spread his wings before coming downstairs with quick steps.

He hadn't fully made it to the bottom floor when the wavy tones of a shrill voice had him stopping. "Leaving already, sir?" For someone as old as this man, he was lethally quiet when he wanted to be.

Orion half turned to meet his hazy gaze, making sure the burnt tome wasn't visible to the man. His schooled features would be hard to read, as he'd been trained to do by the Society of Crows. "Yes. Is there a problem?"

"No, of course not." The man wrapped an arm over his stomach and came one step down the marble stairs, his other hand grasping at the decorative black metal railing. One more step down and then another. "Did you find what you were looking for?"

He took a deep breath to calm his sudden irritation at his nosy behavior. His aura expanded, turning a deeper shade of black around him.

"*Let's show him what happens to the ones that question us,*" hissed a voice near his ear, and Orion's hand twitched with the vibrations of his magic.

"Are you intent on wasting my time today?" he asked

instead, and the man's expression shifted from inquisitive to cautious.

"No, sir. However, if you were to find anything in the forbidden area, I'm bound by my duties to record it."

"*Let him try to take it from us.*" The voices weren't helping with his mood, and Orion had to take a calming breath to quiet them.

He had to give the old geezer something; the man was persistent and not too afraid of him. Orion guessed the keeper had to deal with his father often, whose temper was known to be short, much like his own. "I didn't find anything other than burned books, Ellis. I'm sure you already know that," Orion said and turned to leave but paused. "I will be back tomorrow."

By the time he was out of the library, the shadows of daylight stretched over the castle halls. The air was warm and humid, almost as suffocating as the forbidden area in the library. However, the pleasant smell of summer blooms surrounded him as he walked at a quick pace toward the dining hall.

The book ground into his side, and his throat tightened as he thought it might be falling apart with friction. He took a corner and inspected the empty place; surely everyone was back in their homes, eating or working to serve the king.

He took the book out of its hiding place and looked around once again. He didn't have time to find answers right at this moment, so without preamble, he sent it away to his room, the scent of magic burning his nostrils.

Orion was greeted by the smell of roasted pork and buttered potatoes when he entered the dining hall. His gaze settled on the king, who sat at the head of the table. One of his cohorts was draped over his lap, her thin arms wrapped over his shoulders while his face worked the nape of her neck.

Her half-closed lidded gaze snapped to Orion. Her eyes were a rich brown that contrasted against her very pale skin. Her hair was long and straight, the color of spun gold. He slowed down, hesitating near the table.

"The prince is here, sir," she purred. A smile curved her plump pink lips.

Orion cleared his throat, shifting the weight of his body, not knowing if he should look elsewhere or pretend this was normal. "You called, Father?"

The king lifted his face, and his cobalt eyes darkened as he studied Orion closely. "You are late."

"I got caught up in the library."

The king hummed, straightening in his seat. His hand draped over his mistress's hips, his other holding a half-full glass of wine to his lips. "I don't like waiting. Don't let it happen again."

"You were . . . entertained without me."

The king narrowed his eyes at his heir. "Sharp tongue, like your mother."

Orion swallowed, remembering the shape of the ghost. Burnt and shallow, pointing at a book in the library. Dead.

The female sitting on the lap of the king straightened, her skin turning pale as her aura bloomed a darker shade of black; the scent in the air soured with her displeasure. He guessed she didn't like the reminder of the queen, especially when coming from her lover's lips.

Orion took a seat by the king and proceeded to fill his glass with some of the grape wine in front of him. Then he piled his plate with a healthy serving of meat.

"The forest fires, were they handled?" the king asked. "Have you found a guilty party yet?"

"What you mean to ask is, have I found a human to blame?" Silence hung heavy in between them, so Orion continued. "I haven't found signs of any human that could lead us to what the guards have been claiming."

"You have a sensible head on your shoulders but are also clouded by biases that might lead you to overlook things our people are seeing."

"This whole place is swimming with prejudices against humans. It's worth a reminder that I'm half one."

The king moved forward in his seat, and the mistress hung tighter to his neck as if afraid he would push her off at any moment. It wouldn't be the first time the king had done so in front of Orion. "Don't use that tone on me, boy."

"You asked me to go with them, and I'm reporting back that there is no human sign in that forest. No use of gray magic will cause such destruction in such a short time."

The king settled onto his seat once again, bringing the grape wine to his lips. "I heard that the witch has been tended to by my healers."

It was a miracle Orion didn't choke on his food, the change of subject was so abrupt. He tried to act casual as he washed the rich taste of pork, potatoes, and gravy from his mouth with wine. "Nava was badly injured by one of the guards."

"She was caught escaping her confinement. Our guard was allowed to punish her how he saw fit."

"I didn't like the way he behaved in my wing," Orion countered. It had been the king who'd told him he was free to make his rules on that part of the castle.

"Don't play the fool with me, Orion. It doesn't suit you."

"I told her she was allowed to walk outside her room if she needed a change of scenery. She wasn't disobeying anyone's command." Silence descended upon them, heavy and infinite, broken only by the hissing of the fireplace by the table.

"And why would you do that?"

"I learned she is claustrophobic." His jaw ached with tension, his need to protect almost overwhelming. "I'm keeping an eye on her, Father."

"But how close of an eye?" the king challenged. "Perhaps too much, as I was also informed you placed her in the green room next to yours."

His heartbeat raced and his hands prickled with sweat, but he didn't cower from his father's scrutiny. "So what? I didn't want her near Devon."

It wasn't even a lie and was something that had been bothering him for days since she'd arrived at the castle. The incessant need to protect her, like it was second nature. It didn't die there. He'd rather face the ire of his father than have her sleep next to Devon, and that thought alone was even scarier.

"*Divert. Now,*" one of the misty voices whispered against his ear.

Shrugging noncommittally, he said in a flat tone, "I don't trust her with my brother."

"You don't trust her near the Crow, but I'm supposed to be at ease with her sleeping next to *you*?"

He didn't believe for a second the king was truly worried about Nava hurting him. The king's aura vibrated with pent-up tension, his expression sharpening. He was trying to find a hole in his tale.

Orion swallowed, counting on his expression not to

give away how he truly felt for her, which might give his father a reason to jail them. The female sitting on the king's lap, Elly or something, shifted uncomfortably, avoiding either of their gazes.

"She is wearing the bracelet that cancels her magic. I'm capable of protecting myself from her, unless you doubt me," Orion countered with a lie that was far too easy to spout, especially since she'd been able to do magic just fine, and he wasn't so sure he was able to protect himself against her at all.

"What about other powers she might have over you?" The king's voice came down an octave. "She is beautiful."

"She is also my brother's fiancée."

"And I'm supposed to believe that makes a true difference? You almost killed two of our guards because they were hurting her."

"I would think after what happened with Herous, the other guards would've learned better than to harm her."

"Why do you care?"

Why, indeed? Orion wasn't sure why he was risking it all for a woman he didn't know, and he shouldn't care as much as he did. He had been telling himself he wasn't wicked, unlike the blood that ran through his body. Even though everyone back in the Iron City liked to remind him his very essence was evil, he wanted to be more. "Because I'm not a monster." Or at the very least, he hoped to avoid being one.

"She entered this palace without an invitation from either of us, which is punishable by death."

"I believe my brother when he says it was a miscalculation. When I left the city, I told him I would be gone for a month at maximum. It's natural he would come looking for me. He was all I had while I was there, and I accepted staying with you if you respected some boundaries, which includes my family."

The king stayed quiet for too long for Orion to feel at ease. This man's wisdom and wickedness were not to be outsmarted. "I see in you the way I used to be, the power, the hunger. You have the level head needed to make decisions in a moment's notice." The king picked a grape from his plate, holding it between relaxed fingers. "But then you speak and sound just like her. Idealism is the murderer of powerful societies, and we have no room for it." His gaze burned like blue fire when it landed back on Orion.

He didn't need to tell his father that idealism had saved his heart when he'd been a lonely child in an unwanted place. It wasn't his craving for power that allowed him to be human and pardon people the Society of Crows wanted dead for no reason other than wanting freedom.

Human or fae, he'd rather just be true to himself.

CHAPTER TWELVE

ORION

"I thought the next time I saw you, the cat would be dragging you in." Devon's voice carried through the walls of his room, his ebony eyes studying him. "It surprises me that I'm disappointed she wasn't the one bringing you to me."

"I have no idea what you're talking about," Orion said flatly, making his way into the room without waiting for an invitation. The door clicked behind him, and his brother followed him, crossing his arms over his chest.

He already looked ten times better than he had the day he arrived. His sunken cheeks had filled some. The darkness under his eyes had lifted.

"I have many names for her—cat, kitten . . ." Devon used his fingers to count, his lips twisted into a shadow of a smile. "*My* fiancée."

Orion flinched at that last word. Devon calling Nava his fiancée had his blood boiling. The smirk barely reached his brother's eyes, however, and it was as if he knew deep inside the word alone would grate at him. "I see," Orion growled.

It was odd with the way Devon held himself around him, like a wound that had festered between them. They had been close just four months ago, before he'd come to this place . . . unless something was off.

Devon could be under a spell that was forcing him to be here, acting strange. Manipulated by the same beautiful woman who had *him* under a spell.

Clearing his throat, he took a step closer and changed the subject. "You look thinner than four months ago." He studied Devon's complexion with a frown.

The aforementioned moved with floating steps toward the sitting area by the hearth, unbuttoning his deep blue jacket before taking a seat in the plush gold chair. "Arkimedes, brother, your manners are horrid. I would think they would beat you into shape in this hell, teach you better."

"Just call me Orion."

Devon tilted his head, showing straight teeth behind a tense smile. "Changing names in such a short time seems rather abrupt. Are you determined to stay here, then?"

Orion shrugged, making his way to the chesterfield sofa in front of his brother. The silk cream fabric was soft, with golden botanical patterns that shimmered with the light of the fireplace. His brother chased his every move, like a caged animal waiting to bite. His chest constricted at the realization that behind the false confidence, Devon was terrified of him. The only family he truly had hated him.

Orion laced the fingers of his hands tightly, bouncing both legs as the uncomfortable silence descended over them. "Arkimedes reminds me of someone I wish to leave behind." His throat thickened, and it was hard to swallow. Not knowing what to do with his hands, he raked his fingers in his hair. Arkimedes B. Valeron was a name associated with so much pain. With feeling like he didn't belong, like he wasn't wanted. Always feared. A monster.

"Ah." Devon allowed his body weight to rest on the back of the couch, crossing his ankle over his knee. "The tormented act."

"It's not an act. If someone were to offer you a chance to turn the page, to start fresh and not be who we were, you would also take it in a blink of an eye."

"I'm sure it doesn't hurt that you turned out to be a prince."

"You know me well enough to know I don't care about status or money."

"Yet somehow you always end up with both." Devon sneered, and Orion sat back, mute for a moment. His brother's eyes burned with a fire he hadn't seen before.

"What's happening here?" he wondered after a moment of extended silence. "Did we have an argument I'm not remembering?"

"You have no idea."

"What?"

Devon let out a heavy breath, his jaw tightening. "Never mind."

"Speak your truth. What's happening?"

Devon opened his mouth, and gurgling noise came out. His cheeks turned red, and he tried again. Silence, not one word. His thick black brows met in the middle. "Fuck."

"Are you under a spell?"

"You know well enough I wouldn't be able to tell you. But no, I'm not under a spell, per se. I'm under something much bigger."

"What, then? Is it something Nava did to you?"

Devon's eyes widened when no words left his lips again, and then he was up from his seat, a heavy groan leaving him as he walked around the room in a frenzy. "I guess I won't be able to say what I really want to about it."

She *had* cast a spell on his brother! Orion's body heated as he also stood, his hands turning to fists. "I will have her break it now."

"Calm down." Devon waved him off. "She can't break it. Only I can once I fulfill my end of the . . . bargain."

That damn woman would be the end of him. Orion hesitated but took a seat again. "So the match, when was it ordered? Can you break it?"

Could it be broken? Had it been an order from the Crown itself or was it a mere suggestion that his brother had blindly jumped into because of her breathtaking beauty? His skin prickled with anticipation as he waited for Devon to answer.

When no words came, Orion sat forward. "It's rather odd they matched you so quickly, and I find it suspicious you are suddenly here, under some sort of magic bond. She shouldn't be matched to you."

His brother barked a laugh and let his body unceremoniously fall onto the chair in front. "Oh, tell me how you are feeling, I beg you."

He should leave before this ridiculous jealousy came out in any way that could harm their trust further.

Leaving before asking Devon the questions that had brought him here in the first place was ridiculous. The scent of spice wafted, and the palm of his hand heated before the charred tome he'd taken from the library last night materialized in his open hand.

Devon wrung his hands together before straightening in his seat. Leaning forward, he studied the book and then raised his eyes slowly to meet Orion's.

"I have been searching for information ever since I arrived as to why my mother took me to that orphanage when the kingdom clearly wanted me here. Something is not adding up—"

"And you brought me a barbequed book to solve your mystery because . . . ?"

"The wing in the library that held the history of the kingdom and the royal archives burned around the time I was taken." Orion shrugged and placed the book on the polished wood coffee table in front of him. "I paged through it this morning, and there are some pages that are legible but in an old fae language I can't understand."

"Ah, there it is. I told you the language arts class was important to not fully flunk, didn't I?"

"You also love to dish out the 'I told you so' with no remorse."

"Touché." Devon's grin reached his eyes for the first time, and Orion relaxed a fraction in his seat.

The memories of ditching class to go and master spells while Devon stayed behind were still fresh in his mind. Like they'd happened yesterday, not when they had both been in their teens. His brother could speak many languages; they always came easy to him.

"We all have our strengths and weaknesses." Orion's lips twitched into a smile. "You and I both know I'm abhorrent at languages."

"Indeed." Devon grinned before leaning forward to inspect the book, his fingertips going over the charred cover with a gentle touch. "I'll page through it, but I won't make any promises."

"Thank you."

It had been hours, and the cool air of morning had turned warm and humid. Long ago Orion and Devon had abandoned their coats and moved to more casual positions in the same sitting area. They talked little as Devon scribbled on a clean parchment, his knuckles stained with black ink as the feather plume scratched the paper.

The document being so incomplete by the destruction of the fire made it harder; it didn't help that it disintegrated if held the wrong way.

The whole experience was like déjà vu. Devon hunched over a table, muttering unintelligible words as Orion sipped on whiskey from a gold cup, biting the inside of his cheek not to ask for the tenth time if he had found something of use.

"Don't you have anything better to do?" Devon asked finally, reaching for his own drink. "I can't translate this damn thing with you breathing down my neck. The least you can do is go and get me food."

Feeling his cheeks warm at his brother's words, Orion raised to his feet. "I will get something."

"And you'd better believe I require payment for this."

"What kind of payment are we talking about?"

"For starters, I would like to leave this room once a day, at least." Devon dipped the tip of his quill inside the pot of ink. "And I would like to see the cat."

Orion's back tensed over, his stomach churning suddenly as heat settled in his chest. He hadn't mentioned to Devon that she'd been hurt or the fact that she was able to do magic even while wearing the jewelry. "I will see what I can do." He forced the words through clenched teeth. "You probably can guess that I was barely able to save you two. It's a fine balancing game."

"I have seen you accomplish harder things." Devon tapped the dirty pages on the table. "This is not easy. Call it a favor for another favor."

Orion nodded before he left the room.

CHAPTER THIRTEEN

NAVA

Facing the garden, Nava sat on a cold stone as a gentle summer breeze came through the open doors of her room. The walks in the garden had been short and far between; however, she was happy she got to inspect some of the castle grounds while out. It helped her set a goal of where to go if she were to try transferring again.

Not that she was too eager to do so after her last attempt had nearly gotten her killed. Her back was mostly healed by now, but the mental scars were ever-present.

Her fingers tingled as she focused on the way the air felt against her skin, the wrinkle of magic pushing to come out of the curves of her body. Even though the energy inside her was practically begging to be let out, she'd been hesitant to even try.

What if she transferred into the hall again and Fael realized she was able to do magic? Then he might decide to punish her and call for reinforcements, and Arkimedes might not be close enough to save her from the king himself.

She took a deeper breath and closed her eyes. Her hair moved with the wind. The sounds of people working around the castle were almost as loud as nature itself. The power building in the pit of her stomach swelled as she tried to become one with nature, as Ari had told her dozens of times.

Maybe if she quieted the what-ifs, focused, and believed she could do it . . . she could save Arkimedes. Get back to Ari and fight the demons wreaking havoc in the forest.

The magic was there, buzzing beneath the surface. She just had to learn how to tap into it and let it flow, without letting self-doubt drag her under.

She had tried to run when she hadn't even learned to walk, too preoccupied with what was happening with the Zorren and Arkimedes to focus on her task of learning to transfer, to map the area with her mind and allow her energy to bring her there.

Steadying herself, she emptied her thoughts. Her limbs became lighter, and she focused her attention on the room next door. She wanted to transport herself into the washroom; it was safe and close.

Her stomach became alive with dozens of butterflies lifting, and now it wasn't only her limbs but her hair that billowed like air. Dust and pollen surrounded her before her body disintegrated, cell by cell, becoming one with the air, and she moved quickly toward the washroom, feeling the hot, humid air of the surrounding bath.

Her body became solid again, and she stumbled on shaky legs as adrenaline pumped rapidly through her limbs. *I did it!*

Light-headed, she sat on the bathroom floor to prevent falling due to her weakened limbs; a wide smile spread across her lips as her heart doubled in speed.

"Ha!" She pumped her fist up in the air. For the first time in days, she allowed herself to squash her fear and believe she could do it.

Throughout the day, she transported more times than she could count, taking quick cat naps in between to recuperate her energy, for once happy that no one came to fetch her. The blue sky had warmed to bright orange tones, the highlight burning a trail down the top of the garden hedges and stone paths.

Nava made her way out to the terrace. The sky-blue fabric of her dress billowed in the air, and each small gem that was beaded on the skirt shimmered in the sunlight.

Summer had always been her favorite season, but not this year. She frowned when the hint of burnt wood lingered in the air. She squinted into the forest but couldn't see smoke in the distance. Still, the pit of dread bubbled in her gut.

The dreams of fire and Aristaeus fighting the demons couldn't be a coincidence. If she could smell something burning nearby, there was a possibility Ari was in that forest, losing a battle that she should be helping with.

The sound of metal-heeled boots over stone floors came from the room next door. The terrace mirrored hers, but the whole time she'd been here, the room had been closed. Arkimedes came into view as he stepped outside. His green eyes met hers, and she noticed them softening as he took her in.

He was far, but even in the distance, the sun brightened his features with light gold tones. He wore armor, she realized, similar to the guards'. The insignia of a dead tree on the chest plates called to her. Silver chain-mail mesh wrapped around his arms and neck like a scarf.

She had seen that tree somewhere before, but where? Her mind couldn't reach the memory.

Soot stained his face and armor, and his large wings flicked behind his back, the feathers moving with the wind, catching blue highlights. He hesitated but continued toward her, his gaze dropping to her neck, clearly trying to find remnants of her attack.

The skin of her hands became cold and sweaty, and she was back to being a nervous wreck under his scrutiny.

"It's cold out here," he said as a greeting when he reached the edge of his balcony and held onto the banister.

"It's not too bad." It wasn't a lie. It was cool, yes, but her body was suffocating with a bothersome heat underneath her skin. The coolness of the approaching evening felt good.

"How have you been feeling? Has Leela taken good care of you?" It was hard to hear him, and her brows met in the middle as she came closer.

"I think I heard you right, but yes, she's been wonderful. You didn't need to force her to keep me company, though."

He scowled. "She said that?"

"Oh, no, no. I just—" *know you* "—figured it out."

Arkimedes's wings expanded, so large they barely fit in the area he stood. He flapped them and soon he was landing on her balcony. Her heart threatened to leap out of her chest. She would never be tired of the vision that was him flying.

He tucked his wings behind his back but didn't put them away, like he would have if they were back home. "Have you left your room again?"

She had been dreading the possibility of this conversation ever since she'd woken the morning after the attack, not wanting to explain or lie about how she was able to use magic, especially since she didn't know the answer to that. "Other than the garden walks Fael takes me on, no."

Arkimedes focused on the landscape, his jaw clenching. "I'm not talking about him taking you anywhere."

"I know what you are asking. I'm not sure if you are ready for my answer."

That called his gaze back to her, and she struggled not to squirm under it. "How did you do it?"

Nava shook her head, letting the silence wash over them. "It smells like smoke. Have there been fires in the forest?" Her eyes cut to him.

His frown deepened, and a lick of mistrust reappeared on his handsome features. "You can smell it?"

She shrugged. "I'm sure anyone can smell it. It's pretty strong, no? I mean, I don't see any smoke around, so maybe not . . ." Oh, she had not missed the babbles.

"No, it's not apparent to anyone. But there have been some fires. We don't know what's causing it." He squinted at her, clearly forming his own wild ideas inside that thick head of his.

They didn't know what was causing them. She did. "Before you try to blame it on me, I have nothing to do with those fires," she said sharply. "I have been stuck in this room for days."

"You can also leave this room, apparently." He reached to her wrist, touching her bangle with a finger. "It's active."

"Yes. It works just fine. It just doesn't work one hundred percent with my magic." She fidgeted, trying to prevent anything else from spilling out. It was difficult when it was second nature to want to be open and confide in him.

"So you can bend a magic-canceling jewel and can smell a forest fire that is miles away." Arkimedes was close enough that she had to crane her head back to meet his gaze.

"My magic works with nature." She hesitated when his attention burned through her. "Um, you could bring me along. I'm sure I can help."

"Isn't all of our magic supposed to work with nature?"

Nava scowled. "I'm not exactly like you or—other magic wielders. I guess it's of no use to explain since clearly you are mocking me."

"No. I want to understand what you mean." If he did, why was his voice loaded with irony? "If you aren't the one starting the fires, can you find who is? Are you a soothsayer?" His skepticism dripped off every word, and it grated on her nerves. Sure, this Arkimedes didn't remember her, but that didn't mean he had to be such an ass.

"Stop mocking me."

"I'm asking questions." His voice dropped an octave, becoming dangerously low. His aura billowed out. "How can you do magic with the jewel on?"

"I don't know."

"Liar."

"I don't!" she huffed, crossing her arms over her chest. "My magic is earth-based, not fire, water, air, or dark." Though, that was a lie as well. Nava didn't feel so connected to fire but had been able to call it before.

The kingdoms rarely specified the inclination of one's magic, but magic wielders usually had an inclination or two. It had always been one of Nava's favorite subjects when reading her mother's books.

"You won't leave this palace," he said.

"Why the hell not?"

"Because you trespassed when you arrived here, and the king doesn't trust you."

Well, duh, the king didn't trust her because she was sure he knew she had been there the night they'd kidnapped him.

She wrapped her hands tightly around the terrace's balusters. "Well, for someone who just claimed I wasn't a prisoner when your guard almost killed me, you sure treat me like one."

Arkimedes hovered closer and his body brushed hers, his energy a mist of cool air against her heated skin. "Don't fool yourself. I did that because you are to be Devon's bride."

Nava raised a brow, feeling the wave of dangerous fire churn between them. "In that case, can I at least move next to my fiancé? I sure would love to spend some time with him."

Arkimedes held the railing so tightly his knuckles turned white. Nava was sure it would explode under the pressure of his power at any moment. "You are to stay here, where I can keep my eyes on you."

"One would think you are jealous of your brother, sir."

"Don't flatter yourself." His eyes dropped to her lips.

The swarming heat that took over her body left her breathless, and she pulled away. Being so close strengthened his emotions within her, and she didn't need to feel his jealousy when he was so clearly trying to be an asshole. "Speaking of, when will I see Devon?"

A fake smile appeared on his handsome features. "Are you going to stay out of trouble if you do?"

"Is that what betrothed people do?" Her words came out harsher than she'd intended them.

His nostrils flared. "Good girls do."

"Who says I'm good?"

A wave of burning desire that was all him had her blood boiling. She gulped at his darkening gaze. "No, I supposed you mustn't be." He brought his hand to her face but stopped himself short of touching her. "My name is Orion. Use it."

"I'd rather not, Your Highness." She curtsied, and his expression morphed. Out of annoyance or interest, she didn't know. Maybe it was both.

CHAPTER FOURTEEN

NAVA

The warm air was suffocating, clogging the lungs as she sat on a tree branch, watching the forest burn. Her hand grasped at the blackened wood, still warm to the touch even though it had stopped burning hours ago.

There was no life left in this tree—hundreds of years of memories gone. The knot in her throat became so thick she couldn't swallow. To think of the centuries of magic, life, and love lost to the shadow demons.

This was the end of whatever had been set in motion the day the gods had bound her to her other two parts. Her eyes focused on the branch she sat on, her skin bark and lichen. Long fingers that resembled sticks, and nails of iron that cut through fallen angels, fae, and demons alike. Her power lightened beneath the rough texture of her skin, and soon the burnt tree regained its luster.

What they had burned became alive with her touch. The tree creaked under her, and the ash and soot that covered it fell to the ground. Her body weakened as the tree greedily took all she offered. Soon, leaves sprouted out of the dead branches. Moss regained its emerald-green color.

She took her hand off the wood and her energy dwindled further, *too low if she were to be attacked at that moment. There was no way they could revive an entire forest. No, not even their magic could save the tragedy of what was being lost here.*

Nava woke up with a gasp. Her dreams about Ari were coming to her every night. It was the only connection she had to what was happening out there. Even though she had been asleep for hours, her body was drained and tired.

She reached for the glass of water on her nightstand, something she'd been leaving there every night to battle her parched mouth.

Nava was exhausted but buzzed with the need to be out there in the forest. Knowing her Beekeeper was hurting, alone, made staying here that much more painful. Her unsuccessful attempt to get Arkimedes to take her with him was maddening. A part of her knew she could have tried harder.

Groaning, Nava let her body flop back onto the feather-filled mattress. A commodity she'd never had before. However, in her current state, it was almost suffocating her. Her breathing was quickened as fragments of the dreams she'd been having flashed through her brain.

He didn't trust her, didn't love her, and that alone was heart-wrenching. Telling him they were mated and that he'd been taken from her could help matters, but he might also just send her away to live in town alone. There was no sentimental attachment, just the damn bond.

One of the options was to give him time to fall back in love with her all over again. To trust that he would with time, like he had done last year. She *had* to believe in them.

On the bright side, she'd been successful at transporting the entire day and was ready to risk it farther.

With the Zorren attacking Ari every night, she feared

her time was short. She would try to get to Devon's room tonight and figure out how to remove the bracelet from his wrist. Once he was able to do magic again, they could portal Arkimedes and her back home.

Her heart slowed down, and her body prickled all over. *No.*

Grabbing the silk cover of her bed, Nava pulled it harshly. The fabric tensed under her fingers as a profanity left her lips. She would not kidnap him like *they* had done. Nava had to battle those dark thoughts every day.

Nava just needed a few minutes alone with Devon to figure out how the damn jewelry worked. She had been trying to remove it for days with magic and other small objects in the room, to no avail.

A knock on the door had her jolting in her spot. Leela came in, holding a tray with food. The scent of eggs and bread wafted through the air, along with black tea. The fae put the tray on the bed's foot and rushed to the doors of the terrace to open them wide, the way Nava liked to keep them.

"Good news today. His Royal Highness has requested for you to join him for lunch." Leela was practically shaking with excitement, her face blushing as she walked back, filling the ornate porcelain cup with steaming tea.

"Really? No outing to the forest today?" Nava wrapped her silk robe around her body, hoping her question would get her more answers than she had gotten from Arkimedes yesterday. Her leaving him outside the afternoon before had struck a nerve, she was sure of it, and was likely the main reason he'd set this little lunch date. It might be the perfect time to try to get him to bring her along or maybe slip some information that he could use to help Ari.

"I guess not. Aren't you excited?"

She was and wanted to wear something other than blue

to celebrate the occasion. Didn't these people like variety? Judging by the orange dress Leela wore every day, Nava got the impression they had designated colors.

"Would we be alone?" She tried to sound casual, but the shake in her voice gave away her nerves. She picked a light blue day dress with embroidered silver flowers down the bodice. It draped down wider than the ones she'd been wearing lately, in layers of distinct tones of blue.

"That one is gorgeous. He won't be able to take his eyes off you," the young fae gushed, rushing to take it out of Nava's hands. "Neither of them will."

Oh, so Devon was joining them as well. The pleasant warmth that had been running through her body dimmed. She had wanted to see Devon, to plot if he had any ideas on how to get out of this mess.

He couldn't plot against her since Arkimedes's life and hers were so intertwined. The life debt would demand he didn't act in any way that would harm them while the bond was latent. That didn't mean she trusted him one bit near her soulmate.

"Where are we eating?"

"Out in the garden—very romantic."

Leela needed to find another hobby that wasn't gushing about Nava's love life, because whatever she was imagining was happening wasn't the case.

By the time she was ready, Nava's brown wavy hair lay past the middle of her back, not half as frizzy as it usually was.

"Leela, your matchmaking skills are really something to behold." Nava shook her head with a smile.

"I apologize for my enthusiasm, my lady. I know they betrothed you to another, but my romantic heart is just— When you two were bickering in the hall that night . . ." She sighed, and Nava's smile grew. "This is the most exciting thing I have seen in the last ten years. Other than this, I only get to clean cobwebs and dust curtains."

"Oh, yes, that sounds dull. At least it's a beautiful castle. Also, there must be gossip that doesn't involve the royals."

"Yes, my lady, but this is so much more exciting." The fae's fingers retreated from Nava's hair with the soft knock on the door. She beamed down at Nava and scurried toward the door with light feet. "The guard is here to escort you to the garden, my lady."

"I'm not your lady, it's just Nava."

Leela nodded and cracked open the door, revealing the looming shape of her mate. Arkimedes rested against the doorframe, his brow lifting as a rebellious strand of hair fell over his forehead. Nava heard a gasp to her left and could only imagine the young fae's face right now.

With the silence that descended, she battled the need to fidget.

"Your Highness." Leela bowed from inside the room, and Nava remembered where she was and who this was supposed to be. Not her rugged soulmate from the forest or the Crow chasing her across an ocean. This was a prince.

She curtsied. "Your Highness."

"Orion," he offered with a secret smile.

Her cheeks warmed at the sight of it. "I like your other name better."

He shook his head and allowed her space to exit the room. Today it was warmer, and within the humidity in the air, Nava could still scent a trace of smoke.

"I didn't expect you to escort me," she said, bringing her hands down the skirt of her dress, straightening nonexisting wrinkles. "Sir," she added for good measure.

"I was on my way there." His eyes grew darker, and he pushed both hands inside the pockets of his ebony tunic.

While the words said something, his inner emotions were a lot more complex. He was excited to see her. Waves of warmth and bubbling nerves pushed through their bond.

Nava had a hard time hiding her trembling smile. He had the gift of an impressive blank expression, but it was hard for him to hide all of his emotions from her. "So, is this lunch to make it up for having locked us away for days? I assume Devon has been treated the same way . . . since I haven't seen or heard of him." She paused, taking a deep breath after she'd pretty much blurted out all of the words.

"I thought Fael was taking you out for walks," Arkimedes shot back, lifting a brow at her.

"Well, who is taking Devon out? You?" And she didn't mean to sound as petty as she did, but the words left her before she'd gotten hold of her feelings.

His lips twitched. "How are your wounds healing?"

"Fine."'

"Are you sure?"

"Yes. Um . . . could you reconsider the option of taking me with you next time you go to the forest?" she whispered, and his face snapped back to her, his eyes narrowing. She wrapped both hands together in front of her.

He let a deep breath out and shook his head. "You don't understand your current situation. Even if I scream that you are my guest, the king doesn't see it that way. There is no walking out, not yet."

Nava *did* understand, but she couldn't just accept it. The forest called to her; Ari needed her there to balance, lend, and borrow each other's magic. There was a lot she had to learn about her own power before she could confront a demon alone.

Transferring was her only choice.

She looked forward and didn't broach the subject

again, and they walked mostly in silence, all the way to a part of the garden she hadn't seen before. They crossed under arches and down stone steps. Sage-green grasses lined the stone pathway, and the tips caressed the stone with the light breeze.

Past that, shrubs of camellias were in full bloom with pink-and-white flowers. Her heart soared as the energy of nature embraced her. Here, she could almost forget the scent of burning around them.

They meandered to a large veranda on the side of the castle. Its roof was molded metal that swirled with leaves and branches. A massive wisteria tree climbed it, draping lavender blooms on the sides.

Nava slowed as she took it all in. The large circular table in the center filled to the brim with food. Tiers of buttery pastries, bowls of fruit, and platters of dried meat and nuts.

Devon stood from his spot at the table, straightening his coat. His hair was slicked back behind his ears, making his high cheekbones and porcelain skin practically glow. "I wondered if I would eat by myself." He crossed toward them, patting Arkimedes's arm as his dark eyes met hers. "That perhaps the approaching summer solstice had already gotten to you."

"What does that even mean?" she asked, taking a seat.

"The solstice affects all magical creatures. Warlocks, sorcerers, and witches are affected the least, as we are the most human—but the fae have curious parties."

"What do you mean by curious?"

Arkimedes took a seat across from her.

"Seductive. Stimulating. Sexual," Devon continued, and his eyes shone with malice.

Nava's face heated. "That answers nothing, Devon."

"He means the fae have sex all night long while the

party is going," Arkimedes said, filling his dainty cup with steaming tea.

Her face slacked, and her whole body grew warm from something entirely different. She pressed her legs close together, squirming under both their gazes. "Oh."

"Oh, indeed." Devon filled his plate with food. "But not only the fae are affected, of course. It's said soulmates are . . . how do you say this without being crass? Well, they go through a heat spell. Like animals, really."

Nava reached for the collar of her dress, her cool fingertips calming her flaming skin. "Huh."

"Whoever has a soulmate around—well, let's just say, all the crannies in this garden will be occupied. Won't it, brother?"

Arkimedes's gaze all but seared her alive. She swallowed, reached for a glass of water in front of her, and drank it all in one go.

"Are you two soulmates?" Arkimedes's growl had her jumping in her seat.

Devon's rumbling laughter filled the space a second later. "No, no, brother. She is not mine."

Damn right she wasn't.

"How did you two become engaged? It takes years for the Society to consider a match, and I have never heard of her before."

"You have heard of Nava—or the possibility of her," Devon said, his face abandoning the lightness of before.

"What do you mean?"

"Does the name Forrest ring a bell to you?" The porcelain cup shook between his bone-white fingers. His onyx gaze deviated from Nava to his brother.

Arkimedes's face dropped. "Celeste's daughter?"

"The one and only," Devon said, popping a ripe green grape into his mouth.

"But she couldn't be. Nava would have to be——"

"Fifteen?" she asked, and his eyes burned through her. "You are not fifteen."

"Ouch, kitten, you must up your face moisturizing rituals." Devon smiled wickedly.

"Devon, you aren't making this easy." She seethed. "But he is right, and so are you. I'm Celeste's daughter and I'm not fifteen."

"Right, and she had you when she was, what, eleven?" Arkimedes's voice was drenched in sarcasm. "She wasn't even pregnant when she left the Society."

"Well, there must be something wrong with your timeline. I'm sure you can see the resemblance—I have been told I look just like her."

"Maybe her sister, but not her daughter," Arkimedes insisted.

"She is her daughter, brother," Devon said. "Her and the potion maker made this wonderful creature, and we—I—discovered her."

Arkimedes paled, but Nava's vision of him glazed over, her skin breaking into a cold sweat. The potion maker? Her father. Why couldn't she recall him?

He was missing completely. Was he alive? Dead? Had he been a part of her life growing up? Her chest constricted as the walls of her mind closed in on her, and she became a prisoner of her panic.

The memories of darkness and emptiness from when she'd crossed the portal slammed into her like an iron wall. There had been two entities the day she and Devon had passed through the shadow lands toward this kingdom. The voice that had demanded payment, and the shape that had loomed closer.

One of them had taken her father away.

Her breaths became shallow, and she sank deep within

herself, putting her half-eaten scone back to her plate, her appetite lost.

"Her skin is lighter. A mixture from her father. And she has the one blue eye like him." Devon reached to the three-tiered stand that held the pastries. He hummed while deciding which buttery cake to pick. "She is also a potion maker. Like father, like daughter."

"You look a lot like her," Arkimedes acquiesced, then his expression shifted. "Are you all right?"

The air left her lungs, and her grip tightened on the edge of the table. She wanted to swallow, but her tongue was as hard as a rock. She couldn't breathe, or was she breathing too fast?

"Nava?" Arkimedes's tone was far away, and his face became closer as his hand rested on top of hers, his touch scalding her skin. Why were they looking at her? Was she speaking out loud? Was she screaming?

A couple of bees landed on the table, crawling over her fingers. Why couldn't she remember how her father looked? Or his name, the sound of his voice? Had he enjoyed singing? Cameron had red hair, so very different from the dark brown of their mother. Perhaps his hair was the same color as his father's.

Nava gasped for air, stumbling to her feet. The chair crashed against the stone floor. She tipped over it when Arkimedes wrapped his arms around her, bringing her straight to his warm chest. Her knuckles whitened as she grasped the silky fabric of his tunic, feeling his breath hit her face as she closed her eyes.

"You're fine." His arm reached behind her back, drawing circles over the fabric of her dress. The touch grounded her somewhat.

Silence descended. Even the birds had stopped singing —or perhaps she couldn't listen to them.

"Ark, take me back home, *please*," she whispered against his chest. She wanted to be back in her house in the Northern Village, wrapped in her favorite, fluffiest blanket that Laurie had knitted last winter.

He scooped her from under her knees. Soon she was flying off the ground, and the flapping of wings moved her hair with the air.

"Take a deep breath, Nava. Don't pass out on me." His voice was like honey, and her skin raised with goose bumps. However, it was the soft beating of his heart that helped calm her down.

Nava didn't remember what happened next, just that she was inside his warm embrace in one moment, and the next she was lying on a mattress made of feathers, under covers of silk and fine cotton. The scent of leather and him pulled her to sleep.

CHAPTER FIFTEEN

ORION

It was not lost on Orion that he'd been the one who'd jumped to comfort Nava when the panic attack hit her in the middle of breakfast. It was even stranger that his brother hadn't reacted at all to the fact that he'd touched his fiancée.

She'd asked him to take her home, like he knew what she meant. Maybe in that moment, when the wave of desperation hit him out of nowhere, he would have taken her anywhere.

Orion sat on the green velvet couch. Flames rolled in the fireplace; however, no heat reached him. His fingertips grazed his lips as he studied the frame of her body as she slept. The waves of her dark hair lay across the mattress, covering the points of her shoulders. He followed the gentle curve of her back and the soft curves of her hips.

He had never burned like this for anyone. To drop whatever he was doing just to get her out of the situation. To want to fly, to fight, to kill. What was going on here?

A sob escaped her lips, and the sound alone had his back straightening. His fist tightened as he tried to rein in his feelings. He would find and hurt anyone who'd harmed her this way. Flipping the sofa over wouldn't help the situation at all. The fact that that was his first inclination as to what to do had him stopping before he did it.

His fingers stilled over his chapped lips, and he blinked away the fog of protective anger that had settled within him. The deep knot in his throat was hard to swallow, but he knew he needed to get out of the room before he just took her in his arms and left this place for good.

To hell with his mission of finding the reasons for his mother's betrayal, her death, his past. He was up and storming out of the room like a soul traveling to hell. He hesitated for just a second before he flew off the balcony.

Nava only represented danger to him. She was forbidden and would only distract him from something he had been searching for his whole life. He needed distance.

The guards were pushing Devon out of the gazebo by the time Orion entered it. His aura bloomed against the greenery, almost as opaque as the night. Their gloved hands immediately abandoned his brother's shoulders, and his ebony hair lay in disarray over his forehead.

"Your Highness!" The two guards took a healthy step back from his brother before one dared to speak. "We thought you would be occupied, and we were bringing the pri—your guest back to his accommodations."

"Was he even done with his meal before you two decided to push him around?" Orion growled, and silence descended.

These two guards were part of his troop, and he usually had to work with them when they went into the woods or to town to deal with any issue that might have arisen. They respected him and were amicable enough that he didn't sense they feared him. However, the scent of the area was sour with the spike of anxiety emanating from them.

He knew his answer then. They hadn't waited for Devon to be done with his food. They had decided to take him away whether or not he had eaten.

"You are dismissed. I will take Devon back into his room *after* we are done eating."

The two men didn't have to be told twice. They pretty much piled toward the exit of the gazebo, trying to get away from there.

Devon looked back with a scoff and straightened the cuffs of his shirt before his pale hands combed his hair back in place. "I thought you had forgotten about me."

"They shouldn't have pushed you around like that." Orion walked to the table and took the seat he had previously occupied, his gaze traveling toward the metal chair that still lay on the floor.

"I'm guessing the cat is fine?"

Orion's attention snapped back, and his jaw ached with tension. It was hard to battle the need to go back to where he'd come from. "She is asleep."

"Rather an intense reaction to scones, if I do say so myself."

"Do you know why she acted that way?" He had lost his appetite in the middle of the commotion.

Devon piled extra food onto his plate as though nothing was amiss. He didn't care what had happened. "Not a clue."

Orion went over everything they had said, trying to find what had triggered it, and it was the mention of her parents—not her mother, but her father. "Did her father hurt her?"

That had his brother looking up from his food, his brow crinkling as he thought over his answer. "As far as I know, the man is dead. Nava was working at the potion shop by herself. Why?"

"She has a potion shop? Where is Celeste in all of this, and why would Nava panic when reminded of her father?"

Devon dropped his pastry on the dish and dusted his hands. He was buying himself time from speaking. "She is elsewhere. You know how she is—hiding all of her family from us."

"How did the Society find them? Did you . . . ?"

"I found her, which is why I got stuck in this predicament in the first place." His sigh of annoyance was telling, and damn if his brother's reluctance didn't make him confused. "But enough of that. I found something with the . . . item you brought me."

The book. Orion perked up in his seat.

Devon pulled something from his pocket and slid it to Orion over the table, while his other hand took the bone china cup that no longer held steaming tea. "The translation might be off. I'm a bit rusty."

Orion looked around him but found no one was around. This meant little, as his father had spies everywhere, even in the damn vegetation. He opened the folded paper; Devon's neat scrawls were familiar. "It's not much," he commented, looking at his brother over the paper.

"There wasn't much left in what you brought me. Most of what was there was not important—recollections of yearly expenses on improving the garden and some updates to the town. There was a brief mention of the Society visiting, but the juicy bits were burned. I did find a few tidbits that might interest you."

Orion dropped his gaze back to the parchment. The

more he read, the slower his heart drummed. The sudden dizziness that hit him had his head spinning.

The child of royal blood came to this world sick, poisoned by evil, and was taken into the world of shadows, away from the land and our people.

Did this writing mean him? The world of shadows was considered the transition place. Where souls went to get winnowed to a better or worse fate. Purgatory.

He swallowed and fought the urge to crumple the paper in his hands; he kept coming back to the words sick, poisoned, evil.

Evil.

Had his mother led him to find this book to show him that she'd had a reason to get him away? She had not killed him . . . but people considered him dead until not long ago.

"Oh, you got the tortured face on. Am I going to have to convince you this might not be about you?"

"No."

"This could be any other royal, Arkimedes."

"It doesn't matter." The thickness in his throat told him otherwise, and he wished it was true. "This is something I can work with, ask questions."

"If you were evil and sick, the king wouldn't have received you with open arms. But by all means, we can just leave and be done with this madness. Go back to our city and—"

"I'm not going back to the Society of Crows, Devon. I

don't want to go back to that life, I told you. I feel this is where I'm supposed to be."

Silence took over for a moment before he continued reading, but the leftover paragraphs just spoke of resistance toward accepting the human soldier in the royal guard. No mention of the queen.

"Oh, there was something else. I didn't get to write it down, as I was in the middle of reading when the guards came to get me. The book mentioned a prophecy. It was at the end of the book, and since most of the pages were charred, the dates were a bit difficult to access."

"There is likely another record of it in the library."

Devon nodded with a hum. "It would be strange if they only tracked it in one book."

Orion folded the paper his brother had given him before putting it inside his pocket. Now he had a task—go back to the library and find that prophecy. "Thank you, Devon."

"Sure. But the true payment is not being stuck inside that room. I would like to see the cat again, at some point."

Orion nodded, even though he felt cold and sick at the idea. He had to battle this urgent need to keep them apart. Nothing good was going to come out from trying to prevent her from seeing him, not when they were engaged, and she was a distraction he didn't want or need. "I will see what I can do."

CHAPTER SIXTEEN

NAVA

*N*ava pressed the sliced cucumbers against her swollen eyes. She'd cried until she had no tears left. This morning, the redheaded fae who'd tended to her for the last week had woken her up by opening the balcony windows.

Leela had gotten one good look at her face and disappeared from the room for almost an hour. She'd returned with sliced cucumbers and a juice she'd claimed would help with heartbreak.

How the young fae knew about her broken heart was a mystery Nava wasn't sure she'd ever find the answer to. She appreciated her immensely.

"He is off riding today," Leela said as she worked on Nava's hair, untangling the mess of curls that had matted over while she'd slept.

"The prince?" Nava's voice cracked.

"There are rumors circulating the castle that he flew you here yesterday. That there was a fight in the garden between him and your fiancé."

Nava's lips slacked when she realized that Leela thought her sorrow today was due to a romantic upheaval. Not the fact that she'd lost her father. She cleared her throat before she went down the same path. "If they fought, they didn't do it over me."

"Why are you so sad then?" Her eyes shone behind thick black lashes. "I'm an excellent listener, my lady. I know I talk a lot, but I promise whatever it is, it won't leave this room."

Nava tightened her lips. If only she trusted her. But her mother had taught her to believe in herself and her family. Her eyes ached from the lack of moisture, and she blinked rapidly, trying to bring some back. "It's—it is heartbreak, but not the romantic sort." Nava took a deep breath and pressed her palms against the dressing table's top, letting the coolness of the wood ground her. "On my way here, I lost something very dear to me. Something I won't ever get back—" Nava swallowed the ache in her throat. "I'm not ready to speak about it."

Leela stared but nodded. "I will bring my lady some grape wine for this evening."

Nava's lips turned. "Now that's what I was hoping to hear you say."

The fae left not long after. Nava looked at her reflection in the quiet morning. She had been a potion maker since she was a teen. Her blood sang when she sat on her stool to ground herbs and play with metals and oils. She loved helping people, but it was more than that. Being able to create had given her purpose.

Now, all the memories of potions were gone—most of them, anyway. And even if she remembered making them, the techniques were murky, as if someone had punched holes in the recipe.

It was all gone, all she'd fought to learn for the last decade of her life. Her career.

She allowed herself to bask in her pity party for a while longer. But eventually, she reminded herself she was not one to wallow for long. Forrest women didn't let problems take over. She wasn't no one. The gods had given her a task: to protect the world from the demon realm. Her magic was wonderful and alive, even though someone had tried to snuff it.

To think she'd always assumed that when Arkimedes would give her a piece of jewelry, it would be an engagement ring—not a magic-sucking bracelet.

Nava stood from her chair, resolution settling in her stomach. Ari always told her something was holding her back, but it wasn't something. It was someone. Herself.

She would leave this castle and get to that forest to see her Beekeeper at whatever cost. He called for her, night after night. The bees crawled the walls of her room, blending against the warm tones of the stone, a reminder that she was still very much a creature meant to protect.

Nava stood and dashed to her armoire, rummaging until she found her old clothes. Brown pants and a white shirt. She pulled on her well-loved boots; they fit her like a glove, the leather worn and caked with mud.

It was time.

After what happened, Nava wasn't ready to attempt transportation all the way to the forest. She had to tackle it differently. First to the garden, and then to the forest from there. Easier said than done, but hunger for the result gave her resolution a well-needed push.

She looked at the expanse of the garden. This would be a long distance to go, and she was going there half-blind. Her connection to Ari, and his need for her, would guide her there. Sort of.

"Stop being a chicken." Her knuckles whitened with her tightening hold against the banisters. "You've got this. You are a badass Beekeeper."

Apparently a crazy one at that.

She closed her eyes and held her breath, focusing on the mental image of the garden and the meadow between the palace's grounds and wilderness. Her insects crawled over her skin, answering her calls.

Nava reached down into the bond, trying to sense where Ari was, feeling the tug across her bond, calling for her, as she wished to be there. Letting out her breath, she transferred away. Down the terrace, hugging the rock walls of the palace. However, she veered back inside again. To the lower floors and inside an open window.

No . . . No . . . No.

Walls of large wooden bookcases that extended to the ceiling caged her in, with volumes upon volumes of aged manuscripts, ancient if the musty scent was anything to go by. She materialized in the darkness of the vast room.

Nava held herself behind the cabinet, the wood smooth under the pads of her fingers. It smelled like leather, beeswax, and old paper. Why the hell had she ended up here? It was the complete opposite of an open garden filled with plants.

She eyed the tones of books warily, remembering all the hours she'd spent hunched over some like this in the manor before she'd met Arkimedes. Forced to read hundreds of pages of boring history lessons and ancient politics that didn't help anyone.

Nava was much more of an outdoorsy sort of learner.

She absorbed new information from experience; she craved the feel of nature's air against her skin.

What a waste of time. Just when she closed her eyes to transfer again, she heard them.

"Look for them again," Arkimedes growled, and Nava stumbled back, hoping the shadows of the heavy furnishings would hide her from view.

"I will, Your Highness. I—I'm trying. The king ordered we burn all the books that mentioned the queen—" The man paused, and she heard the shuffling of feet.

Nava held her breath, too afraid to call anyone here to her in the room's silence. It was now clear that she had ended up in that library because of Arkimedes; he had been in despair and calling for her. Nava now knew her soulmate was hunting for answers about his past.

"I'm sure there are more here, and I hate to think you are holding information. I need to know what happened before my mother left the kingdom."

"Before you were born?" the other man asked, and the candlelight flickered as Arkimedes's magic burned through the air.

"Yes. I know when something doesn't add up, and I need more information."

"I will turn every book, every page, in this library."

Silence descended, and for a moment, Nava thought they might have left. She stood still, her back pressed against the cool wall.

"What about the prophecy?" Arkimedes's voice lowered, and for a while, nothing broke the heavy silence.

"The prophecy," the old man repeated, clearly buying himself time. "I don't know what—"

"Save yourself the trouble, Ellis. I know about it. Where is it?"

Nava let her body relax against the heavy bookcase, breathing slowly as she listened.

"Someone stole it from this library around the time you were taken, s-sir."

"Are there any records of it?"

Nava peered behind the wood corner of the shelf. The old fae pointed at a spot, his twisty old finger shaking. She followed the direction of where he pointed, finding a section of the library burned to the ground. The metal gates were still black with burn marks, and soot extended along the walls and ceiling.

"They are all gone," he said.

Arkimedes said nothing, but the churning disappointment in her stomach told her more than he could say with words. "You may now go."

"Sir," the other man said, and Nava heard the distinct dragging of feet.

She took a deep breath and chanced another glance behind the rack she hid behind.

Arkimedes pinched the bridge of his nose, closing his eyes. "Come out of the shadows, Nava."

Her throat ached as she tried to swallow, making her body as small as she could between the heavy bookcases. She could try to transfer now to avoid this terrible situation.

He exhaled, and she could feel his annoyance pulsing down their bond like a wave. She hesitated but stepped out of the shadows. The sun pierced through the massive windows behind him, grazing their skin.

He considered her in silence, and his already sullen expression darkened. "What are you wearing?"

"My old clothes. I'm tired of the dresses," she whispered. He prowled toward her, and she shuffled back, pressing her back against the bookcase. A rim of fire haloed around his wings. He towered over her.

"Why are you wearing traveling clothes, and how did you get in here?" His voice was significantly lower than what he'd used with Ellis.

Her body shook from the top of her head all the way to the tips of her toes. Based on her fast heartbeat, scared didn't cover how she felt. And the heat pooling between her legs confirmed this. Her libido was back with an appetite. That horny bitch never knew when to lie low. "Back away, Arkimedes."

"Don't call me that name. How. Did. You. Get. Here?" His body was less than a foot away from her. Tendrils of darkness rose from his body. Oh, he was pissed. "This area is warded. No one but the royals are allowed in."

"What about—Ellis?"

Both his hands caged her in. So much for having him trust her.

"I said, back away!" She pushed against his chest with all her strength, but he didn't move an inch.

"That was the custodian, the only other person allowed to enter." His gaze narrowed on her. "You shouldn't be able to enter."

The solstice was affecting them both, she realized. Nava had been off-kilter ever since she'd woken up, her blood flowing hot under her skin; her thoughts about her mate weren't just focused on how to escape but more about how to get him trapped somewhere, preferably under her and wearing a lot less clothes.

Still, she would not let him think he could talk to her this way, even if she was secretly loving it. She was technically in a forbidden area of the castle—and had gotten caught eavesdropping. Those were semantics.

"Stop whatever this is, *now.*"

"I'm going to ask you one more time, and then . . ."

Nava lifted her chin, narrowing her eyes at him. She called upon her magic, and it came soaring through her veins with the heat of her scorn. She dissolved midair as Arkimedes staggered forward, his hands desperately grabbing a breath of pollen, dander, and dirt.

CHAPTER SEVENTEEN

NAVA

 ava's legs buckled when she materialized between sculpted hedges in the garden. She took in her surroundings with a heated breath. The emotions inside her weren't hers alone but his as well. She bolted forward.

She transferred three times, each occasion bringing her closer to the forest. Her energy flared along with her adrenaline; however, transporting so many times in a row made her dizzy.

The pounding of gravel under her steps and the clear buzzing in her ears muffled all other noise. The large flapping of wings came behind her, and then Arkimedes had landed with a mighty roar. She turned and her eyes widened when he met her gaze.

His frown deepened. "Nava, stop."

She ran as if her life depended on it. Repeated inside her head that Ari needed her. Arkimedes also deserved to see this side of her, of them. Her actions only kept feeding his mistrust. Something had to change.

He groaned when it became clear Nava would not listen to him. "Stop!"

She turned back around but ran faster. Her strides down the path led to an imposing copper gate, rusted in mint-green color with drips of white and dark browns. Walls made of stone caged in the garden. Here, so far from the castle, the heavy scent of smoke lingered heavier than before.

They were playing cat and mouse, and the excitement of it made her blood simmer. Whatever the gods did to magical creatures like them in the solstice was not helping.

The gate's intricate designs let her see beyond the carvings to a misty forest where Ari awaited her. She could almost feel Arkimedes's heat as his steps boomed closer. If he caught her, she knew somehow it would take a lot to convince him to let her leave.

But if she made it out and Ari found them . . . then maybe it would spark his memory. His fingertips brushed the end of her hair, and her body lost matter, floating in the air and through the holes of the closed gate.

"Fuck!" His voice sent a thrill of excitement down her back. She almost smiled as she materialized back on her own two feet outside of the castle grounds. "Dammit, Nava."

He flapped his wings and was over the gate and heading toward her. He had to be using his magic to propel his movements.

The exhilaration that ran through her was a mixture of magic and something more primal. The strong wind stirred her hair before a wall of steel landed on top of her, sending her flying to the ground. An iron arm snaked around her waist and twisted her in his grasp.

The air escaped, and she shut her eyes, awaiting the

impact, but all she saw were dark feathers that wrapped her in a protective cocoon.

His muscles reverberated with the impact of the landing. Arkimedes grunted in pain, and the soft, velvety texture of his wings touched her skin.

Nava was draped over him, her arms pulled around his chest. She felt the quickness of his heartbeat under her cheek. This was the closest she had been to him in so long. Her mark soared at the touch. His wings spread open, letting the warm light of the day fold over them. His dark lashes lowered as he blinked multiple times, confusion flashing through his features. One of his hands came to his chest and massaged the spot where his mark lay.

Nava stirred, feeling the long expanse of muscle tense under her movement. He was hard wherever she was soft, their angles and curves perfectly molded to fit one another, just like their souls. His pupils dilated, and the thrill of desire that traveled through her body left her breathless. Whatever this nonsense Devon had been blabbering about, it was not untrue.

Arkimedes rolled over her, and his warm breath hit her cheeks. "Don't run away again," he commanded.

"Or what? You will lock me away in the dungeons?" She'd heard castles had dungeons. Her complete ignorance on the matter was not lost on her.

"I will tie you to my bed if I need to."

Her mouth went dry. Now, *this* was the kind of submission she could get behind. "I would like to see you try."

His gaze dipped to her lips, and her heart leaped. Maybe he would kiss her and his curse would lift. She kept thinking if she made him break this iron grip he had on his feelings, he might remember her.

He clenched his jaw and pushed away from her as if she burned him, leaving her on the ground, lamenting the loss of his body heat. "If you leave again, I will." His voice sounded throatier than usual. However, his eyes burned with the intensity of the promise. He meant every word.

"I need to be in the forest," she whispered. "I can't be locked in that room forever."

"Even if you survived that forest, the king will hunt you down, and this time I won't be able to stop him." His hand went over his face. "They will kill Devon too."

Nava was about to tell him she didn't care whether or not the Crow was killed but hesitated. Not only would that reveal the lie of their supposed engagement, but she wasn't sure that was the case anymore.

Did she hate the man? Yes. Did she want him dead? Maybe not . . . and it had to be due to how important he was to Arkimedes because the Crow couldn't be growing on her.

No way.

She rushed to get up from the ground. "I would not leave"—*you*—"permanently. I will be back before sunset."

"The forest is dangerous right now, and the king doesn't trust you."

"What about you?" Hope bloomed in her stomach as she held his eyes.

His lips tightened. "How did you get into the library? How were you able to disappear like that?" He inspected her, as if she would grow an extra head at any moment. "How can you work your magic while wearing the bracelet?"

She pressed her lips together. "I already told you I don't know."

He reached for her wrist with gentle fingers. "What spell did you put on me?"

"None. I swear." She swallowed and knew she had to take a leap of faith. Lying would only push him away further. Plus, she hated lies. "I haven't lied to you. I don't know why I could enter the library, but I know my magic is different—and I can show you."

He dropped her wrist and brought his hands over his face, taking a deep breath. "How?"

"You can come with me to the forest," she started, and he was already shaking his head.

"It isn't safe in the forest right now."

She knew this! His words only lit the fire within her to be out there. "No, it's not. But it doesn't mean I don't need to go." She took a step toward the trees behind her and called to Ari, hoping he would hear her.

His brows dipped, and he followed her. "If the king finds out you were here, it won't be good. This is not a matter to take lightly. My rational mind tells me I shouldn't trust you, that this is strange." He moved his hand around them, pointing at their surroundings.

"Then why are you trusting me?"

"I don't know." He groaned. A spike of annoyance rushed over her body. Hers or his? Likely both of them. She could feel Ari nearby, could sense her strength growing. A bee landed on her shoulder, and Arkimedes's eyes came to it.

"Nava . . ." His brows raised as a spark of recognition lit his face, his eyes never leaving the insect as another landed over her hand. He paled, staggering back. "I have seen this before."

"Ark—"

"Don't call me that."

"Do you want to be a prince that badly you have to abandon who you were?"

"No, but does it matter? It's who I was meant to be." He stirred under her scrutiny, but his expression hardened.

"I don't know why you think you can talk to me like you know me."

"Maybe I *do* know you," she snapped. "You must not fully trust what you are being told around here, either. Because something doesn't fit, does it?"

"And you do?"

"I know where you were four months ago, and it wasn't here or the Iron City," she said but hesitated to continue telling him, too afraid that the truth might spook him.

Arkimedes hadn't wanted or planned to leave the Iron City ten years ago to go to an island in the middle of nowhere to find her. If Nava told him, he might ask what had happened with Devon, and she feared the truth would make this harder.

She needed Arkimedes trusting Devon so they could get him out of here. If he didn't trust either of them, she would be screwed. "I'm going in that forest, whether you or the king try to stop me. Unless you plan to take me to that castle against my will." For a moment, she really thought he would take her up on it, and she wasn't ready to go down without a fight. "Aren't you at least curious about what I have to show you?"

His tense pose relaxed a fraction, his eyes narrowing on her. "Fine."

Nava turned around and headed into the forest before he could change his mind. She let her intuition guide her. Here the air was thick and dry; moats of dust and ashes floated in the air as if gray snow was falling from the sky. Even though she couldn't see a trace of flames anywhere, it was sweltering hot the farther in she went.

Her eyes watered as she moved forward, knowing Arkimedes followed closely behind. The knot in her throat thickened as bees came to her. The forest differed from the ones in Grey Island. Moss didn't hang from every surface, and the trees were sparser, with a gentle mix of conifer species and others, like pecan and maple trees. Their energy embraced her, welcoming her.

Her body was weightless as she walked forward, the tentative smile she wore had her cheeks aching. But it wasn't only happiness that had her giddy.

This was home, the scents of wood and soil. The rattling of the leaves as the wind passed through them. Her body refilled with energy she hadn't known had been depleted until this very moment.

The treetops waved with unnatural force, and Arkimedes pulled her behind him, his magic exploding into a plume of black ink that embraced them in a protective shield. "Stay behind me."

"It's fine. I know who it is." She pressed her hand against his back, right underneath where his wing protruded from his coat. A creature of wood and bark landed in front of them, crouching on the ground before he stood over seven feet tall, looking down at them with black eyes.

"*It's nice to see you, dearest.*"

"I wasn't allowed to leave. I had to escape today—and barely made it."

Ari stared in silence. "*Blackness hugs the mind of our protector like poison.*" The Beekeeper turned his head to the side, studying Arkimedes with an expression that morphed into one of worry. "*That is why he didn't bring you along the last few times he has been in the forest.*"

"He doesn't remember us," Nava said and heard the loud intake of breath coming from Arkimedes. She chose not to turn to face him, not to dwell on the lack of recognition on his face. With a few strides toward the Beekeeper, she placed her hand on top of one of his wooden legs. "It's good to see you again, Ari."

The creature nodded. *"You have finally let your body unleash some of your power. You have transferred. I can sense it in your skin."*

Even though Ari didn't speak out loud, the creature's mouth ticked up in a prideful smile, and that alone took some of the burden that weighed her heart. She turned to Arkimedes, who was staring open-mouthed at the both of them.

"I have never seen a Beekeeper this close before," he breathed.

If only he remembered all they'd gone through, their adventures, the knowledge they'd both gained, their life together. "You have," she whispered.

He turned toward her, a brow raising. "How would you know?"

"It's easy." She shrugged, but her eyes stayed on him. Unblinking. "You have seen *me*."

And to prove her point further, she lifted her hand, and bees came flying down, circling her palm. Tens. Hundreds of them. The buzzing grew louder, and Arkimedes staggered back. His eyes widened as he followed the swarm.

Ari grasped her shoulder, and their energy blended together, soaring with their nearness. *"He doesn't quite remember us, but the memories are still there. Trapped under an enchantment."* The Beekeeper's eyes shifted to Nava. *"You, dearest, lost something greater. The shadow man's touch was on you."*

Her body crumpled down, or maybe it wasn't her physical self, but everything inside. An emptiness in her heart grew like a black hole, sucking the energy she had just regained.

She didn't want to be reminded of it, not now. She had cried enough already.

"It can't be. A human can't be a Beekeeper." Arkimedes shook his head, but his eyes traveled from the bees to her.

"Surprise." Her lips turned into a weak smile, but the heaviness that lingered in her heart was anything but happy. "The Zorren have been coming to our dimension more and more. Ari needs me here."

"The Zorren?" Arkimedes repeated, his skin growing pale. "We suspected it was humans using dark magic to burn the forest, but we didn't expect demons."

"I sent one back to their realm a couple of days ago. There is one more I have tracked down. They have opened a gate in this forest, but my power alone doesn't let me find it."

"Does he talk to you?"

"Yes, we are connected." The three of them. However, she hoped Arkimedes didn't see the mark carved in Ari's chest. She didn't want to have to go through the soulmate-bond thing while she had to deal with everything else. Cowardly? Perhaps. But after realizing she'd lost her father and her ability to make potions, she was determined not to lose Arkimedes as well. "He says there is a gate opened in the forest, but he needs our combined forces to find it."

"We have seen the destruction scattered around the west side. They've killed a few hunters, and our farmers claim the land has been poisoned."

"We should go there, right?" She turned to Aristaeus, who quietly observed them.

"There is a legend that claims the god of the night had two children. One with a mortal, and one with the goddess of the moon. Both offspring were so wicked, they were cast away to roam the earth. One became the first fae to walk on this land. The first Dark One, our protector's ancestors."

The information, though shocking, didn't pertain to their current predicament. "So?"

"What's happening?" Arkimedes's brows crinkled with worry.

"The Zorren power works similarly to the Dark Ones. They feed

on life and were created by the other sibling, whom you met. His claws have been on you, dearest."

Nava's lips slacked. The shadow that had taken her memories was the person commanding the Zorren? Which one of the two? "What?" Her body went cold, shaking at the memory of the dark shape with an icy voice that had ripped a part of her soul open. "Didn't you think that information was important to tell us before?"

"*The gods work in mysterious ways. Them making our protector the Dark One's princeling was a surprise to me, but it makes sense, as Arkimedes's power works similarly to theirs, and so different to ours.*" Ari sounded passive, clearly not understanding why she felt so upset about this new information.

"Nava," Arkimedes started, "what's going on?"

She hated lies, and not being able to unload all this information on him right now was difficult for her. "Did you know he was a prince before?" she asked, ignoring Arkimedes's gasp.

"*No.*"

Nava let out a sigh of relief, but the creature continued speaking. At least Aristaeus wasn't a liar, unlike Arkimedes, who had lied about them being soulmates the year before —and her, who was doing the exact same thing now.

"*But I suspected his powers were connected to the gods in a more direct way after I saw him fighting against the bounty hunters.*"

Arkimedes grasped her arm with a gentleness that wasn't reflected in his impatient tone. "Are you talking about me?"

"Yes, we are. But we don't have time to get into this right now." The scent of smoke was too strong around them. She wrinkled her nose. "We have to find the gate and try to close it."

Arkimedes was ready to argue, but he closed his mouth and nodded instead. "Are we heading west?"

"*With you two here, I should be able to close it for the time being, but more will come.*"

"What did he say?" Arkimedes shifted his body weight around, his shoulders tense. He stared watchfully at the Beekeeper as she repeated what Ari said. "With the both of us?"

"Later," she promised, laying her hand over his arm, and they stared at each other in silence. "I will tell you more later, I promise."

"All right."

CHAPTER EIGHTEEN

ORION

They trailed the forest with haste; dew saturated their clothes from the slick leaves of the low-hanging branches, and it was harder to move in the muggy surroundings.

His wings were too large to walk in such a confined space. They slowed him down, and he'd been fighting against the urge to put them away every damn second. If he wanted not to be an outcast for once in his life, all he had to do was to learn and adapt.

His ability to do so had saved him when he'd been picked by the Society of Crows at the age of five.

The sun trickled down the path as they moved farther east. The forest rapidly changed from healthy and living to the sicker nightmare he had been fighting against. Hanging in the air was a disease of evil that burned in his lungs. The foliage withered with brown-and-black tones and crunched under their feet.

"It's gotten much worse." Orion turned toward Nava. Clenching his jaw, he studied the area. "It wasn't like this a couple of days ago."

The Beekeeper creature whimpered, and Nava's expression shifted as the shock of the visuals hit her full force. The mystery of this woman drove him mad—she was reckless and an enigma he craved to unravel.

Seeing the mask of fortitude she slid over her features was endearing. Her face appeared stern, but her hands trembled as she held onto a burnt tree. Those strange eyes flashed to every corner visible. "How much longer until we get to the gate?"

"We are close."

"You two are synchronized!" she said with a smile that reached her eyes, the freckles on her cheeks multiplying. His heartbeat raised, and he wished his body stopped reacting to her this way.

She had given him a half-reasonable answer as to why she could do what she had, but it didn't mean she was trustworthy. No matter what his senseless body was telling him, he had to keep his distance.

He lifted his brow, staring blankly at her.

"What? You both said the same thing at the same time. Find some sense of humor, you two."

His lips twitched, and he struggled to school his features from her curious eyes. It was peculiar that the mythical creature spoke with her.

They reached the area where the open gate quivered in the air. The forest became hazy with smoke, and their travel slowed down as they moved forward, keeping their steps as quiet as possible.

There were no noises here, no animals, no rustling of the leaves with the wind. The air hung stagnant with something malicious. In this destruction, even their breath echoed.

The ends of his hair stood on end when a smoky shape fluttered between the trees. Orion's steps froze alongside the rest of them. He was not wearing his armor or carrying any of his weapons—not that a metal sword could help him against a demon.

Immersed in this destruction, Orion's power rejoiced at the possibility of battle. It always hungered to take energy and life.

Something warm called to him, like a lover's embrace. Orion turned to his side and let out a breath when encountering the beauty of Nava's aura. Yellow and blooming like the sun. Her power embraced her as she prepared for the evil presence that approached them.

The smoke took shape, and a demon formed in front of them. A giant insect-looking thing that could come from anyone's nightmares. Taller than seven feet and looming with a snarl that showed ebony teeth behind a gaping hole.

The Beekeeper's stance widened and his magic billowed around him, yellow like hers—no, his was gold, shimmering like metal. Orion's own aura exploded around him, mist, smoke, and shadows that looked so alike the ones around the demon.

The Zorren's eyes traveled to him, shining red as it also realized how alike the two magics were. Orion's stomach sank deeper. No wonder people always feared him.

The child of royal blood came to this world sick, poisoned by evil, and was taken into the world of shadows, away from the land and our people.

The words written on Devon's parchment flashed through his brain as fire bloomed from the demon's clawed hands. Soon, a ball of fire came their way—toward Nava. It burned a path of charred dirt and everything that once had been alive and green.

Nava gasped when the heat scalded their skin. Panic

bloomed inside him, and without thinking, he stepped in between her and the enchantment. His shield of black ink came over them, and the fire bounced off, dissipating in the air. His energy dwindled.

"It shouldn't take it long to fire back." He heaved out of the way as the Zorren ran to them, its segmented insect legs kicking ash and dirt in the air, steam pouring out of its wide mouth.

The roots of the burnt trees moved, and the dirt groaned under their feet. Orion struggled to keep standing, gazing at the two Beekeepers by him. Nava shone like a beam of light, her anger burned into her beautiful face. She strode forward as the branches swung low toward the demon.

The Zorren weaved out of their reach. The wood of the tree withered away in large coal chunks.

Roots lifted from the ground, not just from one tree. All around them lifted, causing a tremor on the forest floor and forcing Orion to take flight. The land stayed still as the demon tried but eventually failed to run from the attack.

The forest soon pinned it under roots, rock, and debris, and the evil thing screeched as fire lit from its skin, charring everything in its path. The trees burned, and the soil melted with stone, but the woodland didn't release its hold. The three of them ran to the demon. From this close, its features were even more horrifying. Its snappy movements were jarring to his eyes.

It smelled like charred flesh and burnt acid. Orion lifted his hand to it, and soon the smoke around the demon started dissipating, rushing to his extended fingers. The creature's eyes widened as its fire dimmed; a high-pitch scream left its mandibles again, lacking some of the energy it previously had.

It was never easy seeing the life of a living creature

flicker away under Orion's destructive pull of energy. The demon's eyes became vacant as his magic fed from it.

With the destruction surrounding them, his human compassion dwindled, and instead, the bitter tug of resentment took over, and he wasn't sure he wanted to fight against it this time. Why was it on him to always turn away from his natural urge to steal energy from someone else, even when it was against something as evil as this demon?

His depleted energy soared, but with it came an increase of rage and bloodlust.

A small hand wrapped around his arm, momentarily distracting him from the strange veil of anger that had come down over him. He shook his head, trying to clear his thoughts as he focused on Nava's face.

"Are you all right?" she asked, her brow crinkling. One blue and one brown eye studied him closely.

"Yes." His voice came out hoarse, and he wondered if using his power to suck out that evil energy had affected his thoughts. Had the malicious essence of a demon somehow clouded his thinking, made him angrier and ready to enjoy killing it?

The Beekeeper creature held the demon by its neck, and the gold of his power enveloped them both. Soon the Zorren's body turned from burnt matter to vines twining around it. Nature soon devoured the body of its adversary. The only remnant was a pile of ash on the ground of what now appeared to be a fallen tree.

He cut his gaze from the Beekeeper to Nava. Her face had been tense before, but now it rested at ease with her surroundings. Sensing him, she met him with a raised brow.

"Your magic . . . is incredible," Orion breathed as her hand dropped from his arm. He had all but forgotten about her touch.

"I know." She smirked, and the air of laughter escaped him before he could stop it.

"Who knew your ego was this inflated?" he teased back, a warm feeling spreading from his stomach and through his body. Maybe he didn't need to hide from her, just now when his darkness had been at a high point. Instead of fearing him, she had grounded him.

He paused at his problematic thoughts. It was beyond worrisome, especially since he knew near to nothing about her, other than she was Celeste's daughter, a Beekeeper, and was engaged to his brother.

"Someone has been feeding said ego for a year. I blame him." Her smile faltered after the words left her lips, and her eyes searched for something in his face that made the pit in his stomach grow.

Whatever she was looking for wasn't there. A spark of a memory, perhaps. But his mind only drew blanks, only pieces of dreams that involved her body with much less clothing. His cheeks warmed, and he turned his gaze away.

"Ari says we should close the gate before another demon appears."

He guessed Ari was the creature's name, a much less impressive one than he'd thought. Who would name such a being of life *Ari*? It felt like a dog's name. The Beekeeper responded to her words as if called by them. The situation was bizarre, at the very least.

They didn't have to walk long before the gate came into view. In a land of nothingness, a wide black circle quivered with pent-up power, the wrongness of it palpable in the air.

They slowed down when the pressure of it kept them away. Voices speaking in tongues came from the other side.

"How do we close it?" he asked.

"Ari?"

The Beekeeper stood forward and lifted his arms in the air, sharp fingers spreading, and soon words came out of his mouth. It wasn't something he had heard before, but the words caressed the back of his spine and were beautiful. A language of gods.

He soon realized that not only the Beekeeper's aura surrounded him, but so did hers, blooming as bees descended from the sky. Orion's throat felt clogged as his own aura also billowed, and he was sure Nava's shocked expression mirrored his own.

Strings of yellow, black, and gold flowed between them, like ribbons of woven silk shimmering with magic. Nava's fingers extended, and her power came in waves from the ground beneath her boots.

The creature kept chanting the same words in that language that soothed Orion's darkened soul. He didn't understand the direct meaning—or did he? His mind tickled with a distant understanding. He shouldn't know what the words meant, but somehow he did. It signified the healing of this world, the closing of a gate between realms.

The dark portal closed another inch and then two more, zapping with magnetic power, now barely a sliver. Claws appeared in the black hole, trying to push through the small space, but soon it closed down, and black iron fingers fell to the ground without another sound.

The three of them stopped at once, and the ribbons of magic slowly faded away, back into their depleted bodies.

It had been a while since he'd felt this level of exhaustion. His legs trembled under the weight of his body, the ache of his shoulders apparent as he rolled them. Nava walked like a newborn fawn toward a nearby tree and leaned against it as her head thumped on the blacked texture.

He pinched the bridge of his nose as he took a couple

of deep breaths. This fatigue was unlike anything he had ever experienced, something that took his essence from the marrow of his bones. "How did I know what those words meant, and why did I know what to do? I have never heard that language before."

"I didn't know the language either, but I also knew what it meant," she admitted, and her gaze traveled to the Beekeeper.

Silence followed, and Orion tightened his fists; his stomach churned. "What is he saying?"

"He said it's the lost language of the Beekeepers. Only he knows it fully. Since we are a part of him, it passes the knowledge through the bond."

His back straightened, and he became utterly still at her words. "What did you just say?"

Her skin turned a pale shade of gray, and her eyes dipped toward the ground, her teeth capturing her bottom lip with a sharp bite. "Um—so, perhaps you want to sit down? Or stay standing, no worries. It doesn't make me more nervous or anything." She cleared her throat. "Remember when I said I was a Beekeeper?"

He raised a brow expectantly. Of course he did; she had just dropped the bomb not an hour ago. "Yes."

"There are always two Beekeepers in the world, and with the Zorren coming to this land intent on destroying it, the gods also assign a protector." Nava lowered her gaze to the ground, avoiding him. "Our magic works together. They bonded us to protect the world from destruction."

He stepped toward her, shaking his head. None of it made sense. "Does that have anything to do with me?"

She shifted, restless on her feet. He was closer now, and she hesitated to meet his gaze. "You are our protector, Arkimedes."

His jaw slacked. "What?"

No, I am not.

She flinched, and he realized he had said the words out loud, but the churning of his stomach told him he was not fit to protect anything or anyone. He took lives. He certainly didn't deserve to be one protecting these two creatures of light.

"We are connected and have been so for a year—actually, more like a decade."

"My magic is the complete opposite of yours," he growled. "I'm not at all one of you."

"Maybe that's the point!"

His lips tightened into a flat line. "If we are, why can't I hear him?" he challenged, pointing a finger at the Beekeeper.

Silence came over them again, and Nava turned her face toward the tall, treelike creature. "Aristaeus says you don't let him in—not like I do. He says you have a block in your mind, that you've learned to shield against him communicating with you. Willing or unwilling—"

"I don't want to hear any more of this nonsense," he said and paced away. Not ten minutes ago, he had been deep into thoughts so dark, she would shiver over them. He didn't deserve to be even near these two, let alone protect them.

She cleared her throat once again. "You had dreams of us, right? Maybe those weren't dreams . . ."

Here it was again, the damn memory loss that didn't leave him alone.

"Stop." Arkimedes lifted a hand, while the other rubbed a circle on his forehead.

"Shh." She shot the Beekeeper a pointed look. "Arkimedes, there is a reason—"

"I said I don't want to hear it," he snapped. "We should head back. I don't want the king to send guards looking for me and realize we both left the grounds. It will be bad if he gets suspicious."

"He is already suspicious of me." Nava lifted her arms over her head, groaning in frustration. "He knows I was with you when he took you." She let the words die on her lips, and they both stared at each other.

"Nava." His voice sounded broken even to his own ears. He hated that sound.

Unlike anything his father had told him these last four months, *this* felt like the truth. That alone had his body shaking as it mixed with utter exhaustion. The thought of having lost a decade of his memories was an out-of-this-world notion. He *had* seen them before.

Nava and Aristaeus were familiar in a way they shouldn't be. Devon's distance toward him was like there was a wedge between them that hadn't been there before. The extra scars he'd found on his body didn't lie.

With how much his father needed him to be here in this kingdom, it was no surprise that the king would go as low as to erase Orion's memories.

It made sense, but it still deviated him from his original goal, which was to find answers as to why he'd been abandoned. Why his mother had been killed, and all that had led him here. To have ten years of memories gone.

He didn't have time for strange bonds and falling for his brother's fiancée . . . if that's what she was.

"We should go," Nava agreed, turning to the creature. "We will be back, Ari." She flinched at apparent words he couldn't hear.

"What did he say now?"

"If you didn't want to hear about our connection before, believe me—now is not the time for what he said."

CHAPTER NINETEEN

ORION

*O*rion had hated these woods ever since the ghost of his mother haunted his dreams. It was a daunting task to come every night and hunt for arson when he knew the darker secret that lay behind. As he got closer to the spot he hated the most, his heart pounded alongside the building headache.

He needed a distraction.

"How are you feeling?" he asked, glancing back.

"Tired." Nava's brows twisted as she took in his features. "How about you?"

Apparently, she could read him like an open book. Did this have anything to do with the supposed bond they shared? He sure as hell couldn't read her that well, but now he was wondering if he had been able to. Magical bonds came in all shapes and strengths.

The bond a shifter had with their claimed mate, forged with a bite at the time of selection. The bonds witches had with their covens. The bonds of brotherhoods and sisterhoods, formed with blood spells. Then there was the myth of a soulmate, chosen by the gods themselves. The only chance a soul had to find their other half.

This supposed bond Nava had blabbered about sounded a whole lot like a soulmate bond, except the creature was dropped in there, and Orion believed in soulmate bonds about as much as he believed the king's lies.

"I'm fine," he said sharply. "We are almost there. I'm guessing you won't be able to do your disappearing trick to get to your room."

"Transferring? No, I'm barely able to walk. Be glad I'm not fainting as we speak—I have done that before." Her cheeks turned a bright shade of pink. "Multiple times."

He faced forward, fighting a smile. "There are some areas of the garden that are heavily watched."

"You mean by the creepy flowers?"

"Yes." That was one way to put it. "I'll take you through a secret passage and then fly you up to your room."

"Aren't you also tired?"

He raised a brow, facing her. "Are you worried I'll drop you?"

"Absolutely. I know you think you are invincible because you're the all-powerful Ar—prince, but it's not the first time you have crash-landed with me in tow." Nava pressed her lips tightly together, as if realizing she had given too much of their past, and once again, silence descended upon them. When and why had he dropped her? He hadn't shown his wings to anyone before he came to this kingdom.

The two of them had to be close, and if the dreams were memories . . . intimately so.

"I won't drop you," he promised. "Say I believe this madness you are telling me, that I have known you from before—you claimed the king knows this?"

Nava took a subtle breath but didn't hesitate. "Yes, if you remember the way he greeted us at dinner, then you know there was a threat woven in there."

Orion nodded. "I have learned in my time here that our kingdom's history is messy. The king wants to prevent it from repeating itself. It's hard for the royal kin to produce heirs. Something to do with our blood not mixing well with others, even our own kind—or humans."

This was it, the area of the woods he hated the most. The trees had become thick with age, and even though it had been years since this part of the forest had caught on fire, it was still all dead.

He slowed his steps and turned to meet her gaze. Nava was not looking at him but at her surroundings.

Her eyes were wide and horror shone through her expression. "The Zorren were here too? So close to the castle."

He walked forward, and the tree of his nightmares came into view, so large it commanded reverence. A huge clearing was around it where no other tree could grow due to what he assumed was poisoned grounds.

He was sure this had been a beautiful place, but it wasn't anymore. The tree's charred trunk and branches were all that was left.

"When my mother took me away, the kingdom mourned us for years." He paused, turning away from the horrible imagery that would forever haunt him. "This tree was where the queen was murdered, though it's not the story told to the population."

Nava brought both her hands to her lips, covering her horror.

He wasn't sure why he was feeling so open and vulnerable with her and the Beekeeper, who trailed close behind, but he was. Orion needed to get this burden out somehow. "My dreams of you are not the only ones that have haunted me these past few months." His chest sank lower despite himself.

"You have had nightmares of her dying here?"

"Yes, though very fragmented, and it doesn't really reveal who did it or why she was here in the first place."

"I'm so sorry, Ark," she whispered, her brow wrinkling as she grasped his hand. Her skin was warm, and it lifted some of the heaviness that had settled in his gut. Her touch should have startled him, made him want to shake her hand and put some distance, but that was the opposite of what he craved.

They stood in silence; the looming presence of the tree hung around him like an oppressive force, and he no longer wished to speak a word of it.

"Is this why the kingdom's emblem is a dead tree?" Nava's voice shook him out of his thoughts.

"No." He cleared his throat, debating whether he wanted to keep speaking or just move on. Her gentle gaze brought him back into the conversation, like a moth to a flame. "There is a mirror tree inside the castle, the queen's tree."

"Oh?" Her brows knitted together, but she didn't ask anything else.

"Since there is no recollection of what happened, it's all my own conclusion. But it's possible this was made to look like the one inside to send a message to the king."

"Do you think it's the same species of tree?" she asked, her voice hesitant.

"I think they look too similar for it not to be so. The only difference is this one is burned, and the one inside is asleep and untouched by fire."

"The king hasn't been able to have any more children

after you?" Nava asked, as if knowing to change the subject.

It had been so long since he'd felt he could trust someone. The history of his family came with a heavy load. He hadn't known them personally before coming here to search for answers, but for some strange reason, he cared. "No one but me. After my mother was gone, he took on multiple women to get an heir."

Nava's lips slacked. "I have not read in any books that the Copper Kingdom's king has multiple wives. Though clearly, I have not read enough. How does it work? I didn't know there was a queen in the castle."

"There is no queen. He never remarried." Orion rubbed the back of his neck, the uncertainty of his feeling settled somewhat.

"It explains why he went through the trouble to kidnap you in the middle of the night, all the way from the Grey Island," she grumbled, and waves of images crashed into him.

He was chasing her across a vast ocean. Salt waves crashed against the large ship, the wood groaning alongside the sound of seagulls above. He stood at the end, gripping the rails. The captain had assured him there was an island less than an hour away. The Grey Island, where magic wielders came to run away from the crowns.

A town that held a spell that canceled magic. Willowbrook.

. . .

"Willowbrook," he breathed, and Nava's eyes snapped to him. His skin turned cold and clammy as the memory pushed to come through the haze of his thoughts.

"Yes." Her voice was hesitant, and her lips shook as she studied him closely.

"How long has it been? How many years did I lose?" His voice was barely audible from the noise of the forest.

"Eleven."

The anxious bubbling sensation in his gut didn't allow him to stay in this forsaken place a moment longer. He strutted toward the castle. His breathing was hard as he processed all he'd been told, everything that had happened today. "When did we meet?"

"The first or the second time?" she asked, and he turned to her, raising a brow. She looked so incredibly beautiful under the light of the setting sun with soot marking her cheeks. "We met once eleven years ago and then again last year."

"Why the time gap?" He hadn't meant to sound so harsh. Her back tensed and her eyes shifted away, teeth catching her bottom lip. "Are you going to tell me that's too much for me to hear?"

"It will be too much," she admitted, her rigid tone matching her straight back. For the first time since she had dropped back into his life, true fear took over her expression. He found he hated that look and needed to make it go away.

The air was still muggy, and his skin was rough with the ash that stuck to his sweat.

"Why did the king not remarry?"

Orion stared at Nava, wanting to find answers in the softness of her face, but maybe he wasn't ready for all the truth, not after all he had learned today. "The tree didn't bloom."

"What does that even mean, the queen's tree?"

"Haven't you read about it? It's pretty much shoved

down everyone's throats in history." He slowed his strut and turned to her.

"I have not. I was homeschooled, and history wasn't my cup of tea. There are a lot of nuances of all four kingdoms—I don't keep track of every detail." Her tone took a defensive quality to it, and the way her nose wrinkled was adorable. She crossed her arms over her chest.

"The tree signals when the rightful queen has arrived. It can be an heir being born if it's a girl. But it also can be a betrothed."

"So, the tree bloomed with your mother and then died down when she passed?"

"That's how my father learned she had died." Orion's jaw tightened, and he resumed his walk. "And then he found her back where we just were, in an exact replica of the beloved tree of our people."

"I'm sorry, Arkimedes," Nava said between breaths as she struggled to catch up to him. At this point, he wasn't sure he would bother to correct her using his old name, not when it clearly held some sort of history with her.

"I'm fine. I never even met her." The hollowness in his voice told him that was a lie even though he didn't believe any longer. He cared very much as to why she had suffered such a horrible death. He cared too much.

The castle's magnificent sight came into view between the leaves of the trees as the sun set behind it. Orange and golden hues painted the tops of the buildings and trees, like a pastel painting.

"So—do you believe me?" she asked.

"That my dreams of you weren't dreams but memories being repressed? That I'm cursed?"

She nodded. "Four months ago, when they took you away."

"I believe that something is not adding up."

The palisades became clear behind the wilderness as they stepped out of the cover of the foliage. Nava turned around, her face changing as she took in the forest; it pained her to go back to the castle, and now that he knew the why, he would try to get her out of that room more. Even if that meant having to face the king's scorn.

"We can't enter the garden the same way we came out. Because of the attacks, we've increased patrolling during the night."

The sky darkened, offering them cover. "Are we going to walk all night, then? Or are you just trying to torture me?" She groaned, rubbing her hands over her thighs.

"Torturing you? May I remind you I'm here because you had to go to that damned forest today—"

"Right . . ."

She was an eager, beautiful woman, with a sunny disposition and a breath of fresh air.

Orion patted the wall that separated the wilderness and the perimeter of the castle ground, the pattern he had memorized months ago. The grout cracked, and a line was drawn over stone, between the rocks, forming a door with an arch frame and intricate designs.

"So tell me, Nava. In my repressed memories, I remember you being a curious creature. Are you also an impatient one?" His eyes shone when she approached the door.

"I guess you will have to find out for yourself." She smirked, passing by him. The scent of her wrapped him like a warm hug. Wild berries, earth, honey, and, of course, smoke. The threshold wasn't wide, and her body was touching his. She faced him.

With her skin flushed as she stared into his eyes, he wanted to pull out her thick bottom lip from the ministration of her teeth and replace it with his own. He was suffocating, dying to know if she felt as soft as he imagined.

But as soon as the heated thought surfaced, it was quickly pushed down by guilt. Devon's face flashing through his mind had his stomach dropping. Was she even engaged to him? Had that all been a lie to prevent the king from making an example of Nava the day they'd arrived?

It would explain why Devon had been so unaffected the day of her panic attack, when to Orion it had been anything but. He would be asking his brother questions tomorrow.

CHAPTER TWENTY

NAVA

The warm evening enveloped them as Arkimedes flew to his tower, the white moon and stars peppering the sky's veil. The smoke didn't linger in the air any longer. However, their skin was stained by the demon's scorn, and the scent clung to their clothes. A reminder this was not over.

It'd been a while since Nava had been this close to him, with his arms wrapped around her body protectively. Their feet touched the cool stone of her balcony, but he didn't let go of her. Maybe he was also enjoying their nearness for a change.

She held the cloth of his tunic, feeling the quick beat of his heart under her fingertips, and lifted her face to meet his. They were so close, she would only have to lift to her tiptoes to kiss him the way she craved. "I guess you didn't drop me after all."

"I'm offended you even considered it," he mocked and mirrored her smile. "Safe and sound and delivered to your room." Arkimedes's gaze flashed behind her and into the aforementioned space.

She was still determined to get them out of this place as soon as humanly possible. After today, she sensed she had taken a significant leap forward.

He believed her; he knew her role as a Beekeeper and was guarding her secret of being able to call to her magic, even though she was wearing the bracelet. Arkimedes didn't trust these people. She still wished he would have taken her straight to his room, and by his heated gaze, she knew he was thinking the same.

"This is not my room," she murmured.

"No? Where, then?" He matched her tone.

Emboldened by his question, she pushed forward. "I rather think my room is wherever you are sleeping."

His eyes widened at her words, and his fingers combed his hair back away from his forehead. "You keep playing this dangerous game, Nava—"

"I'm not playing. I want you to take me there tonight—"

"I want to," he admitted. His finger caught her bottom lip and pulled it out from under her teeth. "Is that something I have done before? Take you to my room? Touched you." His hand left her lips and traced down the skin of her cheek. He wrapped his hand around her neck, pulling her closer to him. His body was hot, and that place in between her thighs throbbed in anticipation of more. "Have I tasted you?"

The heat that ran through her was nothing to be trifled with. She breathed, "Yes."

"I keep wondering if you would be as sweet now." He dropped his face down, and her breath caught in her throat as she awaited the kiss that didn't come. "It feels like I'm under a spell, burning for you."

"Why don't you let go?" Was that even her voice? She

couldn't tell anymore. The drumming of her heart muffled everything else.

His darkened gaze dropped to her lips. "Why are you with him?" His brows dipped.

"What?"

"Why does he get to call you his fiancée? Every. Single. Time. You tempt me here, and I want to believe this whole thing." He hesitated. "I believe you, at least the part that you are a Beekeeper. However, Devon hasn't come out and said you aren't engaged."

Her breath left in a whoosh as he stepped away, his hand dropping from her neck. "It's not true that Devon and I are matched. He said this to protect us from the king."

"I almost kissed you. I want to do so much more. My brother calls you his fiancée, even when we speak in private. I need to hear it from him."

An icy wave ran through her veins, cooling the heat that had been burning there before. She crossed her arms around herself. Devon technically couldn't hurt them with the life debt in play, but that only protected their lives. He could very well plot to have them both survive but not be with each other.

She had wanted to appear unaffected, but it was too much for her to take. The change of their relationship, the trust they'd always held for the other's words. Even before accepting their bond, they'd both known to trust each other.

But this was too different, and just as this was all a shock to Arkimedes, it was also to her. She *loved* him, whereas he might lust over her now but had not fallen in love with her yet. He was also determined to call himself Orion; he wanted to play prince and had just told her he had never wanted to be a Crow, never wanted to be Arkimedes.

The man she loved.

"If you need to talk to him to believe me, do so. I would love to be present because I sure as hell don't trust what he tells you."

"*I* trust him."

"Well, you are more naïve now than you were before!" she snarled and almost felt sorry for the way his face fell.

"You came here with him. If anything, your actions don't match your words."

"I'm here trying to save you after you were kidnapped! I had few options at the time. I don't know how to open a portal or work with dark magic. All I know is I came here and you didn't remember me, and you aren't the only one who lost memories."

Silence descended upon them, the thickness in the air strong enough that she found it hard to breathe. Arkimedes's frown softened as he took in her ragged stance. "You paid the price by crossing, not Devon?"

"I lost all memories of my father." Her voice cracked.

His Adam's apple bobbed as he swallowed. "Your reaction in the garden was when you realized he had been taken from you?"

"Yes."

"I'm sorry."

The churning coming through their bond made it all worse. "Good night, Arkimedes." Her feet dragged over the stone when she turned toward her room.

"Nava . . ."

But she closed the door behind her.

The sound of the curtains being pulled aside woke Nava from sleep; the morning sun stretched shapes over the floor of her bedroom. She grumbled and sank her face into the pillow, chasing the last remnants of sleep.

"Good morning, miss!" Leela's voice was shrill with excitement.

Nava awaited stiffly inside her warm cocoon. Maybe the fae would take the hint and leave. It wasn't like she had much to do other than transfer to Devon's room and hope she would find Arkimedes there.

Get that damn conversation over with.

Her whole body ached, from the top of her head to the tips of her toes. Her hair still smelled like smoke, even though she had spent a good hour in the bath scrubbing every inch of her body clean of the grime from yesterday.

"Too tired." Nava's voice came out muffled by the pillow, but soon enough, Leela's cool fingers dragged the sheets away. "Hey!"

"I'm sorry, miss. But the king has commanded the guests to get fitted for the celebrations tomorrow."

Nava blinked groggily. "Can't I just wear one outfit in the closet? There is plenty I haven't worn." She pointed at the aforementioned wardrobe.

"Oh, no, there is a dress code for the solstice celebrations. Plus, if the king commands it—"

"Fine." Nava took a deep breath and got out of bed. The morning breeze that entered from her terrace's open door was cool over her heated skin. Unlike yesterday, it didn't smell like burning and death, and she grinned at their victory.

It had been an amazing feeling, the three of them working together, like the gods had intended it to be.

"You smell like a campfire, miss," Leela commented, helping her onto her robe, her small button nose wrinkling.

These fae and their sensitive noses. "I spent a long time in front of the fire yesterday," she said with a wry smile. When did it become so easy to lie? She used to be horrible at it.

"Oh, that makes sense," she chirped. "Let's get you in the bath, then. Marni is rough around the edges."

"The seamstress?"

"Yes. She doesn't like . . ." Leela fidgeted, pulling her red long hair behind one pointy ear.

"Outsiders?"

"Humans."

Oh, the joys of classism. This was not something new. In Willowbrook, she had been looked down on her whole life for being a "witch." The townsfolk had always whispered behind her back in hushed tones about the woes of Forrests' luck.

"Is there anywhere else I can go to get fitted?" Nava wasn't even sure why she asked when she knew the answer. Even if there was somewhere else she could go, it wasn't like she had money to pay for such things.

"Unfortunately, all royals—and their guests—go to Marni." Leela hesitated. "My seamstress, Renna, is amazing. You would like her. She is just as talented as Marni, but kinder, and beautiful." Her eyes shone with such affection, Nava wasn't sure if this was a family member or something more.

"Is Renna your friend?"

Leela's cheeks turned a bright shade of red. "Yes."

"I see. Maybe something more?"

"Miss!"

"Come on, humor me. I have been stuck in this room forever! I need something to hold on to, hope for what's good in life," Nava continued, and the fae's face turned as red as her hair. However, her eyes shone.

"It's difficult for the kingdom to accept us, not with the Society looming nearer this part of the world."

"Fuck the Society straight to hell."

Leela gasped. "But your betrothed is part of the Society."

"I just said what everyone else is thinking. If you think a girl like me would get matched and just accept it, then you haven't heard me complain enough." Nava laughed, and her fight with Arkimedes flashed through her mind. His jealous outburst, and the mess they were both in.

Leela's shaky lips turned into a tentative smile. "I don't know what we could do."

"You could always leave this kingdom—go to the Grey Island."

The fae's red lashes moved like the wings of a butterfly as she blinked before her thin hand grasped hers, pulling her into the washroom, where a steaming pool that smelled of honeysuckles awaited. "Thank you."

"For what?"

"For your words." Leela's lack of words could mean she wasn't used to any sort of support on the matter. Her voice rang small. "I will set your dress on the bed and make sure Fael is ready to go. Our appointment is at ten." The fae smiled and bowed before she left the washroom, allowing Nava the privacy she had asked for earlier.

How did they keep time in this castle? She hadn't seen a steam clock hanging anywhere in sight. She had seen several sun clocks in the garden when she'd gone out with the guard. Still, everyone here followed time like it was a religion.

She moved her freckled hands over the fading bruises on her neck as she inspected her reflection. Her cool touch was a contrast to her feverish skin. What tomorrow's solstice would bring to her and Ark was . . . worrisome, as

if she needed anything else added to her already complicated life.

CHAPTER TWENTY-ONE

NAVA

A polished black carriage with gold trim awaited them by the entrance of the castle, down dozens of narrow stone steps that were lined with cement banisters. Two guards wearing polished copper armor and long blue capes stood at the bottom.

The beasts pulling their transportation were not horses, nor bulls. They were as wide as the latter, with shiny hides of charcoal gray and ebony. Their necks had long, thick, wavy hair that reminded her of sheep.

"The orrus." Fael's voice had her heart jumping out of her chest. "The beasts are bred by the fae in the high mountains. Stronger than a bull and faster than any horse. Stubborn and the males can get . . . scary if females are around."

"I have never seen one before. Are they bred as a mix between a bull and a horse?"

Fael shrugged. "I'm sure they took inspiration from that, but the high mountain fae are known to have the gift of creation. Once a century or so, they bring to life something new. A plant with medicinal powers never seen before. A creature like this."

"So magic is no issue for them?" That thought alone had Nava perking up. It was a disease that affected every corner of the world. The dwindling of magic, the main reason the Society of Crows was wreaking havoc on people's lives.

"No, they are also affected. Before, they were able to create every decade—then every fifty years, and so on." Fael moved toward the door, and the footman made haste from his path, clearly not wanting to interact with the guard. "It's rumored their magic is not as strong as it used to be."

"Oh."

"Either way, these creatures are protected by our laws because they are made by our magic, and they don't reproduce easily. It's forbidden to hunt or trade them, and they are to stay in our kingdom. Of course, poachers happen, but it's not common that they go unpunished." Fael held the door open for her.

Another poor living creature having difficulty procreating in this kingdom. Nava wondered if it had something to do with the water or maybe the magic that fed the lands.

The orrus snorted loudly, their two-fingered hooves lifting rock and dirt from where they stood, clearly not pleased to be holding still while the three of them got in the carriage.

Standing straight and looking forward, the guards with their impressive dark wings shaded the gravel path; they were taller than even Fael, their mists billowing around them like a campfire. Their gazes burned the nape of her neck as she turned around to get into the carriage, past the footman in orange regalia who didn't say a word and avoided her eyes.

It had been a long while since she'd ridden a carriage. Last time had been in the Iron City, when she and her family had been running from Arkimedes and Devon. She could still remember her mother tightening the ropes that had held their sparse belongings to the back of their wooden ride. Her mother's dark chestnut hair had billowed in the wind, wild, much like her own.

If Nava closed her eyes tightly, she could almost smell the soft notes of rose from her mother's body oil. But as she sat on these black velvet seats, the only scent that surrounded her was leather and musk.

The Copper City revealed itself as the carriage pulled past a tall archway under the castle's outside walls, layered in tiers that descended in circular patterns. Tall, century-old trees lined the streets here, with black lamp posts and uneven cobbled roads.

Nava held the leather handle by the roof as the carriage rushed past impressive-sized manors on either side of them.

"The high fae live here," Leela said and intertwined her fingers over her legs, her blue gaze flashing from Nava to the outside. "Are you well, miss? You are looking rather pale."

Her stomach churned as nausea hit her in waves, coming and going with the rocking of the wood that encased her, closing in like an unwelcome hug. "I usually walk everywhere."

They crossed past another archway, the stone walls shorter than the ones that surrounded the castle, but here the color of the city exploded around her. Bright yellow and beige homes loomed over them. Every inch of the city was covered by a stucco building or ones made with burnt-orange bricks and framed in wood.

The city was alive with people. Unlike what she had

seen in the castle, they all wore different colors. Reds, yellows, whites, and browns. Beautiful patterned silk fabric hung from a particular store, with greens that reminded her of the forest in the Grey Island.

Children played on the sidewalks; some had wings, some did not. The streets were packed full of other carriages being pulled by less-impressive orrus or by horses. Nava swore she even saw a donkey somewhere.

Her nose touched the cool glass of the window, and her breath caught in her throat when the turquoise water of the canal appeared behind the buildings.

"We are close now, miss," Leela said.

Nava met the eyes of a young man with long, camel-blond hair held down by a tall hat. A polished gray suit fit like it had been tailored to him. He smile at her from the sidewalk, tilting his hat up and revealing perfectly rounded ears. Nava blinked and sat back, finally meeting both Fael's and Leela's amused expressions.

"They are not all fae," Nava murmured.

"We have a large population of humans in the city, and in outer towns of our kingdom, there are other fae races and shifters." Fael placed his helmet over his head, covering his salt-and-pepper tresses.

The carriage shook as they went over a large bump on the road, and Nava struggled to keep herself seated and not lose her breakfast all over the place. The damn thing moved even faster than the steam vehicles from the Iron City.

The carriage stopped in front of a row of red brick shops, and the morning sun hit the uneven copper roofs with golden highlights. Nava jumped down faster than any polite lady of society should; Laurie would have been scandalized if she'd seen it. However, her caregiver was far away in the Pearl Island with Cameron, and Nava was too happy to be out of that can to care.

She dusted the skirt of her dress, staring at the orrus through her lashes. The creatures were fast and strong, without an ounce of elegance in their massive bodies. It took her a moment to calm the storm brewing in her stomach before she faced the shops.

These were undoubtedly a place of elegance where people of money would come to get fitted for their clothes. A bit far from the castle, and Nava guessed the royals didn't really come this way, but rather the seamstress Marni would go to them.

"This way, miss." Leela's gentle fingers wrapped around Nava's arm, pulling her toward the shop.

The gentle breeze brought smells of baked goods from the nearby bakery, mixing with the distinct scent of sea breeze from the canal nearby. Light music tones grew from the distance—someone playing a guitar, perhaps a street performer?

She strolled behind Fael's giant frame, his white spotted wings swaying with his every step. His hand rested all too casually on the hilt of his sword as he looked around for anything amiss. Always alert.

Leela walked next to her, chatting vividly about the preparations for the dance. "At the ball, women wear golds or yellow, while the men wear whites." Leela had not stopped talking. Nava admired how she could fit so many words into one breath. "It will be hard to tell who's who with the masks. Except for the royals, of course. Their aura alone gives them away."

Right. Nava still couldn't see Arkimedes's all the time, but she had to assume it looked just as scary as the king's.

Fael tilted his head, staring at both of them with a

raised brow. "Most of us in the guards have the aura as well, Leela."

"But it's not the same, obviously." Leela grinned. "Are you jealous I'm not specifically pointing at the royal guard too?"

Fael choked on a laugh. "You wish I was jealous."

Nava had not realized Fael and Leela were close, but it was clear now with the affection that shone behind both of their gazes. If Arkimedes trusted this man with her protection, and Leela liked him, he couldn't be so bad.

Leela answered an unspoken question while snickering. "Fael and I went to school together. Actually, he was a few years ahead of me. He is an old man."

Nava couldn't help but smile. "That makes sense. I was wondering for a moment why you had gray hair if you were as young as Leela."

Fael's laugh rolled in a carefree way. "To a human eye, we probably look around your age. However, we have to be nearing a century now."

Nava almost choked on her own tongue at his words. Fael didn't appear much older than Arkimedes or Devon, with his copper skin, gold eyes, and smooth face. Leela looked much younger than Nava. Twenty at most.

"Not all of us, even though we are fae, inherit the wonderful genetics of the Rosalors," Fael continued.

"That's my family name," Leela replied, perking up. "But Fael is actually graying now because of the stress, not genetics."

"If you keep going this way, Leela, I will not bring you the honey wine you love the next time I come to visit you."

Leela's lips clamped shut at his words. "What a delicate child you are." She turned to face Nava. "I will bring you some of that honey wine. You would enjoy it, maybe you can share it with your fiancé."

Right. "Oh, you don't have to. I actually don't eat honey." The skin of her face turned warm. "But speaking of Devon, would he get fit with an outfit as well?"

"Oh, yes. I believe His Royal Highness took him earlier in the day," Leela said, and Nava's heart sank in her chest.

It was silly to be jealous of Devon, but her mind hadn't been acting rationally today, and her nerves were still fried from her ride here. Nava clasped her hand together in front of her, trying to hide the need to fidget.

Why would the Crown Prince take her to get fitted for a dress? Not even if he had been courting her would he do such a thing, and he was not. That would raise questions, obviously.

Had he talked to Devon by now about if their engagement was true? If so, had the Crow lied just to make things difficult for them? She wouldn't put it past him to do so.

Even though she liked her current escorts, she would have preferred Arkimedes's company, even after their small fight last night. He had almost kissed her. He believed her. She just needed time to convince him to leave all this madness behind.

"Must be nice to be catered to by the prince." Nava said.

Leela's attention came crashing to her, her face practically glowing as she bounced on the balls of her feet. The fae's plump lips opened to say something but shut the moment she remembered they weren't alone. They had arrived.

Incense hung in the air outside the shop. Notes of patchouli and roses tugged at a ghost of a memory that wasn't present any longer, something she had lost, and it ached for unknown reasons.

Even though she didn't remember her father, who had clearly taught her the art of potion-making, she still had fractured memories of working in her shop. Her roughened hands chopping herbs, of her sniffing oils and boiling potions.

Simone had brought fresh-baked bread in exchange for migraine medicine. She had spent a whole summer trying to teach Cameron the proper way to extract carmine from the cochineal insects. And her shop—it had green walls the color of sage behind the counter.

Nava remembered the imagery and the ingredients were familiar, but she couldn't remember why she had used them. The purpose of it all was lost, much like her father's smiles. It was like watching a dream but failing to understand the meaning behind it all.

Potion-making had been such a large part of her identity. However, she had to keep moving forward. It mattered not what she might be unable to recover, and she needed to focus on what mattered most.

How to get Arkimedes back had to be what occupied most of her thoughts. The rest . . . she could figure it out later.

The entrance to the seamstress's store was an impressive twelve-foot-high archway, framed by decorative sand-colored bricks and a heavy wooden door with glass panels that distorted the inside. A wooden sign hung from a swirling metal arm.

Marni's Woven Magic
Tailored to you

"This is it, miss." Leela's nose scrunched as her sky-blue eyes glared at the seamstress's door. "Don't let her get to you."

"Don't worry, Leela. I'm not a damsel in distress. I know how to handle myself."

Nava lifted her hand to knock on the door, but it swung open before she even made contact. A chime of bells sang as she came face to face with the man she had been dreaming of the entire day.

Her body reacted in kind, burning up just at the sight of him. She focused on the muscles that weren't covered by his light tunic. Black silk tugged over his wide shoulders, and charcoal threads that depicted naked branches. His eyes blazed over her, bright and self-illuminating, and a wave of something warm ran through her, making her dizzy.

Heat. Lust. Want . . . Longing.

That emotion wasn't coming from her alone, but it was being enhanced through their bond by him.

Was this all related to what the solstice would bring for the both of them? It was like she had become starved for his touch even more than normal.

"Nava," he breathed, his gaze lingering momentarily on her lips before shifting to Devon, who approached them from his back.

He wore a light blue double-piece tunic, belted with wider fabric, and dark indigo pants. He seemed less pale than the last time she had seen him, his hair cropped shorter and pulled back behind his ears, allowing his sharp cheekbones to catch the morning light.

"*Fiancée*, fancy seeing you here." Devon approached her with wicked bright eyes, the side smirk on his face growing under her glare.

"Stop with that," Nava said in between teeth, and

Arkimedes stirred next to Devon. It was hard to discern if he looked guilty or plain uncomfortable.

Had they talked? Had Devon poisoned Arkimedes's mind with more lies that would bring on his rejection of her? What if the Crow told him they were mated?

The crawl of panic began to take over her body and mind, her chest tightening and making it hard to breathe. She was going to murder Devon and this stupid charade he had put them on. He was doing this to torment Arkimedes *and* her.

"I would have loved to come with the both of you." Maybe that way, she would avoid the possibility of being bullied by a hostile seamstress, if what Leela said was true.

Devon shrugged. "We wanted to spend some time with just the two of us, like the good ol' days before we were split up by . . . destiny." His eyes flamed.

Nava crossed her arms over her chest, meeting his gaze with equal intensity. "Catching him up on what you have been up to, by any chance?" she asked in a fake sweet tone. "Were you able to tell him all the wicked activities you engaged in while he was away?" She hadn't forgotten that both Leela and Fael stood near them, undoubtedly listening to every word the three of them exchanged.

"We were too busy talking about the future to focus on the past." His hand landed on her shoulder. "Have fun in there!"

The future? What future was he speaking of? One where she wasn't in the picture and would be forced to move to be near but never close to the man she loved? Would she be able to put Cameron through this?

Anxiety took hold of her windpipe, and if it wasn't for her mother's stern voice echoing in her mind to get herself together, she would have allowed panic to burst free and pull her down in its attack.

Nava glared at Devon as he sauntered out of the shop, enjoying himself too much for her liking. She turned to Arkimedes, who walked past her, one hand burying inside the pocket of his tunic.

"I have told Marni to take care of you. I—will see you later." His other hand went through his hair, the way he always did when he was nervous.

"Yes . . ." She looked behind her to see if her escorts were close, but they were far enough away and chatting by the carriage. She drifted closer. "Did you ask him?"

"I did." His eyes softened on her, and that alone killed some of her self-doubt, her anger toward Devon appeasing. "We can talk about it later, alone."

"Next!" A shrill voice came from inside the shop, startling her out of her stupor.

"Nava." Arkimedes bowed, his eyes never leaving hers, before he too strode off from the entrance of the seamstress shop. "Fael, Leela."

"Your Highness," both of them said in unison, bowing, and Nava realized that once again, she had not adhered to the formality surrounding them.

Arkimedes walked past the carriage and toward the shops where Devon awaited him, and she trailed their retreating shapes that disappeared in the streets of town.

"Oh, you are here." A woman's voice flowed to her as Nava came into the shop, the scents here much stronger. A tall, slim brunette walked to her with light feet and a raised chin. She wore a wine-colored gown that fell like a cascade of gems and shiny threads toward the soft ground. Her scowl was so deep it could give Violet a run for her money.

"Good afternoon," Nava said, waving a hand.

The shop wasn't large, the ceilings not as tall as she had expected, but the windows were open, letting in the warm breeze of the morning. Rolls of fabric of all the colors of the rainbow lined the walls. Golden gowns lined the display in front of the store. Draped over mannequins were all kinds of different outfits Nava had never seen before. Wide skirts and narrow bodices.

Gorgeous dresses, dyed with rich pigments. Patterns, textures—this time her heart was racing, not due to forgotten memories, but because she was excited to be here.

Never had Nava stepped inside such a fancy seamstress shop before. The one in Willowbrook made and mended clothes that were simple and utilitarian for the most part. She couldn't have afforded to be in a place like this, even in passing.

Well-preserved rugs covered the floors, and in the center of the room, there was a fitting stand and a wooden mirror next to it.

The woman's umber eyes scoured down Nava's body, making her squirm. "It will be hard work to get a gown made in such a rush."

"I'm sorry, I just arrived in town not that long ago."

The woman glowered and headed to the center of the room, waving her hand toward the stand. "Come this way now, human."

She followed Marni with long strides while her blood heated inside her veins. "My name is Nava, not 'human.'"

Marni scoffed, dismissing Nava's words. "It doesn't matter. I will never remember."

It was her turn to frown. If the woman wanted to upset her with her words, she had another thing coming since Nava had had an internship of hostility with Violet last year.

She shrugged. "Suit yourself." And she stood on the pedestal as the seamstress looked her over.

"Your kind is always one to have such wide hips, not the most appealing."

Nava cleared her throat, swallowing her spike in annoyance. "Good news, it seems you make your gowns to overcompensate for the lack of curves. Maybe mine doesn't need as much padding."

Why had she decided to say it out loud *before* the fae made her gown? Marni's glare told her she would be paying for it later.

The fae walked off to the wall that held mounted rolls of fabric, coming back with a roll of the most garish canary-yellow fabric Nava had seen. It shimmered under the light, iridescent colors as she unrolled it unceremoniously over the ground.

"Isn't that a bit loud?" Nava asked, and the brown eyes of the seamstress met hers with a wicked light behind her pupils.

"I'm afraid I ran out of all the other yellow or gold fabric. It is pretty late to get anything brought in since the ball is tomorrow." She smiled.

Nava studied the wall with the rolls of fabric, where at least a dozen of other yellow and gold rolls leaned against the wall. "There are a few more over there." She pointed in the direction.

The fae didn't even move a muscle to turn around. "Those are for . . . higher-class individuals, dear, not for you." So much for this woman following Arkimedes's command of taking care of her.

Nava frowned but pressed her lips together, unwilling to let Marni enjoy getting a rise out of her. She needed the dress; the king had demanded that she get it from this cruel woman.

She pictured her mother's image in her mind and closed her eyes, calling for her strength.

"Do not let them see you affected by their words. Ignoring them is the best kind of retaliation," her mother had once told her, though right now it didn't feel that way.

"Ow." She jumped when the prick of a pin dug into her skin.

"Stay still," the seamstress growled. She wrapped a strap of a hideous, shiny yellow fabric around her waist and pinned it down. The needle went through the fabric and straight into Nava's flesh once again.

She pulled away with a hiss, narrowing her eyes at the smiling face of the fae. "If you poke me again, believe me, you won't be smiling by the end of the day."

Her smile faltered; maybe it was the slight shake in Nava's body, the glow under her skin, or the bees that crawled the walls of the shop.

"I said I was sorry," the woman said, though it was the first time Nava had heard those words.

She had never been one to care about dresses, parties, or makeup and such. She shouldn't care that these were cheap materials set aside for just humans when fae got something else. It bothered her that the gown being pinned together looked like a badly formed cake, decorated by toddlers.

Her skin itched, as if ants crawled over her, biting every inch of exposed flesh. And with the sound of the scissors cutting the fabric, Nava's chin rose higher. She shouldn't care, but she was woman enough to admit it bothered her. However, she would make the most of it.

Fuck the king, his curse, and this woman straight to hell.

CHAPTER TWENTY-TWO

NAVA

By the time Marni was done measuring her for what was to be the most hideous dress the whole kingdom would ever see, Nava was ready to leave and never see her again. The air was cool against her skin when the door of the shop slammed behind her.

Her steps faltered when, instead of Fael and Leela waiting for her, Arkimedes met her eyes from across the sidewalk. He leaned against the carriage, one of his hands resting on his hip, while the other bounced off his leg as he spoke with Devon, whose back was facing her. She saw the footman feeding the orrus, ignoring everything around him.

"Well, this is a surprise," she said, trying to sound casual, but the shake in her vocal cords gave her away.

"You two have been complaining a lot, so I thought we could see the city." Arkimedes pushed off the carriage. Was this a trap of sorts? It sounded too good to be true. Had Devon spoken lies to Arkimedes and this was when they dropped her in the woods to fend for herself?

Devon tilted his face toward her. "Lighten up, kitten."

Nava swallowed and took tentative steps toward her soulmate, searching his face for anything that signaled trouble.

Arkimedes opened the door of the carriage and made space for her to jump in. "Have you ever visited the Copper City before?" he asked when she stood by his side, the scent of leather wrapping around her.

"No, I have only been to the suburbs of the Iron City and the Grey Island," she admitted and looked back at Devon, who buried both hands inside his pockets. "Is this a trap?"

Arkimedes's surprised laughter was a welcomed melody, and his eyes crinkled with amusement. "A trap?"

"Well, yes. Yesterday you weren't happy . . ." She looked back at Devon before raising her chin up in the air. "I don't trust you two all buddy-buddy like this."

"For once, I will agree with Devon and say you need to relax." Arkimedes shook his head, and a caress of his amusement crossed the bond, creating butterflies in her stomach. "It's nothing bad, I promise."

Nava pursed her lips, hesitating just a moment before hoisting herself inside the carriage of hell and waiting by the farthest corner. Devon came in next and sat in front of her with a rogue, elegant pose that required a lot of practice. "What did you tell him while alone with him?"

"Me?" His brows lowered over his eyes, clear confusion tinting his pale features. "What could you possibly mean?"

What she meant was she didn't trust him one bit, and the nervous churning in her stomach was driving her insane. Had Arkimedes asked Devon about their fake engagement, and had Devon told him the truth? "I don't trust you—that is what I mean."

Devon stared at Nava with an unreadable expression before shrugging a shoulder. "I have been working on our combined task. What have *you* been doing? Other than panicking in public and letting the whole castle know he would drop anything to take you away."

Nava's stomach churned at the memory of that morning when she'd realized she had no memories left of her father. The hole that festered in her chest ached with her loss. "I didn't mean to lose my mind that morning. The king already knows who I am; I don't believe for a second they are believing our story. They kidnapped him, and they saw me while doing it." Nava's hands turned to fists, and she hated the guilt creeping inside her. It wasn't like she had full control of what had happened to her that morning. The trigger to her panic attack had not been expected.

Devon looked past the open door. Arkimedes talked to the footman, giving directions perhaps? She didn't know. "The king and his close guards kidnapped him. The rest of the population, I'm sure, thinks he showed up to claim what's rightfully his. Now the whole castle whispers that the prince has it for his brother's fiancée. A human. What a scandal."

"You are enjoying this."

"Enjoying this mess?" Devon's false politeness melted as his brows met in the middle. "I'm tied to protect you two without having a say in the matter. I have hated you both for a year. Don't get things twisted, cat."

"You don't hate him. So stop trying to make me think otherwise." Nava checked on Arkimedes once again. He was still chatting away and pointing in the distance, possibly hearing their conversation. "What did you tell him?"

"The truth."

"Your truth?"

"Who else's?" He smiled.

Nava's annoyance turned into concern, the burning

fire in her veins cooling down as she studied the Crow's face. "Don't do anything that would hurt him, Devon. Please."

Devon ignored her words, his onyx eyes following the movements of his brother outside. "When we met, him and I, we had no one but each other. Unwanted children who were given a chance at greatness." Nava was sure he meant the magic in the world. The balance the Crows believed to upkeep. "He always thought of it as servitude. I saw it as a new opportunity to have something worth fighting for. Unwanted by the rest of the world, we found a family in each other." Devon let the weight of his body lean into the seat behind him. "In less than fifteen years, he got not one but two families who wanted him."

"You mean the Valerons?" Nava whispered, not wanting Ark to listen. "They weren't a family to him at all. He hates them."

"Yet they still wanted him." His eyes shifted away from her. "He gets to be a royal, have the gods give him a beautiful mate who travels across the world to save him against all odds."

Beautiful . . .

She stilled in her spot, her heart hammering against her chest, and she let the air leave her lungs. Alarm bells rang in her ears, telling her to get out of there, to disappear and avoid the uncomfortable sickening feeling that awakened within her.

It was the first nice thing Devon had ever told her. However, she didn't want him to think she was beautiful. She preferred him thinking of her as anything but.

He straightened in his spot. "Don't let it get in your head. I find women beautiful. It's not you, it's what you represent."

Her muscles relaxed a fraction as air entered her body

once again, and she brought her hands over the fabric of her dress, whipping away the cold sweat that coated her skin. "You are jealous of the idea of me . . . ?" She looked around, expecting to find Arkimedes by the door. What the hell was he up to out there?

"Jealousy is such an ugly word."

"You want a soulmate?" she asked in a whisper.

"Don't we all?"

She hadn't, not one bit. Had fought it every minute of a decade. Arkimedes had fought it tooth and nail last year. "You're envious of all he's gotten when he didn't even want it, aren't you?"

Devon opened his mouth but shut it when Arkimedes's head popped into the carriage. "We are ready." His eyes shone with an eagerness she hadn't seen before; her heart skipped a beat at his tentative smile, as it showed a shadow of dimples.

What was going inside that head of his? Before he was taken, she'd been able to listen to some of his thoughts. That was not the case now—their bond was hurting from the lack of memories. Was he taking them around to see his city? Hoping they would love it as much as he did?

The weight of iron dropped in her stomach, the metallic taste lingering on the back of her tongue. She had been with him not only in the Northern Village, where they had their home, but also in Willowbrook, and not once had he looked this way.

Would he want to leave with her if he did regain his memories—and would she even want to take him away? She brought her hand over the aching spot where the three circles of her soulmate mark formed a flower.

His black wings were there one moment, fitting in the cramped area, and then gone the next, the scent of spices flowing in the air. Her eyes lingered on the smooth plane of his back as he took a seat next to her; she contained her urge to drag her finger over it.

He turned to her, called by her thoughts, and dropped his gaze to where her hand massaged the spot on her chest. His brow crinkled. "Are you all right? You seem uncomfortable."

"Yes, I'm fine. It's just this dark box of a carriage reminds me of a coffin."

His lips pulled to the side into an amused smile that showed straight teeth. "A coffin?"

"Uh-huh. With all this shiny, dark fabric . . . and the pattern." Nava swallowed, moving her fingers over the polished wood of the wall next to her, but held his gaze. His expression softened as he studied her. His fingers twitched closer over his lap, and her lips parted as waves of heat bloomed in her stomach at the intensity of his expression.

Longing. Caution. Concern. Want. So many emotions, she had a hard time picking which ones were hers and which ones were his.

"Ugh. Get me out of here."

She jumped when Devon's voice interrupted the silence. Her face warmed as she tried to ignore his words and annoyed expression. Arkimedes's surprised chuckle had her whole body melting into her seat. He didn't smile enough, let alone laugh, and this carefree expression just fed her doubts further.

"The king would be disappointed to hear that his carriage looks like a coffin," he teased and relaxed in the seat, but he didn't stop searching her features, as if trying to uncover what she was hiding.

Intertwining her fingers over her lap to prevent flapping her hands around, she faced the window as they started moving. "Where are we going?"

"The market, and then maybe we can ride through the oldest part of town. It's a bit bumpy. But there is a lot of—"

"History?" Devon asked with a mocking smile, and Arkimedes side-eyed his brother but proceeded to ignore him.

"Street vendors and art. Does that sound good?"

Breathless at the shine behind his irises, she didn't think she'd seen him so eager since she'd met him. He was happy.

She cut her eyes to Devon, making sure she wasn't the only one seeing this, and by his brother's softening expression, it wasn't just her.

Arkimedes loved it here, and it was a disaster.

By the time they made it back to the castle, the evening light had taken over the sky. Watercolor shades of blues and oranges matched the beautiful silk scarf Arkimedes had gotten her in one of the markets earlier in the afternoon.

She hated to admit she'd had fun. Though she'd been apprehensive at first, life in the city had been contagious. Since Arkimedes's wings had been hidden from view and he hadn't been wearing his crown and regalia, they'd gone unnoticed. Just three humans walking around town.

Time had passed, however, and her body had acted a bit off-kilter. Too swollen in areas it shouldn't be. Even though the night was cool against her skin, she was too warm to stay in her dress a second longer. Having left Devon back in his room, she and Ark walked together down the corridors of the castle, trailed by Fael not far behind.

"Did you have fun?" he asked as they approached the green room.

"I did. Very much so."

Memories of eating frog legs for the first time flashed through her mind. Devon had told her they were chicken skewers; it was her own damn fault for trusting the Crow with anything. She'd been halfway through her second skewer when Arkimedes asked her if she had eaten frog before.

In her defense, it sort of tasted like chicken—with a bit of a swampy aftertaste. Their combined laughter still chimed inside her head, making her smile.

Their rooms grew closer, and with that, the tension in her stomach multiplied, a sort of giddiness she hadn't experienced before. It was what she imagined being courted a regular way felt like. Being walked to her door, unsure what to expect from it.

Unable to look away from him, she was drawn like a moth to a flame. His face had relaxed from the weight of mistrust that had darkened his aura after what they'd done yesterday with the Zorren, and the lightness of today's outing.

He was breathtakingly handsome, and the fact that she was not allowed to reach and kiss him had her aching when she shouldn't be. Fael hung back as Arkimedes leaned against the doorframe, his gaze flashing around the corridor before coming down to her. Nava's back hit the cool texture of the door behind her. Her blood drummed in her veins, and her fingers twitched with the need to grab the lapels of his tunic and bring him in. She missed the way his lips felt against hers, soft but demanding. The softness of his tongue, the burn of his stubble against her cheeks.

"You weren't lying last night," he whispered, and

Nava's gaze snapped back to Fael. She gathered her soulmate trusted this man more than he did the rest of the guards. Why? Nava didn't know, but she didn't feel comfortable speaking about yesterday here.

She brought her hand to his chest; his skin burned the pads of her fingers through the fabric. They were both running too hot and treading dangerous territory. "I wouldn't lie about that." Withhold truth, yes. But out of necessity.

"I'm sorry for how I reacted. I was— I have been feeling a bit off-kilter."

So was she. Nava grasped the collar of his tunic and pulled him in just a fraction. He was close enough she could see the spots that moved in his irises and the darkness of his lashes as they dipped.

Nava had to get out of this hall immediately. They had company. "I should get in. I need a good shower." Or ten to cool down. She reached for the doorknob with a shaky hand, struggling to grasp at the metal. "Good night, Ar —sir."

His pupils dilated. "Good night, Nava."

The door clicked closed, and she leaned against its surface for too long, grasping her chest, trying to calm her fast-beating heart and talk herself out of doing something ridiculous like inviting him in.

The reason why she shouldn't was not sounding too important. She struggled to remind herself that there were lies in between them. That being intimate for them was more than just a good time and tousled sheets.

Lying with Arkimedes when he was in a solstice-induced spell was not her goal here. Her nerves were on edge after the day she had today.

She focused on something else. The burning fire in the corner, the fresh scent of a summer night, the memories of the afternoon they had. Nava wanted to hate this city as a whole, but it had been nice to get to know something new, something bigger than where she had been in the past.

Nava walked toward the fireplace, dropping the sleeves of her dress and pushing the gown past her wide hips and down her legs. She wiggled out, her body coiled tighter with each step she took, and the gentle breeze of the early evening enveloped her, cooling her skin.

Her only clothes was a light chemise, made of sheer silk. A low neck and beautiful embroidered straps that tied it to her shoulders. It was light as a feather over her, but even that felt suffocating.

She pulled it down her arms when the ends of her hair raised on end and a pleasant sensation in her stomach blossomed.

Arkimedes's gaze burned across the expanse of her balcony and through the fabric of her curtains. She guessed he'd been outside getting some fresh air—or maybe he'd heard her and had been waiting for her.

Raw and on edge, she closed her eyes and took a deep breath. She should get her robe and meet him outside to talk about what had almost happened yesterday. Ask him details of what Devon and he had discussed.

Her body had other ideas. The pleasurable heat of desire that had started in her stomach spread to the apex of her thighs, making her lose her train of thought.

She smiled and took her time to untie her clothes, and with each brush of her finger over her skin, the desire grew wild. It didn't feel like her fingers were the ones grazing her skin but his instead, rough with calluses and holding the promise of more.

She had memorized his touch long ago. Was it wrong to tease her mate when he didn't know he had no choice but to want her? To hell with that. Life wasn't fair. They had a history that had been stolen from him—from them. She needed to get him on board.

Nava pushed the garment off her body, and after a calming breath, she peered behind the waves of her dark hair and the gauzy fabric of the curtains. Across her terrace, the shadow of a large body loomed behind the banisters, two large wings spread wide.

His bright green eyes lit within the night. She couldn't help the coy smile that grew as she pushed her drawers down the curve of her backside, dropping them to the ground with an unceremonious thump.

She gasped when the inferno in her stomach bloomed. His desire pushed through the bond like wildfire, incinerating everything and leaving her breathless. If she focused enough on her memories, she could recall the scent of his skin. Pine, leather, and something that was solely him. Naked and burning for him, she closed her eyes, drunk from the arousal that devoured her. Nava brought her fingers between her breasts, past her stomach. Her moan would have been embarrassing if she'd been in her right mind.

She didn't want to miss a second of his reaction to her, focusing on his shape outside. The silver light of the night rimmed the silhouette of his body, marking the sharp contours of his muscular arms as he held himself stiffly to the banisters.

Her mouth tasted sweet with anticipation, her body drumming as heat pooled between her legs.

His wings beat, and in two powerful movements, he was up over his balcony and landing on the very edge of hers. Her heart skipped a beat, but she didn't cower or pick up her discarded clothes. Meeting his gaze, she moved one of her hands past her breasts and down her navel, her skin forming small goose bumps and reacting to her touch.

His chest heaved, and she could tell—could *feel*—his all-consuming need. He was burning for her and just holding himself back. Arkimedes was outside looking in, but here with her as well. She could almost feel the warmth of his body behind her as the weight of his hands pulled her to him. Her body hummed and the softness of her fingertips became rougher and more desperate over her stomach. She recalled how it felt to be his.

Nava had a very good imagination, and memories of the last time his hands had dipped into her soft warmth were still vivid in her mind. She took a shaky breath and massaged one of her breasts with her hand, bringing the other down to the place where she ached for him.

She gasped with the touch, and Arkimedes flinched outside, taking a step closer to the doors, his face becoming clear. His irises were no longer bright and green. Chills ran through her body; she expected he would barge in at any moment and take her. He might be even surprised that she would let him.

Arkimedes stopped, and his whole body went rigid as he held himself from taking a step farther. Nava's lips moved on their own into a slow, lazy smile, and she dipped her fingers inside herself.

Moaning, she leaned against the door, hoping Fael wasn't able to hear her but not caring enough to stop since she wanted her mate to be affected.

Her body melted with the movement of her fingers over her most sensitive spot. She recalled the memories of his lips trailing down her neck and her back. The weight of his hard body pressed against her backside as his fingers entered her in and out, and she forgot it wasn't really him doing it.

Soon she was crossing the edge, gasping for air as she came under her touch. She opened her eyes and met his gaze. It wasn't hard to see all the places where he was affected by her. His wings flexed in the air, and the wind moved outside. Nava grabbed one of the sheer curtains and pulled it closed, not blinking or looking away.

Standing still and giving him a full look at her naked body, she smiled before turning around and walking off to the washroom, putting an extra wave in her hips and sensing the weight of his eyes on her until she disappeared into the room next door.

CHAPTER TWENTY-THREE

NAVA

Three fae paraded into Nava's room the next morning, wearing light dresses made of billowy fabric that skimmed their lithe frames. Two carried the yellow monstrosity Marni had made for her, and Nava itched just at the sight of it. Their sapphire eyes fixed on her, dancing with mirth.

Nava sat by the fire; even though she was running hot, the fire produced no heat, and the sound of crackling wood somehow soothed her. With a thump, she closed the book Leela had snuck in for her earlier in the week and made her way toward the door, ignoring the fact that bees had been crawling over the walls of her bedroom ever since she'd woken yesterday morning and had doubled during the night.

It was worrisome, and she was trying to ignore it for now since she wasn't feeling threatened at the moment.

Fael peered in from the hall, his brows raising as he took in the gaudy garment. "I don't think I have ever seen anything as terrible as that." His white teeth made an appearance, showing a straight smile and crinkles to the side of his eyes. "Marni hates you even more than I thought possible."

The three fae wearing burnt-orange clothes, who Nava had at first assumed were servants of the castle, might indeed be the seamstress's minions, as their garments were not orange but different tones of red. They huffed a laugh as they crossed in front of Nava, eyeing her mockingly. She waited with a mask of indifference plastered on her face until they had left her room.

"What did you do?' Fael asked.

Nava brought her hand over her chest, her lips parting in offense. "Why do I have to be the one doing something? She is evil!"

Fael laughed, nodding. "True, but still . . . what did you do?"

"I threatened her, but that was after she pricked me multiple times—and she had already chosen the fabric by then."

"She pricked you?" His face fell as he straightened to his full six-feet-plus height. "The prince won't be pleased to learn this."

Oh, great, now she had to protect the evil seamstress's life from her soulmate's scorn. "Don't tell him, please. I don't want to burden him with something so silly. Plus I took care of it myself."

"You know I can't just keep the secret, right? I swore allegiance to the crown, and to him."

That was good to know. "Why him?"

Fael moved closer, his brows dipping as he checked his surroundings. "He is our future. If he is hell-bent on protecting you and your . . . fiancée, then so shall I." He paused, his deep gaze scanning the room before he eyed her as if it was the first time he had ever seen her. "He put a target on you the moment he placed you in this room."

He added in a whisper, "I told him as much, but he is stubborn."

"Why are you telling me this?" She matched his tone, and his deep, gold eyes softened. "You were there, weren't you? The night he was taken from me?"

His lips tightened. "I can't speak about it, not now or ever. But it's not only the catty behavior you should be wary about. While the prince knows he must protect you, he is not aware of whom might try to hurt you and Mr. Black."

Except he did now. Fael wasn't aware that Arkimedes had learned what had happened to him.

"I will be careful."

"And I won't leave my post, under any circumstance. I made a vow to him. You can trust me, Nava."

She nodded, though she wasn't sure yet.

He held her eyes and reached to close the door. "I'm sorry about . . . all of it," he finished, and the door clicked behind him as he left the room.

Leela arrived at her room not long after, carrying a tray with food. She stopped dead in her tracks when she saw the gown hanging by her armoire.

"What is that?" She rushed to the end of the bed, putting the tray on the mattress as she stormed over to inspect the dress.

Nava stood by the tray of food, picking at the flaky pastry, lost in thoughts. When she came out of their home the night Arkimedes was taken, she'd seen several Dark Ones, hidden by the shade of the night and the darkness of their power. How many of the royal guards had seen her? How many knew this "Devon's fiancée" lie was just a charade to buy them time?

Had the guard who'd almost killed her also known she'd been with Arkimedes the night he'd been taken? Had Herous been aware she was the same woman who'd come outside in her nightgown and had tried, but failed, to save him?

The king knew. Did that mean he was counting down her days? Was he going to try to kill her tonight when the castle was especially loud and busy? Yesterday she had gotten a taste of freedom, but today she was forced to face her reality once again. She was seeing the light at the end of this drab mess. With Arkimedes believing her, she had gained something big.

The food, rich in butter and salt, was bland in comparison. She moved her jaw, forcing the bite down.

She didn't have time to wait for him to fall back in love with her, and dread tasted bitter because she knew the secret looming over her—their soulmate bond—needed to come out. But after seeing him so happy in this town, after yesterday . . . What if she ruined it all by coming clean?

She stuffed her mouth with a larger bite of bread to quiet some of the blooming anxiety.

"Is that your dress?" Leela asked.

"Yes," Nava said with a full mouth. Eating was one of her default coping mechanisms. Sleepwalking was how her anxiety presented itself. She had nowhere to go in this castle while locked in this room. "The minions also delivered a wooden box, but I haven't opened it yet. I'm afraid she sent me someone's hand or ear as a souvenir."

Leela's face paled. "Do you think she would do such a thing? That would be a war call!"

"It was a poor joke!" Nava rushed to say, shaking her head. "Please ignore me."

"Huh." Leela eyed the aforementioned object warily, and then her gaze met Nava's and softened. "Come, miss. Let's start getting you ready for the celebration tonight."

Nava wrapped her robe around her body and sauntered toward the dressing table, sitting the way she had for the past few days. Her skin was heated and flushed, her body sensitive and swollen, her mind not as sharp as it usually was.

"The party is not until later tonight. It's pretty early to get ready," she commented as Leela started brushing her hair with a musical hum.

"Solstice celebrations are for everyone to attend," she chirped with a grin. "Including us."

"I like that. Maybe that way, I won't be by myself." Nava smiled.

"I'm sure your fiancé will love keeping you company . . ." Leela hesitated. "Even while wearing that dress."

A surprised laugh escaped Nava's lips. "Please don't hold back how you hate my dress, it won't make me more self-conscious or anything."

"Sorry." The fae's hands stopped all movements in Nava's hair, and she looked sheepish. "I noticed the tension between you and your fiancé yesterday. There is history there, though maybe not romantic?"

"Not romantic."

"What about the prince? I know it has been all in good fun, me teasing you about him. But that night when you first arrived, when you two were speaking in the hall . . . it just seemed like there was more." Leela hesitated, sliding her fingers over Nava's hair, her gentle hands resting on her shoulders. "Do you feel more for him than for your fiancé? The way he looked at you yesterday was different. I have never seen him look at anyone that way."

Nava met Leela's eyes through the reflection.

"I knew it! I'm fantastic at reading. If the gods had given magic to my family line, I bet I could have been a soothsayer."

It didn't escape Nava that Leela had always known Arkimedes was important to her. That they were more when nothing had pointed to that, other than him placing her in the room next to his.

A small voice inside her head, one that sounded an awful lot like her mother, told her she was being too trusting of this girl she had just met. It was hard not to let herself be at ease with the fae, not when her eyes were so round like a doe's or her smile so genuine.

Perhaps Nava was starving for female friendships. To meet a girl who, unlike Violet, wasn't trying to insult her at every corner. Someone who didn't think bonding came over the aftermath of war or a very painful training session. A friend like Simone.

"Has he spoken with you about what he might feel?" Leela continued, undeterred by Nava's silence.

"No. Not at all. We are just friends."

Though friends didn't strip naked and proceeded to intimately touch themselves to give the other one something to dream about. But those were semantics.

The faerie pouted but let the subject drop as she worked in silence over the intricate hairstyle.

Had Arkimedes taken care of his needs while thinking of her the night before? Nava couldn't believe she had been that bold, and her cheeks heated at the memory.

"Please say nothing about Devon and me outside these walls, Leela," Nava blurted, wishing she had been better at keeping her feelings under layers of self-preservation.

"Of course not." Her brows knitted together as she took in the monstrosity Marni had made for her. "This won't do. That hateful wench did this on purpose to shame you in front of everyone."

"That much is clear to me." Nava sighed, rubbing the bruised skin on her thigh where the seamstress had pricked her multiple times. "All the other dresses she had hanging in her shop for the occasion were beautiful."

The loud canary-yellow tulle mocked her from where it hung. The voluminous sleeves made of gaudy sheer fabric and that orange sash in the middle of the dress worsened the already appalling silhouette.

"I will take your measurements. I can't bring you to Renna's shop or the king will have my head. But if I rush there, maybe she has something on the rack that you can use for tonight. Our prince won't be able to look away from you."

Nava laughed again, shaking her head. "I'm pretty sure he won't be able to look away if I wore that horrible thing. No one will."

"Oh, yes, but for different reasons." Leela walked toward the dress and pulled at the fabric, scrunching her nose.

"Wouldn't it get you in trouble?" Nava asked. "My pride can handle this dress tonight. Maybe I'll even make it work for me somehow. I'd rather do that than have you catch the scorn of King Oberon." If only she had learned to sew. Laurie had tried to teach her multiple times but to no avail. Nava had refused.

Leela reconsidered, her skin glistening as perspiration cropped up on her powdery skin. "I might get in trouble." The fae's forehead scrunched. "But maybe we don't have to get you a new dress. Perhaps we just have to alter this terrible thing. It will drive me mad to not do something about it. I despise Marni."

"There is nothing that would make it worse," Nava

agreed. "Maybe we can take the sleeves and high neck off."

"And the sash has to go as well." Leela peered inside the garment, and her frown deepened. "Honestly, miss, I doubt this will even hold through the night. It's not properly sewn."

The evil seamstress had had less than a day to sew the whole dress. The lack of proper technique did not surprise Nava. However, maybe she had intended for it to fall apart and ridicule Nava mid-dance. The ballgown had been the least of her concerns earlier when Marni's helpers delivered it. Something had entranced her into the horrors of the way her body was awakening. Not even Fael's words were registering.

The heat taking over her senses, her increased libido, and her mind being stuck in passionate memories and their almost-kiss from a couple of nights ago—none of it was helping matters.

Bringing her hand over her fast-beating heart and her soulmate mark, she took a sharp breath. Nava needed to get herself together. It wouldn't matter if she was wearing a potato sack, if she could not keep it on once she got a good look at her mate tonight. "Do you know anything about the solstice and how it might affect . . . people?"

"Do you mean magic-wielding humans?"

"Sure, anyone really."

"Well, it affects all of us fae much like a full moon affects lycans. We gather to celebrate the longer days, for healthier crops, which means a healthier kingdom." Leela rubbed at the yellow dress, not paying attention to Nava's fidgeting.

"I wonder, if I say I'm sick, would that work for me not to have to go to the celebration?"

"They will send the healers, and they will know if you are in fact ill," Leela warned. "Are you feeling unwell?"

"No. Maybe?" Nava pulled the belt on her robe, deviating her gaze elsewhere. "The healers weren't nice when they tended to me last time. What's with the people of this kingdom hating humans?"

"We're split in between the ones who dislike humans, especially after the queen—" Leela cleared her throat and wandered around the room. But Nava could fill in the blanks now.

The queen had stolen their heir away. A precious prince who wasn't easy to replace, not if what Arkimedes had told her about the royals having difficulty making babies was true.

"But these last ten years, the hate has grown like a rotten thing. The king used to trade with your kind. We used to get delicious chocolate from the Gold Kingdom." Her expression turned dreamy. "And traveling musicians from the Pearl Islands used to tour our land."

Nava's heart shrank at hearing about the islands, where Cameron, Gavin, and Violet were, searching for knowledge about how to battle the Iron Crown and the Society of Crows. Trying to find ancient laws set eons ago that would protect magic-wielders over the crown's army drafting and coupling laws.

It was Gavin's and Violet's hope that there had been a law signed by all kingdoms at some point that protected things like soulmate bonds or families' rights. It was a long shot but worth researching.

"I saw a lot of humans in town yesterday."

"Oh, yes, our locals have always been here. However, they've grown more resentful over getting pushed to the edges of the city. Most of the homes near the castle are fae homes," Leela continued.

"That's horrible, the king shouldn't have so much hate toward his own people."

"I don't believe he does. Not truly." Leela's gaze searched the room. Nava remembered the first day Leela had come to keep her company. How the room had reacted when she'd spoken ill of the queen. Nava wondered if she was waiting for a similar reaction. "He made a human his queen, after all," Leela added after a moment of silence, taking Nava out of her musings. "It's said he loved her, making the betrayal even more heartbreaking."

Nava wasn't sure the king could love anyone or anything. Not if he'd kidnapped his son, erased his memories, and forced him to stay here against his will. "Why are they so sure she betrayed him?" Nava asked.

Leela pressed her lips together, shrugging one slim shoulder. "The king says so, and it must be true since he defended her for years."

If her instinct was correct—and it usually was when it came to her mate—she was sure Arkimedes didn't agree with the sentiment. Something was off, and he was determined to find it.

"I will fetch some needle and thread to fix this monstrosity before the ball. I'm not amazing with sewing, but I know a little, miss. I can help you if you allow me to do so."

"Have at it, Leela. You will make it one hundred times better."

If what Devon and now Leela had told her was true, the way magic worked with soulmates during the solstice would make her irrational when it came to being intimate with her mate. She needed to stay away from Arkimedes B. Valeron, and maybe this dress would help her with that.

CHAPTER TWENTY-FOUR

NAVA

Nava caressed the top of the box, her fingers slipping over the red polished wood. The emblem of Marni's boutique was etched on top with gold foil accents. She undid the clasp, and soon her eyes encountered a feathered, canary-yellow mask to go with her dress. "Does the king allow himself to partake in the ball?"

"Yes, the whole court will be present. He always has his hands full with his ladies . . ." Leela lowered her gaze back to the gown. *Riiiip.* She pulled away one sleeve of Nava's dress with a grin. "I have a good feeling about this, miss. She built it so poorly, I'm able to remove these layers with almost no issue."

"That makes me feel better." Nava grabbed the sash, using the small scissors Leela had provided to cut some of the thread that attached it to the dress. Once the sash was off, it revealed a nice, narrow bodice.

Leela walked to the closet, opening the doors and examining the gowns hanging in there.

Nava stared, curious. "If you are looking for a new yellow or gold gown to magically show up there, I hate to break it to you but I already checked, multiple times."

The redhead laughed, shaking her head. "Oh, no, I want to borrow some pieces from some of the gowns you have already worn."

"Are you looking for something specific?"

"A sash . . . some tulle, anything really." Leela's delicate brows met in the middle. Her lips pursed as she moved the gowns around. "I don't remember them being so dark before."

"Dark?"

"Yes, weren't they all light blue?"

That piqued Nava's curiosity. She strolled to the closet, eyeing the colors of her dresses. Leela was right—they were still blue, but much darker. Some indigo, others navy. "I swear I haven't done anything."

"Of course not. The room is charmed to tend to your needs," her friend said, and it sounded like a practiced speech. Something she repeated often, likely to other guests of the castle. "I have never seen it change dress shades before, but it must go with your mood or something." She shrugged and picked a gown from the bunch.

"Callisto mentioned it, and I forgot to ask her . . . Is it a room thing or is the castle somehow magical?"

"The king's magic feeds the castle—and our kingdom in a way I don't claim to understand, but it's what we're told."

Nava looked around the room, to the ceilings and floors, feeling watched as her spine prickled with aware-ness. "Can he hear us?" she whispered.

"He shouldn't—"

"Shouldn't and couldn't are not the same."

"He has spies everywhere." Leela's words became almost silent, but she smiled after the room had grown too cold. "His power used to have more of a reach decades ago. I'm sure he has better things to do than spy on you."

Think again, Leela. He was her enemy.

They worked through the morning and into the afternoon. By the time Leela made her way out of Nava's room, the dress looked less like an overly decorated cake. They had picked apart one or two of the other gowns, taking a bit of embroidery from an underlay skirt here, some soft white tulle there.

It was not a masterpiece by any stretch of the imagination, but just the fact that Marni would be upset about them altering her gown had Nava smiling.

Her dress didn't look like two women had pulled it apart at the last minute this morning, and even though it wasn't the most beautiful gown she'd seen, it was pretty enough.

"I will try to bring you a mask to the ball to replace the one Marni gave you. But it gets very busy, I might not be able to find you," she vowed before leaving

Fael peeked through the door, his brows lifting as he met their creation and whistled. "Now that's what I call a full transformation."

"Aren't you going to get changed?" Nava asked when it was just the two of them left. His black aura was a soft, billowy mist, barely perceptible and nothing compared to the royals.

"No, I can't leave the post unattended."

Guilt boiled in her stomach. "That won't do. Maybe I can come with you so you can get changed. I mean, I won't come to see you get changed, of course. What I mean is I can be close by."

Fael's laughter rolled over the room. "Miss Nava. Have you seen how the prince can kill by lifting his hand? It takes the royals just half a minute to break one's soul apart." The guard cleared his throat and shook his head with a tentative smile. "I won't change to anything else than my armor. It lends me better opportunities while I'm there either way."

Nava swallowed, standing on shaky legs. She didn't want to give away the fact that to her, Arkimedes wasn't scary. He was home. "I guess people do like a man in armor."

"It's my preferred outfit for any occasion, and unlike the rest of the crew, we aren't forced to wear white."

She grinned. "I bet you get lots of attention."

"Oh, you have no idea."

Rich red runners flowed down wide spiral stairs, leading to a music-filled room. Crisscrossed columns lined the ceilings, reminding her of the waffles Laurie used to make for breakfast. Her stomach churned, and Nava wasn't sure if it was from nerves or hunger.

The room was vast, with decorated columns and polished marble floors where couples wearing gold, yellow, and white swirled around the dance floor. She found a band in the corner, playing unusual instruments.

Fael walked next to her as they came into the crowd. Laughter filled the air, and Nava met the curious gaze of a mask-wearing fae who snickered at the dress. She would have cared in a normal situation, but the heat soaring through her made it hard to give a crap about the disastrous puffy yellow nightmare she wore.

"How are we going to find Leela?" Nava turned to

Fael, who stood a good head and a half taller than her, towering over most people.

He dropped his gaze; golden eyes shone behind a black mask. He lifted a bushy brow. "With that dress, it's more likely she will find you."

Nava lifted onto her tiptoes, trying to find her friend among the crowd. However, her eyes deviated away from their original task, hunting for someone else instead. "Is it too naïve of me to expect that Ar—er, I mean, His Royal Highness to join me at any point tonight?" she asked, wringing her hands together, avoiding the man's knowing look. "I mean, I know he is going to be busy, and I don't expect for him to come to talk to me alone, but since Devon and I are his guests, I hoped . . . You know what? I don't care."

And she shouldn't care! Nava had spent a good portion of the day planning how to *avoid* him. She did want to tell him her life might be in danger, just in case the king decided to attack her tonight when there would be so many people he could put the blame on.

So her mind had settled on having a quick chat with her mate. It would be an in-and-out sort of conversation. *"My life is in danger. Keep an eye on me, but stay away from me. I love you."*

Nava wouldn't utter the last three words, but she would say the rest and then quickly disappear. She would not say they were soulmates when they were both in some sort of lust frenzy.

"I'm sure he will extract himself from duty to be with you at some point." Fael's chin pointed to a spot in the room she had somehow missed. A long table rested above the crowd. It was made of carved wood and painted in rich ebony tones that masked the dangerous aura of the two men sitting behind it.

A banquet of delicious-looking fruit lay in front. The royals wore stark white outfits with gold emblems and decorations. Nava focused on Arkimedes, drinking in his handsome features. The coat he wore hugged his shoulders, and a golden mask covered the top half of his face, made to mimic his features.

"I just hope that when he does, he finds a moment when no one will miss him," Fael said, bringing her out of her thoughts.

"I need to tell him something quick, and then I will be away." Would he recognize her if he saw her?

Nava swallowed, feeling her body buzz with need. He shouldn't be there, chatting with random women, eating and drinking, instead of here, with her. A distinct sensation boiled within her, one she had not felt in a while. Jealousy.

He wouldn't feel attraction to anyone—she knew this from experience. It didn't mean the king wasn't pushing his own agenda.

It took her a moment to notice that all the women sitting at the royal table had black auras in various shades of intensity. Not as opaque as the king's, and without the creepy appearance of random body parts, very similar to Fael's.

The king's women possessed the Dark One's power. Nava felt her lips part as she took all of them in. Varying in different shapes and skin colors, the cohorts were undoubtedly fae, judging by their pointy ears and the wings behind their backs.

"They all have auras," Nava said, wandering closer to take a better look. "I thought all fae who possess the power were part of the guard?"

"They were once part of us," Fael agreed.

"He forced them to be with him? He took advantage . . . ?" Nava's face warmed. The women didn't appear unhappy where they sat, talking and laughing. They looked at complete ease, unlike the rigid set of Arkimedes's shoulders.

"He didn't force them. They volunteered to give the kingdom a chance for an heir, as we thought our prince was dead." Fael's stern gaze traveled down from the table and met Nava's. "I must admit, some of their choices surprised me . . ." His words trailed as his brows met in the middle. Sadness lit behind his dark lashes, morphing his features and dulling his bright skin.

"I see. Why them when there is a kingdom full of people?"

"It's not for me to tell." Fael put the helmet onto his head and placed a hand on her back, but the sensation his touch gave her was all wrong.

The fire in her veins demanded to be touched, but not by him. Nava stepped away from the guard's hand. She focused back on the royals' table, meeting Arkimedes's gaze from across the room.

Her throat bobbed as he leaned forward, holding the weight of his body on his arms over the table. From this far, she couldn't see the play of muscles in his arms, though her vivid, heated mind could provide her plenty of details.

Frozen in her spot, pinned under his gaze, she was too close and not close enough at the same time. His bright green eyes were brighter than all the other fairies next to him.

"Fiancée, you decided to show up." Devon sauntered into her line of sight, his voice like a drop of ice melting over burning skin.

"I preferred when you called me kitten," she said. It was the first time she'd seen Devon in such bright colors, and he looked almost as white as a ghost under such shades. His hair was slicked back, and the dark circles under his eyes made the pupilless orbs pop.

"I much prefer this new one," he said, stopping next to her with a bored stance. His gaze drifted toward Fael. "Guard."

The fae grunted. "I will get something to drink but will be close. Do not step away from here without me."

It was then that she noticed the glass of red liquid in Devon's hand. "Where are your guards?" she asked.

"I lost them a while ago. Fae get rowdy with the wine," he said with a side smirk. "You, however, don't need such a thing to be in trouble, do you?"

She swallowed, and her eyes shifted toward the table where Arkimedes sat, his eyes burning through the crowd, fixed on them with the intensity of the seven suns. "Is—is there anything wrong with the wine, or do they just drink too much?"

"Everyone knows the fae spike their wine during a celebration such as this to liberate themselves. They like the lack of repercussions or censorship." Devon swirled the liquid again, which spilled down his ivory skin and onto the floor. He dumped half of the contents when no one was watching.

Nava lifted a brow. "What are you doing?"

He took a step forward and lowered his face to her ear. "The guards gave me this wine to drink, no doubt with some wicked intent." One of his hands grasped her lower back, and his lips caressed the shell of her ear.

"You are going to get it all over your white clothes," Nava said, taking a healthy step away from him. She didn't need her dress to become more of a horror show.

"Does it look like I care?" Devon paused and shortened their distance again. They were far enough from the dance floor and other people that most wouldn't be able to hear them. "Neither of you can stay here." He grabbed her arm, something he hadn't done before. Things had changed between them in a matter of days.

She tried to pull away, but his hand held her still. "Let go of me," she said between her teeth.

"Calm down," he whispered. "We don't want to call attention now."

Nava blinked and pulled her head back, meeting Devon's calculating gaze. "Do not touch me again."

He smirked but dropped his hand from her body. "Tell me, have you told my brother that you are soulmates? Does he know why he is burning for you right now? Why he wants to tear away every inch of that dress from your body? And to hell with the consequences."

Nava's cheeks burned hotter than before, and she wouldn't have been surprised if she combusted at any moment. She cleared her throat before speaking, but her insides fluttered with need.

She gazed at her mate from across the room, and her throat became drier than a desert. "If it's such a big deal, why didn't you?"

"I have been busy translating a book for him and assuring him we aren't engaged." He looked around before focusing on her again. "I also thought it was none of my business."

Nava swallowed, and the pit in her stomach grew, weighing a ton. She couldn't tell Devon that she was afraid Arkimedes would reject her. That she was giving him time to fall back in love with her, which was a stupid plan, but it was better than kidnapping, which had been her other idea.

Nava had to be cautious about how much she shared with her mate, and how fast, especially since he'd been so distrusting of her. She didn't want to lose him.

Well, maybe she'd tell him today.

"I'm afraid we are in danger tonight at this party," she admitted. "What if the king plans to get rid of us? It's such a busy night . . . Arkimedes might be distracted to notice us gone."

"He won't be distracted from you tonight."

Her cheeks burned. "Well, still, I thought I would stay away after I told him my concerns."

Devon pondered her words. "Yes, it's a possibility. Why do you want to stay away again?"

"Be-because of consent? I don't think it's a good idea for me to be near him. We aren't in our right minds right now, and it seems wrong to take advantage of him—" Why in the hell she was opening up to this man, she didn't know. Nava must be more distressed than she'd thought.

His laughter shook her out of her panicked thoughts. "Take advantage? You won't be able to avoid him."

Nava's mouth opened and closed a few times before the words bubbled out. "How could you possibly know that?"

"I was not locked away in a non-magical island for a decade like you. I have seen things. Read many other things . . ." Devon lowered his voice. "You have your head on your shoulders now, but at some point, you won't care whatever noble reasonings you've told yourself, and neither will he."

In other words, he would look for her—and she would do the same. She had to get him out of here, and they had to go somewhere away from prying eyes.

Devon's eyes traveled over her shoulder, and his brows dipped. "He doesn't like me being this close to you, but he is not moving away from that damn table."

"It's better not to call for the king's attention," Nava reasoned and was proud of her own self-restraint not to look around.

"Let's dance."

"Um, no thanks."

"Look, I want it as much as you do, believe me. You have to get out of here, and I might be able to go back to my room if I'm leaving with the two of you." Devon scratched his chin with a long pale finger.

Nava shifted the weight of her feet, wanting to squirm out of this dress. The uncomfortable throbbing between her legs grew ever so present. She clenched her thighs together to relieve some of the pressure, to no avail.

Maybe she didn't care if everyone here saw Arkimedes devour her. It might make them understand he was hers, and nothing the king could do would separate them.

Oh, no.

"Good, now she gets it. Let's dance." He offered her his hand, and her stomach dropped as she took it. A year ago, she would have scoffed in horror if someone had told her she'd dance with her archnemesis. The one who now had become an ally of sorts.

The ground became soft the farther onto the dance floor they went. Nava looked down, finding stained white coats and shimmery golden fabrics. She watched as the fae and humans shed their clothing. The dance floor was packed, winged people moved alongside wingless partners.

Some wore more clothes than others. She had never seen anything like it. Devon led her forward to the center of the room. Nava wasn't sure she wanted to be so close to all these soon-to-be naked people.

She wrinkled her nose when the Crow turned to face her, lifting his brow.

"Don't tell me you are a prude."

"I'm not!" Nava glanced around her as the strangers of this kingdom writhed against one another in a seductive dance that looked too intimate. She took in the crowd and was astonished by how quickly the party was developing into some sort of orgy. What was going on here?

Devon held her too close for her liking, and her skin prickled with the sensation of being followed. "Don't step on my feet."

"Oops." She smiled when the tip of her heel met his soft boot. "Have you come up with a way to get him out of here? Because, other than giving him time . . . I haven't."

"He is not leaving this place, not until he unravels whatever he's trying to find from his past," Devon whispered. "Unless you break the spell he is under and he somehow evolves to the man you met last year. Which is not the Arkimedes of a decade ago."

She wiggled in her spot, feeling like ants crawled over her skin, the sensation making her lose her footing on the dance floor. "How do I break the spell? I thought the one casting it formed a counter-spell. I doubt the king will offer me the solution."

"You've got that right."

"Well, then what? Is there a way to gain back memories that were taken?" Devon nodded, and her heart stumbled on a beat. "Like-like all memories, even the ones that were taken from me?" Her voice sounded too small.

His face softened. "Cat."

"What?"

"Yours are gone."

She shouldn't have asked. Nava didn't have the luxury of falling apart in the middle of the ball. Her eyes blurred, and she deviated her gaze, focusing on anything but Devon, not wanting to see an expression that mocked her —or, even worse, pitied her.

Devon gave her a moment to collect herself, and she allowed the beautiful music to carry her sorrow, wishing she had her brother close, to get lost in one of his famous bear hugs and find solace that at least she still had him.

"So that's it then?" Devon's words had her mind sharpening back to this reality. "You have been gaining his trust, hoping he'd choose to leave with you in just a couple of weeks?"

She scowled. "Do you have a better plan? I'm open to even your suggestions."

"We can poison his mind to have him kill the king and then take over the kingdom. My debt will be paid, I will be free, and this mess will be your problem."

"You know what? I changed my mind. Your plan sucks." She huffed. "And so we are clear, you will not be free after this." She had to take this man back with her to the Northern Village in the Grey Island or Roman would never allow her back.

His smirk grew to one side. "Watch and learn, cat."

"Nava is a bee, brother. Not a cat." Arkimedes's voice came out dangerously low.

She jumped in her spot, and Devon's hands loosened from her body, dropping to his sides as if he knew he shouldn't push his luck. Her skin raised into goose bumps as she turned to face Ark. This close, he towered over her, standing every inch the prince he'd turned out to be.

His aura flickered, letting her know he was not amused. His temper was not controlled, which in return made his magic act out. It was the only time she was able to see it. "I will steal your dance partner now." It wasn't even a question.

"I'm sure I get a say in the matter," she grunted. However, there was a secret part of her that rejoiced at this alpha display.

Arkimedes took a deep breath, his eyes shining with a heavy dose of amusement. "Can I have this dance?" But his hand was already grabbing for hers before he even heard her answer, pulling her toward him as his wings tucked behind his back. The fairy lights bounced on his feathers, bringing out the blue iridescence shades.

She stumbled forward, steadying herself against his chest. His heartbeat drummed under her fingers, erratic beats that told her his adrenaline was pumping hard. From this close, Nava took in the woven patterns of his coat. Someone had made it, with beautiful embroidered shapes of feathers and tree branches that held no leaves, like the insignia of this house.

"I will leave then." Devon bowed and met her gaze from the side as his lips formed the words *"Get out of here."*

Arkimedes's eyes bore into her, as if reaching for her soul. His other hand grabbed her lower back, bringing her closer to him. Her body quivered when his fingers trailed up, reaching the bare skin of her back.

She breathed as a spark traveled through her with his touch, and for a moment, it was only the two of them. Even though everyone could tell who he was by the shining crown of thorns that lay over his styled head of hair, he was still wearing a mask.

"What would your kingdom say, seeing you dancing with a human? Isn't that scandalous?"

He lifted a brow. "I would like to see them come and tell me to not do it."

Oh, he was long gone. She had a six-foot-three problem on her hands. Literally.

She didn't want anyone to interrupt them, aware of what was going on between them after her talk with Devon. Nava needed to get out of here, fast, if the tremble of her knees and the throbbing in her center was anything to go by. "I'd rather avoid anything that would upset your father if possible. I don't need him getting any ideas to make me disappear."

"No one is making you disappear," he breathed, and his fingers dug into the skin of her back as he lowered his head to her ear. "I'm afraid my head is not in its right place, especially after last night."

"What happened last night?" she asked in a thin voice, remembering the way she had touched herself when she'd known he was watching.

"You tell me." His lips touched her ear, then moved to her neck, breathing her in.

Oh, god. It was too much. Nava was going to ignite into flames on the spot if he continued on.

"It seemed like you were tempting me to come to you and finish what you'd started."

"I was."

"I'm here now." His tongue slipped over her neck, and her toes curled in her shoes at the sensation that spread through her.

She had to battle to keep the moan inside her mouth, but her eyes rolled back when his teeth nipped at her skin and his wide hands brought her closer to his body. Nava's dress was too tight over her skin.

What if his father was watching them now? It would be hard to explain why Arkimedes was kissing her neck at the moment.

Devon's plan to get too close to her to get a rise out of her mate had worked. Now she had to do her job to get them out of here somehow, away from prying eyes. Maybe gather some courage and confess.

She lifted her gaze toward the table. An ebony-skinned concubine sat on the king's lap, caressing his face as her curves and narrow wings hid most of him from view. They were kissing, and the image was too intimate to linger on.

Alertness descended over her fogged mind. "We should try to not call for attention." She pushed away from him, but desire burned hotter within her as she touched him, grasping the lapels of his coat.

Why should I care? Everyone else seems to be doing it.

"No one cares." His lips traced the side of her cheek, so close to her lips that her body shook with anticipation. But she cared; they weren't a cheap one-night stand. If there was something she'd learned last year, it was that destiny didn't mess around. If soulmates became this heated and uncontrolled during the solstice night, it meant something.

She was scared—maybe a bit paranoid. But she didn't want to regret whatever happened here. "Did you drink some of the wine? I heard it clouds your judgment."

He pulled back a few inches, meeting her gaze, and for the first time, his expression cleared. His gloved finger caressed the side of her jaw, where his lips had just been. "Everyone knows not to drink the wine at these parties."

Nava had his attention; it was go time. "It's hot in here . . . I need some air." No one paid any attention to them.

"Right now?" He glanced around, appearing more lucid. "It is getting a bit . . . intense here."

"Let's leave," she whispered. "Maybe you can show me parts of the garden I haven't been allowed to see. I would love to be close to nature, but maybe somewhere where there aren't any creepy flowers?"

Arkimedes's grin slowly spread, and he nodded, stepping away from her. "There is a place I would like to show you." His hand still held hers as he pulled her through the sea of people on the dance floor, toward the large doors that led them to one of the many halls of the castle.

She caught Devon's eyes on their way out. He was

leaning against a far wall and nodded as they walked past. Straightening in his place, he walked behind them.

Last Nava saw him, he was going up the wide staircase Fael and she had descended. She assumed he was returning to his room, but one never knew with Devon Black. She was too far gone to care.

CHAPTER TWENTY-FIVE

NAVA

The sky had turned into marbled shades of apricot and purple by the time they made it out of the castle. Fae filled the wide corridors, dressed in elegant attire. So caught up in their conversations, drinking and laughing, they missed even Arkimedes's imposing shape.

Arkimedes and Nava soon walked out to the garden, and when his hand grasped hers, she had almost forgotten this man walking next to her was not *her* Arkimedes. His burning touch was disorienting. She would have to focus on ice buckets or festering wounds. Anything to bring herself to a more level head.

"Not many people come to this part of the garden anymore," he said after they had walked in silence for a while.

Twisty trees with thick green foliage lined each side of the path with manicured symmetry. Her feet clicked over brick terracotta stone, still warm from the afternoon sun, and lightning bugs flew low to the ground, adding to the festive ambiance.

Her heart soared at the sight of it; it was magical being here on the castle grounds, surrounded by masked people in beautiful dresses. When she was young and prisoner to her mother's strict rules, she had always daydreamed about attending one of these.

If she closed her eyes and forgot everything, Nava could almost fool herself into believing this was a normal courtship. That they had met at this age, not when she'd been a teenager. That their meeting and bond wouldn't have sent her mother into a frenzy that had taken her entire family to a different continent.

Maybe Arkimedes would come and get her for the ball, and they would spend time kissing and hiding from prying eyes before a deeper engagement was announced. Maybe if she saw the positives of this terrible situation, she could enjoy falling for each other again.

Her eyes prickled as she focused on their intertwined fingers. A puzzle piece made by an expert, they fit just right, like their souls. Where she was weak, he was strong. Where he lacked confidence in himself, she had it for the both of them.

The string instruments played a beautiful ballad even here, and the percussion of the drums hammered along with her heart. She wondered if the king had a poor band hidden somewhere but didn't care to try to find them in the darkness.

The path continued as they went under an arched gazebo that held white wisteria, hanging low enough to graze her shoulders, and soon people became less of a common sight; the few they crossed here were busy doing other things.

Cedar box hedges lined the perimeter, growing alongside flowers that vined over them. The grass grew wild and uneven, and flowers of all colors rose within the grooves of the rickety brick pathway. The beauty of this area in its wild state took her breath away.

They went under a tall arbor that could have been made of metal or wood, but she couldn't tell with the platinum light of the moon. There, in front of them, was one of the most breathtaking images she had seen. A large pond with turquoise water, no doubt illuminated by magic.

Waterlilies floated above, and in the center, an island held a massive tree that stood twenty feet tall with a wide, knotty trunk. Its texture shimmered in silver tones, and its branches mimicked roots, twisting up in the air.

The sight left her speechless. She had seen this before —no, not this, but one that was made to look the same. Except that one had radiated death and suffering. This was beautiful and full of magic.

"My father brought me here a few weeks after I got to the Copper City."

"How did he find you the first time?"

"I was asking questions, which called the guards' attention." He laughed, shaking his head. "They didn't like that a Crow was nosing around town. Fael found me wandering around. Plus my aura gave me away." He turned to face her and looked at ease while speaking with her. Not guarded. He looked like her Arkimedes, not Orion.

Her heart ached at the sight. "Did they bring you to see His Majesty?"

"Oh, yes. I mean, they had no grounds to arrest me but made it clear it wouldn't go well for me if I resisted the invitation."

"Little did they know," she said with a shaky smile. "I mean, you look like a copy of your father. Same nose and eye shape. Even the lips are the same."

"When you aren't looking for it, it's hard to see it.

Especially because my father doesn't like people looking straight at him."

Nava did remember Fael's warning the day she'd arrived at the castle. "Right."

"I'm not sure if those memories are from this time around or the previous time I was here when in my twenties." Arkimedes brought his hand over his head, frowning at the tree. "He wanted to show me my mother's tree. He claimed the future queen will bring it back to life . . ."

Nava didn't want to face him with those words. Oh, no, those were too scary for her to dwell on. Before tonight, Nava had never *truly* considered the fact that he might want to stay, if not for Devon telling her Ark wouldn't leave until he accomplished whatever he was looking for.

Even then, she wouldn't have believed it if she hadn't seen the way his face had shone when exploring the city yesterday.

She'd been dreading that he might not want her if he learned who she was. Now she had gained that trust back, and he was within arm's reach. What would she do if he didn't want to leave with her? Would she feel okay bringing Cameron to this place? Away from the safety net of town?

Even if the king accepted that they were mates and wouldn't just make her go away, would Cameron, Laurie, and Nava be safe in a city that hated humans? So close to the Society of Crows.

Arkimedes's crown glistened under the moonlight, his feathers swaying behind him with the light breeze as they got closer to the tree. She needed a new plan, that much was clear. After the solstice, she would tell him about their bond. Then they could decide what to do together. Any other option was too heartbreaking to consider, and her mind wasn't in the right place at the moment.

She reached the stone banister that separated the pond

from the land, and her stomach fluttered when he got closer and the warmth of his body seeped through the fabric of her dress. She turned to face the tree once again. It was clear this was the muse for the kingdom's emblem. And for the queen's killer.

A giant dead-looking tree in the middle of a wonderful garden. So tragically similar to the one in the forest.

"So, this is the queen's tree . . . ?"

Arkimedes nodded, and his brows pulled together as he took it in. "When we were together, did I tell you how I grew up?"

"You told me they dropped you into an orphanage when you were a one-year-old boy."

His throat bobbed. "She was killed after she dropped me—though the literature claims she killed herself."

"How could she have? Didn't they find her tied to that tree?"

"Exactly the questions I have been asking," he said in a low voice before turning to face her. "But she was a magic wielder, and that is their response to all of it. They have erased from all records that her body was there."

"Why?"

"The king said it was to prevent the kingdom from appearing weak. If we couldn't protect our queen, who's to say we could protect our people from harm?"

"Well, that's manipulating true events, it's a lie." Nava huffed. "I hate lies."

Guilt bubbled in her gut. Was she doing the same? No, she wasn't lying, per se. She was . . . momentarily holding the truth.

"Someone attacked her multiple times, once while pregnant. The books don't go into details, but most of the records are still there." His lips tightened.

Nava's heart sank with each of his words. A memory

of what she'd heard that day in the library flashed through her mind. "Is the prophecy you are looking for related to this somehow?"

"Your guess is as good as mine." He leaned over the rails, looking at the tree with longing. "It's strange to feel this need to find answers when I didn't know her. But it's a question I have asked myself all my life. Why didn't they want me?"

Nava's heart squeezed in her chest, and she reached for his hand, hoping he wouldn't shut off at the touch. Instead, he wrapped his fingers around hers, his skin feverish. "Turns out, they wanted you very much, but your mother taking you doesn't appear to be the move of someone who doesn't want her baby. It's like she was trying to protect you."

"Right." He nodded. "But from whom?"

"Well, the king kidnapped you and took your memories away. My vote is on him."

"My father wouldn't hurt me. Why go through all the trouble of bringing me here if that were the case?" He had a point. "There is also a book I found that mentions a child born sick, being dropped in the world of mist and shadows."

Her skin became cold as dread spread over every inch of her body. "You think that was supposed to be you?"

"What if that's why my mother did it? What if they believe I was sick somehow, and she abandoned me in that orphanage to prevent my father's people from—killing me?"

"Could the book be referring to her dropping you in the orphanage?"

"I guess it could be. The book was burned in a fire. The dates aren't clear, but its scripture is written in an old language, and it appears to be older than me."

She remembered Devon speaking about helping Ark with a translation. This had to be it. "Too many fires in this castle are linked to you and your mother. If you add the Zorren to the equation, it seems like too many to be a coincidence." She dragged her finger over the stone of the banister before meeting his shocked gaze.

"I had not considered the demons."

"You just found out about them. Well, actually, you have known about them for a long time, but you don't remember, thanks to your dear father." Nava wanted to be there for him and help him with whatever he was going through. Just like he had helped her last year, when she had been the one searching for answers about her nature. She'd gone from hating and fearing magic to embracing it.

She changed from being a scared, closed-minded person to— Her thoughts stopped. Was that what she was now? Scared of something different, of a new world she didn't understand? No, surely not.

No one could blame her for her reservations about this place.

"Do you think the prophecy holds the information about why she took you away?"

"I'm certain about it. Like you said, too many coincidences." His body was so rigid, she almost could see his aura become solid around his body, his magic taking over.

Nava dragged her hand over his arm in a soothing motion. "Have you gotten a clue of who might be behind it? Multiple people?" She hesitated. "The king?"

Arkimedes shook his head. "Whatever feelings he has harvested since her death weren't there when she was alive. The root of it all began with heartbreak. He loved her, and he believes she betrayed him."

"By taking you away?"

"I believe she did it to protect me. Maybe that's a part

of that idealistic self he likes to tell me I inherited from her."

Nava tightened her hold around his forearm, winded by the wave of sorrow that pushed through the bond. She took a shallow breath. "If she was being targeted while living here, he betrayed her before she took you away. He didn't protect her from whoever killed her and then hid the truth from the people."

They stared at the tree. Even this far from the party, the music drifted in the air, reminding her why she'd run away from the crowds. Even though she wanted to keep learning what he had been up to when away from her, something else boiled beneath her skin. A primal need to be closer to him.

"The tree has been dead for twenty years," he said.

"You mean thirty-one years?"

He turned to face her and let go of a deep sigh. "Yes, it's still hard to wrap my head around the time change."

Nava wondered if they kept this conversation, they might fool nature from calling upon them. "I know it looks dead, but it's not." She squinted at the tree, and there she saw it, white and yellow waves of magic vibrating out, pulsing with magic.

"What do you mean?"

"I can sense it's alive—vibrating with energy." She smiled and focused on it. The light of the moon bathed the shapes of the branches, and there in the silhouette, Nava spotted hundreds of small black dots peppering the twisty shapes. "It's one of my Beekeeper superpowers," she teased, though it wasn't a lie. It had been one thing that was unique about her. The way she could see nature's waves. "And I can also see it's budding."

Arkimedes's head snapped back to the tree, his eyes widening. "I see nothing."

"I mean, they aren't opening yet, but I see the start of leaves—maybe even late-summer flowers?" She was not sure why she felt such excitement about the prospect, but her heart soared at the idea of bringing this news to him.

"Nava," he gasped, bringing her attention back to him. His voice didn't sound as elated as she'd thought he would be by the news. "In the life I don't remember, were we married?"

"W-what do you mean?" she stuttered, not liking where this conversation was going. Her neck pickled with the quick building of anxiety. This had better not mean what she was starting to think.

His brows dipped. "Did we get married back on the Grey Island?"

They hadn't even talked about it . . . much. Though she had hoped it was the next step. More of a symbol than anything. "No."

"Don't lie to me."

"I'm not!" She took a step back, and the pleasant heat that had been present in her body the entire afternoon came alive in another way. "And do not talk to me that way!"

"This tree has been dead for twe—thirty years because the queen of this kingdom was murdered."

She swallowed and stepped back one more step. This was going the way she didn't want to go.

"I told you, it's linked to the new queen. It hasn't budded for anyone until you arrived here. I was here last week, and it was dead."

"What makes you think that means we are married? Your father has ten women with him. Surely one of them kicked this tree back to life." And she knew she was reaching for excuses when the truth was pulsing in her mind. She, the soulmate of the Crown Prince of this kingdom, had arrived a week ago.

"He has five women," he corrected, "and they have been with him for over a decade. So no, what are you hiding, and why?"

She needed to get them out of here before she ended up trapped into being a queen, which was not something she wanted at all. She took another step back, her heart drumming. "I recommend you to track everyone who's entered this palace in the last week since she has the possibility of giving your father another child, and then we can leave this place and be in peace."

Arkimedes strode forward, and she hit the hedge with the side of her body. "I have been thinking of you for months. I can't get you out of my mind for even a moment. If we weren't married, were we in love?"

Nava swallowed the thick knot in her throat, which felt like it lead to her stomach. "Yes."

He placed his hands on each side of her head, and she squirmed at the intensity in his eyes. "You can't keep pretending to be with Devon. We need to tell my father, and you will become my bride here."

"Arkimedes. Can you even hear what you are saying? The king took you from our home and conveniently left me behind. He knew who I was when Devon and I arrived. He was ready to have us killed. I'm just a human, and everyone in this kingdom hates humans."

His lips parted. "Not everyone hates humans, Nava."

"I'm not a queen." She had to steady herself, to not lose her calm. "I'm a potion—I mean, a Beekeeper, and we need to protect the forests from the Zorren. Being king and queen is not a part of that."

"It's a part of who I am," he countered; however, his

eyes glazed over. His expression changed as if a fog had come down his mind.

"Ark," she breathed. Her body shook with something primal spreading over her like a tsunami wave.

"We can talk about it later." His eyes dropped to her lips.

"Not later." She half pushed against his chest, not really wanting to get him away from her. "I'm not staying in a place where everyone hates me, where I don't know what will happen to me. Look at the dress that wench made for me just because I'm a human!"

"I like it." *Off you. Now.*

Nava blinked. Were those his thoughts bouncing in her head? It had been a while since she had heard him so clear. Their connection was sharpening as the night grew closer to midnight.

"It itches all over." The words tumbled out of her lips. She lifted her hands, dropping them on his shoulders, and he stood closer, resting his forehead on hers. "She did this even after you told her to 'take care of me.'"

"I will deal with her tomorrow."

"*No,* just let me complain without murdering someone with your shadow power."

Arkimedes's eyes danced, and his hands caressed the side of her dress over her rib cage. "My shadow power?" He hummed, and that side smirk was all she needed to forget about the whole queen ordeal.

"What else do you call it? Either way, don't go kill Marin, please."

He kissed the side of her cheek with an open mouth, and goose bumps awakened in her body. The arousal that had been simmering under her skin, just waiting to be released, bubbled out on a moan.

What had she been blabbering about? She couldn't

think about it with his lips trailing down her neck and with one of his hands tightening on her hips, bringing her flush against his body.

He pushed her toward the hedge. Sticks and leaves dug into her back, and she let her head fall, exposing more skin to him. Their breaths became heavier, and a flow of emotion overtook her. This felt right. She was supposed to be here with him—why was she so worried about everything? She brought her hands to the back of his neck, grasping his hair.

His lips trailed up close to her ear. "When you touched yourself last night, were you thinking of me?" His breath caressed the side of her cheek and down the wet path he had created a moment before.

Nava swallowed as heat pooled in her stomach, growing like wildfire. "Yes." She tried to get her leg around his hips and groaned at the layers of fabric that prevented her from feeling him pressed against her.

She needed to get this dress off. It was suffocating her. There had been a reason she didn't want to do this here, but right now she couldn't care.

Another moan escaped her lips when he traced a pattern over her chest, his knuckles gingerly grazing her nipple.

"Ark . . ." Her voice came as a desperate cry, and his lips crashed over hers in a demanding kiss.

It was wet, soft, and hard all in one. His tongue wasted no time diving into her mouth, claiming her like he had been thirsting for years. He tugged at the collar of her dress, and a rip clamored as the yellow fabric floated to the ground, exposing her under the sheer lace chemise. Arkimedes lost no time, cupping her exposed breast and kneading it with his rough hand.

She had missed him like she hadn't had him for years, not just days.

He pulled away just enough to drink her in. "You are beautiful," he said against her lips, and his wings wrapped around them, black like the moonless night, hiding them in plain sight.

"Thanks." Why was she thanking him? Her mind had the worst timing to come up with the most awkward response known to mankind. She felt her cheeks warm. "I mean, thank you for noticing. I'm ruining the moment. Again."

He smiled and pecked her lips, meeting her gaze with an expression that had softened. Her heart stumbled in its beats. This was how he had looked at her that last night in their home, right before he'd been taken. Like she hung the moon and the stars above.

The reprieve from his heated kisses lifted the fog that had been in her mind for a while, telling her this was too dangerous. They shouldn't be exposing themselves like this in the middle of the garden, even if not many came around this place.

His lips captured hers again, and her skin burned under his day's worth of stubble. She wrapped her arms around his neck and pulled him closer. Whatever magic was running through them was too strong to ignore. His lips trailed down her neck again, across her chest, and closed in on her nipple.

And it felt too good. Why was she so nervous about being here either way? There was no one else around them, not even the creepy flowers. His tongue flicked over her nipple with a punishing pace, and she writhed against him, feeling like she might come apart just from that touch.

She heard the ruffling of leaves and tensed with the

noise, the daze clearing from her mind once again. The heat on her skin didn't subside; it demanded more.

Sensing her sudden change, Arkimedes pulled away, his brow furrowing, illuminated by the light of his gaze. "Is everything all right?"

She nodded but stayed quiet, listening. The breeze picked up, and she heard the sound again, realizing it had been the wind.

His wings shifted, revealing the bright night above. "Are you sure?"

"Yes."

He shook his head, as if trying to clear it. "I can't think straight. Please tell me to stop if this is not what you want."

"You are all that I want." She caressed the side of his jaw and down the side of his neck. Why was she fighting this? "But I don't want it here where someone can find us. You aren't forgettable, and I'm not dressed to run."

Arkimedes kissed her again, sucking on her bottom lip, and her toes curled and her mind faltered at the last thought. To heck with caution. She was going to have him now, and she didn't care if anyone got a peep show.

His arms snaked around her body, and soon his wings were flapping and his lips abandoned hers. He lifted her in the air and carried her off toward the castle.

CHAPTER TWENTY-SIX

ORION

The flight back to his room's balcony didn't take long. Nava trailed kisses down Orion's neck, and goose bumps raised over his skin.

"Stop that." Orion tightened his hold on her as his wings moved to slow down their descent and stabilize them for landing. She had been right—the wide skirt of this dress was the least convenient garment he had ever encountered. If only for this, he should pay a visit to Marin when he was back in town.

She didn't stop, however, her tongue tasting his skin instead, and the groan that left his mouth was not a noise he remembered ever making before. His booted feet hadn't finished touching the floor before her lips met his, and he lost track of all thoughts as his blood raced.

He wished he could blame magic for making him this painfully hard and in a constant state of hunger for this woman. But even though tonight his self-restraint had withered to nothing, he had been craving her for months.

His teeth captured her thick bottom lip, and she moved her hands from his chest to the back of his neck, her fingers digging through his hair. Her tongue was divine torture; he didn't know where he wanted it most.

They kissed like rogue teenagers escaping the prying eyes of their caregivers. Enjoying the way her body responded under his touch, he brought his hands down the sheer fabric of the dress, over the naked planes of her back, and down her wide hips to the alluring globes of her backside. Tugging her closer to him, he smiled as she gasped against his lips.

It was not lost on him that *this*—them—was not new to her as it was to him. The pressure of not letting her down weighed in his chest more so than he had ever felt before. She was important to him. Whether he remembered why or when it happened, she had been the main source of his thoughts for months.

He knew deep in the marrow of his bones that what he was craving was more than her body, and that alone sobered his heated thoughts.

He broke the kiss and met her dazed gaze. "Did you drink some of the wine?"

"No, it's not the wine." Was that guilt flashing through her eyes? Did she feel this craze as well? A heat that didn't subside and made his focus narrow on just this. Being close, having her in his bed at this moment.

She dropped her hands from his neck before inspecting her surroundings. She hesitated before she strolled into his room. The fireplace came alive in a soft roll as she made it past the billowy curtains that flowed with the night's breeze.

With the tall ceilings and the dark furnishings, she stood out like a beacon of yellow light. Much like her magic had been that day in the forest. She fit in here, like she was meant to stay forever. In the dim light of the fireplace, she studied her surroundings, taking in all the details that made the room his.

The flames marked an orange highlight over the soft edges of her curves, and just like that, an intense need to protect her washed over him. She had come through a dark portal, losing something dear to save him from . . . his father.

There had been little time to get to know her, but he already admired her tenacity, strength, and stubbornness.

Nava walked toward the four-post bed in the middle of the room. Her fingers drifted over the black sheets, then she turned to him and air escaped him all at once.

Gone were the inner thoughts of someone falling in love, and back was the intense burning he was no longer able to hold back.

She walked toward a large mirror that leaned against the wall by the bed, at least eight feet tall and towering over her frame. In the dim light of the room, her dress, or what was left of it, was muted in the cool light of the night, and it reminded him of her bees.

Orion approached her, following each one of her movements through the reflection. He wrapped a hand across her stomach, steadying her after he brought her back to meet him. His lips came down over the supple skin of her neck, trailing toward her shoulder, where he lowered the strap of flimsy fabric that still held the bodice to her body.

It was too much and not enough. His body was ready, straining with desire and tension. She grasped the ends of his hair, trying but failing to keep his face locked in place. Her skin raised in goose bumps as his lips trailed down the skin of her back. He stored the memory aside for later.

If he closed his eyes and blocked their surroundings, just

focused on her and the scent of berries and something wild and earthy around her, he sensed the talons of recognition clawing their way back to him, invigorated by the fire burning in his veins. His lips abandoned the ministrations as he pulled back, unwrapping the ribbons that secured the corset to her body. The fabric loosened and pooled over her chest and down her hips, falling to the ground with a thump.

Her breasts were still under the chemise that covered her, but he could see the clear silhouette. Orion stroke one, and she melted against him.

Nava met his gaze through the reflection with heavy lids, and he was struck by the weightlessness of his stomach and the flutter of his heart. His hand covered the entirety of her right breast and he massaged the supple flesh, bringing her against his straining erection. The rest of her clothing was off in an instant, the scent of magic wafting in the air. Naked in front of him, she stared at him, and they shared the same look. Clarity.

Orion needed her now. He dropped his hand from her breasts, down below her navel. She held her breath when his fingers reached her center, and her face morphed as pleasure overtook her. She was wet and ready, and he was going to burst.

She let her head fall against his shoulder. He slid his finger inside her, arching it to find the spot that would make her squirm. In and out, he let her sounds spur him on alongside her moans.

She trembled in his arms, holding her breath for a moment before her orgasm ran through her body, like waves of ecstasy that bloomed and colored her skin. His stomach tightened, and the pleasure of an orgasm built within him. His breathing faltered as he tried to calm his body and not come all over his pants like a teenager.

What the hell was that?

Breathless and confused, he swallowed down and focused on the woman in front. "I have wanted to do that for so long," he said in a tone he almost didn't recognize. Orion wanted to taste her and not be so gentle when making her shout his name as he filled her.

Nava turned around and captured his lips with hers in a demanding kiss. Orion growled against her lips and dropped his hands to her hips, pushing against her in a way that almost calmed both of their needs. But she needed more of him if her clawing at his back was anything to go by.

She fumbled over the hidden buttons of his coat. It didn't take long for his large hands to replace hers, and soon his white coat fell to the ground, joining the pile of clothes already there. She touched his chest like it was something to be revered, not the marked planes of skin he saw day after day. Goose bumps appeared on his chest when her lips crashed down, her tongue peeking out to taste him, over that weird mark in the middle of his pecs.

She continued down and over the bulges of his abs, licking and nipping as she went, and he could barely hold himself together as anticipation built. But it wasn't only his need to have her wrap her lips around him; there was also a growing sense of worry.

That he couldn't hold a candle to the man she was used to. Maybe he wasn't good enough, not in his current broken state. A shadow of the man he was sure she loved.

She untied the leather strings that held his pants up, and he tried to swallow the knot that had formed there. His blood was boiling too hot, and he was too turned on for his sudden nerves to cool him. Her lips continued across the muscles of his pelvic bone.

His pants loosened as she pushed them down with an eagerness that matched his mood. Nava met his gaze as she wrapped her hand around him, giving him a tentative pump.

A breath caught in his throat just before she took him in her mouth and swallowed him whole. He grunted, holding himself against the mirror with one hand, entranced as he looked at her.

His mouth opened in a silent cry as he grasped her hair. Soon her curls were falling loose over her back and face, and she hollowed her cheeks. She *knew* it would drive him crazy.

He gasped, and the memory of her wet thighs had him breathing harder. He wanted her so badly. Nava read him like an open book and picked up her pace.

"This is going to be over before it starts if you keep—" His breath stuttered.

She pushed forward and sucked him all in.

He pulled out of her eager mouth, colorful words escaping his lips before he wrapped his arms around her and lifted her with ease. His lips crashed over hers. "I want more than just your mouth."

She bit his lower lip before her tongue soothed the sharp pain left behind, and his cock bobbed in response. He couldn't let her go, even if he was damaged. "We have the entire night."

In a whirlwind motion, he turned her around, and her eyes met the reflection. Every inch of her body was exposed, illuminated by the warmth of the fireplace.

Orion's wings expanded, dark like the night outside. He hadn't slept with many women. At first it had been difficult with his duties with the Society to find time to court anyone. Then it had become clear it was pointless to fall in love when his destiny would be chosen by someone else. Much like what had happened with everything in his life.

Then there were the dark, misted shapes that followed his every move. Not many were eager to deal with those. But this kind of attraction, the jealousy with Devon—or with himself—was something new. Too scary at times.

He pressed against her and brought his hand to her stomach, and his lips traveled to her neck once again. "Hold on to the mirror and bend over for me."

The goose bumps that ran across her skin spurred him on. His body hummed with anticipation. He pushed down on her lower back as she followed his command, her round backside lining up just where he wanted it.

He settled behind her, digging into each side of her hips. His cock slid up and nuzzled at her entrance. To make a further point, Nava wiggled her hips. He kicked aside one of her legs, widening her stance, and pushed into her.

Orion dropped his head to her shoulder. His arms shaking, he held himself against the wall as a swarm of feelings and pleasure that hadn't been there before took over him. Like his own, but different somehow.

A rush of moisture ran through her as he set a punishing pace. Her hands slid over the mirror with a screech.

The coil wound tighter with each passing second as he entered her, threatening to snap something within him. Nava's legs trembled, but he held her, pushing her against the mirror fully. Her whole chest and torso slid over the slick surface, and his pace grew erratic.

Her breath caught in her throat, and then stars exploded behind his closed lids. A wave that shook him to his core had him emptying himself inside her.

They might have stood in that spot for seconds, minutes. When he opened his eyes, she grinned at him.

And the burning heat that had accompanied him all day lowered to a simmer inside his gut.

He took a step back and couldn't help but grin as she wobbled on her feet. Maybe he had fucked her good enough to have her forget the other man who shared his name and body but not his memories.

She turned and wrapped her arms around his neck before he kissed her.

"I hope you aren't tired because I don't think you'll be sleeping much tonight." He swept her off the ground.

Nava wrapped her legs around him like she knew how this would go, and without another word of warning, he dropped her onto the bed.

CHAPTER TWENTY-SEVEN

NAVA

The room was still dark when Nava blinked her eyes open. Soft rays of sunshine extended over the dark stone floors, hinting at an early summer morning.

She couldn't have slept for longer than a couple of hours, judging by the coolness in the air and how late it had been since their last heated exchange. She ached in the best possible way—a delicious burn inside her thighs, her body still tired from a night of a magical-induced frenzy. The warmth of his body was familiar behind her and still sent her heartbeat galloping in a rush.

She snuggled closer to him, her head on his chest. His fingers caressed the planes of her back.

"I didn't know you were up." His rough voice broke the silence of the morning.

"Hard to sleep with you next to me."

"Last I checked, you fell asleep on me before I was done with you."

Her cheeks warmed, because she had, in fact, fallen asleep on him. "I only have so much energy. Some of us are full-blooded humans."

"What happened yesterday . . . I've never felt anything like that before."

"Me neither." Though she didn't know if he was referring to the weird solstice heat or being with her. Intimate contact always meant the deepening of their bond.

The heat that had burned through their bodies while on the dance floor, it was hard to put what she felt into words when so much had happened in a matter of hours. Her normal thoughts had been fogged, but not gone. She'd been present and able to make decisions, though maybe freer to lean on what she'd wanted.

A prickle of concern trailed her thoughts. The outcome of the sex, the longing—those had been something she'd half expected after all the warnings. For Arkimedes, it had been all new. Their craving for one another came with who they were to each other, but . . . he should have known of their connection before it had gotten to this.

She should have pushed harder to tell him the truth, past her own selfishness.

Turning her face toward the balcony, Nava evaded his gaze. "I should get to my room before Leela comes looking for me." Her stomach revolted at her action, or the lack of.

"They are very punctual in their morning rounds, her and Callie."

His words made her pause, and she shifted back to meet his gaze. "Callie—is that Callisto?"

His bright green eyes focused on her, his expression sharpening to focus. Nava hadn't even given a thought to whether a female fae would be the one tending to her mate while no one else knew of their bond, and the new information sat in her stomach like a bag of rocks.

"Has she come into your bedroom before?" She focused on the door, frowning. "Is she the one coming to wake you every morning?" Weren't there societal rules about this? Nava was sure there should be something like that.

Arkimedes's slow grin lifted the corners of his mouth. "What's happening inside that fiery head of yours?"

She narrowed her gaze at him. "Has she?"

"Are you jealous?"

She huffed, bringing the sheet over her chest to make sure her mark was covered from sight. Now that the morning sun made it more visible, she was glad their heated frenzy had hit them in the middle of the night and not during daylight. She moved her body away from his. "I don't get jealous. I don't have a reason to be."

But the what-ifs came rushing back to her. What if the king had been pressuring Arkimedes to find a suitor? That was something they did in court, right? Laurie had never pushed her to learn much about this. It wasn't like Nava was ever supposed to be exposed to a situation that would make the study worth their time. Little had they known . . .

The burning embers of something angry lit in her stomach. Nava had no reason to be annoyed with him, not when he didn't remember her and was a victim here. But whatever possessive nature their bond brought upon them was hard to battle.

"Good." Arkimedes angled toward her as his hands chased after her hips. "Where are you going?"

"I'm going to my room to allow you time to get yourself dressed before she shows up."

His rolling laughter almost thawed the ice in her veins. "I don't want you to go. Stay with me."

"No." But her body was already sinking back into the mattress. Damn the tone of honey and sex in his voice; she had no defense against it.

His warm hand wrapped around her stomach,

bringing her flush to his body, his lips tracing the skin of her back. The intense heat from last night was mostly gone, but his lips were getting her there once again. "I haven't looked at a woman the way I see you ever since—" His words got lost somewhere, and she turned to meet his distant gaze.

"Ever since . . . ?"

"I can't remember. The memory evades me." Arkimedes frowned. "But even if I did, I'm not sure if I have ever felt this way before."

She grinned, and hope bloomed in her chest. It had taken him much longer to admit his feelings for her a year ago. However small, this progress was good. Maybe the idea of waiting for him to fall for her wasn't as ridiculous as she'd thought. "You will get your memories back," she said. Devon thought so.

However, there was a possibility that he would never remember the last decade of his life. Much like she would never remember her father again.

They both stared at each other in a heartbreaking silence, and Nava couldn't handle that pain in his features a moment longer. She cleared her throat. "Has she seen you without clothes?"

A shocked roll of laughter came out of him. "No, bee, she has not." His expression softened.

There it was again, her nickname.

With the light of the early morning flooding the room, she allowed herself to relax in his embrace. It had been a little over a week in her time since he was taken, but it had been much longer for him.

She lay down, facing the canopy above her, closing her eyes as her mind reeled. Unable to imagine the confusion he must have felt from being apart from her, not knowing what was happening.

Even knowing he was taken, she had been perplexed as to why her health had faded in a matter of hours. It made sense now with the time difference between the kingdoms. Maybe her soul had always known they'd been apart for longer than well.

His touch raised goose bumps as he trailed his hand from her shoulder, making a path to her heart.

"What's this?" His whole body tensed as he stared at her chest, his calloused finger tracing the raised edges of her soulmate mark. The warmth in her body drained away, replaced by the icy caress of panic. Her scalp crawled and she put both her hands on top of his. He pulled out of her grasp as if she had burned him and sat straight in the bed, his eyes widening, his face losing all color. "Is this some sort of trick?"

"No, no." She sprang up, reaching for him.

"You'd better start talking, and I hope this is not what I think it is."

Nava sat straight and fought the urge to fidget under his scrutiny. She covered her chest, and the taste of guilt was bitter. "I wasn't sure when to tell you."

He hissed out a breath, and in a blink, he was standing by the side of the bed, his wings spreading as his eyes took her in. "You had plenty of time yesterday when I was asking you if we were married."

"I didn't lie. We aren't married—and I didn't want to divulge our information in the middle of the garden."

He leveled her with a look that made her shut her mouth. "You were diverting about you being the future queen. You know well a soulmate overwrites any marriage in the eyes of our gods."

"I don't want to be the queen."

"Don't change the subject," he growled.

"You changed the subject, not me!"

This was the most ironic thing she'd ever thought could happen to her, the complete mirror image to what had happened almost a year ago when their situations had been reversed. After all, Arkimedes had hidden that he was her soulmate for almost a month before the truth had come out, thanks to Violet outing him as a member of the Society of Crows.

"I wanted to tell you ever since I first stepped foot here! It was hard with you not remembering even meeting me. You thought I had bewitched you, Arkimedes," she rushed to say.

He walked around the bed, picking up his discarded pants from the night before. "That is not an excuse."

"I tried to tell you yesterday . . . for a moment." But Nava knew she hadn't tried, not really. She crossed her arms over her chest, her blood boiling. "You don't get to be mad at me for this."

"What?"

"You did the same thing to me last year and—"

Arkimedes's lips parted before his aura exploded around him, black and sinister like fingers and arms emanating from his body. "I don't know what the hell you are talking about, Nava! I don't remember anything of what you are telling me. I'm trying hard to trust you, but how can I when you are lying to me about no less than being my soulmate!"

The temperature of the room lowered, and Nava pushed back against the headboard, her heart hammering. "I was waiting for you to trust me before I dropped the soul bomb," she blurted. "I was waiting for the right moment."

He pinched the bridge of his nose and took a shaky breath, the black tendrils of his power coming closer to his body as he regained some of his control. "You can't be here. I need to get you out of this castle unharmed."

"What are you talking about?"

"I'm talking about the enemies I have inside these walls! The people who tried to kill my mother when she was pregnant."

Oh, that was rich. "So yesterday you didn't care when you told me we should go to your father and get married, but today you want me gone so you can keep going on your solo mission?"

"I was not in my right mind yesterday!" His voice might have been the coldest she had ever heard. "This place is too dangerous for you because it's not only my father who has his eyes on you."

She brought the sheets up, trying to shield herself from him. "I won't leave without you, and even if I wanted to—which I don't—I couldn't. We would both die."

"You said the king had taken me from our home, that he knew who you were the whole time." Arkimedes's tone dropped, and she met his gaze. "And you didn't think to tell me we are bonded?"

Her lips shook, and desperation clawed at her from within. "That is why we have to leave, *right now*. Back to our home. We can put Devon back in the prison. Roman might not even be mad since it would've been just a few minutes for him. Next time we will be prepared if they come for you—"

"Back to our home? You mean a place I have no recollection of, to a life I don't remember?" He looked away from her to the side of the bed, his jaw coiled with tension.

Nava gripped her hands, and the prickle in her eyes told her she was close to losing it. This was going wrong. She needed to fix it. Rushing up to her feet, she shuffled to him. "You will love it there like you did before."

"And I'm just supposed to blindly believe this?" Arkimedes scoffed, shaking his head. "I have been alone without a family my whole life, wondering why I'm this way."

"You know a portion of what they tell you here is not true," Nava said. "They are lying to you. They kidnapped you from our home. Took away your memories and our lives together!"

"And you haven't been?"

She flinched, her shoulders tensing. "I have not lied to you until this moment, and even now I was going to tell you as soon as I thought you were ready."

"What gives you the right to choose when I'm ready or not?"

The words got stuck in her throat. She lowered her face, and tears fell down her cheeks. "I was afraid. This has also been a tremendous shock to me, Arkimedes."

"The Arkimedes you knew is not me, and it is about time you understand that." A cold mask descended over his features, and she knew the conversation was over. "In this castle, I'm Prince Orion, and I will not follow you blindly across the world. I'm not leaving."

Tears swelled in her eyes as her heart split open. It was as if she was losing him all over again. This kingdom had stolen him from her. Stolen their memories, their lives, their identity.

Now it was her and him. A sob escaped from her lips, and his already closed expression softened.

His pain and confusion swirled within her, and even though she didn't want to go, she knew they needed space. It hadn't been easy for her when she accepted that Arkimedes was her soulmate. Even then, she'd had an entire month to fall in love with him. He'd had but a handful of days to fall for her. She was asking him too much.

He needed time. The one thing she didn't know how much she had left to give since the king might strike her at any moment. She guessed that now that Arkimedes knew of the danger they were both in, things would change.

Maybe he would tell the king, and the two of them might lock her away, safe from physical harm but away from him. No, Arkimedes wouldn't do that to her, even as angry as he was.

She swiped at the tears that wet her cheeks. "Even if you don't remember, you have had a family for some time now, and you are not alone."

With those parting words, her body became air, pollen, and dust, floating out of the window and toward her room.

CHAPTER TWENTY-EIGHT

ORION

A soulmate. He'd had a goddamn twin soul all along, and no one had deemed it important for him to learn the truth.

His blood boiled as he stormed into the solarium. His brother sat at the table, drinking tea from a small bone cup. He raised a brow as Orion loosened the button of his coat and shrugged it off. It was too hot to be wearing so many layers outside in this sweltering heat.

"Did you know?" he demanded, tossing the offending piece of clothing over the black painted metal chair.

Devon placed the cup on the table, his face giving away nothing. "So I'm guessing the solstice brought the truth out, *finally*."

Orion pushed one of the chairs, the noise of metal scraping over the brick ground the only noise around them. His magic burst out of his fingertips. "You didn't think of telling me that my—" He stopped himself and took a calming breath. His brother's challenging smirk was anything but apologetic. "You don't care a thing about what could have happened to us if—"

"On the contrary, I'm *forced* to care about your relationship," Devon snarled and pushed off the chair, fixing his white cravat with both hands. "And for the record, I did tell her to tell you. Maybe that way, we would be out of this place by now."

"Well, she didn't, and I'm not leaving."

Devon shrugged, walking around as he looked at the purple flowers that hung from the winding plant above them. "I'm sure she was mistaken to be afraid of your reaction—you are taking it quite well."

A prickling sensation crawled down his spine, and he rubbed his fingers together, trying to calm his speeding heart. "I never wanted a soulmate, but I have wanted her every minute of the last four months, even when I thought she was your . . . bride-to-be."

"Oh, the joy that gave me." His eyes shone, and Orion didn't know if he wanted to punch that smirk off his face or just keep asking questions. "The world gives you what all of us mundane people want, yet you are too good for it, as always." Devon's eyes blazed on him.

"I don't need your passive-aggressive shit right now, Devon." It was confusing to know what his real feelings toward Nava were when he now knew magic forced some into him. His need to cherish and protect her had been there since the first day. Those were magic-induced, right?

The way his heart skipped a beat when she smiled or his stomach dropped with her magic; her stubbornness drove him mad in the best and worst ways. Those were real. Orion wiped his hands over his face, pacing around.

What he felt had grown to more than something physical, more than good chemistry and desire. The way she challenged him, her sense of humor and laughter. He had been in awe of her magic and the beauty of what she truly was.

Too good for him to taint. She intrigued him, and it wasn't just a magic-induced want. This was real.

Devon returned to the table, his dark gaze studying him before he lowered back into his chair. "Last year when we met, you didn't want to be without her. As a matter of fact, you wanted to stay in that place."

He didn't want to be without her now either, but the man he'd been before . . . that was scarier than even the bond he had formed with Nava. Why had he stayed on the Grey Island and forgotten about his own duty?

Orion needed to protect a whole kingdom, yet he had forsaken them all.

The fact that he had gotten kidnapped from his own home said a lot about how relaxed he had become, not only putting himself in danger but Nava as a result. "I don't want to remember who I was four months ago."

Devon paused halfway in reaching for the forgotten cup. Lifting both brows, he faced him. "Are you saying you can remember if you choose to? Or is this more of a—"

"I was able to get a memory back a few days ago. I remember chasing them across the ocean to the Grey Island. I have an idea of what spell was used to fog my memories, and I could use some of the dreams I have had to unravel more."

"But you don't want to?"

"What kind of man would have stayed on an island full of deserters when this whole kingdom fell into despair because of it?" His voice grew heavy, and he remembered the ghost of his mother, burned and blackened. His heart soared with the need to find answers. "It's likely I didn't even set wards to protect Nava. I knew who I was and the fact that my father would come for me at some point, and I didn't do anything to prevent it."

Devon's long, pale fingers wrapped around the handle

of the cup. "Those were my exact thoughts last year. You grew soft there, brother."

Orion nodded and sat on the chair with a heavy sigh. He needed to get the keys for the bracelets from the king. He didn't claim to understand the ins and outs of how the magic worked in this kingdom, but with them, the king could track both Devon and, most importantly, Nava. He couldn't get her out of this place and into temporary safety while she wore the bracelets.

The tree burned bright red. Hissing demons surrounded it. Its wide trunk trembled as the rolling flames devoured the previously green leaves with orange and yellow shades. She screamed, her throat raw from her pained cries and the burning smoke. Her skin blistered as the heat crept closer. But she was too weak to move against the ropes around her body.

Her voice soon gave away, breaking with pain so raw and unlike she had ever felt; however, deep within her soul, she was calm. While this was the end of this life, she had succeeded in a way. It had been a fool's errand to come to this forest to make sense of this madness. To see if it was him after all. To have him call these demons away. Maybe her death would be what he needed to finally rest in peace.

Then darkness coiled in from the sides of her eyes. For a moment, she floated over the burnt tree in the forest, anger and sorrow stealing in her breaths, but she couldn't moan out loud. She couldn't reach those she loved anymore.

Her most beloved had killed her.

Orion inhaled, and it took him a panicked second to understand in the haze of sleep that he wasn't really in that forest. Every inch of his body ached as if he had slept on the hard ground instead of his feather-filled mattress. It had been days since the nightmare of his mother's passing had plagued his sleep.

He peeled the sheets from his sweaty skin, which felt like sand rubbing his body raw. The atmosphere of the room changed with a heaviness that lingered. He wished he could say it was the first time the suffocating sensation of being watched had loomed over him, but it happened right before the ghost of his mother appeared to haunt him.

Looking around the room with his heart beating in his throat, he expected the burnt corpse to appear in front of him at any moment now. But his room remained empty. He took another breath and rested his face in his open palms, wishing he knew better what the spirit wanted from him. It was known that spirits remained in this realm because their souls were restless and needed closure.

Orion had been grasping at straws. He'd considered he had been the one killing her, the heir born sick. But how could he have, when he'd been just a toddler when she'd been killed, and on another continent? Her last thought was always that her most beloved one had killed her—could that be his father?

The sun rose behind the banisters of his balcony, tinting the sky in gold tones as the warmth hit his face. It was too early for most in the castle to be up, and the scent of smoke lingered in the room—could be his mother somehow or an impending attack from the demons.

It had always been strange that he was able to smell them before anyone else in the castle could. That was, until he'd gone to the forest with Nava and found out he was somehow linked to the Beekeepers, the natural enemies of the Zorren.

If he were going to be dispatched early to fight them,

he needed to make it to the king's room and find the keys to the bracelets before then. He finished tying the straps of his trousers and reached for one of his favorite black tunics. It had dark gray embroidery that depicted leaves and flowers sprouting out of a branch.

He traced the silk thread, his mind going back to the night of the solstice when he'd kissed Nava in front of the queen's tree. She was his future—*his* queen. He shifted his hand over his chest, trying to massage away the sudden ache that bloomed there. Did he want that longing? She was in love with a man who wasn't him—one who had his face but didn't share his beliefs.

What if Nava hated the person he was today once she realized he was determined to stay this way? Pressing his lips together, he finished doing up the clasps of the tunic and walked out of the room.

The first month of him being back—or stolen back— the king had shown him his private library. He had seen the bracelets and the keys displayed in a glass case. That was when he'd learned how the jewelry worked. The ins and outs of their magic-canceling properties, the fact that they didn't affect the royal kin, and that they were trackable by the king himself.

The library was adjacent to the king's bedroom, but Orion also knew the king was likely visiting with one of his ladies. So if he was quiet enough, he might be able to get the keys without him being the wiser.

Both libraries in the castle were closed off to everyone but the king, Orion, and Ellis, the keeper of the records. The doors of this particular one were ebony with gilded nature-inspired patterns and gold handles. He opened them quietly, and his footsteps were muffled over thick, red-and-wine-patterned wool rugs.

The room was vast, with large arched windows at the

end, black ornate frames, and painted glass on the top panels. The pink and orange shades of the morning outstretched over the floor. The small sitting area by the fireplace had three large winged chairs in front of it; the scent of leather and old paper hung in the air, mixing with the soft notes of lavender and flowers—maybe camellias—from an arrangement on the coffee table.

On the far left wall, floor-to-ceiling bookcases held thousands of leather-bound books in various shades and stains.

The clear glass display case for the keys was past the bookcases, perched against one of the stone walls. There were many magical artifacts inside. A blade with three large rubies in the handle, an old book that was held together by worn bindings. He searched for the wooden case of the bracelets and the smaller one that held the keys . . . but it was missing.

He gripped the handle, and the glass shook with his pent-up emotion. If the keys weren't here, that meant they were in the king's room, which really complicated things.

Groaning, he pushed away, gazing around the room, hoping to find them misplaced somewhere else. His eyes came upon a wooden panel hung next to the glass case like art. He didn't remember seeing it there before, but it called his attention now.

He approached it, studying the intricate carvings of wood and gold details; the king stood tall with both hands extended in front of him as he dropped a child toward a sea of clouds. Orion's heart started to beat at double speed, and he traced the carvings, so similar in detail to the one on the throne room's door. The one that had the queen holding a child.

"Orion."

He jumped in his spot, dropping his hand off the wood

panel like a child caught doing something wrong, which he guessed was accurate.

Orion turned to meet his father's curious gaze. The king strolled into the sitting area of his private library, holding both hands behind his back. The light rolled over his silk robe and matching wide pants.

Behind him, the doors that connected the library to his private chambers were open wide, which hadn't been the case before. Entranced by his search for the keys and the strange art piece, Orion hadn't heard it open.

"Father." He dipped his head into a bow, his skin prickling as a drop of sweat formed at his temple.

"I didn't know I was supposed to expect you this morning or I would have had breakfast served here. It's already difficult enough to get you to join me for dinners." The king sat on one of the large leather chairs by the fireplace, crossing his legs and hands in front of him, his eyes shimmering like the cat that caught the bird.

He was in trouble. So much for his half-baked plan to sneak in here and retrieve the keys. Orion didn't want his father knowing he was hunting for a way to remove the tracking bracelets from Nava and Devon. "I had a dream about the queen again," he said after clearing his throat, going for a partial truth in hopes of distracting his father.

The king stiffened on his seat, his features shadowing with a haunted expression. "She is still visiting you in your dreams? She hasn't visited mine for quite some time now."

The queen more than haunted his dreams. She appeared out of nowhere, especially if Orion was in the library. "I kept searching in the main archives but haven't had much luck finding much about her, or me for that matter. I didn't want to bother you if you were busy with one of your cohorts."

The king's eyes went vacant as his lips twisted into a

grim expression. "How did she look in your dream? Do you remember?"

Orion shook his head. The first time he told the king he dreamed of his mother, his father had asked many questions. A man starved for any piece of information that would fill a void. However, Orion had always felt very protective of these particular dreams. There was a reason the queen wasn't haunting his father, so he would work this up on his own.

"You aren't finding anything in the main library? I should have a talk with Ellis about his lack of help."

"You know well most of it's burned to the ground, and the keeper breathes on my neck the whole time. I don't need him hovering any more than he already does." Orion hesitated in his spot before making his way to where the king sat and taking the other seat. "You did say I was allowed to check this library . . . if I ever needed it."

The king pushed forward, assessing him with increasing interest. "*If* I were to be in the room, Orion. However, this will be all yours. There is no need to rush into anything—your mother is gone, and you can find all the answers soon enough."

Of course he hadn't missed that part of the information; the whole point was he had assumed the king was occupied elsewhere. He looked at his father. Old, thin skin over youthful features. A weird combination that had taken him long to get used to.

"What is that?" he asked, gazing back at the mounted wood piece he had been staring at. "It looks so similar to the one in the throne room."

"It's art. I like to collect it." The king's pleasant features shuttered, and the prickling sensation in the back of Orion's head increased. This was more than art, an aged intricate carving that showed the king throwing a child to mist. A complete opposite to the one of the queen holding a small prince in her arms.

Had this been the one next to the queen's panel in the door and had been replaced at some point? If that was true, why? His father had always been okay with letting the kingdom believe she had taken him away, but what if people questioned why that had happened?

It made him wonder if the king had ever tried to get rid of him when he'd been a child, which might be the reason why his mother had run away with him in tow. Had his father killed his mother in retribution?

Orion itched to be out of there, or to stay and check every single one of those books and find answers. His search would have to wait, however; he couldn't rest until Nava was out of this castle and safe.

"The forest fires woke me this morning, Orion. It has been your job to catch the culprits *before* they get out of hand. They are already getting closer to our city."

"The fires are not caused by humans like the guards are telling you."

"Then by what?"

Orion hesitated before releasing a breath. "The Zorren. I saw one the other day—"

"The demons are crossing to these lands?" The king stood from his seat and paced around the area toward the bookcase. "No one else has reported this to me before."

"It's the truth."

"I need proof. The high fae are convinced the humans that call themselves the Fallen Crows are behind this mess and are demanding retribution. If the demons are the ones wreaking havoc in our land, killing our forests and poisoning our soil, I need some of the guards to back your word—or for you to bring me proof."

"They become ash when killed. How am I supposed to

bring you anything but ash?" Orion pointed out, shaking his head.

"Their nails are made of iron, deadly for our kind—yet you are half-human, so picking one up shouldn't be a problem. Cut one of their hands, and bring me the nails."

Orion stood from his chair and bowed to the king. Last time he'd seen a Zorren close enough to see said nails had been with Nava and the other Beekeeper, Ari. That day, it had been just one, but lately there were many more, if the fires were anything to go by.

"I will leave to get them for you then." He walked around the living area, scanning the shelves and the display case where the keys were supposed to be.

"Take as many guards as you think you will need," the king said. "I can feel the kingdom becoming stronger ever since you arrived. Our magic feeds the castle, and the spells that connect this structure to the city, to the lands beyond, work out the rest."

It was the same words the king had said to him the first time he'd been in this castle, learning he was the stolen heir. At the time, he'd half believed them. However, when he returned four months ago, the land had been dry. The castle walls cracked under the demands of a hungry kingdom. A high power that demanded things he didn't claim to understand. The citizens, animals—everyone had been struggling.

Not because of the lack of magical-born children, like in the Iron Kingdom, but because of the lack of children in general. The land and the citizens had become barren. A curse placed on this kingdom eons ago, eased by the power of the king. Lifted by the queen's tree.

Orion paused by the door. He had seen the city regain life, though he wasn't sure if it was due to him returning or just the change of the seasons. "I don't feel different."

"Our power eases the way the magic flows. It allows other magical creatures to help us. The queen's tree is the missing puzzle. A kingdom is barren without its queen."

Oh, the tree was already alive—his father was not going to like the how, but the process was in motion. Orion considered telling the king about the tree and that Nava was his soulmate. It would stop whatever plot his father might be brewing to hurt her.

However, he held himself back; even though he believed his father wanted him to stay, he wasn't quite sure what had happened to his mother. And now with that wooden panel, the rock of dread in his stomach just grew heavier.

What if his father sent Nava away, kept her alive but hidden, and then erased his memories of her? Orion wasn't willing to give her up to whatever fate that was. Sure, he had not wanted a soulmate, but he wasn't going to give her up.

"It's our job to find the queen. It might be time for you to start courting women in the kingdom."

His skin went cold. "I'm not interested."

"Orion. Our kingdom depends on our bloodline to be alive to keep our land strong. The spells that make it run are linked to us. I have told you this. We need your children."

There was one woman in Orion's life he would tie himself to, and he had already chosen her, in his past life and in this one. He opened his mouth to say the truth, but his father continued.

"A fae woman, of course."

"Why does it have to be a fae? The queen was human."

"She was my . . . biggest regret." His voice sounded sorrowful. Orion wasn't sure what the mistake was. "It would make our fae blood too diluted for the spells to keep working. You are half-fae and already struggle to keep the voices at bay. A quarter fae . . . They wouldn't be strong enough to hold them back from taking over."

While he had told Nava they should go to the king and get married the night of the solstice, Orion wasn't sure Nava wanted the life of living in this castle as a queen, which was the life he wanted.

There was also the fact that she was in love with a version of himself that didn't exist anymore. She was the only woman he was interested in, but he wasn't interested in marriage, at least not now.

"I'm not marrying anyone in your court," he growled with a finality that shocked the king. "I will bring you the proof of the demons."

The king nodded and waved his hand in dismissal.

CHAPTER TWENTY-NINE

NAVA

It had been a day since Nava had seen Arkimedes, and the hours dragged by. At least this time, she wasn't forced to stay in her room for the duration of it. Smoke hazed over the sky, thicker with each hour. She stood almost immobile in the wide hall, staring in the distance; wingless fae walked behind and in front, minding their own business as they took care of chores around the castle.

The cool stone column grounded her, and she searched for a sign of a forest fire nearby. It would be her excuse to leave at this moment and damn the consequences.

A few dozen bees crawled over the banisters and walls, camouflaged against the warm tones of the surrounding marble. It hadn't taken the Zorren long to return, and the pressing need to be out there in the forest with her Beekeeper was growing like a weed.

She had hoped the next time she escaped this castle, Arkimedes would be with her. It had been ignorant to think this would be anything but difficult.

Deep inside, she knew his reaction was her fault, that

she had acted in a similar way a year prior when he'd hidden the truth from her. It was a humbling experience to choose to lie to protect oneself, knowing the truth always came out to hunt you down.

Maybe it was time to admit that, buried within the crevices of her heart, she had half expected the curse would break if they kissed or lay together. That foolishness had driven her to hide the truth from him for longer than she should have. Like her lips would be magic on their own.

It didn't help her morose mood that she was also worried sick about Ari. Knowing he was fighting their battle on his own was another kind of torture. Nava was being pulled in both directions, torn apart by her love and her destiny, which were supposed to be one and the same but weren't fitting properly.

She rubbed her eyes, and her mind took her back to the nightmares that had plagued her dreams the night before. She had slept little, between dreams or memories of being hunted by demons and Arkimedes's hard features telling her she had to leave.

With the scent of ash and burning wood, she knew he had to be thinking of the Zorren, and the Beekeeper as well. At least Cameron was safe, away from this danger. Nava closed her eyes and swallowed the heavy knot that had formed in her throat.

Please be fine. She trusted Gavin, Violet, and Laurie to keep the vibrant teenager at bay. Still, he was a ball of energy and curiosity, and she hoped he was staying out of trouble.

If she didn't make it out of this mess alive, at least she knew he would be okay.

Out of nowhere, her heartbeat sped up, bringing the nervous reaction down her body as her stomach did somersaults. Arkimedes was nearby. She straightened and turned, searching for him in the empty halls.

"Is there something wrong?" Fael was next to her in three strides. He had been waiting while she got some fresh air away from her room.

The thudding of heavy boots on stone came soon after, quick steps and the screeching of metal as Arkimedes turned the corner, followed by five of his guards. Like the rest, he wore his copper armor, layers of chain mail under his breastplate, and cognac leather belts that held its placard in place. His face, much like the rest of his outfit, was marked with soot and dirt. His golden skin gleamed with sweat. Vibrant green eyes sharpened over her, and his expression turned from fierce to haunted when he noticed she was there.

He held his helmet in the crook of his arm as the group strode toward them, and her heart matched their quick steps. They didn't stop when they walked past her and Fael. His gaze barely held hers before he turned around, abruptly facing forward, and continued his journey down the corridor.

Not a word or a sign of a greeting. The Zorren were back, and he was back to fighting them on his own, and it was all her fault.

"Are you ready?" The fae next to her sensed that something was off, his voice gentler than she was used to.

"Yes, I guess so." She hesitated. "Have there been forest fires nearby?"

Fael's face turned solemn as he nodded. "Been fighting them all summer."

"Do you know what might be causing them?"

He paused as they walked down the corridor to her room. "We believe it might be an attack from an organized group of the citizens who are unhappy with the king, though there is no proof of this theory. Yet."

It was vague but also wrong. Still, Nava was glad she'd gotten an answer at all. It might mean that Fael was trusting her more, and she would take that as a win on this bleak day. "Are there many unhappy citizens in the city?" Curiosity had gotten the best of her again. Her worst quality, her mother had said. But if you didn't ask questions, how were you supposed to get answers?

"Isn't there always at least someone unhappy?" Fael raised his brow as he examined her. "Let me guess, you are one of those people who like politics?"

"It's more like I'm here for the foreseeable future, and I'm curious by nature."

His lips tilted into a smile. "Yes, I guess you are going to be here for a while." Nava didn't like that comment one bit. "Our kingdom is vast, and the city's usual lack of presence from the Society of Crows made it an ideal place to migrate years ago."

Now, that piqued her interest. "The Crows don't monitor you as much as in other kingdoms?"

"We are the only kingdom in which the king possesses magic greater than the most powerful Crow."

"The prince was once a Crow," Nava commented.

"And now they have lost him." Fael's brows deepened into a frown. "We didn't know he was there, rumors of one of our kind being spotted in other kingdoms wearing black and blue. It could have been anyone."

They walked in silence, and her mind hoarded all the new information. She wished her room wasn't so close so she had more time to get answers.

"The Crows are less inclined to come searching for people here and avoid confrontation with us, just like we do with them." Fael let go of a tired breath and rubbed his prominent brows. "A while back, the king signed a new arrangement with the Society. To maintain amicable terms, they were to keep their quarters here and still hidden; in return, they would make themselves scarce from the kingdom."

"So this group, are they upset about it enough to burn a forest?"

"Oh, yes, but they are a minority. The rest of our citizens understand that one king and his army can't battle the Society if they rile up the other three kingdoms against us."

Arkimedes's mother had to have known the crown was less likely to search for him if he was part of the Society. So why leave him in an orphanage instead of leaving him with them and staying herself?

From what Arkimedes had told her, the Crows didn't take people who didn't volunteer, and the young they took were homeless magical beings. The queen would have been recognized by them, and they wouldn't have taken the child of a royal. Leaving him in an orphanage, knowing he would develop magical traits like no other, meant direct transference to the Crows, without the Copper Kingdom ever being the wiser. Had Arkimedes thought of that?

Both their mothers had been masterminds of their own plots with their children's lives. Nava's mother had cursed Arkimedes so he couldn't come to Willowbrook and get close to her, time that had turned into a decade. Then had gotten herself killed by his magic in return and had left a notebook behind with answers for whenever Nava felt like asking questions.

Which was why she was determined to ask as many questions as possible. Still, she didn't understand why the queen would want to escape and leave her child to strangers, to suffer as a misfit for life.

Fael's voice took her out of her musings. "Our kingdom is more of a mixed-race population. In the last few decades, humans have been growing angry against the fae."

Not a shocker. "Does this have anything to do with the obvious animosity that exists from the fae toward the human?"

"The question is, what came first, the chicken or the egg? Tonight the king has demanded that I escort you and your fiancé for dinner."

The change of subject gave her whiplash. She guessed Fael didn't want to talk about the subject any longer. Nava tightened her fists, feeling the sharp sting of her nails biting her skin and the soft buzz of her magic coming alive. She didn't want to be anywhere near the king, especially now that there was this rift between Ark and her.

It was easier to direct her anger toward the man who had kidnapped her soulmate, instead of her own faults.

Fael swatted near his face, and it took her a while to recognize he was trying to get rid of a bee. She let go of a deep breath and called her insect off.

"Is this a casual affair, where the king might murder Devon and me without Ar—Prince Orion being around?"

Fael looked around, alarmed, and then lowered his face to her as he hissed, "Be quiet or you will get yourself killed, for real." He straightened. "But no, the prince will be there. You just have to be ready before sundown."

"Fine."

The beautiful archway of her bedroom door came into view, and she dreaded the loss of information about the queen and whatever was happening with the fires.

Ever since the solstice, it had been eating at her about

why the women of the king's concubines were all Dark Ones. Fael had been disappointed about this.

"I have another minor question," she said with a voice she hoped sounded neutral and small. He turned to her, his lips set into a sharp line. "It's about the king's women. I'm just curious because I never knew they were once part of the Royal Guards."

"Ah, yes."

"Were you involved with one of them?" Ugh, why did her brain keep doing this to her?

"I beg your pardon?"

"In a relationship, perhaps . . . with one of the cohorts?"

His face fell. "Wow, you humans do know how to ask inappropriate questions."

Nava took a shaky breath, her cheeks warming with embarrassment. "It's not all humans, it's me. I have a problem with curiosity and lack of a mouth filter."

Fael shook his head. "One of them is my sister, Rhoan."

"Oh, and her choice disappointed you?"

He placed his helmet on his head, hiding the crestfallen expression that had flashed across his features. Nava got the impression no answers would come, which would be fine since she was being extra nosy. "I don't like it because he will never love her the way she does him."

"How do you know that?"

"It's said the queen and the king were soulmates, and we all know once they find each other, they don't fall for another person."

Nava's throat felt thick, and she darted her gaze away so the fae couldn't see her anguish, remembering Arkimedes's cold expression toward her a moment ago. "They couldn't be. She has been dead for decades. I know this because—my parents were soulmates, and they died close to one another. He wouldn't have survived this long."

"Our king is the closest one gets to a direct offspring of a god," he murmured with a shrug, clearly thinking this was answer enough. "He has been alive for centuries. Much longer than any fae I know. However, he never took a wife until the tree bloomed." Fael's eyes were bright behind the slits of his helmet, much like Arkimedes, except his were bright amber and gold.

"So you think the tree blooms when a soulmate crosses paths with the royal heir?" This would mean everyone would know she was Arkimedes's soulmate within weeks at the most when that tree finished blooming.

"Why else hasn't it done it in centuries?"

Nava fidgeted with her clammy hands, and Fael studied her expression.

"Your heart is beating quite fast."

Great time to learn he could hear her heartbeat. Could Arkimedes do so as well? That secret keeping, annoying man wouldn't have told her so if he could. He was also part human, so maybe that didn't give him hearing superpowers.

"I have a lot of reasons to be nervous in this castle, Fael."

He didn't look convinced; however, he proceeded. "Laws of life don't affect our king like they do all of us, much less a human." The fae paused as they arrived at her room. "I don't know, or want to know, what Prince Orion and you have going on. I swore to my prince that I would protect you. But the king won't allow you two together. Our prince is too precious to us. If you care about your life and his, let him go because there won't be a new human queen in this kingdom."

Nava wanted to scream that she didn't want or care to

be a queen here. She hated this kingdom, the king, and, so far, almost all the guards. However, her stumbling heart made her hesitant to voice her thoughts. The city had been a breath of fresh air, and Arkimedes had been so happy.

She had never wanted to be a queen, but neither had she wanted to be a Beekeeper or a magic wielder. Both things she now loved. That had also been the case with Arkimedes and their bond. Nava had been so sure she didn't want a thing to do with it.

Last year, she had learned to open her mind when life threw her into uncomfortable situations. Ultimately, it would be Arkimedes's and her choice, not these people's.

Her eyes prickled with fiery tears that rolled down her cheeks without her permission. "I can't stop it, and even if I could, I wouldn't," she said and turned around, slamming the door behind her. It felt like the entire world had gone against them, and it was difficult to breathe as a sob escaped her lips.

She hadn't cried this hard since remembering she had lost all memories of her dad; at the time, she'd mourned not only him but her identity. All the information her father had given her about potion making was all gone. This kingdom wanted to also take away her soulmate. To hell with them.

Nava made her way to the bathroom, wanting to splash cold water on her face to calm herself down. This kingdom had taken almost all she loved. Had stripped her down and had her fumbling for days. It might be time to tell the king she wasn't going anywhere, and that the tree was already blooming.

CHAPTER THIRTY

NAVA

The outfit constricted Nava's pacing across the room. It was a tan gown, almost the exact color of her olive skin, with shiny ebony beading that formed beautiful panels. It had surprised her to find this beautiful gown in her closet earlier in the day, especially since it wasn't blue. She and Leela had noticed the day of the ball that her dresses had been getting darker.

Was this something that happened with the change of seasons? The magic feeding things like this, the garden, or the fireplace is still a mystery to her.

The bodice hugged her curves until it reached her hips and then flowed like a mermaid's tail toward the floor. She was grateful the neckline was modest enough that it didn't reveal her soul mark. Nava let her hair fall wild over her shoulders. Today, for the first time since arriving, Leela hadn't come to fix her tresses into something more elaborate.

Nava didn't have time to worry whether her hair was proper for the king and his court, not when the forest was burning and she had to prepare herself and her magic for a possible confrontation.

Taking a deep breath to calm her nerves did nothing when all she could smell was smoke. Bees crawled over the walls and floor, no doubt answering her subconscious calling. It was hard to transfer to the forest when Fael and a new random maid had been checking on her at every hour.

Suspicion rose within her whether Arkimedes had expected her to leave the castle when the fires restarted and had upped her guard and maid rounds to be random and often.

She huffed at the spike of annoyance within her. Maybe tonight at this dinner she could talk some sense into him. If not, she might have to leave and deal with the consequences later.

Fael's gravel voice boomed over her frazzled senses. "It's time for dinner, Miss Nava."

She stood, debating whether leaving at that very moment was the best chance she would get. No one could stop her if she did.

The knock on the door startled her. "Nava?"

What was she thinking? That she would leave her soulmate here when he had lost his trust in her after her lies? No. She couldn't harm their already fragile bond any more.

Her heart shrank as she pushed down the sudden need to cry. Not wanting to be in this situation for a moment longer, needing to be near Aristaeus, but having to stay here instead, playing with pretty dresses and fearing that someone might kill her if she strayed out of this room for long.

"Be right there." She took a fortifying breath to ready herself for the night.

Devon's indigo suit and cobalt velvet cravat reminded her of the one he'd worn the day he walked into her shop almost a year ago. "You are looking rather ravishing today, cat. I would have loved to match your gown color today, but I'm afraid all my clothes are the same shades of blue." He picked her hand up in a blur, his touch scalding and wrong.

Before his lips could touch her skin, she pulled her hand away. "Do *not* put your lips on me," she hissed.

His lopsided grin became a full-toothed smile. "No fun. So who do I have to bed around here to get a different color outfit?"

The origin of such a dress was still a mystery, and in the middle of her fogged-out thoughts this afternoon, she hadn't stopped to think whether or not it might be a good idea to wear it. Should she have questioned it more? "The clothes just appear in the wardrobe. I found it and thought it would be nice for a change from the regular blue clothes."

Fael's eyes had just caught up on her outfit as well. If his furrowing brow was anything to go by, he was not happy with this news. "I thought the dress was indigo." He stepped closer, his gold eyes raking down her body. "Only the royals wear black."

"What?" She shook her head, her bottom lip trembling as perspiration built up. "Then it must be indigo."

Except it wasn't. Nava lowered her gaze to the gown sleeves, semi-transparent black. She hadn't seen Leela since the day of the ball; earlier in the day, she had gotten dressed on her own, not questioning a thing. What if this wasn't a dress facilitated by magic? Maybe someone had placed it there to get her in trouble.

Or maybe . . . the changing in the tree somehow signaled the magic of the castle to change this as well?

She exchanged a look with Devon. "Do you think someone was trying to sabotage me tonight by putting this gown in my wardrobe?" Leela? The thought alone made her heart shrink. Part of her never had trusted the friendly questions. What if this was one of Leela's partner's creations? She was a seamstress, after all.

Devon shrugged. "Probably."

"We don't have time to do anything about it," Fael said. "We are going to be late, and that will get more attention than the gown itself."

Her skin turned clammy. "I should go back and change."

The fae grunted in front of them, shaking his head. "No time. We have to be there before they close the doors."

Or what? What could be worse than appearing in a crowded dinner wearing the royal colors in front of the king?

The garment itched on her skin. Maybe it wasn't Leela but Marni's doing, as a form of revenge for the way she and Leela had changed the horrid yellow gown the night of the ball. Nava had wanted to blend in with the crowd, not call more attention to herself. This was what happened when one didn't have their head in the right place.

"I have a bad feeling about this," she whispered in the same rhythm as her stumbling heart.

They turned a corner around the hall, which became busier with the sheer number of people gathered by the entrance. This was not a regular quiet dinner with a few people from the court. Fael took them across the crowd toward a room they had never been in before.

It was like a secondary throne room, similar in shape,

with an impressive ceiling made of beams that formed an intricate honeycomb shape. Large stained glass windows lined the sides. The late sun's rays made the colors of the art cascade onto the crowd in a shimmering rainbow. Nava spotted the royals at the center of the room. Both sat on their large ebony thrones.

The king's aura swarmed around him like spilled ink in water, and his cerulean eyes snapped upon her as if called by a magnet. Nava's legs shook under her weight just by the sheer fear running through her veins.

She had been so self-assured earlier, thinking she would be able to confront this man, tell him who she was. Nava shouldn't have worn the damn dress. It would have been better to be naked, judging by the prickling sensation of all eyes fixed on her.

Trying to look elsewhere was proving to be impossible. She found herself a captive to the king's deepening scowl, and the warm swarm of panic that raged in her stomach wasn't only her own. Arkimedes's emotions were so strong they sent hot and cold flashes through her body. Her steps slowed down, and she was too dizzy to keep walking.

Arkimedes's hands tightened on the arms of his chair, his body tense. Feeling off-kilter and dizzy, she tried to get air back to her lungs. The light warning of insects crawling over her arms was a clear sign this was moving to a fight-or-flight situation.

Had this always been meant to be a setup, about a stupid dress that would end up getting her killed?

An icy hand grasped hers, bringing her hand across the crook of an arm. The velvet touch of fabric distracted her for a moment. "Look at me, *now*."

Devon's distant voice cooled the raging flames inside her, and she took another step forward, following his pull. If she could break eye contact with whatever magic had her locked with the king, she might be able to blend in the crowd.

"Close the doors." A deep, masculine voice that felt like honey to her senses broke the murmurs in the crowd. Arkimedes's voice had been all but collected, showing some traces of the tension Nava felt through their bond.

The words had the desired response since the king's gaze had broken contact, which freed her from whatever she had been paralyzed under. It had felt too similar to the way she froze when the Dark Ones took Arkimedes from their home. Or the day she'd been frozen in the middle of the Northern Village by Devon a year ago. Mastering these sorts of spells should be at the forefront of her learning at this point.

She took a couple of quick breaths, filling her lungs with precious air as Devon pulled her into the multitude. People followed their retreating steps toward the back of the room, surprise reflected on their beautiful faces. Everyone was a fae in here, except for Devon and Nava. The two of them stood behind the crowd, illuminated by the light of the candelabra. The scent of incense and expensive perfume hung in the air. Nava allowed herself to release the panic that had her nerves tense and frantic.

Since this was not a dinner where she could talk to the king and maybe convince him to not kill her, she would gain nothing by standing like a lamb awaiting slaughter. She needed a plan A and B and C.

Inspecting every inch of the room to find a way out, she clutched Devon's arm like a lifeline. Her enemy had become her savior tonight, and the realization wasn't lost on her. She didn't want the warmth that bloomed in her stomach, thawing the feelings she harbored toward this man.

But she was grateful for Devon's help—even if it was to save his own life due to the life debt.

"Next time, maybe stick to the damn blue colors, yes?" Devon murmured close to her ear.

She glared at him. "You think? I did ask Fael multiple times to let me go back and change."

"It would have helped if you weren't so ignorant about the kingdoms. It's known everywhere that black is the royal color inside this castle."

But she didn't know this, not when she had learned so little of the four kingdoms and their cultures. Her mother had always intended for her and Cameron to be sheltered. To live inside a non-magical island where no king could ever harm her, let alone kill her. "It wasn't my choice to know so little about . . . the world," she whispered. However, the words didn't ring true. Her mother had been gone for years now. What excuse did Nava have to turn a blind eye to everybody outside the Grey Island for so long?

She avoided Devon's gaze. Being vulnerable in front of this man was not her idea of a fun evening, but he had just saved her, and that left her a bit off-kilter.

Devon hummed, studying their surroundings. His sharp jaw caught the highlight of the candlelight like a blade. "The universe is intent on shoving you out into the outside world, despite Celeste's attempts."

Nava allowed her eyes to drift back to the man and her shoulders eased. The universe, the gods of this world, destiny. They all had picked their players in a game she and Arkimedes were forced to play—dragging this man alongside them.

She was a woman tied to a kingdom hell-bent on killing her, and she needed to find a way out.

There were three large doors around the circular room, each one closed with a couple of guards at each side. For a supposed dinner, this was suspicious. Were they expecting trouble?

If the worst came to pass, she could transfer out through one of the door crevices. Maybe if that happened, Arkimedes could save Devon and not have to worry about her. She reminded herself that the only person who knew she wasn't helpless was her soulmate, and she trusted him with her life, even in their rocky circumstances.

Nava focused on Arkimedes, who rose from his seat as if called by her thoughts. His skin was clean of all the soot from earlier in the day, which meant he had been back in his room and had avoided seeing her. She would know, as she'd waited for him on the balcony after she returned from her walk.

His green eyes met hers across the multitude of fae around them, and the room went quiet at his solemn face. "The forest is burning," he said, and murmurs erupted around. Nava could hear the angry inflections in their whispers.

"The humans are doing this."

"It's too close to the city."

"Silence." The king's voice boomed over the room, and every whisper quieted in an instant.

"We have been using our best guards to locate the culprits. Following leads, as some of you suspected a local group from the village was responsible for the attacks. However, this is not the truth. The royal guard and I have been battling demons in our woods for the last week."

Nava's stomach dropped as she clasped her hand over her chest, feeling the bond toward this man, toward nature, ache. Murmurs of panic and alarm spread like an echo in a cave, and Arkimedes found her again. "Today we battled at least fifteen."

Even Devon was quiet, though she felt his eyes burning on the side of her face.

"Be at ease, my people. It's not the first time I have encountered the Zorren in my life." The king stood from his throne, and for the first time since Nava had arrived at this castle, she could see his pale features through the mist of his power.

His almost translucent skin lacked the natural glow Arkimedes had, and for someone so beautiful and young in appearance, his jaded expression didn't hide an ancient air about him. Fael had said he was the oldest fae he had ever met, and according to Leela, both she and Nava's guard were pretty old themselves, to Nava's twenty-six.

"I don't believe it's a coincidence my heir came back, led by his need to help his people. His magic, much like my own, feeds the castle you stand in tonight, the roads you drive and ride on. The grounds this very city is built upon. I have no doubt with our powers combined, we will have no problem finding and fighting this new foe knocking at our doorstep."

He came back . . .

She studied Arkimedes's features, the way the copper crown rested on top of his thick brown hair. He looked at peace with the king's words.

Nava's mind reached deep within herself, and the bitter taste on her tongue grew more pronounced. Her eyes snapped to the kingdom's emblem stitched on the backs of both thrones. A dead tree, with roots and branches that mirrored one another. The queen's tree.

Nava knew this already; she had talked about it with Arkimedes when he showed her both the real one and the one in the forest where his mother had been killed. But the nagging sensation that she was forgetting something told her it wasn't a memory from this kingdom, but from a different one.

Nava's throat closed in, her vision hazing. When she arrived in the kingdom, her first reaction to the emblem was that she had seen it before. Not in a book or in a dream, but etched onto the blades that decorated her soulmate's cabin walls a year ago.

There had been two swords. One said his name, Arkimedes B. Valeron. The other had the image of this kingdom's tree. It had been the sword he'd taken with him to battle, choosing this weapon over the one from when he was a Valeron, a Crow.

"He always wanted to be back," she breathed.

Arkimedes had been here like he had told her and had left, maybe intending to return to what he'd always perceived as his destiny, the one he was so adamant to fulfill now. He had wanted to be back because the kingdom needed him. Had his plans been derailed the day he found her when he'd been forced to run away across the world to survive and not die?

Her mother's choice had made it so. Because they were soulmates and being apart after finding each other meant death. He'd had to run away from this life because of her.

"The royal army will begin preparing for an attack, and until further notice, all civilians, *including humans*, are banned from entering the forest. This is for your protection, and defiance to my command will be your end. By my hands or the demons," the king finished and sat again.

The heat in her body swelled, setting her nerve endings aflame.

A dry cackle escaped Devon's lips. "I guess he didn't tell you he always intended to be back."

Swallowing, Nava turned around, not able to look at Arkimedes any longer with the guilt that sank in her stomach. No wonder he didn't want to leave. He had already sacrificed a decade of his life to wait for her, alone and unwanted in that forest she was trying so hard to force him back into.

Devon was in front of her in a few strides. "So are you this quiet because of the Zorren?"

"Oh, no, I know about the Zorren," she breathed. "I didn't put together that he knew he was a freaking prince."

"Ah." Devon's eyes shone with mischief. Like he had been waiting for this kind of dessert. "So he didn't tell you last year he had a big life responsibility awaiting him elsewhere? He does like to keep his things quiet."

Nava's jaw ached as her vision blurred with unshed tears. "I didn't know."

"You don't know many things, cat. However, I figured he told you, with you both being . . . so close."

Had her mother known? She hadn't mentioned it in her diary. Nava's heart was pulling and pushing her toward angry feelings her mind didn't think it had the right to go to. "He is a man of secrets," she said, lowering her gaze to the floor, trying to calm her erratic breathing. Horror clutched her at the thought that he had given up so much for her.

"He had been back for three days the day we found you. We wanted to check on Celeste, and her involvement with a shady group, before he went to the Society and explained he had to leave." Devon's casual tone in the oddest moments always surprised her.

Shady group—Nava filed that comment for later. Right now she didn't want to ask about her mother.

"Would the Society have let him go?" Was that even her voice? She sounded so beaten down.

"Of course. The Society has no claims over the crown's

heirs. The king and Arkimedes alone are dangerous enough to piss off, let alone with an army of Dark Ones."

Nava swallowed. "That's why he wants to stay now. He always wanted to be back here."

Devon's smile faltered into a grimace. "Arkimedes of ten years ago wanted this. The man I met last year was not the same brother I knew, for better or for worse."

Nava loved the man he was; she was hopeless at loving him even now when he was a stranger wearing her lover's skin. "How much longer do we have to stay in this room? I'd rather leave when the king is not looking to murder me."

"The doors are still closed, so unless the prince or that guard who follows you around comes to get us out, we are very well stuck in here."

Nava raised her hand to her temple, trying to massage away her building headache. She would have liked to leave this kingdom, but now things were different. She had more information that made her own selfish needs take pause.

She wished Arkimedes had confided in her, but she also understood him. Circumstances had made her walk the steps of someone who withheld information due to fear, and she wouldn't be so quick to judge him again.

Maybe he didn't want her to feel the way she did now —like she had stolen his life away.

She had to believe he had been trying to protect her from a kingdom that hated humans. From a place that might be dangerous for her, as he didn't know why he'd been abandoned in the first place. She understood now that however misguided either of their reasonings were, the truths they withheld weren't meant to hurt one another.

CHAPTER THIRTY-ONE

NAVA

When the prince of the Dark Ones walked to you in a crowd, it was expected the eyes of every stranger to follow. No longer frozen by the king, Nava could study everyone around them. There had to be at least a hundred people inside.

She spotted the king's cohorts near the two thrones. Unlike the night she'd seen them for the first time, tonight they wore armor. Some made of aged copper, some shiny new metal. Their blackish auras billowed around them as they stood waiting for their king.

All of them held their helmets in their arms, their hair pulled back or braided, awaiting a battle to come soon. Nava wasn't sure if she was feeling jealous of them being able to fight or admiration that they would choose to do so, even when they were no longer part of the guard.

The fae parted ways to allow Arkimedes to cross toward them with long steps. He wore a black suit with gold embroidered details on the jacket. By the time she had to crane her neck to meet him, she could hear the screeching sound of the doors opening in the distance.

"What are you wearing?" he asked between his teeth, his eyes blazing as he studied her.

"It was in my wardrobe," she blurted, battling her need to fidget. "I assumed everything in there was acceptable for me to wear."

"There was nothing black in mine," Devon piped in, studying his fingernails with a quirk of his lips.

Arkimedes glared at his brother. "We've gotta get you two out of here."

They walked out like souls traveling to purgatory. The tight skirt of the dress and her pointy heels made it difficult to keep up with the two giants on either side of her. Neither spoke as they went up the stairs toward the prince's wing.

When the halls were quiet and no one was around, she couldn't hold the silence any longer. "If what makes you so mad is that my dress is black, you have to know I didn't do it. I didn't even know black was the royal color until Fael came to get me. I have no reason to want to get myself killed." Plus, there was the thought she'd had before that maybe his own magic had pushed the change to start.

"I know, Nava." Slowing his walk, he turned to her, his voice below a whisper. "I believe our connection was what made it happen."

Ha! She had been right; the change of her dress was related to Arkimedes's and her connection.

"Like my father said, my magic is linked to this land. The moment you arrived here, it knew who you were because of our bond. The tree is alive, and the clothes have shifted." It was the first time he'd looked at her so intently since their argument.

"Why didn't it happen sooner?"

"I wouldn't say it has been long. We have been here for, what . . . a little over a week?" Devon chimed in. "But the king did say both their magics are connected to this place . . . so it might have something to do with the king's feelings about you."

Nava remembered the day Leela spoke about the queen in her room, how the air had shifted. Had that been related to this as well?

"When Fael brought me to this castle, my clothes changed from the Society of Crows' uniform to a deep black shade in a matter of days," Ark said. "There is no fooling this magic from what runs through our blood."

For once, Devon's face was not one of mocking triumph. "We need to leave, *now*. If the king finds out she is your . . . you know what, he can hold her to get you to do things you might not want to."

He was an expert in evildoing, after all. Was that what he'd intended to do last year when he captured her in battle? He had been so sure Arkimedes would follow. She held her tongue; it wouldn't help their circumstances for her to pick a fight with Devon at this moment.

They had stopped in front of Devon's door, and Arkimedes's hand hovered over the door handle. "I won't leave when my kingdom is being attacked by the Zorren."

"So what then? We stay here and wait for the king to take her . . . and kill me?" Devon challenged, stepping into the room without a look back.

Arkimedes's eyes landed on her. A pained expression that matched the churning in her stomach stared back at her. He had not said the words, but the dread building in him . . . she felt it clear through their bond.

Nava shook her head, wanting to reach to him and hold his hand, but her throat tightened with the realization that she didn't feel like she could. "Whatever you are thinking . . ."

"It will be better if we speak in Devon's room," he said

instead.

Her stomach dropped, and cold shot through her body. With the screeching sound of the door opening wider, he shifted his body and waited, silent.

Nava straightened her back. The prickle of her magic came alive under her skin, and white bees hovered over her, a protective shield to guard her breaking heart.

The room was as opulent as she had imagined it. With natural drapes and white-and-gold couches. The floor and fireplace were polished white marble, and the click of her heels echoed in the quiet room, right before the door snapped shut behind her.

Devon cursed out loud, his wide eyes staring at her as the bees circled her body. "Has she been able to do magic all along? Why the hell are we still here, Nava?"

Her chin shook with pent-up emotion as Arkimedes's morose mood pushed through the bond. He didn't even need to speak the words for her to know he wanted them to be separated.

"Devon . . ." Arkimedes warned, but the Crow continued.

"We could have been gone a day after we arrived at this place! Just get this thing off me." He lifted his hand and shook the bangle.

"We can't remove it from you or I would have done it already, Devon. It will poison you." Arkimedes took a step closer to her. She was shaking, the adrenaline of all that had happened in that circular room and the pent-up tension finally catching up to her.

He stood a bit too close to her, but instead of calming her nerves, it made them flare up. She knew he didn't want to be close to her. This was his own nature telling him to be so when he so desperately wanted space.

At this point, Nava wasn't sure her pride could let her

enjoy it, not when her gut told her something was wrong.

"So, what then? We stay in this castle?" Devon lifted both hands over his head and dropped them in frustration. "And what's with the demons? How long have they been attacking the kingdom?"

"A week or so before I was brought back. The king thought they were fires from a particularly warm summer. Then it was thought to be arson by the Fallen Crows . . ."

Devon cursed, and recognition tainted his pale features. Nava turned to Arkimedes, her lips parting as her mind went into overdrive. The Zorren had been attacking this kingdom for a while, not because of her and Ari being here. Had they been waiting? Was it a coincidence?

Not once had Aristaeus told her that they needed to go back to the Grey Island so the demons would leave this kingdom. Did this mean the three of them were where they were supposed to be, against all odds?

Had she been the only one trying to be out of here when she should have been focusing on something else?

"You are right, Devon." Arkimedes's eyes burrowed into her instead of looking at the Crow. His forehead crinkled as the color drained from his features. "You two are in danger here. If the king doesn't know you are my soulmate, Nava, he will soon. It would have been easier for me to protect you had you been a regular human. Even though there is a stigma, the king doesn't hate humans."

"He hates soulmates? I heard around here that he and the queen were soulmates."

"Before I knew about us, I didn't believe in the whole concept of it myself, so I brushed it off as hallway rumors."

"What are you saying?" She turned to face him. He was so close, his scent wrapped around her like the hug he wouldn't give her.

"You and I have to go, while he stays here playing prince." Devon's voice was like a bucket of ice over her, and Arkimedes's warning gaze flashed over her head to the man behind.

"You can't seriously consider this," she said, crossing her arms over her chest. "We can't be apart. It will hurt us. It almost *killed* me. Plus, I'm not leaving when the Zorren are wrecking the forest. You . . . you know better."

"I don't intend for you to leave the city. You will be close but removed from the king's reach." He raised his hand toward her but hesitated before his fingers reached her shoulder. "I will be coming often to see you, and it will be easier to plan where to go from there."

What he was not saying was how he needed space away from her. Arkimedes wanted to keep her close enough so his soul wouldn't hurt, but far so his heart wouldn't get too attached. Nava wasn't sure who she had pissed off in a previous life, but she must have done a mighty good job at it.

Devon's voice broke the silence. "Are you thinking of us staying in the Society's safe house in town?"

Nava turned her head to the Crow, and her back crawled. She would rather stay in the forest than step foot inside a Society of Crows' house. She had grown more accepting in the last year, but not this much. "Absolutely *not.*"

"My father is bound by the treaty he signed not to enter that safe house. He can't destroy or harm the property either."

"Ask me if I care. I'm not stepping a foot inside that safe house."

Arkimedes pinched the bridge of his nose with two fingers. "Why not? Your mother was part of the Society."

"Yes, and I ran away from the two of you for a whole

decade, just so I could keep my freedom from the Society. You seem to think you have control over me." She took a step closer and tapped her pointer finger over the hard planes of his chest, waves of anger burning in the pit of her stomach. "I'm not serving myself on a gold platter to them."

His hand captured hers in a gentle move, holding her as he studied her features with a puzzled expression. "There won't be any Crows there, other than Devon."

"My answer is still no."

"Nava. There is no other place I can think of where the king can't just pluck you from while in the city." His gaze turned wild and pleading. "I can't leave the city to burn."

She swallowed and pulled her hand away from his grasp, taking a healthy step back as her heart stuttered. "Wouldn't it send an alarm to the Society if nonmembers enter?"

"You will be invited by one of us."

"I'm not talking about me, Ark. Can either of you still walk in there? You deserted them over a decade ago, and Devon has been a prisoner for a year . . . which might have made them start their pursuit of another possible escapee. We all know how much they love those."

"What?" Arkimedes's face lost all color as he looked back at his brother. "What did you do?"

"She is such a charmer, isn't she?" Devon's voice dripped with venom. "Why don't you dig into the memories you are so desperately avoiding and see for yourself?"

With those words out, it wasn't about the Society's safe house or the fact that she believed Arkimedes wanted space. Time slowed down. She searched for answers in his expression, and the sudden tension in his shoulders gave it to her.

Did that mean Arkimedes had access to his memories of her and had been avoiding them?

"Nava . . ."

She hadn't meant to say her question out loud. "Are you avoiding your memories from the last decade? From us?"

"It's not the time nor place to talk about this."

In other words, yes. The ground beneath them shook as the pulse of her magic left her body in a thunderous wave.

He could work on recovering his memories, to love her again, to know all that had happened in the last ten years that had made him choose her over this. But he was making a different choice now.

She took a step back when he tried to come closer, presumably to calm her from unleashing an earthquake in this castle. The buzzing of her bees became stronger, and she battled her own need to disappear from this place and not come back.

Beyond her broken heart, the love she had for this man was strong enough that she knew being away meant their deaths—and she couldn't do that to him, nor to Cameron or Ari. Nava steeled her spine and called for strength she didn't know she had left. "If going to this safe house will buy us time, then I guess I will go there, but I won't play by these prisoner rules anymore. I will be going into that forest, with or without your consent." No matter what happened, after tonight she would be transferring to Ari every day.

Nava had lost Arkimedes, even though she had done all she could to prevent it. She had lost her identity as a potion maker and had lost her father. Memories she could never gain back, unlike him.

Her stomach churned and her skin turned warm, yet it

wasn't anger alone, but despair. Hadn't he given up ten years for her, living like a hermit in a cabin in the woods, cursed to be a bird every night by her own mother? Unable to reach his soulmate or the destiny he had once believed was his.

Maybe it was her turn to suffer from a distance.

"So, let me get this straight. You want the both of us to go to the Society's house and pray we aren't caught by the guards on our way out?" Said Devon.

"No, *I* will take you tonight. We will leave after the sun goes down," Arkimedes said. "The guards are being dispatched to the forest tonight. The king is going as well. I'm to stay inside the city walls to keep the wards from collapsing in case we get more attacks than expected."

"So the king will find out you helped us escape and hurt you? No, thank you. We will all go or I won't be going anywhere."

"The only way he can hurt me is if he gets *you*." The way his expression shifted from worry to affection, then back to the former had her head spinning. "Tonight while he is out, I need to find the key to take the bracelets off you, which he keeps in his room. But I will come back and stay with the two of you in the safe house."

"So, you aren't staying in the castle?" she asked.

He shook his head, and there was a fair amount of hesitation flowing through their bond.

A horn echoed out in the gardens, along with the loud steps of metal on stone, as soldiers marched over gravel pathways to the forest. Their copper armor shone pink and brass under the golden shades of the setting sun. The three of them walked to the balcony and held onto the railing that was still warm from the day. Over a hundred Dark Ones headed to the outer walls of the castle, and in the very front, hidden by darkness, was the king himself.

CHAPTER THIRTY-TWO

ORION

It was hard not to make promises to Nava when she looked at him the way she did just now. Her lip quivered as her eyes dipped to the floor. Orion was ready to throw caution to the wind and do whatever she wanted from him.

It had to be a bond-induced drive that didn't line up with what he *needed* to do. Before she arrived at the castle, his strive to find answers had taken precedence. Why he'd been abandoned when he was just a toddler. What made his mother's spirit haunt him, repeatedly showing him a horrible nightmare of the night she died.

He had a bigger role in this kingdom, one he accepted before he ever met Nava, this time around . . . eleven years ago. Because of a soulmate, he'd abandoned this purpose—a whole kingdom—to the mercy of lost protection.

Still, he battled his primal need to say to hell with his role and the answers he always searched for.

Sensing her emotions through the pit of his stomach made his decision-making weak at best, and that alone was reason to break this irrational need to be what she needed him to be. He appreciated she wasn't asking for more than he was ready to give right now.

Orion brought his hand over his chest, massaging away the throbbing ache that built underneath. The guards marched toward the walls, and beyond them, a black smoke of fire already lifted in the air, clouding the forest behind.

"Do we leave now that the king is out of sight?" Nava swallowed. "We should be there too . . . Ari needs us."

Devon turned around to face them, his pale fingers tapping over the stone railing. "Who is this Ari person I keep hearing about?"

Orion ignored his brother's question. It was worth putting a pin in the way his stomach churned at the idea of revealing the Beekeeper to his brother. Then the flash came to him like a cold winter's breeze.

Devon held Nava by her neck, his face twisted with rage. Blue fire burned behind him in houses built on the sides of large trees. He made it to them fast. "Devon, let her go." The bitter taste of panic and dread coated his tongue.

Devon's grip tightened against her throat, and the smell of magic wafted around them. "And why would I do that?" Menace dripped off each word. "Keeping her will ensure you don't kill me, brother."

"If you don't let her go, I will kill you," he promised and meant every single word.

His breath tore out of his lungs as he shook off the memory and took a step back. He wished he could ignore that vision—the betrayal that churned in his gut. Orion stormed back inside the room.

His heartbeat drummed against his rib cage, and the

air was too thick to get enough into his lungs. Were all the people he thought of as family meant to betray him?

"Are you all right?" Nava's heels clicked on the marble floor. Her voice was like a healing salve over a wound he had just reopened. She was by his side in a blink, grasping his forearm, blue and brown eyes studying him closely.

"I—" He cleared his throat, as the touch alone grounded him. "The king can take care of the demons tonight. It's better if you are away from him while he doesn't know you are my mate."

Why, if Devon had attacked her, was he here with her? Now her hostile predisposition toward his brother made sense. Why was she trusting him?

Everything fit into place. Devon was under some sort of bond. That much had been clear when they had talked about it, a life debt or a blood bond by the trust Nava had with him not hurting her.

Nava had said she almost died when the king took him from the Grey Island . . . and Devon had been in prison. Had the desperation of almost dying forced her hand to trust Devon, even after what he'd done to her?

They had traveled through a portal to get to this kingdom, and Nava had paid the price. She had lost memories that were too dear to her, which led her to a panic attack.

There was one person in this world who would do anything for him, and that wasn't his father or his brother, but this woman. Just like at one point in the last decade, he had dropped everything that made him the man he was for her. His identity as he knew it hung from a fine thread.

"I don't understand why we have to run and hide. If the rumors are correct, your father had a soulmate he loved. He should understand that he can't kill me and keep the heir he so desperately wants."

"My mother might have been his soulmate, Nava, but

she ended up dead after she betrayed him. He won't look at this with a rational mind."

"Not to stir the pot further, but if he already took your memories once, he could do so again when he finds out you have let us go." Devon's voice was claws and poison gripping his gut, and the images of him hurting Nava were hard to ignore.

He closed his hands into fists and allowed his breath to even out. "I now know what he did to block my memories, which would lead me to a better defense against another attempt, but . . . it's always a possibility."

Orion was battling and losing a war against what he desired and what needed to be done. He needed to get the keys or else they would be tracked. Them being able to move around the city without trackers would give them freedom enough to live outside the castle while he figured out what needed to be done. With the kingdom, his past— and his future. Many questions were swimming in his mind, and he couldn't make a decision when lives depended on him.

Orion didn't want to keep Nava from being around nature even for her protection, especially when things like the Zorren were wreaking havoc.

With the new memory of what happened in the Grey Island with Devon, Orion couldn't leave Nava alone in that house with his brother while he was so far away in the castle. "We will go first to the king's room to get the keys and then head to the safe house."

"Why do we need the keys so badly?"

"I, for one, would like my magic back, especially if we are going to be hunted by the king and his dogs."

Nava's brows furrowed as she crossed her arms over her chest. "Who's to say you won't betray us when you get your magic back? Are you even still under the life debt?"

Ah, a life debt. "Who do you owe your debt to, Devon, Nava or me?"

Devon's lips pulled into a lazy smile. "Like I said, search your own damn memories."

"Enough with this. It's your life debt, Ark. You saved him last year from me." Nava cleared her throat, looking uncomfortable. "He had me and was hurting me—was hurting so many. I was angry, and I didn't know what I was doing with my magic."

His throat went dry, and he wished the images didn't flash through his mind the way they did.

Bees swarmed towards Devon from the sky, stinging him until he lay too still on the ground. He had asked Nava to stop.

Orion's heartbeats were too heavy. "I—remember it," he admitted. Nava's lips parted as she searched him for more. Hope glowed behind her dark lashes. "Did you call for the life debt?"

"I was running out of time, and I didn't know how else to get here."

Devon let out a heavy breath and walked to the sitting area, where he fell onto one of the chairs. "I have tried to leave multiple times, once during the solstice. The faes were too drunk and occupied to pay attention to me. I just had to slip past the gates, make it to the safe house, and wait for a member of the Society to come." He shrugged one shoulder and met Orion's gaze. "They have tools to get rid of jewelry like this bracelet—or the plan B was that I would bargain with the king after."

"Why are you telling us this?"

"I couldn't leave." He swung his head back with a dramatic sigh. "Not because of the debt, which is still active, but because . . . I had been searching for you for a decade, Arkimedes. Sometimes we do unimaginable things to try to get our family back. What I did doesn't make me different from the king, but I doubt anyone in this room has a clean conscience to condemn me for it."

Nava's mouth opened but shut soon after, and her guilt and shame flooded Orion's stomach like a tsunami.

"The reason we need to take the bracelets off is not because they cancel magic, Nava. It also allows the king to track you two."

"Oh."

"The location of the safe house is a secret only members of the Society know. Having a beacon leading him straight to it would mean you two would have to stay inside the house and not help with the Zorren situation."

"So we find the key and then head there?"

"This is the first time in the last four months the king has left the castle—it might be our chance to get the keys and avoid a confrontation."

"I can't believe I'm going to a Society's safe house of my own free will. Let it be known that I'm not happy about this."

Devon's forced laughter bounced over the walls of the room. "Cat, you haven't precisely made it a secret."

Finding the lost memories of what Devon had done last year didn't make Orion's choice any easier. Now there was a decade of secrets, of experiences, that had split them apart.

"I would like to get changed out of the dress that almost got me killed before we leave," Nava said, pulling at the fabric that wrapped around her narrow waist like a second skin. His eyes trailed up her body. He wished he could allow himself to help her out of the dress, if she would let him. But the reasons to keep his distance were present.

She had told him they'd met again a year ago, and that man she knew, it wasn't him. Not fully. And Orion wasn't ready to jump into those shoes. The thought of opening the weight of those memories, woven in a hazy web inside his brain, was haunting him, much like his mother.

Would he abandon it all again for her?

He swallowed and forced his eyes from her body to her face, and she raised a challenging brow at him, having caught him looking at her. His cheeks warmed. "Sorry."

CHAPTER THIRTY-THREE

NAVA

When they left Devon's room, the sky was turning black, away from the ominous gray and orange of the fires burning behind the walls of the castle.

The halls were deserted. The wind whistled through stone crevices, accompanied by the tapping of their quick steps over the marble floor. Her room wasn't far from Devon's, and as they paused outside, Nava noticed the door was ajar.

Had she and Fael left it open in their rush to make it to dinner on time? Maybe a maid had come to bring her dinner. She had not eaten anything since lunch, and her stomach growled at the reminder.

She walked forward, already anticipating the comfortable fit of her pants and well-worn boots over this tight gown. Nava hadn't taken three steps when Arkimedes's large hand grabbed her shoulder.

He stepped closer, and his lips touched the shell of her ear; the whisper of his breath sent goose bumps down the expanse of her skin. "Let's go to my room instead."

His aura was thick enough that it enveloped her body like a cool mist. She turned her head and met his intense gaze with a nod. Devon stood behind, observing everything around them. Both men moved like trained warriors, assessing for anything that could signal trouble, while she had just been coveting food and comfortable boots.

It hit her that the two of them had trained since boyhood to be like this. While she baked cherry pies with Laurie or gardened with her mother, Ark and Devon had been forged into weapons.

Arkimedes opened the door to his room and entered after, leaving her outside in the hall with Devon. From where she stood, the room was dark; the light coming from the glass doors of the balcony cast rays of silver on the floor. It was too quiet around them, making her extra aware of the loud sound of her breaths.

"Clear."

At some point, she had stopped breathing. She turned to Devon to make sure he was following before entering the room.

It felt like ages since she had been here. Her eyes lingered over the bed as memories crashed through her of the night she and Arkimedes had shared here before he'd learned her secret and everything had gone wrong.

The room was cold enough that she took notice, but the flames in the fireplace rolled to life soon after the thought crossed her mind.

The scent of spices burned her nose and she focused on Arkimedes, who stood in the middle of the room, both hands extended in front of him, while dark mist spread out of his fingertips and leaked into the walls and floor.

The making of wards was a spell she had started to learn a month ago. There hadn't been much of a need for her to master it after Devon's soldiers had been placated.

However, her mate had insisted she learn the basics just in case.

Just as she turned her palms up and called on her magic to ward this room for something she didn't know, Arkimedes opened his eyes and faced both Devon and her, frowning.

Her gut churned with an uneasiness that didn't belong to her. "Is everything all right?"

"I don't know. But we are closer now to the king's wing. We should head there as quickly as possible and then get out of here. You will need to bring your clothes to you. I'm afraid someone was in your room, and we should try to avoid a trap."

She swallowed; her scalp crawled with the sensation of being watched. This learned magic, wards and calling spells, was something she was very new and self-conscious about.

She wouldn't have been ashamed to have Ark watch and even instruct her on what to do, but this was not her normal soulmate, and now they were joined by none other than Devon Black.

"Calm down, cat, it's just a spell," Devon said, reading every single one of her insecurities that were no doubt painted on her face.

"Shut it."

His smirk grew wider, and Arkimedes stepped forward, his brows knitting together. "What's the problem?"

"I almost forget I might know more about your soulmate than you nowadays," Devon gloated, and that had both Nava's and Arkimedes's frown become more pronounced. "Celeste and the potion maker had Nava living in a non-magical town. The poor thing had barely any knowledge of magic when we met last year."

Arkimedes's eyes cut to her at the same time her cheeks burned.

"I know how to make a calling spell."

"Good, then you won't have to run in heels and that gown," Devon said.

Ark started, "I could go and—"

"You'd better not offer to get me my things from that room, Arkimedes, if you know what's good for you," she said, not even bothering to turn to face him, but by the cackling of Devon's laughter, she could imagine his face.

Nava swallowed the knot in her throat; she had learned earlier in the year that you could call on your things. Which was why Arkimedes couldn't manifest her clothing or the keys the king now held in his room.

It was why last year he could call the things that were in his cabin—though she'd never gotten him to explain how he could get fresh bread while they were traveling.

Nava walked to the bed and took a seat in the corner, opening her hands and closing her eyes. She pictured the armoire of the green bedroom, the musty scent inside, the now-black gowns, and the area where her clothes lay, neatly folded over.

Nava remembered the details of the white linen fabric of her shirt, the rough cotton of her pants. The worn leather of her boots, still caked with mud from her back-yard. She wanted to bring anything she wore the day she'd left the Grey Island. Everything from those days was so far away now, but it represented a level of comfort she hadn't been able to reach.

Her skin turned warm as her magic became alive in her veins, right before the weight of her clothes appeared in her hands.

Devon's soft cackle turned into full-blown laughter, causing Nava to snap her eyes open and find to her horror that alongside her pants, shirt, and boots, her undergarments had appeared as well. Folded pieces of lace and thin fabric on top.

Bringing all her clothes to her chest to hide any evidence the Crow could see, she schooled her features and faced them both with what she hoped was a cool expression. "I know it has been a while since you have seen a woman's undergarments, but don't let it get you too worked up."

Devon choked, and she dared to look at Arkimedes, whose red face showed mirth, a smirk tilting his lips.

She stood from the bed and made her way into the washroom to get changed and put her embarrassment behind her.

By the time she got out of the room, wearing the clothes that fit her a bit too loose, she found Devon and Arkimedes talking in hushed tones, the latter removing cufflinks from the black shirt that peeked out of the sleeves of his jacket. "So what now?"

"Well, we—"

The knock on the door had Arkimedes stopping mid-sentence, his back straightening as he looked at the door with a deepening frown. No one spoke or moved a muscle.

"Your Highness, are you there?" Fael's familiar voice came from the other side of the door. "I haven't been able to find Miss Nava ever since dinner."

Arkimedes stood very still for a few heartbeats before he prowled to the door. Pausing in front of it, he looked back at Nava; the intensity in his gaze mirrored the turbulent feelings coming down the bond, making her nauseated.

He cracked the door and peeked through the hole, then without another word, he opened it fully. Fael stood in the doorframe, wearing his customary copped armor, holding his helmet in the crook of his arm.

Fael raised a bushy brow when his eyes met hers. "Well, now I know why I couldn't find her."

Arkimedes moved back into the room with no welcoming words. "Were you the one who opened her room?"

"Yes, I was worried something had happened, especially after what went on during dinner with the king."

"Sorry, Fael, I didn't mean to worry you," Nava said with a tilt of a smile, and the fae's golden eyes landed on Devon, then back on her, tracking down her body, catching the change of outfit.

"You are helping them escape?" Fael entered the room, his wings swaying with each step as his gaze traveled again over each of them, reaching Arkimedes last.

Nava paused and tightened her fingers around the fabric of her pants. Her shoulders tensed as the air crackled with tension.

Arkimedes shrugged off his black jacket and tossed it over the bed. "You recommended I do, a week ago if I remember correctly."

Nava's mouth fell open wide.

Fael crossed his arms over his chest with a wary expression. "Yet you were determined to keep them here. What has changed?"

Besides the king paralyzing her in front of everyone earlier?

Arkimedes's aura thickened enough that she was able to see it, the scent of magic spiking in the air. "What changed was I didn't know I was taken from a home I shared with her." His voice dropped lower. "I thought I had to save my brother from being under her spell. Turns out the one enchanted is me. You could have told me, yet you chose to leave me in the dark."

Fael's frown softened, his posture tensing at Arkimedes's tone. Devon, who sat on the edge of one of the chairs by the fireplace, stood and crossed the room with his iconic lazy steps, as if expecting a show at any moment. However, Nava could feel that Arkimedes's emotions didn't match his tone. He was calm enough; if anything, a tinge of panic started to burn in the middle of it.

He was acting angry, though he wasn't. Plans were forming inside that head of his, and that alone gave her pause.

"I swore I would follow you, my prince. But I can't defy a direct command from the king himself. His magic prevents me from doing so."

"Did he force you to swear your allegiance to me when I arrived to this kingdom? To make me feel like I had someone to trust?" Arkimedes's calculated moves were that of a predator. He opened his shirt with swift fingers, revealing light golden skin over muscle. Unlike the last time she had seen him, his ribs were bruised and his skin red. Had he been burned earlier in the forest but hadn't gotten around to seeing a healer?

She found herself taking a step toward him, her mind clawing at empty spots of memories where the potion for burns used to be. Arkimedes lifted his hand and a new, clean shirt flew out of the closet to his hand, making her gasp.

Show-off. No one else in the room cared about the flying garment or the lack of clothing.

"I swore to follow you 'till the end eleven years ago because I, like everyone in this kingdom, feared for our future. I wanted you to stay then—or to return to us of *your own free will.*" Fael's sincere tone shook at the end with pent-up emotion. "I was forced to come the day we took you, and I remembered her, which is why I offered to get them out of here."

Fael had told Nava earlier in the day that there was no future for her and Ark here, so she didn't expect the man to be trying to help her get out earlier.

The fae's chin pointed to Nava, who was already halfway toward Arkimedes. What the hell was she doing? She had no way of healing his wounds without a potion, even if she wanted to. Yet she *needed* to press her palms against his skin. To heal.

Maybe Fael had been right and she had been dropped on her head at some point.

"After what happened today with the dress—and what followed in the room with my father—I have to take them out of here to a safe place until the Zorren threat is removed and I'm able to talk with the king and not fear their safety."

"But he will follow the bracelets' trail," Fael protested. "Are you leaving us in the middle of this attack? What about the king's health? It ties to the health of this castle . . ."

Guilt churned in her gut like a festering disease. Had she been hoping Arkimedes would do that this whole time when these people were so desperate?

Arkimedes's eyes met hers. "I have to get the keys and then take them away. I'll be back after they are out of the city."

Out of the city? She'd thought he'd said the place they were going to was inside the city, but hidden. So he wasn't telling Fael about the Society's safe house. This gave her snippets of how far his trust went. Still, she was not understanding where all of this was going.

Devon brought his hand to his chin, scratching it as he

followed the conversation with interest. Had he figured out what was happening? It would be extra annoying if he had, especially since she had a direct tap to Arkimedes's strongest feelings and all she was getting now was calm expectation, with a healthy dose of worry.

"I can get the keys for you, sir. Let me do this to mend what I have done. The king will believe it was me who let them go. I have been vocal about how wrong it was that we took you that way from the island. You won't have to answer for this or lose whatever memories you have just regained."

Wait. Arkimedes hadn't been trying to lead Fael to this point, right? He would never be okay with letting an innocent man sacrifice his freedom and possible life for his own neck.

"I will go with you to the king's room, in case there are any spells that might delay it or harm you in any way."

"What about them?"

"They will wait for us here in the room." Arkimedes's gaze flashed to Devon, so quick she might have imagined it.

"Ark," she started, but Devon's fervent headshake distracted her long enough to miss stopping this madness from happening. Fael was already crossing the threshold and out of the room. Arkimedes walked behind the guard, buttoning his new shirt and avoiding her gaze. She grasped his arm, stopping him from going any farther. "You can't seriously consider letting Fael throw himself to certain death when the king learns he betrayed him," she whispered.

His gaze was distant when it landed on her, but he couldn't fool her. His gut churned with building dread, tasting bitter in the back of her throat. He wasn't thrilled to do this. "It will buy us time to get you two out of here."

His eyes bore into her before dropping to her lips, and his yearning exploded in her so strong her lips parted on a gasp. Then he stepped away, and the warm dizzying sensation was replaced by cool dread that pooled in her stomach.

"But you—you wouldn't let an innocent man get hurt like that," she pleaded, and that had him turning to her, his jaw clenching.

"The Arkimedes you remember wouldn't, but that's not me, Nava. It's about time you accept that." He paused, swallowing deeply, then whispered, "Become dust and leave."

She followed his retreating shape, her words getting caught on the knot forming in her throat, but he left the room without looking back. Then the door clicked shut right in front of her face, leaving Devon and her inside.

Nava gripped the door handle, which didn't move or budge, and she pounded on the wood as heat bubbled in her gut. "You asshole!" She was going to murder him, not only for locking her inside *again*, but for being such a dickhead. "I hate this new you!"

She turned in a whirlwind and ran to the balcony door. She had promised herself she wouldn't be a prisoner in one of these rooms again. The balcony door didn't move an inch, even though she shook it and pulled at it with all her strength. Bees crawled out of her skin as her magic awakened with her building panic.

Nava couldn't breathe. She didn't want to be responsible for Fael's death in the wake of his sacrifice. The king would kill him for it. Glancing at the glass of the door, she swallowed a second before she slammed her fist onto it. Pain extended past her knuckles and fingers, down her arm; however, the glass didn't crack, nor did it even shake.

"What . . . ?" Her clothes were too tight. She was going to combust with anger and desperation.

"This is very entertaining, but you should stop before you break your hand. I'm afraid neither of us can help you heal, and we will be running soon enough."

"I can't believe you are fine with this. Actually, never mind, of course you are. But Arkimedes . . . he is so ready to throw that man into certain death just to save our skin." Her throat thickened, and soon tears welled in her eyes.

"Calm down, cat. Even the Arkimedes I knew from a decade ago wouldn't do that—unless there was something else brewing beneath the surface."

She paused her movements at once, blinking as her heartbeat slowed down. He had been very calm, acting angry even though he hadn't felt it. "Do you think . . . he doesn't trust Fael?" she ventured.

Devon, who had been standing in the same spot as when Fael had been here, walked to where Arkimedes kept his armor hanging by the wall. So similar to how he had displayed his swords back in his cabin. The Crow picked the long sword, the moonlight shining over the blade's sharp edge.

Her bees flew around her with a warning—something was off. Ark's words before he parted rang in her head. They would make sense to no one but the two of them. Only Arkimedes knew she was a Beekeeper, capable of becoming dust. He had told her to leave.

"I think he realized he was being betrayed and tried to take the threat away from here."

"What are you doing?" Nava took a step back; her skin turned yellow as her power raised to her call. Was Devon going to attack her?

"He locked us here for protection, meaning he believes there is a chance we won't be alone for long. I can't open a portal and get us out of here. Do you have any better ideas?"

So he wasn't locking them in, but locking people out. "But we saw the king and the guards leave. Do you think it was a setup? It looked convincing. The fire . . ."

Oh, she hoped Aristaeus wasn't fighting this mess alone.

The pieces of the puzzle that Arkimedes had solved clicked for her all at once. He had been acting all along while Fael was here. Nava looked into Devon's eyes and knew she could leave him now, like Ark had told her to. Transfer out of this room under the crevices of that door and save herself.

He had been her enemy a year ago, but he wasn't that anymore. The realization hit her in the gut, along with acceptance. She couldn't leave Devon to fend off a group of Dark Ones when he was here because of her and couldn't use his magic.

"How long do you think we have?" Bees crawled over her body, and her stomach churned with anticipation.

Devon's eyes widened over her. "Believe it or not, cat, I'm not a soothsayer." She glared at the Crow and reconsidered her previous line of thought. "But probably not long. I'm guessing the king left guards behind just in case the prince decided to do this. If I were the mastermind behind this, I would have left enough of them to restrain him."

"You mean like you did with Mortimer when you had him stabbed?" she hissed, and her bees buzzed closer to Devon. Now real ones crawled down the crevices of the door, coming to her call.

"I asked him to *restrain* Arkimedes." Devon's face turned red, a vein popping on his forehead. "With magic, not with a physical injury that could have killed him."

Nava shook her head, refusing to go down that hole of memories that might sway her from staying and fighting alongside this man. "Back on the Grey Island, there were enough Dark Ones to restrain him and portal him back here." She exhaled. "They are going to kill us and take away his memories again."

"They will *try*. But they don't know they should fear you, cat. It will be their biggest mistake—take it from someone who has learned that lesson."

CHAPTER THIRTY-FOUR

ORION

Orion had been on this side of the castle twice—maybe trice since he'd found out he was part of the royal family. It seemed like such a long time ago but, at the same time, like it had just happened yesterday.

Large windows lined the walls, with metal black frames and intricate art that told stories of a millennia with bold colors that reflected onto the ground. This hall was so grand, it was hazy in the distance. Orion found it difficult to keep his steps calm but determined while walking next to Fael, a fae who had sworn his life to him but was betraying him in such a bold manner.

He was sure this was some sort of setup crafted by his father, but he didn't want to act irrationally and give away that he had sniffed the plan. His mind was somewhere back in his room, where he had left Nava. If his fears were confirmed, they would be in much more trouble than he.

Orion's gut churned with images of Nava getting hurt, and the fear racing through his veins felt like frozen water. Not a muscle of his face twitched under his well-crafted mask, and having put away his wings earlier in the night allowed him easier movements.

They turned a corner toward the king's room. Here in this wing, there was a clear lack of art, and they crossed many rooms that were often occupied by his women this late in the day. The couple of times Orion had been here, the halls had smelled of lavender and roses.

Right now, it smelled like smoke, ashes, and sweat.

The moan of the wind had the ends of his hair lifting on end, and just as the memory started to come to him, they walked across a marble sculpture of the queen holding a sun. A crown of thorns lay over her head, much like the one on top of his head. Orion's throat tightened as he focused on her face. Gentle doe eyes, small but sculpted lips that tilted into an innocent smile, and long, wavy hair that hit the top of her hips.

She couldn't have been older than seventeen when this had been made, which meant she'd been just a kid when she joined the messy, dark world of her father's magic. Orion's features weren't much like hers, as he had inherited all of the king's shapes, quirks, and malice.

That lovely figure had now haunted him through these very halls for the past four months, demanding some sort of justice he had been unable to fulfill.

They slowed when they reached the king's room; the door awaited ajar, which was the first indication this was too easy and he was about to walk into a trap.

He reached for the doorknob. The cool metal under his hand warmed with the ire raging beneath his calm mask. He pushed the door open to reveal a grand space. The fireplace came on, much like it did all over the castle, providing the dark quarters with the gentle orange light of the fire.

Orion's magic bubbled out of him, like waves of rage

unleashing over the walls of his body, the cage the power was always suppressed in. "Tell me, Fael, what do you think is going to happen when we cross the threshold to get the keys?"

Fael stared wide-eyed at the power that billowed out of Orion like the fires outside of the castle walls. "Sir?"

Fragments of memories crashed into him then.

He ran barefoot down the wooden steps of a narrow staircase. The landing room led him to a short hallway and a small kitchen. He moved with the familiarity of someone who had used this space many times before. He rummaged through the contents of the cabinets, looking for a bottle of wine he had picked up earlier at the market. The flash of lightning illuminated the room briefly before thunder rolled in. The hairs on his neck stood on end as if called by static, and there he sensed it. The mild scent of spice hung in the air, masked by the familiar smells of his home.

A clear edge to cayenne that was more like his magic than Nava's earthy tones.

Arkimedes turned to the doors that led to their backyard. They appeared closed, but not quite. He walked to it, his heart picking speed as he inspected his surroundings. The living and dining areas were connected and, much like everything else around him, quaint. He was able to see everything.

Still, the sensation of being watched grew stronger. The wrongness of his surroundings closed in. Shadows in the room elongated, morphing into men with large wings. Fae from the Copper Kingdom. His family's kingdom.

How had they found him?

The wine bottle slipped from his grasp at the same time the grip of multiple spells crashed into him. They didn't know Nava was upstairs, and if they did, they were uninterested in her. He gasped for air and stumbled to the dining table; one of the chairs fell to the ground.

The fae stepped out of the shadows, his wings pale gray and spotted. Golden eyes shone behind a copper helmet. "We aren't here to hurt you, my prince."

Arkimedes's magic pushed against ten—twenty—spells that caged him in. It was hard to find a hole to sneak some counterattack when these spells wove around him like a skilled spiderweb. Too many materialized.

"Stop. Please," he gasped between labored breaths.

Fael's hand wrapped around his bicep, yanking him away from the table. He had used too much strength or Arkimedes was too weakened by their magic. His hand slipped from the wooden table, and with his loss of balance, he fell forward, but the fae caught him before he collapsed against the table.

His forehead hit the edge, however, and pain erupted down his brow as a warm drip of blood trailed down the side of his face.

"Your father is tired of waiting," Fael said near his ear, and then many of them came around, grabbing his arms and pulling him out of the house.

"Ark?" Nava's voice echoed around the room, a tinge of fear spiking through the bond.

Stay. He begged that Nava wouldn't come for him and be hurt by these people. He closed his eyes and threw all his strength into a paralyzing spell. He was too weak to hold her for long, but maybe it would buy time so she wouldn't get caught in the cross fire.

The rain hit his body, and his bare feet dragged over muddied grass as the group of fae walked in silence to the edge of the property, outside of the wards he set to prevent portals to open inside his home.

It was naïve of him to think they wouldn't come.

Orion opened his eyes, dazed by the memories that tightened his gut. Nava's voice had been so familiar, and the panic of her being hurt was something he had felt even when he didn't remember who she was, back when she'd been attacked in the castle.

The guards shouldn't have been able to sneak up on him so easily, even with all their magical strength. He—*Arkimedes*—had been too distracted that night because of Nava to detect he was being ambushed.

Devon had been right; he had grown soft while living on that island. Even though right now Fael—who was working with his father—intended to repeat the ambush, Orion had all of his senses awakened. He was ready for this.

"Were you going to stab me in my back again when we walked inside this room or out here in the hall?" he asked, raising his brow as he turned to the fae next to him.

Fael's helmet fell to the ground as the spell Orion unleashed hit him full force. It wasn't different from what they had used that night when they kidnapped him away from his house. Strings of magic woven together to subdue and repress, closing like a cocoon over a man who had betrayed him not once but twice.

Fael gasped as he fell to the ground, both hands grasping at his throat as Orion's claiming magic pushed between the webs of the other lighter spell and took away fragments of his power. "Stop. Please."

"I asked that same thing when you took me away from my home." Orion's voice became colder, so similar to the one used by the king.

He didn't remember all that had happened in that old life on the Grey Island; a part of him was clawing at any chance to remember, wanting that warmth that represented safety and love—and her. But Orion had to remind himself that it was a weakness that had gotten him captured. A distraction to what he had wanted to do for so long.

To find the reason for his past, unravel the whys of his power. To find out what had happened with the queen.

"Who is waiting for me inside my father's room?"

Fael's arms shook as he was barely able to hold his body weight from the ground, and Orion lifted his hand to the man, fingers pulling strings off his essence, taking apart his power.

"*Yes, let's show him what happens when we get played,*" a voice echoed in his mind. It had been a while since he'd lost control of his darkness enough for the spirits to come alive.

"*Fool me once, shame on you. Fool me twice, shame on us,*" said another, and Orion's jaw hurt as he tasted blood from biting hard.

"That's how I know you are my son." The king's voice, soft and mellow, echoed from the empty room ahead. The shadows trembled, and similar to how it had happened that night on the Grey Island, a Dark One walked out of the shadows.

Orion's throat tightened at the sight. What was his father doing here? He was sure he had seen him riding away to the forest. Had it been a decoy, or had he portaled his way back here while Orion had been talking to Nava and Devon in his room?

The king's steps were sure, and the sound of his silver armor didn't make a noise as he walked to the door. The shadows twitched, and soon the king's females walked out of every dark corner of the room, wearing the armor needed to fight the Zorren. Yet here they were, ready to fight *him* instead. He wasn't a fool to think he could defeat all of them. There was no chance of getting inside that room with so many Dark Ones and finding the keys to release Nava and Devon.

They were the closest guards to the king, always with him, ready to defend him in case of trouble. Had the king grown tired of his insubordination and was going to kill him as well? To hell with all of the reasons why he was supposed to care about his estranged son.

"I'm sure you don't want to take Fael's soul, Orion. His life is worth a lot more to our kingdom as a loyal guard. He just brought you back home."

"Against my will."

"Are we holding you against your will now?" The king opened his palms, stopping a mere foot away from him.

Orion hadn't considered leaving the castle until this moment, when he had been so clearly set up. For what? Was the king planning to kill him? Not if all he said about the kingdom needing him was true, and he knew that was the case.

Would he try to take Orion's memories away once again? He pulled his magic back a fraction, using some of his newly acquired energy to knit a shield around his memories. He wasn't as proficient in such spells, but he had been taught to fight mind attacks in the Society. The shields were similar to the spell he was under. Strings that layered together like strands of silver.

"I want the keys," he said instead.

"So you can release *my* prisoners?" The king's expression hardened. "I don't think so, son."

Orion's power thickened, mimicking the king's. If he were to get attacked now by all of his women *and* him, Orion wouldn't be able to hold his own for long. He layered the silver strings faster.

Orion's gaze flashed toward the women, who were approaching at a slow pace so as not to spook him, waiting for a sign. One of them—Fael's sister—shifted forward, catching some of the light from the hall. Her worried face was barely masked as her energy bounced off the room.

Her hand tightened around the hilt of her weapon, and Orion wondered if these women, who he had always sensed were bitter about his return, were looking forward to whatever might come out of this.

"Nava and Devon won't stay in this castle after tonight," Orion said, shifting back half a step, and Fael's still-warm body grazed his leg. Not dead . . . yet.

"Of that, we are in agreement."

Orion's stomach churned, his head prickling with worry. He hoped his wards would keep them safe for a while, but things weren't looking too positive here with so many Dark Ones waiting for him.

Nava should have left by now; even if she were tracked, her Beekeeper magic would keep her a step ahead. He doubted the king would kill him, but her . . . that was another story.

His jaw tightened hard enough that his temples throbbed. "I won't allow you to hurt them."

The king's smile didn't reach his eyes. "I would love to see how you intend on doing so." His voice wasn't mocking or happy. "I'm sure you have noticed I have the power of a kingdom behind me . . ." It wasn't quite the power of his whole army, though he guessed some had gone out to battle the demons.

"You promised."

"You like to bring up the promise I made to you. Yet you broke yours of returning to our kingdom ten years ago. Instead, you went to live with my enemy in that pitiful town you called your home." The king had abandoned all masks of politeness. His facial features twisted with anger, revealing aged skin and wrinkles that hadn't been present before.

"I wouldn't remember that I broke any promise since I have no memories of the last decade."

The king scowled. "You made peace with the man who helped your mother escape and took you away with her."

He had to be talking about Roman, the high commander of the Iron City's army. A soldier who once had been a high-ranking member of his father's guards. The only human he knew who'd been one.

From what he could remember, Orion hadn't seen the man since they had been in the Iron City, and they weren't close. Roman was busy with the armed guards for the kingdom and had little dealings with the Society of Crows. Orion's brows knitted, and he took another step back from his father.

This wasn't buying him any time; there was no way to get what he needed from that room and leave unharmed. The room's shadows moved as if listening to a mental command he was not privy to. Maybe he could call on the keys magically instead. If the castle already recognized him as the heir and prince, perhaps it would allow the keys to come to him.

It was something he hadn't even tried.

He pictured the aged brass skeleton key in his mind and called to it. His body warmed; the energy of his surroundings responded to him. The castle did recognize him—but the keys didn't come to his hand.

The king's smirk grew wider, but this time his eyes shone with a delight Orion didn't share. He lifted his hand, opening his palm wide. "Is this what you are calling for?"

Dammit.

"Our magic is interconnected, Orion. I can sense what you are trying to do. Whether it's to ward your room or call on *my* things."

Orion swallowed, and the weight of stones settled in his stomach. "I don't want to fight you."

"Of course you don't," the king said and took a step out of the room, his black aura increasing in size. Much like it happened with Orion's when he was ready for a fight, the shapes of people came out of the mist. Arms, faces—a trail of nightmares. "You will lose. But worry not, son, I will take away these memories, and tomorrow you will be free of them."

Them. Orion didn't think his father was referring to his memories, but having both Nava and Devon disappear. Orion's wings popped out with the increase of tension running through his body.

He gasped when a surge of energy hit his body, draining whatever it could take. The king's eyes shone brighter with unnatural cerulean light, while the storm of his inky power mixed with his.

His legs wavered, but he pushed back. The voices of the fragments of souls became louder once again. Probing in anger, demanding bloodshed. He took a step toward the king, flexing as their magic pushed against one another.

Then the extra waves of magic pushed onto him all at once as five—six—other fae attacked him with the same shadow magic. He struggled not to fall as the pressure extended down his muscles. An angry cry left his lips before he fell to the ground, pain extending from his knees to his hips.

"Coward." The word left his lips before he could think twice; the claws of magic fingers wrapped around his mind, and the memory of the night he'd arrived here flashed behind his closed lids. It had been too similar to this. Many powers used to subdue him while his mind was stripped open.

"I don't need to be just to save my kingdom."

The floor beneath his hand shook and he twitched forward, closing his eyes and focusing all his power to peel away the inky fingers that clutch his mind's shield. His head throbbed as pain extended through his temples.

"You learned to shield me," the king said with a strange waver in his voice that could be mistaken for pride, had he not been torturing him alongside his concubines. Orion's anger burned deeper in the pit of his stomach as flashes of what they had done to him before came back.

He pushed against their hold, stumbling up to his feet and leaping toward the king, who looked surprised for the first time. Orion's fist connected with his father's cheek, and the energy of his adrenaline drained with the contact.

They both stumbled into the room and to the commotion of winged women rushing in. Long nails dug into his arms and chest as the women pulled him away from his father. The king lifted to his elbows and cupped his wounded chin as a trail of blood dripped from the corner of his mouth.

"They trained you well," he said. His crown straightened on its own.

Orion guessed his father was referring to the Society of Crows, and right now he was thankful for their training as well. He moved against the hold of the women; words escaped his lips even though he didn't know what he was saying. His magic took from them, fed from all it could get. Some of them even dropped him, backing away from the pull of his power.

"Hands off my heir. His magic will feed on yours if you touch him." With the king's words, the women dropped him to the ground, but their magic kept pressing into him, paralyzing him.

The king stood from the ground, and Orion's arms shook as his father's power came harder now. It was too much—too many of them against him. The silver shield of his mind was struggling against his hold, the clawing of the king's power taking away strand after strand.

Maybe he should have stayed with Nava and Devon. Sure, he hadn't expected the king and his cohorts to be waiting for him, but facing all of this alone had been his choice.

With Devon being part of the Society, it was unlikely his father would kill the man. His memories might be altered much like his. But Nava . . . Orion's sudden decision of going at this alone weighed on his chest as fear gripped him. Adrenaline pumped through his system, dimming the ache that kept building inside his head.

His body turned cold, and he reached through the bond inside him, tugging at the cord that connected them. The warmth of it seeped through his bones with the soft drumming of a heart.

She was alive—but for how much longer?

CHAPTER THIRTY-FIVE

NAVA

The only sounds around them were the hissing of the sword as it cut through the air every time Devon swung it, the tapping of Nava's boot heels on stone, and the soft rolling of the flames in the fireplace.

How long had it been since Arkimedes left with Fael? Ten minutes? An hour? No, it couldn't have been that long, even though it felt like time was crawling by. Her gut flipped, raising up a wave of nausea that had her slowing her steps as the prick of anxiety grew larger.

"Would you stop it?" Nava snapped, turning to Devon, who put the sword down for a fraction of a moment before swinging it again and lifting a brow in defiance.

"I haven't used this weapon before. It will be good to get used to its weight before we have company."

A weapon, of course. She had been so paralyzed by all that had happened, she hadn't thought about her own defense against the possible attack.

Storming toward the wall where Arkimedes's armor still hung, she looked at the heavy copper plates and mesh. The scent of smoke still hung around it, and traces of soot stained its surface. The leather straps twisted at the ends, warped by the heat of the fires.

She stepped toward the weapons next. Much like in his cabin, another long sword rested upon wooden hooks on the wall. No special markings, just a plain sharp blade that would cut through people as if they were made of butter.

Nava had never been good with swords when she learned weaponry with her mother. Daggers, yes. Bow and arrow made her fingers hurt, but she had been decent with archery at some point.

Her eyes traveled down the wall of well-displayed weapons, and the knot in her throat thickened. Arkimedes had never asked to display anything like this in their home in the village, even though it was something he liked to do.

Had she been so into her own wants and needs that she had forgotten to pay attention to what he desired? Or had he always known the island was a momentary home for them? Maybe he had been waiting to tell her this truth, to find the right time to explain that he didn't want to stay there.

She swallowed, and the almost permanent ache in her heart bloomed larger.

Under the sword's wall mount, there were three knives. Not quite daggers, but closer than a sword was. She picked the two most similar to the daggers she'd learned to fight with, the ones she'd lost when she portaled into this kingdom.

The metal was balanced and heavy in her hands. The edge of the blade reflected her eyes back, and the leather that wrapped the handle was soft, stained a rich ebony color.

"It has been a while," she admitted. "They might not come. Maybe they will attack him instead—"

Devon put the sword down. "Let's hope they don't, and

that he will come back with the keys so we can get the hell out of here."

Nava opened her mouth to answer him when the door handle dipped for the first time. The prickle of dread bloomed in her skull, and a heated silence descended. The door shook as someone outside tried to pry it open. Her heart raced as it happened a couple more times before a more forceful attempt was made.

Muffled, angry voices came from outside, then the first spell hit. The heavy door screeched under its pressing power. Once. Twice. The door shook but didn't open. Her skin went damp all over, her stomach swooping with anticipation.

Their heavy breathing became louder as another spell hit again. The room became unbearable with the scent of magic. Her eyes watered as the door trembled in distress.

A loud pop boomed, and a heavy crack extended from the ceiling, down the stone of the wall, across the doorframe, and through one of the doors.

Then someone hit it full force, and even though the door was still there, it moved a fraction, the broken pieces showing sections of exposed pulp. Nava hesitated before looking at Devon who, unlike her, had walked to the door and was standing on the side with the sword, ready to attack.

Where he stood, it would be easier to get anyone who entered through the hole. She walked to the other side, hoping to imitate someone who had been taught and had fought much more than her.

The crack extended farther as a heavy body hit it full force. The masculine voice coming from the outside was clearer when the wooden door began to collapse and the gap grew larger. Nava couldn't tell what the person was saying or the responses of the fae near him, but they were angry.

She trembled as her magic rose within, her skin glowed bright yellow. She had to do this again, fight for her life like she had last year. The building dread in her stomach wasn't just hers, which meant Arkimedes was in trouble, and he was alone.

She met Devon's gaze from the other end of the doorframe, and time halted right before the door blew off its hinges. Wood pieces flew across the room, and splinters went everywhere. She was protected from them by pushing closer to the wall. The bed screeched, hit by a large piece, and flew across the room as one of the posts broke in half.

She breathed out and steeled her nerves. Four winged men stormed into the room, weapons held high with their dark auras billowing around their bodies.

Devon attacked first, pure stealth and elegant use of the weapon, like an extension of his arms. The first guard who entered had not been waiting for the strike, and the blade went through the gap between the helmet and the bottom of the chain mail, slicing the head right off the body. Blood sprayed out of the severed neck, pooling on the floor.

Bile rose in her throat. She turned away from the body and focused on the guard closer to her, who didn't take long to spot her. He was taken aback by the clear vision of her magic aura blooming off her body. A scream left her lips as she attacked with her knives raised high.

Nava swiped across metal and hit one of the straps of his arm plate. The metal slid over his arms, and the second swipe of her blade hit the chain mail underneath. His magic wrapped around her, but she had practiced against this shadow magic before in all of her training sessions with Arkimedes.

Her body heated in reflex, and the mist evaporated with the touch, then she called her bees. In the past few days, everywhere she went, the insects had always followed. Crawling over walls, camouflaged by the warm tones of the castle stones. Devon or Arkimedes hadn't noticed or maybe hadn't mentioned it.

All at once, the bees flew off the walls and swarmed the other two guards, who were jumping on Devon with both magic and weapons. Maybe they thought he was the biggest threat—and the Crow had been right. They'd underestimated her. The guards, the king, even Arkimedes.

She was a Beekeeper, a sorceress, and she would show them how wrong they were.

"Bees everywhere!" one said with a hoarse scream. From her peripheral vision, she saw a large man jump back, avoiding Devon's blade. He swatted around his face as thousands of bees descended upon him.

His pink copper armor became a moving brown shade when her insects crawled over, searching for a crevice to get in. He ran closer to the bed, his panicked breathing one of the noises in the room. His aura turned black and heavy.

"I can't get them off!" he screamed, and the man who had attacked Nava turned toward him long enough for Nava to jump on him. Her skin was bright, and it illuminated this corner of the room, cutting through the darkness that surrounded him.

She slammed the blade of her knife in the gap where the chain mail met his helmet, and warm blood splattered her hand and the side of her cheek. Pulling back, she held her gag reflex as the man staggered to the wall, dropping down while holding his neck.

Devon was on the third man, his face shiny with sweat. The Dark One's aura surrounded him. However, the guard was overtaken by bees and was struggling to see anything beyond what was in front of him.

Her body temperature was high, and the stone beneath their feet swayed under their steps. The guard by the bed fell to the ground, screaming. The bees made it through the eyeholes of his mask and the crevices between his chest and arm plates.

Their screams echoed in the room, and she heard the sword cut the air once again and a pained cry a moment later. Looking at the last guard by the broken bed sent her a flashback of how her bees had attacked Devon last year and how Arkimedes had stopped her. The man's shaky arms held him on, and there was not a visible inch of his armor.

Nava swallowed and walked to the man, leaving Devon behind. Every step she took, the bees swarmed around in a protective circle.

"Help," she heard someone say. It might have been him or her subconscious yelling at her to hold off and exercise some humanity. He had come here to hurt her— maybe kill her—but Nava didn't need to be like these people.

She called off her insects, and all at once, they flew off his body, and his shaky arms gave way as he collapsed to the floor.

Silence descended upon them, and Nava found she could take a deep breath. She heard Devon's steps by the door. His eyes were wide as he looked at her, presumably remembering all that happened to him before.

"We need to get to Arkimedes," she said and wiped the blood off her hand onto her pants, trying to distract herself with anything else than whether or not she had killed the man or how much easier it had been this time.

"He would want us to go to the safe house."

"Too bad he isn't here to call the shots—and I'm going there, whether he wants me to or not."

Devon nodded, a smirk pulling his lips as they both exited the room. "I did say you seem like a fit mate for him."

Except Nava didn't like to think she would have stormed into a trap on her own. Ark—Orion—had done that. She was much more of a team player than a lone wolf. With the threat of the attack gone for now, she could fully sink into the changes of her mate.

How he had chosen to be alone, had decided he didn't want the memories of their life together. The ache in her chest grew as she stopped by the door. If he didn't want what they had, for whatever reason, she would have to be fine with it, even though it wrecked her.

Nava had been afraid of this very thing happening when she withheld the information about their bond. She wouldn't have abandoned him before and wouldn't now either.

CHAPTER THIRTY-SIX

NAVA

It was not the first time Nava had tracked Arkimedes after he had been taken. Back in the forest when Devon attacked the Northern Village, she had been new to their bond and magic as a whole. Now, as they ran down the wide hallways of this castle, she could sense his presence. It called to her like a beacon.

The halls were empty, dark, and quiet. As if everyone around them had left to battle. Had the royal guard left to keep the demons at bay? Was Aristaeus on his own? Or had the king just kept a few guards here to take care of them?

Nava peered around the corner to check that it was empty. The area where Arkimedes's quarters were was beautiful, decorated, clean, and elegant. But this place was on another level. The runner that covered the ground was plush and muted their hurried steps. There were marble statues or urns placed on pedestals on each side of large windows. Nava could guess this was the king's wing.

Her lungs burned, and she gasped for air with the exertion of running nonstop. If she survived the night, she had to start exercising more often.

Out of nowhere, her heart faltered from a building pressure inside her, a constricting sensation that came through the bond, followed by a wave of searing pain. Nava stumbled, and one of her knives slipped out of her fingers as she gasped, bringing both hands over her stomach.

"Are you all right?" Devon took a step toward her, and Nava took long breaths to calm the ache.

"Arkimedes is in trouble." Her voice went cold, a whisper. "We aren't far."

"Then we shouldn't be running there and alerting them of the fact that we were able to fight the guards they sent," Devon whispered back, reaching for her but stopping short of touching her before pulling his hand back.

Her closeness to Arkimedes made the ache through the bond more real, and now that both she and Devon held still and quiet, voices traveled the distance.

Nava raised her eyes to the Crow. "I will transfer there. We aren't that far from where he is." She pointed in the direction, though she wasn't sure he would follow. "It will give me a better shot of a surprise."

"Transfer? What the hell are you talking about?"

Nava straightened, ignoring the throbbing pain deep in her gut. She didn't have time, nor did she want to explain to Devon what she could do and why she could do it. Nava closed her eyes and focused on Arkimedes. She had done it before, coming to him when he needed her that day in the library.

She could do it again now that she was able to control her skills. Peering around the corner again, she spotted a large statue nearby. If she transferred there, she would have a better vantage point to assess the surroundings and come up with another plan if needed. It wouldn't be smart if she accidentally appeared in a spot that would put her life in further danger.

Nava's body became light and transparent as it floated through the air. Devon's gasp was the last thing she heard before she moved across the hall toward the statue, but before she made it all the way there, Arkimedes's clear cry of pain came from inside the room with the open door.

Her speed increased as she crossed the threshold of the room. Inside, the image was clear. Arkimedes kneeled on the ground, with his wings spread out across the floor, his arms barely holding him up.

There were six women still dressed in armor nearby, and Nava didn't have to understand the Dark Ones' power to know they were all attacking her soulmate at the same time.

She had no body, but the emotion still swelled within her, bright and bitter anger. She swirled around the room like a cyclone, sending their long hair flying over their confused faces.

The king stood a foot or so away, his hand outstretched as his aura billowed. The cool air of his mist had the same cayenne notes she always sensed on Arkimedes, but there was something old in there too, like aged leather and parchment

Nava's body began to gain substance as her emotions became stronger, blurring the lines of her transferring phase with her corporeal one. She had promised weeks ago when these people took Arkimedes that they would pay. For weeks she had been frozen from making the wrong move, for fear of the what-ifs.

It all happened fast. She became flesh and blood behind the king, still holding a long knife. Quicker than she could think, she grasped the king's shoulder with the other hand. With a swift, steady move, she brought her blade against her enemy's throat, and the whole room went quiet.

"Release him, or I will make sure this is the last thing you do," she said, ice in her words. There was no lie behind the meaning. Nava wasn't bluffing.

The king gasped, his back going rigid as he realized who was behind him. She couldn't see Arkimedes, not with the tall mass of the king's body in front of her.

Her soulmate groaned on the ground, and a sharp pain extended past their bond, indicating no one was listening to her—yet.

Nava lifted up on her tiptoes, holding the knife tighter against the king's porcelain skin. A drop of blood trailed down the silver blade that didn't shake or waver. "Call off your bitches from the prince. *Now.*"

"Do as she says." The king's words came out choppy as Nava brought her body closer to him, making sure she didn't lose her grip and not caring one bit if she cut him in the process.

Warmth swirled inside her gut. Relief mixed with a tinge of panic that was solely his. He regained his breath once all their spells lifted from him.

"If you hurt our king," one of the women started, her voice aiming to sound menacing but coming out panicked instead. The way Nava would have sounded if their roles were reversed.

"Be quiet," Nava snapped. "Now give Arkimedes the keys to the bracelets."

The king's jaw tightened, and his bright blue eyes met hers from the side. "This is impossible. You shouldn't be able to do magic. The bracelets are active. I can sense their magic. The only way they wouldn't is if . . ." His eyes widened, at a loss for words. He lifted the two keys hanging from a pale twine and threw it across the room to where Arkimedes was.

When Ark's eyes met hers across the king's shoulder, her body was inundated with a warm swirling sensation that took over. Something that felt a lot like awe and a touch of adoration made her stomach swoop.

He took a deep breath and reached for the keys with a shaky hand before struggling to get on his two feet, his black wings disappearing from view a moment later.

"What are you planning to do, Orion? Run away and forsake our whole kingdom again?" the king asked.

"We didn't forsake the kingdom, Father. Y*ou did*." Arkimedes's lips tightened into a thin line as he wiped his shiny forehead and took a step toward the door, his gaze never deviating from her. "You won't chase after us, and you will stop trying to kill Nava."

Devon appeared in the doorframe, holding his sword high. Arkimedes backed away in his direction and handed him the key, which he used to remove the bracelet from his pale wrist.

The jewel hadn't finished hitting the marble ground when the air crackled with static and a black portal started to form next to the Crow. Like a dot of spilled ink suspended in midair.

"Orion." The king's distressed voice broke the silence, and Nava held him tighter, the blade biting his skin deeper. "You can't leave us with the Zorren at our doorsteps."

The Zorren. She hadn't forgotten about those, even if the king had chosen to ambush his son instead of fighting them today.

"We will be in touch," Arkimedes said just as the portal became large enough for them to walk into it. Devon crossed it first, and the whole circle shook with energy, closing a fraction. Her soulmate stared at her, and she knew by the stubborn set of his jaw that he wouldn't leave with her still so close to the king.

Her body became lighter as her legs floated in the air, then her body and her arms, and just as her fingers started to become transparent, the king turned to her, his face pale.

"What are you?"

A Beekeeper, a sorceress—his son's soulmate.

Nava brought her face a bit closer to his ear, riding the wave of adrenaline still running through her. It was time he knew who he had been trying to kill. "If the queen's tree is anything to go by, I'm the future queen of this kingdom," she said before she disappeared, rushing toward the closing portal.

The whole room went dark, ink and mist exploding in the air as Arkimedes crossed the portal, but none of the king's concubines' powers hit her transferring body.

"Stop!" The king's voice echoed in the room, and she didn't know if it had been directed at her or his women. The portal narrowed to just the size of her hand, and the wind picked up speed, pushing her across the black hole before it snapped close.

The shadow land was empty and quiet, like all life and sound was sucked away from a never-ending room. Nava's shapelessness morphed back into her body, and soon it wasn't all quiet, but her fast breathing was almost as deafening as the pouncing of her heartbeat.

Floating with no gravity, she blinked, and the glow of her skin illuminated her surroundings. Moats of particles hung in the air, and a faint scent of smoke wrapped around her like a cold hug.

"Beekeeper." The voice was like the drop of melting ice on her skin. His voice held pent-up emotion. A mixture of mischief—or was it excitement? A long shape of a creature—no, it wasn't a monster or a demon, but a man—came closer. How could he walk in such a place where bodies weighed nothing?

His shifting expression was confusing. Her stomach churned with dread, and she knew she had to leave there as soon as possible. When she crossed this land before, there had been two entities, the one who'd claimed his prize, her memories . . . and this one. The one whose touch burned.

The closer he got to her, the clearer his face became with the glow of her skin. His features changed to the man she loved. It was the same wide nose, the shape of thick lips and bushy brows. His alabaster skin was jarring with the color—or lack thereof—and his moonlight hair hung down his back, swaying as he stepped closer, long like the king she had been fighting but a moment ago.

She flailed in her spot, trying to move away from this man, floating a few inches as he advanced to her. He looked like her soulmate, but he was her worst nightmare. Panic gripped her throat.

"Nava? Nava . . . ? Where the hell is she, Devon?"

She heard Arkimedes's voice from somewhere nearby. A small hole crackled in the distance and was closing. At first she hadn't seen it because, on the other side, it was still dark, except for the distant lights of a city.

Her skin broke out into a cold sweat as this other entity pursued her. She had forgotten she was supposed to be crossing, not staying here. The soft, earthy scent of her magic spiked as she moved with swimming strokes over the air, and the creature—man—began to run toward her.

He was fast, but she was so close. Her skin tingled the

closer she got to Arkimedes, the real one. The city behind him became so clear and large, she could smell the faint scent of dew and food in the air.

"I don't think so, Beekeeper." A hand wrapped around her arm, thin long fingers coated in a charcoal layer. A scream escaped her lips as an agonizing, bone-melting ache ran through her arm

Her eyes watered as she focused on that lovely face she knew so well, but up close, his features were wrong, wrinkled and translucent like an old piece of wax paper. She focused on her trembling body, her racing heart, then took a sharp breath and brought her own hand on top of his.

She was fed up with these white-haired men trying to suffocate her. Her magic blazed through her veins, and he hissed, ripping his hand away from her. A flash of branches formed over his fingers, much too similar to the way the Zorren had become a tree that day she, Aristaeus, and Arkimedes was in the forest.

Nava took the chance, not wanting to overthink this for a second longer and get trapped inside this world. She moved across the last section toward the end of the portal, and her body fell out like she was being expelled from it.

The city noises were almost deafening. The warm summer night hugged her in a welcomed embrace, a clear contrast to the ice of winter she had been surrounded by in the shadow world. The cobblestone road dug into the soft curves of her body, and she looked around in a daze.

"Hey, hey—are you all right?" A warm hand rested on her shoulder.

Her vision sharpened on the man in front of her, and she flinched as her heart picked up speed.

"Nava?" Arkimedes dropped his hand. His brows knitted in the middle as he assessed her.

It was just Ark—her soulmate—her mind supplied as

she studied his features. The healthy glow of a light gold skin tone and bright green eyes. Her body trembled, at odds with the dread and relief of being near him.

"I'm all right," she said, and even to her own ears, she sounded strained. Adrenaline still ran rampant through her body. She moved back farther before trying to get to her feet.

Arkimedes straightened from his crouched position as he assessed her with worry etched on his face.

Her arms hung over her legs, hunched over while she gathered her thoughts. The stones underneath her dug in, and her eyes drifted shut before she forced them open again. Devon, who had been standing nearby, came toward her, extending her a hand. Her limbs were heavy like a bag of rocks, the feeling all too familiar, and she knew that at any moment she would pass out.

She gripped the offered hand, and the Crow pulled her up with a swift move.

"Thank you," she whispered.

Devon dropped her hand and offered her the keys. The object was foreign now, like that problem had been years and not minutes ago. She didn't move a muscle to grab them, and soon the Crow snatched her wrist and took the bracelet off.

He disappeared from view after, presumably to dispose of the jewelry somewhere where the king couldn't trace it back to the safe house.

Arkimedes's eyes bore into hers before dropping down her body, stopping at her arms. "What happened?" he asked, taking a step toward her. She had to bite the inside of her mouth and urge her body not to back away in a panic.

It was just Arkimedes—*not* the shadow man. This was

not an illusion. They were in the Copper City. He sounded and smelled like her soulmate.

She looked at her arm and gasped at the bright red burns in the shape of a hand, her skin already bubbling into angry blisters. "Oh."

"Did my father do this to you?"

She met Arkimedes's gaze and took a step back when he reached for her again, swallowing the bitter taste in her throat and the sudden need to leave. "It wasn't your father."

It was you.

ABOUT THE AUTHOR

"Abbey Fox has always loved storytelling. Ever since she was little, she created characters for fun and got immersed in their life stories, worlds, and magic systems. This naturally progressed onto writing. Her first story being a cringe worthy teenage high school Romance, which she wrote at the age of thirteen in a notebook that was half falling apart by the time she wrote the end.

As time has gone by, she has dived into writing other genres, from YA Fantasy to Mystery Romance, Romantic Soap opera Sci-fi. Now she focuses on her love for Adult Fiction in the Fantasy Romance/ Paranormal Romance genres.

Her debut novel is coming out later this year. It is part of an enthralling series set in a magical world where soulmates are real and power corrupts the kingdoms.

When Abbey is not writing, she enjoys spending time with her husband and her four-year-old son. She also enjoys tending to her indoor tropical jungle and painting fun characters with watercolors. "

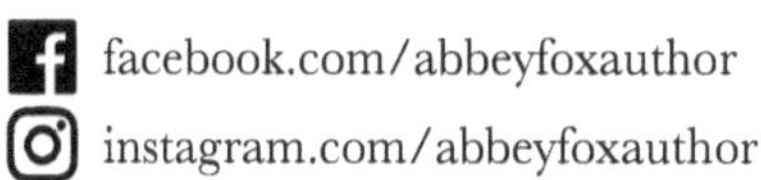

facebook.com/abbeyfoxauthor

instagram.com/abbeyfoxauthor

DANKSAGUNG

Für meine fantastische Lektorin Helen Jenner und das gesamte wunderbare Team bei Bookouture, die diese Geschichte mit mir zusammen möglich gemacht haben. Außerdem möchte ich Kim Nash und Noelle Holten danken – dem besten Team für Öffentlichkeitsarbeit aller Zeiten.

EIN BRIEF VON D.K. HOOD

Liebe Leserinnen und Leser,

ich freue mich sehr, dass ihr euch für meinen Roman entschieden habt und mir mit *Schenk mir Blumen* in die spannende Welt von Alton und Kane gefolgt seid.

Wenn ihr gerne über meine neuesten Veröffentlichungen auf dem Laufenden bleiben möchtet, melden euch einfach über den folgenden Link an.

www.bookouture.com/bookouture-deutschland-sign-up

Über Jenna Alton und David Kane zu schreiben, hat mir große Freude bereitet und ebenso gerne habe ich Shane Wolfe in das Team aufgenommen. Ich glaube, es wird mir viel Spaß machen, auch künftig immer weiter in sein Fachgebiet einzutauchen. Ich selbst bin ein großer Fan der Forensik und finde es spannend, was man alles über Tatorte in Erfahrung bringen kann.

Wenn euch mein Buch gefallen hat, würde ich mich sehr über eine kurze Rezension und eine Weiterempfehlung an eure Freunde und Familie freuen. Ich finde es immer wieder schön, von meinen Leserinnen und Lesern zu hören, denn es vermittelt mir während des Schreibens das Gefühl, dass ihr hier bei mir seid und mit meinen Figuren mit fiebert.

Daher würde ich mich sehr freuen, von euch zu hören. Kontaktiert mich einfach über meine Facebook-Seite, Twitter oder meine Webseite.

Er verspürte ihr gegenüber Respekt und tiefe Zuneigung. »Wäre der Fall damit also abgeschlossen, Ma'am?«

»Ja.« Jennas warmes Lächeln ließ ihre Augen funkeln. »Fall abgeschlossen.«

Er erwiderte ihr Lächeln mit einem Grinsen. »Dann können wir uns ja jetzt um Ihre Tanzschritte kümmern. Bis zum Herbsttanz werden Sie auf dem Parkett glänzen.«

»Genau das weiß ich an meinen Deputys zu schätzen.« Jenna kicherte. »Ehrgeiz.«

»Und warum hat er ausgerechnet *junge* Mädchen ermordet?«

Kane seufzte. »Dazu äußert er sich nicht. Aber wer kann schon die Gedankengänge eines Psychopathen ergründen?«

»Ich hätte im Leben nicht vermutet, dass er ein Mörder ist. Er wirkte immer so nett und fürsorglich. Ich kann nicht fassen, dass ich ihn sogar noch als Notfallseelsorger hinzugezogen habe.« Jenna fuhr sich mit beiden Händen in die Haare und starrte ihn an. »War er überhaupt Pfarrer?«

»Ja, und ich nehme mal an, er war als Prediger unterwegs, um sich jungen Mädchen nähern zu können. Eigentlich keine schlechte Tarnung, wenn man darüber nachdenkt. Wer würde schon einen Pfarrer verdächtigen?« Er verzog das Gesicht. »Er ist uns durchs Netz gegangen.«

»Als er Emily angriff, hat er auf mich wie die Verkörperung des Bösen gewirkt.« Jenna blickte zu Wolfe. »Wie geht es ihr?«

»Sie macht sich immer noch große Vorwürfe, dass sie mir nicht von Aimee erzählt hat, aber nachdem sie den Mord an Julia verhindern konnte, geht es ihr etwas besser.« Wolfe lächelte aufrichtig. »Sie hat das Gefühl, einen entscheidenden Beitrag dazu geleistet zu haben, den Mörder ihrer Freundinnen zu fassen.«

»Das ist doch schön. Ich freue mich schon darauf, wenn sie ihr Praktikum hier fortsetzt.« Jenna strahlte in die Runde. »Ich bin sehr stolz auf mein Team. Wir waren das einzige Sheriff-Department im ganzen Bundesstaat, das Jones' Blutbad stoppen konnte, und haben direkt noch einen weiteren Mörder von der Straße gefischt. Sie beide haben ausgezeichnete Arbeitet geleistet, und Rowley und Walters ebenso.« Sie räusperte sich und schaute sie von unten herauf an. »Aber kommen Sie jetzt bloß nicht auf die Idee, sich auf Ihren Lorbeeren auszuruhen. Ich werde weiterhin die Peitsche schwingen.«

Kane lehnte sich in seinem Stuhl zurück und schaute sie an. Er musste zugeben, dass Jenna sie zu Bestleistungen anspornte.

gehe davon aus, dass Jones hier vor Gericht gestellt wird? Wird er im Bezirksgefängnis bleiben?«

»Ja, ich gehe davon aus, dass auf Grundlage dieser Befunde unsere ursprüngliche Anklage wegen versuchten Mordes an Emily auf Mord ersten Grades an Felicity, Joanne, Kate und Aimee ausgedehnt wird.« Jenna schaute bedrückt in die Runde. »Was uns nach wie vor fehlt, ist das Motiv. Warum hat Jones gemordet?«

Kane tippte auf einen der Ordner auf dem Schreibtisch. »Das Ministerium hat uns eine Akte zugeschickt. Sie hatten ihn schon länger auf dem Radar. Ich weiß nicht, wieso sie ihn nicht bereits vorher auf Verdacht verhaftet haben. Er ist schon seit Jahren als Tierquäler bekannt. Als Schüler auf der Highschool ist er von der örtlichen Polizei mal mit dem Ertrinkungstod eines Mädchens in Verbindung gebracht worden, er wurde jedoch nie angeklagt. Er hat die Schule als Jahrgangsbester abgeschlossen und hat ein Stipendium für sein Informatikstudium bekommen.« Wolfe blickte sie an. »Wie wir bereits angenommen haben, war seine Mutter eine Prostituierte und hat ihre Freier mit nach Hause gebracht. Sie haben in einer winzigen Wohnung gewohnt und aus dem Durcheinander von Jones' Aussage geht hervor, dass seine Mutter ihn wohl zum Zuschauen gezwungen hat und sich die Männer zum Teil auch an ihm vergriffen haben. Außerdem hat seine Mutter an den Prostituierten des Ortes Abtreibungen durchgeführt, bei denen er assistieren musste. Das Ministerium hat ein Foto seiner Mutter beigefügt, auf dem sie knallroten Lippenstift trägt.«

»Gibt es da drin auch irgendeine Erklärung für die Blumen?«

Kane zuckte zusammen. »Ja, wenn seine Mutter sauer auf ihn war, hat er ihr Wildblumen gepflückt, woraufhin sie ihm verziehen hat. Er hat sogar gesagt: ›Sie alle wollten, dass ich ihnen Blumen schenke‹.«